BORROWED
New HEARTS
and
Selected Stories

BORROWED
New HEARTS
and
Selected Stories

RICK DEMARINIS

SEVEN STORIES PRESS
New York / London / Toronto

Original collections were published under the following imprints:
Under the Wheat (University of Pittsburg Press, Pittsburg, 1986)
The Coming Triumph of the Free World (W. W. Norton & Company, 1988)
The Voice of America (W. W. Norton & Company, 1991)

New stories have appeared as follows: "Feet" and "Borrowed Hearts" were published in the *Antioch Review*; "Novias," " A Romantic Interlude" and "Hormone X" were published in *GQ*; "Fault Lines" was published in *New York Stories*; "The Singular We" was published in the *North Atlantic Review*; "Experience" was published in the *Paris Review*; a short version of "The Boys We Were, The Men We Became" was published in the collection *Under the Wheat* and in the *Rio Grande Review* under the title "Good Wars; On the Lam" was published in *Zoetrope*.

Published by Seven Stories Press
140 Watts Street
New York, NY 10013
http://www.sevenstories.com

In Canada: Hushion House, 36 Northline Road, Toronto, Ontario M4B 3E2, Canada

In the U.K.: Turnaround Publisher Services Ltd., Unit 3, Olympia Trading Estate, Coburg Road, Wood Green, London N22 6TZ U.K.

Library of Congress Cataloging-in-Publication Data

DeMarinis, Rick, 1934
    Borrowed Hearts: New and Selected Stories / Rick DeMarinis. —A Seven Stories Press 1st ed.
ISBN 1-888363-98-3
1. United States—Social life and customs—20th century—Fiction.I. Title
PS3554.E4554B67 1999
813'.54—dc21   98–55233
                                                         CIP

9 8 7 6 5 4 3 2 1

Book design by Cindy LaBreacht

Printed in the U.S.A.

FOR CAROLE

Contents

BORROWED HEARTS (New Stories)

Sometimes I think I have known Rick DeMarinis all my life but it's really only been thirty-three years since we met as a couple of pups taking a poetry workshop from the estimable poet and teacher, Richard Hugo. This was at the University of Montana and the year was 1966. It was my first workshop and I felt completely out of my league. Most of the other participants were a few years older than I was, some of them had had careers, some had been in the military, some had wives and children, some even ex-wives. This latter fact left me a bit dumbfounded as I hadn't thought of having a first wife yet.

After that workshop Rick moved from Missoula to begin a teaching career in creative writing that has taken him to Seattle, San Diego, Phoenix and now El Paso.

Although we have been fast friends and in frequent contact during these past thirty-three years, I was as surprised as anyone that Rick would eventually come to be regarded as one of this country's premier short fiction writers. Not that he wasn't promising—but then back in those early years, that's all any of us were—all promise, no real accomplishment. But Rick was as sturdy as a rock in

Introduction

BY JAMES WELCH

his determination to unleash that bizarre imagination that lurks just beneath the surface of one of the gentlest natures I have ever known.

Like most writers, Rick's early work appeared in the small, small magazines that come and go but are so important to literature in this country. The early stories were just fine, carefully made, satisfying to read, but they lacked that DeMarinis signature that his faithful readers now look forward to and recognize at once. In fact, his first big success was a short novel called *A Lovely Monster*, a hilarious, chilling, touching send-up of the Frankenstein myth. This was followed by three other works of longer fiction, all masterfully done, but Rick came into his full power with a collection of stories titled *Under the Wheat*, which more than deservedly won the Drue Heinz Literature Prize for short fiction. In these stories, we begin to meet those bizarrely normal people that have populated Rick's work since. We begin to think these could be the people next door; then we think, My God, if these are the people next door, what is this world coming to? Are we them?

Sometimes we are them. We've been caught in loveless marriages; we've paused to reflect on the meaninglessness of our lives; we've gotten drunk at parties and tried to seduce the host or hostess; we've been told by our bosses that we just don't measure up. These things happen in our lives and we end up moving on. Rick DeMarinis is a master at exposing these moments and the emotions that go along with them—surprise, lust, enlightenment, embarrassment, wisdom, that awful sense of absurdity that strips us naked and leaves us standing on the edge, exposed and vulnerable. And yet there is a *c'est la vie* quality that rescues Rick's characters from maudlin self-pity or bitter hopelessness. In fact, the reader finds himself laughing, almost awkwardly, at the plight of many of these characters. Maybe we're laughing at ourselves—we see something of ourselves in these poor wretches.

But Rick isn't above helping us along in our almost helpless laughter. He has a genius for comedy and the comic moment that can occur in the most miserable circumstance. Choose virtually any story in this collection and see if you don't come away with a couple of out-loud laughs and several stifled giggles. At the same time you are thinking, almost guiltily, My God, that's awful, why am I laughing?

But to think that humor is the only strength, or even the most salient feature, of these stories is to miss their underlying humanity. Even the most fabulous of them—"Your Story" comes to mind—is grounded in human desires, determinations and the inevitable frailties of flawed people. Even the more despicable characters—like Stan Duval, the pretentious stepfather in "Experience" or Price Billetdoux, the thieving con man of "Billy Ducks Among the Pharaohs"— have their moments of vulnerability. In "Under the Wheat," Lloyd, who knows his missile systems and weather, is not very bright when it comes to interpersonal relationships and is perhaps a little willfully cruel about them. Yet, we stand shoulder to shoulder with him and gaze into the distance at a "thick tube hairy with rain" and wonder, along with him, if the incipient tornado will touch down, and if it does, will it change Lloyd, and if so, for better or for worse?

Lest I give the impression that Rick DeMarinis writes only about the ostensible "losers" in our society and that they are readily identifiable by their occupations and circumstances, let me say he writes about all aspects of society, from truckers to people who live in gated communities, from scientific whizzes to door-to-door salesmen. But I personally think Rick is at his best when he writes about children, particularly teenagers. One might imagine, given the kind of unsettled and unsettling adults in these stories, that the children would be equally screwed up. For the most part, this in not the case. In fact, more often than not, it is the young people who seem the most mature. Certainly they are the most observant. If one is seeking a reliable narrator, look to the children.

In "The Boys We Were, the Men We Became," a longish story written in several parts, each one denoting an advance in time, we are introduced to Bernard, a boy of indeterminate age. As in many of these stories, the father is a wreck (he actually comes home from the Second World War fat!), the mother a sweet, accommodating woman who wants things to work for everybody. After the father just picks up and leaves one day, she goes through a string of men, none of them what we might call a "catch." Bernard's observations concerning these men are almost astonishingly accurate. He figures them out in no time flat. Yet he is capable of being conned by her latest suitor (who eventually becomes his stepfather), when he claims to have been a hero in the French Resistance during the war. When his mother tells him that "Frenchy" actually spent the war on a GM assembly line Detroit, Bernard, embarrassed, says, "So what if he's lying... as long as what he's saying is true." It is to the author's credit that he gives this mature, reliable boy/narrator a chink in his credibility. He is human, after all, and that's what these stories are all about. And the fact that Bernard, in adulthood, ends up working as a security guard in a large department store after being sacked from his job as an engineer with Lockheed only adds to the poignancy of how we live our lives.

Borrowed Hearts is a major work by a writer who has toiled in the trenches of pure literature to emerge as one of America's finest storytellers. That I was there at the inception of Rick DeMarinis' remarkable career is both humbling and exciting. Thank you, Seven Stories Press, for giving this work the platform it deserves in a collection that spans his whole career. Perhaps Rick will now receive the attention he has so richly earned over the years. And now, dear reader, have a go at it. I think you will share my unalloyed excitement and my deep pleasure.

From UNDER
THE WHEAT
(1986)

D own in D-3 I watch the sky gunning through the aperture ninety-odd feet above my head. The missiles are ten months away, and I am lying on my back listening to the sump. From the bottom of a hole, where the weather is always the same cool sixty-four degrees, plus or minus two, I like to relax and watch the clouds slide through the circle of blue light. I have plenty of time to kill. The aperture is about fifteen feet wide. About the size of a silver dollar from here. A hawk just drifted by. Eagle. Crow. Small cumulus. Nothing. Nothing. Wrapper.

Hot again today, and the sky is drifting across the hole, left to right, a slow thick wind that doesn't gust. When it gusts, it's usually from Canada. Fierce, with hail the size of eyeballs. I've seen wheat go down. Acres and acres of useless straw.

But sometimes it comes out of the southeast, from Bismarck, bringing ten-mile-high anvils with it, and you find yourself looking

Under the Wheat

for funnels. This is not tornado country to speak of. The tornado path is to the south and west of here. They walk up from Bismarck and farther south and peter out on the Montana border, rarely touching ground anywhere near this latitude. Still, you keep an eye peeled. I've seen them put down gray fingers to the west, not quite touching but close enough to make you want to find a hole. They say it sounds like freight trains in your yard. I wouldn't know. We are from the coast, where the weather is stable and always predictable because of the ocean. We are trying to adjust.

I make five hundred a week doing this, driving a company pickup from hole to hole, checking out the sump pumps. I've found only one failure in two months. Twenty feet of black water in the hole and rising. It's the company's biggest headache. The high water table of North Dakota. You can dig yourself a shallow hole, come back in a few days and drink. That's why the farmers here have it made. Except for hail. Mostly they are Russians, these farmers.

Karen wants to go back. I have to remind her it's only for a year. Ten more months. Five hundred a week for a year. But she misses things. The city, her music lessons, movies, the beach, excitement. We live fairly close to a town, but it's one you will never hear of, unless a local goes wild and chainsaws all six members of his family. The movie theater has shown *Bush Pilot, Red Skies of Montana, Ice Palace,* and *Kon Tiki* so far. These are movies we would not ordinarily pay money to see. She has taken to long walks in the evenings to work out her moods, which are getting harder and harder for me to pretend aren't there. I get time and a half on Saturdays, double time on Sundays and holidays, and

3

thirteen dollars per diem for the inconvenience of relocating all the way from Oxnard, California. That comes to a lot. You don't walk away from a gold mine like that. I try to tell Karen she has to make the effort, adjust. North Dakota isn't all that bad. As a matter of fact I sort of enjoy the area. Maybe I am more adaptable. No, scratch that. I *am* more adaptable. We live close to a large brown lake, an earthfill dam loaded with northern pike. I bought myself a little boat and often go out to troll a bit before the car pool comes by. The freezer is crammed with fish, not one under five pounds.

There's a ghost town on the other side of the lake. The houses were built for the men who worked on the dam. That was years ago. They are paintless now, weeds up to the rotten sills. No glass in the windows, but here and there a rag of drape. Sometimes I take my boat across the lake to the ghost town. I walk the overgrown streets and look into the windows. Sometimes something moves. Rats. Gophers. Wind. Loose boards. Sometimes nothing.

When the weather is out of Canada you can watch it move south, coming like a giant roll of silver dough on the horizon. It gets bigger fast and then you'd better find cover. If the cloud is curdled underneath, you know it means hail. The wind can gust to one hundred knots. It scares Karen. I tell her there's nothing to worry about. Our trailer is on a good foundation and tied down tight. But she has this dream of being uprooted and flying away in such a wind. She sees her broken body caught in a tree, magpies picking at it. I tell her the trailer will definitely not budge. Still, she gets wild-eyed and can't light a cigarette.

We're sitting at the dinette table looking out the window, watching the front arrive. You can feel the trailer bucking like a boat at its moorings. Lightning is stroking the blond fields a mile away. To the southeast, I can see a gray finger reaching down. This is unusual, I admit. But I say nothing to Karen. It looks like the two fronts are going to butt heads straight over the trailer park. It's getting dark fast. Something splits the sky behind the trailer and big hail pours out. The streets of the park are white and jumping under the black sky. Karen has her hands against her ears. There's a stampede on our tin roof. Two TV antennas fold at the same time in a dead faint. A jagged Y of lightning strikes so close you can smell it. Electric steam. Karen is wild, screaming. I can't hear her. Our garbage cans are rising. They float past the windows into a flattened wheat field. This is something. Karen's face is closed. She doesn't enjoy it at all, not at all.

I'm tooling around in third on the usual bad road, enjoying the lurches, rolls, and twists. I would not do this to my own truck. The fields I'm driving through are wasted. Head-on with the sky and the sky never loses. I've passed a few unhappy-looking farmers standing in their fields with their hands in their pockets, spitting, faces frozen in expressions of disgust. Toward D-8, just over a rise and down into a narrow gulch, I find a true glacier. It's made out of hail stones welded together by their own impact. It hasn't begun to melt yet. Four feet thick and maybe thirty feet long. You could stand on it, blind in the white glare. You could tell yourself you are inside the Arctic circle. What is this, the return of the Ice Age?

Karen did not cook tonight. Another "mood." I poke around in the fridge. I don't know what to say to her anymore. I know it's hard. I can understand that. This is not Oxnard. I'll give her that. I'm the first to admit it. I pop a beer and sit down at the table opposite her. Our eyes don't meet. They haven't for weeks. We are like two magnetic north poles, repelling each other for invisible reasons. Last night in bed I touched her. She went stiff. She didn't have to say a word. I took my hand back. I got the message. There was the hum of the air conditioner and nothing else. The world could have been filled with dead bodies. I turned on the lights. She got up and lit a cigarette after two tries. Nerves. "I'm going for a walk, Lloyd," she said, checking the sky. "Maybe we should have a baby?" I said. "I'm making plenty of money." She looked at me as if I had picked up an ax.

I would like to know where she finds to go and what she finds to do there. She hates the town worse than the trailer park. The trailer park has a rec hall and a social club for the wives. But she won't take advantage of that. I know the neighbors are talking. They think she's a snob. They think I spoil her. After she left I went out on the porch and drank eleven beers. Let them talk.

Three farm kids. Just standing outside the locked gate of D-4. "What do you kids want?" I know what they want. A "look-see." Security measures are in effect, but what the hell. There is nothing here yet but a ninety-foot hole with a tarp on it and a sump pump in the bottom. They are excited when I open the access hatch and invite them to climb down the narrow steel ladder to the bottom. They want to know what ICBM stands for. What is a warhead? How fast is it? How do you know if it's really going to smear the right town? What if it went straight up and came straight down? Can you hit the moon? "Look at the sky up there, kids," I tell them. "Lie on your backs, like this, and after a while you sort of get the feeling you're looking *down,* from on top of it." The kids lie down on the concrete. Kids have a way of giving all their attention to something interesting. I swear them to secrecy, not for my protection, because who cares, but because it will make their day. They will run home, busting with secret info. I drive off to D-9, where the sump trouble was.

Caught three lunkers this morning. All over twenty-four inches. It's 7:00 a.m. now and I'm on Ruby Street, the ghost town. The streets are all named after stones. Why, I don't know. This is nothing like anything we have on the coast. Karen doesn't like the climate or the people and the flat sky presses down on her from all sides and gives her bad dreams, sleeping and awake. But what can I do?

I'm on Onyx Street, number 49, a two-bedroom bungalow with a few pieces of furniture left in it. There is a chest of drawers in the bedroom, a bed with a rotten gray mattress. There is a closet with a raggedy slip in it. The slip has brown water stains that look like burns. In the bottom of the chest is a magazine, yellow with age. *Secret Confessions*. I can imagine the woman who lived here with her husband. Not much like Karen at all. But what did she do while her husband was off working on the dam? Did she stand at this window in her slip and wish she were back in Oxnard? Did she cry her eyes out on this bed and think crazy thoughts? Where is she now? Does she think, "This is July 15, 1962, and I am glad I am not in North Dakota anymore"? Did she take long walks at night and not cook? I have an impulse to do something odd, and do it.

When a thunderhead passes over a cyclone fence that surrounds a site, such as the one passing over D-6 now, you can hear the wire hiss with nervous electrons. It scares me because the fence is a perfect lightning rod, a good conductor. But I stay on my toes. Sometimes, when a big cumulus is overhead stroking the area and roaring, I'll just stay put in my truck until it's had its fun.

Because this is Sunday, I am making better than twelve dollars an hour. I'm driving through a small farming community called Spacebow. A Russian word, I think, because you're supposed to pronounce the *e*. No one I know does. Shade trees on every street. A Russian church here, a grain elevator there. No wind. Hot for 9:00 a.m. Men dressed in Sunday black. Ladies in their best. Kids looking uncomfortable and controlled. Even the dogs are behaving. There is a woman, manless I think, because I've seen her before, always alone on her porch, eyes on something far away. A "thinker." Before today I've only waved hello. First one finger off the wheel, nod, then around the block once again and the whole hand out the window and a smile. That was last week. After the first turn past her place today she waves back. A weak hand at first, as if she's not sure that's what I meant. But after a few times around the block she knows that's what I meant. And so I'm stopping. I'm going to ask for a cup of cold water. I'm thirsty anyway. Maybe all this sounds hokey to you if you're from some big town like Oxnard, but this is not a big town like Oxnard.

Her name is Myrna Dan. That last name must be a pruned-down version of Danielovitch or something because the people here are mostly Russians. She is thirty-two, a widow, one brat. A two-year old named "Piper," crusty with food.

She owns a small farm here but there is no one to work it. She has a decent allotment from the U.S. Government and a vegetable garden. If you are from the coast you would not stop what you were doing to look at her. Her hands are square and the fingers stubby, made for rough wooden handles. Hips like gateposts.

No supper again. Karen left a note. "Lloyd, I am going for a walk. There are some cold cuts in the fridge." It wasn't even signed. Just like that. One of these days on one of her walks she is going to get caught by the sky which can change on you in a minute.

Bill Finkel made a remark on the way to the dispatch center. It was a little personal, and coming from anybody else I would have called him on it. But he is the lead engineer, the boss. A few of the other guys grinned behind their hands. How do I know where she goes or why? I am not a swami. If it settles her nerves, why should I push it? I've thought of sending her to Ventura to live with her mother for a while, but her mother is getting senile and has taken to writing mean letters. I tell Karen the old lady is around the bend, don't take those letters too seriously. But what's the use when the letters come in like clockwork, once a week, page after page of nasty accusations in a big, inch-high scrawl, like a kid's, naming things that never happened. Karen takes it hard, no matter what I say, as if what the old lady says is true.

Spacebow looks deserted. It isn't. The men are off in the fields, the women are inside working toward evening. Too hot outside even for the dogs, who are sleeping under the porches. Ninety-nine. I stop for water at Myrna's. Do you want to see a missile silo? Sure, she says, goddamn right, just like that. I have an extra hard hat in the truck but she doesn't have to wear it if she doesn't want to. Regulations at this stage of the program are a little pointless. Just a hole with a sump in it. Of course you can fall into it and get yourself killed. That's about the only danger. But there are no regulations that can save you from your own stupidity. Last winter when these holes were being dug, a kid walked out on a tarp. The tarp was covered with light snow and he couldn't tell where the ground ended and the hole began. He dropped the whole ninety feet and his hard hat did not save his ass. Myrna is impressed with this story. She is very anxious to see one. D-7 is closest to Spacebow, only a mile out of town. It isn't on my schedule today, but so what. I hand her the orange hard hat. She has trouble with the strap. I help her cinch it. Piper wants to wear it too and grabs at the straps, whining. Myrna has big jaws. Strong. But not in an ugly way.

I tell her the story about Jack Stern, the Jewish quality-control man from St. Louis who took flying lessons because he wanted to be able to get to a decent-sized city in a hurry whenever he felt the need. This flat, empty farm land made his ulcer flare. He didn't know how to drive a car, and yet there he was tearing around the sky in a Bonanza. One day he flew into a giant hammerhead—thinking, I guess, that a cloud like that is nothing but a lot of water vapor, no matter what shape it has or how big—and was never heard from again. That cloud ate him and the Bonanza. At the airport in Minot they picked up two words on the emergency frequency, "Oh no," then static.

I tell her the story about the motor pool secretary who shot her husband once in the neck and twice in the foot with a target pistol while he slept. Both of them pulling down good money, too. I tell her the one about the one that got away. A northern big as a shark. Pulled me and my boat a mile before my twelve-pound test monofilament snapped. She gives me a sidelong glance and makes a buzzing sound as if to say, *That* one takes the cake, Mister! We are on the bottom of D-7, watching the circle of sky, lying on our backs.

The trailer *stinks*. I could smell it from the street as soon as I got out of Bill Finkel's car. Fish heads. *Heads!* I guess they've been sitting there like that most of the afternoon. Just the big alligator jaws of my big beautiful pikes, but not the bodies. A platter of them, uncooked, drying out, and getting high. Knife, fork, napkin, glass. I'd like to know what goes on inside her head, what passes for thinking in there. The note: "Lloyd, eat your fill." Not signed. Is this supposed to be humor? I fail to get the point of it. I have to carry the mess to the garbage cans without breathing. A big white fire is blazing in the sky over my shoulder. You can hear the far-off rumble, like a whale grunting. I squint west, checking for funnels.

Trouble in D-7. Busted sump. I pick up Myrna and Piper and head for the hole. It's a nice day for a drive. It could be a bearing seizure, but that's only a percentage guess. I unlock the gate and we drive to the edge of it. Space-age artillery, I explain, as we stand on the lip of D-7, feeling the vertigo. The tarp is off for maintenance and the hole is solid black. If you let your imagination run, you might see it as bottomless. The "Pit" itself. Myrna is holding Piper back. Piper is whining, she wants to see the hole, Myrna has to slap her away, scolding. I drain my beer and let the can drop. I don't hear it hit. Not even a splash. I grab the fussing kid and hold her out over the hole. "Have yourself a *good* look, brat," I say. I hold her by the ankle with one hand. She is paralyzed. Myrna goes so white I have to smile. "Oh, wait," she says. "Please, Lloyd. No." As if I ever would.

Myrna wants to see the D-flight control center. I ask her if she has claustrophobia. She laughs, but it's no joke. That far below the surface inside that capsule behind an eight-ton door can be upsetting if you are susceptible to confinement. The elevator is slow and heavy, designed to haul equipment. The door opens on a dimly lit room. Spooky. There's crated gear scattered around. And there is the door, one yard thick to withstand the shock waves from the Bomb. I wheel it open. Piper whines, her big eyes distrustful of me now. There is a musty smell in the dank air. The lights and blower are on now, but it will take a while for the air to freshen itself up. I wheel the big door shut. It can't latch yet, but Myrna is impressed. I explain to her what goes on in here. We sit down at the console. I show her where the launch-enabling switches will be and why it will take two people together to launch an attack, the chairs fifteen feet apart and both switches turned for a several-second count before the firing sequence can start, in case one guy goes berserk and decides to end the world because his old lady has been holding out on him, or just for the hell of it, given human nature. I show her the escape hole. It's loaded with ordinary sand. You just pull this chain and the sand dumps into the capsule. Then you climb up the tube that held the sand into someone's wheat field. I show her the toilet and the little kitchen. I can see there is something on her mind. Isolated places make you think weird things. It's happened to me more than once. Not here, but in the ghost town on the other side of the lake.

Topside the weather has changed. The sky is the color of pikebelly, wind rising from the southeast. To the west I can see stubby funnels pushing down from the overcast, but only so far. It looks like the clouds are growing roots. We have to run back to the truck in the rain, Piper screaming on Myrna's hip. A heavy bolt strikes less than a mile away. A blue fireball sizzles where it hits. Smell the ozone. It makes me sneeze.

This is the second day she's been gone. I don't know where or how. All her clothes are here. She doesn't have any money. I don't know what to do. There is no police station. Do I call her mother? Do I notify the FBI? The highway patrol? Bill Finkel?

Everybody in the car pool knows but won't say a word, out of respect for my feelings. Bill Finkel has other things on his mind. He is worried about rumored economy measures in the assembly and check-out program next year. It has nothing to do with me. My job ends before that phase begins. I guess she went back to Oxnard, or maybe Ventura. But how?

We are in the D-flight control center. Myrna, with her hard hat cocked to one side, wants to fool around with the incomplete equipment. Piper is with her grandma. We are seated at the control console and she is pretending to work her switch. She has me pretend to work my switch. She wants to launch the entire flight of missiles, D-1 through D-10 at Cuba or Panama. Why Cuba and Panama? I ask. What about Russia? Why not Cuba or Panama? she says.

Besides, I have Russian blood. Everyone around here has Russian blood. No, it's Cuba and Panama. Just think of the looks on their faces. All those people lying in the sun on the decks of those big white holiday boats, the coolies out in the cane fields, the tinhorn generals, the whole shiteree. They'll look up trying to shade their eyes but they won't be able to. What in hell is this all about, they'll say, then *zap*, poof, *gone*.

I feel it too, craziness like hers. What if I couldn't get that eight-ton door open, Myrna? I see her hard hat wobble, her lip drop. What if? Just what *if?* She puts her arms around me and our hard hats click. She is one strong woman.

Lloyd, Lloyd, she says.

Yo.

Jesus.

Easy.

Lloyd!

Bingo.

It's good down here—no *rules*—and she goes berserk. But later she is calm and up to mischief again. I recognize the look now. Okay, I tell her. What *next*, Myrna? She wants to do something halfway nasty. This, believe me, does not surprise me at all.

I'm sitting on the steel floor listening to the blower and waiting for Myrna to finish her business. I'm trying hard to picture what the weather is doing topside. It's not easy to do. It could be clear and calm and blue or it could be wild. There could be a high, thin overcast or there could be nothing. You can't know when you're this far under the wheat. I can hear her trying to work the little chrome lever, even though I told her there's no plumbing yet. Some maintenance yokel is going to find Myrna's "surprise." She comes out, pretending to be sheepish, but I can see that the little joke tickles her.

Something takes my hook and strips off ten yards of line, then stops dead. Snag. I reel in. The pole is bent double and the line is singing. Then something lets go but it isn't the line because I'm still snagged. It breaks the surface, a lady's shoe. It's brown and white with a short heel. I toss it into the bottom of the boat. The water is shallow here, and clear. There's something dark and wide under me like a shadow on the water. An old farmhouse, submerged when the dam filled. There's a deep current around the structure. I can see fence, tires, an old truck, feed pens. There is a fat farmer in the yard staring up at me, checking the weather. I jump away from him, almost tipping the boat. *I am not the weather!* I want to say. My heart feels tangled in my ribs. But it's only a stump with arms.

The current takes my boat in easy circles. A swimmer would be in serious trouble. I crank up the engine and head back. No fish today. So be it. Sometimes you come home empty-handed. The shoe is new, stylish, and was made in Spain.

I'm standing on the buckled porch of 49 Onyx Street. Myrna is inside reading *Secret Confessions:* "What My Don Must Never Know." The sky is bad. The lake is bad. It will be a while before we can cross back. I knock on the door, as we planned. Myrna is on the bed in the stained, raggedy slip, giggling. "Listen to this dogshit, Lloyd," she says. But I'm not in the mood for weird stories. "I brought you something, honey," I say. She looks at the soggy shoe. "That?" But she agrees to try it on, anyway. I feel like my own ghost, bumping into the familiar but run-down walls of my old house in the middle of nowhere, and I remember my hatred of it. "Hurry up," I say, my voice true as a razor.

A thick tube hairy with rain is snaking out of the sky less than a mile away. Is it going to touch? "They never do, Lloyd. This isn't Kansas. Will you please listen to this dogshit?" Something about a pregnant high school girl, Dee, locked in a toilet with a knitting needle. Something about this Don who believes in purity. Something about bright red blood. Something about ministers and mothers and old-fashioned shame. I'm not listening, even when Dee slides the big needle in. I have to keep watch on the sky, because there is a first time for everything, even if this is not Kansas. The wind is stripping shingles from every roof I see. A long board is spinning like a slow propeller. The funnel is behind a bluff, holding back. But I can hear it, the freight train. Myrna is standing behind me running a knuckle up and down my back. "Hi, darling," she says. "Want to know what I did while you were out working on the dam today?" The dark tube has begun to move out from behind the bluff, but I'm not sure which way. "Tell me," I say. "Tell me."

The Billetdoux front yard should have told me right away that the job wouldn't amount to much. The lawn was overgrown with spikey weeds, what grass there was had died a number of seasons ago, deep tire ruts oozy with muck grooved the yard, and a rusty tub filled with crankcase oil sat on the warped porch. But I had just turned eighteen and was still untuned to the distress signals the world volunteers with unfailing reliability.

Price Billetdoux—he pronounced his name "Billy Ducks"—answered my knock. He was in pajamas and bathrobe, even though it was midafternoon. He stood before me, dark and grizzled, blinded by ordinary daylight. When he focused on me he shoved his hand into his robe pocket as if looking for a gun.

"I'm the one who called," I explained quickly. I held up the newspaper and pointed to his ad. "I want to try it, photography."

"Amigo," he said, pulling a crumpled pack of Camels from his bathrobe, "come in."

I followed him into the kitchen. There was a plump girl at the stove peeling an egg off a skillet. She was also in pajamas and robe. She had stringy, mud-colored hair and very small feet. She looked about twelve. I figured she was Billetdoux's daughter.

Billy Ducks Among the Pharaohs

"Pour us a couple of cups of java, will you Shyanne?" he said to her.

The girl dragged two cups out of the sink, rinsed them, and filled them with inky coffee. She moved listlessly, as if she had been sick and was just recovering.

Billetdoux lit his Camel, drank some coffee, made a face. He had haggard, bloodshot eyes. Dark, tender-looking pouches hung like pulpy half-moons under them. He squinted at me through the smoke, sizing me up. Then he explained the job. No salary. No insurance. No fringe benefits. No vacations. Everything I made would be a percentage of the gross. I would go from door to door, trying to get housewives to let me take pictures of them and their children. I would offer them an eight-by-ten glossy for only one dollar. That was the "bait." How could they refuse? But when I went back with the print, I would also have a portfolio of five-by-sevens, three-by-fives, plus a packet of wallet-size prints. The portfolio would cost anywhere from $5.95 to $11.95, depending on how many prints were purchased. Of course, if they accepted only the eight-by-ten "bait" item for a buck, there was no profit or commission.

"You can make a hundred or more a week if you're good," Billetdoux said. "And your hours are your own. I've got a boy over in Sulphur Springs who nets one-fifty."

I admitted that I didn't know the first thing about taking pictures, but he fanned the air between us as if to not only clear the air of cigarette smoke but also the heavy cobwebs of confusion from my mind. "I can show you how to take pictures of prize-winning quality in ten minutes, amigo. The job, however, is salesmanship, not art."

He took me down to the basement where he kept his "photolab." We had to pass through a hall that led to the back of the house. Halfway down the hall he stopped next to a door and tapped on it softly. Then he pushed it open an inch. I saw a woman with wild gray hair lying in a bed. She was propped up on several pillows. She also had the sickroom look, just as the girl did. Her eyes were dark and lusterless and her skin looked like damp paper. There was a guitar lying across her lap.

"I've got to break in a new boy, Lona," Billetdoux said. "I'll get you some breakfast in a little bit." Lona, who I assumed was Billetdoux's wife, let her head loll off the pillows until she was facing us. She didn't speak, but her large, drugged-looking eyes seemed to be nursing specific, long-term resentments. After Billetdoux closed the door, he whispered, "Lona is very creative, amigo."

The basement was a hodge-podge of equipment, stacked boxes, file cabinets, work tables, half-finished carpentry projects, all of it permeated with the smell of chemicals. He shoved stacks of paper around on his desk until he found a small brass key. He opened a cabinet with this key and took out a camera. "We'll start you on the Argus," he said. "It's simple to use and takes a decent picture. Later on, if you stick with me, I'll check you out on a Rolleiflex."

He took me step by step through the Argus, from film loading to f-stop and shutter speed. "I'll go around with you the first few days," he said, "to show you the ropes. Then you're on your own. You're a nice-looking boy—the housewives will trust you." He winked as if to suggest that trusting the likes of me and Billetdoux would be the biggest blunder a housewife could make.

We went back upstairs to the kitchen. "How about some breakfast?" he said.

I looked at my watch. "It's after three," I said.

"It is? No wonder I'm so hungry. Where the hell does the time run off to, amigo? Well, how about some lunch, then? Could you go for a bite of lunch?"

"Sure," I said. I hadn't eaten breakfast either.

"Shyanne," he called. "Honey, would you come in here?"

She came in, looking slightly more haggard than when I first saw her.

"Shy, hon, fix us some lunch, will you? The boy here and I are starved."

"There's no bread," she said. "Or meat."

Billetdoux pulled open a cupboard door. "How about some Cheerios, then?" he said.

"Fine by me," I said.

He poured out three bowls of the cereal, then added milk. He handed one bowl to Shyanne. "Here, hon," he said. "Take this in to Lona, will you? She hasn't eaten since yesterday."

"No one's eaten since yesterday," she said. "Except me, if you want to count that measly egg."

Billetdoux grinned darkly at me, embarrassed. "Time to make a grocery run, I guess," he said.

We ate in silence. The milk on my cereal was slightly sour. A big, late summer fly droned past my ear and landed upside down on the table, where it exercised its thick, feeble legs. A loud, nasty voice broke into the homely sound of our spoons tapping on the Melmac bowls. I heard the word "swill" hiss from the hallway. Shyanne came in, carrying the bowl of Cheerios. "Lona doesn't want cereal," she said, dumping the milk-bloated O's into the sink. "She wants Spam and eggs."

"What about toast?" Billetdoux said.

"Right. Toast, too. And hashbrowns."

He leaned forward, his eyes damp and tired-looking. "Listen, kid," he said. "Can you loan me ten bucks until tomorrow? I'm a little short. I had to get a new transmission put in my car last week. Cost? It's legal robbery!"

I took out my wallet. I still had about fifty dollars from my last job. I gave him ten.

"Thanks, amigo. Splendid. I won't forget this. This is above and beyond, amigo."

Shyanne plucked the ten out of his hand. "I'll go to the store," she said.

"Don't forget cigarettes," Billetdoux said.

Billetdoux told me how to snowjob a housewife, but the first door we knocked on was answered by a kid of about six or seven. I looked at Billetdoux, who was standing right behind me. "What do I do now?" I asked.

"Is your old lady at home, buster?" Billetdoux said.

The kid started to close the door. His little sister, naked and grimy, stood behind him, a gray pork chop in her muddy hand. Pale green bulbs of snot plugged her nostrils.

Billetdoux pulled a bent Tootsie Roll out of his pocket and gave it to the boy. The boy accepted it, visibly relaxing his doorway vigil. "Mummy not at home, huh?" Billetdoux said. "Well, that's all right. That's no problem at all." To me he whispered, "In a way, amigo, it makes our job easier."

He pushed the door all the way open and we went in. "Set the flood lamps up like I told you," he said. "Remember, the mainlight sits back about seven feet. Put the fill-light about three feet behind it, but over to the right. That way we get an arty shadow."

I opened the equipment case we'd carried in and took out the lamps. I set them up on their stands. While I was doing this, Billetdoux set two chairs up in the middle of the living room. I moved the two lamps so that they were the proper distances from the chairs.

"Hey, buster," Billetdoux said to the boy. "Your sis got any clothes? Why don't you be a good scout and hunt up some drawers for her, okay? We don't want to take what you might call filthy pornographic pictures, do we? And wash off her snot-locker while you're at it."

I set up the tripod and attached the Argus to it. The boy pulled a pair of pink panties on his sister. I took the pork chop out of her hand and set it on the coffee table. I used my own handkerchief to clean her nose. Billetdoux sat them down in the chairs. He stepped back and looked at them in the unmerciful glare of the flood lamps. "Good enough," he said. "Now, amigo, you are going to have to work on their expressions. Right now they look like starving Lithuanian refugees about to be processed into dogfood by the S.S. Not a cheery sight, is it?"

"Smile, kids," I said, bending to the Argus.

The kids looked dead in the viewfinder.

"*Smile* won't get it, amigo," Billetdoux said. "Smile is the kiss of death in this racket. You might as well ask them to whistle Puccini. No, you've got to bring out some personality, whether they've got any or not. You want to get something on their faces their mama will blink her eyes at in wonder. You want her to think that she's never really *seen* her own kids. Got the idea?" He knelt down in front of the kids and raised his hands like an orchestra leader. "I want you kids to say something for Uncle Billy Ducks, will you?" The kids nodded. "I want you kids to say, 'Hanna ate the whole banana,' and I want you to say it together until Uncle Billy Ducks tells you to quit, okay?"

He stood up and said to me, "Take ten shots. Press the shutter button between 'whole' and 'banana.' Got it? Okay, kids, start saying it." He raised his hands like an orchestra leader again and started the kids chanting the phrase. I hit the button too soon the first time, too late the second, but I gradually fell into the rhythm of their sing-song chant and was able to snap their pictures on the simulated smile generated when their mouths were open wide on "whole" but starting to close for "banana."

I took ten pictures, then shut off the floods. Billetdoux was nowhere in sight. I felt uneasy about our being alone in the house with these kids. The heat of the floods had raised a greasy sweat on my back. Then Billetdoux came in. He had a pork chop in his hand. "There's some grub in the ice box, amigo, if you're for it," he said. "Make yourself some lunch." He bit into the pork chop hungrily. "I'll say this," he said, chewing fast. "The lady of the house knows how to fry a chop."

Billetdoux began rummaging through the drawers of a built-in sideboard that filled one wall of the small living room. "Hello, there," he said, lifting a pair of candle holders out of a drawer. "Take a look, amigo." He hefted the candle holders as if weighing them for value. "Solid sterling, I believe," he said. He slipped them into his jacket pocket. Then he continued rummaging. The kids didn't pay any attention to him. They were still mumbling "Hanna ate the whole banana" as they watched me taking down the floods. I worked fast, sweating not just from heat now but from fear. "Hello hello hello," Billetdoux crooned, dumping the contents of a big black purse on the dining room table. "Coin of the realm—silver dollars, amigo. Cartwheels, 1887. The real McCoy, not the phony pieces of buffed-up tin they pass off as silver dollars these days. The landowners here appear to be silver hoarders... shameful, no?" He picked up one of the silver dollars and bit it lightly. Then he shoveled the big coins into a pile and began to fill his pockets with them. "It's rotten to hoard money like this when there's so much real need in the world today," he said, his voice husky with moral outrage.

"Let's go," I said.

"One momentito, por favor, kid," he said. "Nature calls." He disappeared into the back of the house. I snapped the equipment case shut, picked it up and headed for the door. I heard the sound of water hitting water followed by a toilet flushing. As I opened the front door I believed I could hear him brushing his teeth vigorously.

I waited outside, down the street. He showed up in a few minutes, his pockets bulging, another pork chop in his felonious hand. He had an electric frying pan under one arm and a desk encyclopedia under the other. "You didn't get any lunch, amigo," he said, his forehead furrowing with concern. "What's the matter, no appetite? You got a flu bug? Here, this chop is for you. You need to keep up your strength in this business."

I put the equipment case down. "You're a thief!" I said, realizing that this surge of righteousness was about ten minutes late.

He lowered the pork chop slowly. He looked astonished, then deeply hurt. "Say again, amigo? Billy Ducks a *thief?*"

"You heard me," I said, unmoved by his dismay.

"You're too harsh, amigo. I assure you it will all go toward an excellent cause. Look at it this way, try to see it as a redistribution of wealth. It's good for a society to have its wealth redistributed from time to time. Otherwise you wind up like the Egypt of the Pharaohs—a few tycoons eating chili and caviar in their plush houseboats on the Nile, and everybody else straining their milk shoving big slabs of granite around the desert. Does that make sense to you? Is this an ideal society?"

"How am I supposed to go back there with an eight-by-ten glossy of those kids?"

He raised the pork chop thoughtfully, then bit into it. "Well, amigo, you won't have to. This was just a practice run. I'll develop and print that film and see what you came up with. Consider it basic training. Boot camp. This is boot camp."

Boot camp lasted a week. Billetdoux was a good salesman. He almost always got into a house, and when he didn't, he vowed to me that he'd come back with a vengeance. I didn't ask him what he meant because I'd begun to suspect that he was crazy. I guess I should have quit after that session with the kids but I figured that once I was out on my own, his activities and mine would be separate. He was a thief, he was crazy, but I wasn't. He would develop and print my film and pay my commissions and that would be the extent of our relationship. I wanted the job badly enough to gloss over my own objections. I liked the idea of taking pictures door to door. It was better than working in a saw mill or on a road crew or baling hay for some stingy farmer. I'd be out in a nice neighborhood every day, I'd meet interesting people, no foreman looking over my shoulder, no time clock to punch.

The last day of boot camp Billetdoux parked his car—a 1939 Chevy whose interior smelled of moss—at the edge of the most exclusive neighborhood in town, Bunker Hill Estates. "Top of the world, amigo," he said, sipping black wine from a square bottle. The neighborhood was lush and hilly, the houses sprawling and surrounded by vast, perfectly tended lawns. "The land of the Pharoahs, amigo," he said. "Makes me jumpy, going up against them. I need this little bracer." He offered me the wine bottle and I took a sip. It was sweet, thick wine, like cough syrup.

We got out of the car and started walking up the steep street toward the looming estates of Bunker Hill. Billetdoux began laboring right away, wheezing, barely able to put one foot in front of the other. I was carrying all the equipment, but he acted as if he had the full load. "I don't feel so hot, amigo," he said, stopping next to a tall, bushy hedge. His face had gone white, his mouth a torn pocket: The Mask of Tragedy. There was a short picket fence on the street side of the hedge. Immediately behind the fence was a narrow flower bed, then the hedge. Billetdoux stepped over the fence and into the flowers. "I'm sick," he said. He unbuckled his belt. He took off his jacket and handed it to me. He dropped his pants and squatted into the hedge until only his pale, stricken face showed. A dark eruption of bowel noise broke the tranquil air. Billetdoux sighed. "Lord," he said. "What a relief. Must have been that goddamn chokecherry wine. Aggravates my diverticulitis." He smiled weakly. I stood there, holding his jacket, the full weight of the incredible situation beginning to impress itself on me.

A small dog, alerted by the commotion, came snapping up to Billetdoux. The dog was perfectly groomed. It looked like an expensive blond wig that had come to life. Billetdoux put a hand out to it, to appease it or to ward it off, and the dog bit his finger. Billetdoux fell backwards into the hedge, disappearing. The dog went after him, lusting for blood after his initial success with this hedge-fouling trespasser. Then they both emerged, Billetdoux roaring to his feet, the dog in frenzied attack. "Son of a bitch," Billetdoux said, picking the dog up roughly by its collar, a satiny bejeweled affair. "I hate small dogs like this, don't you, amigo? Probably eats anchovies and cake."

I looked up and down the street, expecting a crowd of curious Bunker Hill residents attracted by the ruckus, but the street remained empty and serene. It was the serenity of people who knew who they were, enjoyed it, and who believed in their basic indispensability to the great scheme of things. Pharaohs. Serene Pharaohs untouched by the small and large calamities that nipped at the heels of people like Billetdoux and me.

I turned back to Billetdoux. He was squatting back into the hedge, the dog firmly in his hand. "I really hate these lapdogs," he said, "but sometimes they come in handy."

"What are you *doing?*" I said. But I could see very well what he was doing. He was using the small dog that looked like a wig for toilet paper.

"It's all they're good for, dogs like these," he said, a sinister joy playing on his lips. "Bite my jewels, you little pissant, and I'll feed you to the flowers."

The dog whined pitifully. Billetdoux tossed it aside and stood up. The dog burrowed into the thick hedge, making a shrill whistling noise. "I feel much better, thanks," Billetdoux said to no one's inquiry as he buckled up. I handed him his jacket and he slipped it on, squaring his shoulders in the manner of someone who has just finished important business and is ready for the next challenge. He stepped over the picket fence. "Well, don't just stand there, amigo. Time, like the man said, is money."

We continued up the street, stopping, finally, at the crest of the hill. Billetdoux leaned on a mail drop. "Look," he said. "You can see the whole town from up here. Lovely, no? See the smoke rising from the mills? See the pall it makes across the town's humble neighborhoods? Wouldn't it be nice to live up here where the air is pure, where all you can smell is flowers and money? What do you think, amigo? Think I should buy a house up here with the Pharaohs?"

"Sure," I said, thinking of the ten bucks I loaned him that first day, the twenty I'd loaned him since, thinking of his wife and child, his wrecked yard, his mildewed Chevy.

He laughed bitterly. "No way, amigo. I couldn't take it. Too stuffy, if you know what I mean. A man couldn't be himself up here. I'd wind up playing their game... Who's Got It Best."

We walked along a narrow, tree-lined street called Pinnacle Drive. Billetdoux pointed at the street sign. "Here we are—the top of the world. The Pinnacle. Everything is downhill from here. That's the definition of pinnacle, isn't it? Isn't that what they're trying to tell us? You're damn straight it is."

It might have been true. The houses were two and three stories, wide as airplane hangars. Giant blue-green lawns were fitted with precise landscaping. Three to four cars gleamed in every garage.

We stopped at the biggest house on Pinnacle Drive, a slate gray, four-story saltbox affair with a seven-foot-high wrought iron fence surrounding it.

"What do you see, amigo?" Billetdoux said, his voice cagey.

"A house. A nice house."

"A nice house, he says. Look again, amigo. It's a monument, dedicated to arrogance, greed, and the status quo."

I looked again. I saw a nice house with a long sloping lawn studded with beautiful shrubs, a piece of metal sculpture—a seal or possibly a bear—curled at the base of a majestic elm.

"You're stone blind," Billetdoux said when I told him this. "You'll never be a real photographer. You've got scales on your eyes big as dinner plates. Stick to mothers and babies—don't take up real picture-taking. Promise me that, will you?"

Billetdoux stepped up on the stone retaining wall that held the iron fence. He grabbed the bars and began to yell. "Hey! You in there! We're on to you! We smell your goddamned embalming fluid, you fat-ass Egyptian mummies!" He began to laugh, enormously entertained by his performance.

Twin Dobermans came galloping up to the fence. The drapes of the front room moved. The Dobermans leaped at the fence, going for Billetdoux's hands. "I bet they've got us covered with tommy guns," he said, stepping off the retaining wall. "Look at those front doors, amigo. Eight feet tall and wide enough to run a double column of storm troopers through them. Now tell me, do you honestly feel there is warm human activity blundering around behind those dead-bolted doors? No, you don't. Tight-assed, nasty, withered old Pharoah and his Pharaohette live in there, stinking up the place with embalming fluid. Christ, amigo, it turns my stomach." He sat down suddenly on the retaining wall and covered his face with his hands. His shoulders heaved, as if racked with sobs, but he made no sound. "Lona is sick," he said, half-whispering. "That's why I steal things. You called it right, kid, I'm a thief." He looked at me, his face fighting a severe emotion that threatened to dissolve it. "These people get a head cold and they fly to the Mayo clinic. I can't even buy medicine for Lona." He took out his handkerchief and mopped his face with it. "Give me the Argus, amigo. I'll show you how to take a picture."

I opened the equipment case and handed him the camera. He began snapping pictures of the house. The drapes of the front room moved gently as if the house was suddenly filled with breezes.

"I'm looking at those doors," he said, sighting through the camera. "I'm looking at the shadow that falls across them on a severe diagonal due to the overhang above the steps. The effect, amigo, is grim. Now I'm sliding over to the left to include a piece of that window. This is interesting. This is the geometry of fear— a specialty of the Egyptians." He snapped a few more pictures, then handed me the camera. "Everything makes a statement, whether it wants to or not," he said. "It's up to you, the photographer, to see and record it—in that order. *Seeing,* amigo, that will come with maturity."

Billetdoux was full of himself. His eyes were shining with the power and accuracy of his perceptions. He looked stronger and more self-confident and even healthier than ever. He looked brave and intelligent and generous and sane. I raised the Argus and took a picture of him.

The front doors of the house opened. A tall, silver-haired man in a jumpsuit came down the steps shading his eyes to see us better. Seeing their master approach, the Dobermans renewed their attack. They leaped at the fence, turned full circles in midair, came down stiff-legged and gargling with rage.

"Down, Betsy, down, Arnold," said the silver-haired man when he reached us. "Is there something I can do for you gentlemen?" he asked, a genuinely friendly smile on his handsome face. He was elegant and calm and undisturbed by us.

Billetdoux shoved his hand through the bars, offering it to the old man. "We're doing some freelancing for the *Clarion,*" he said. I waved the camera for proof.

"Ah, journalists," said the man, dignifying us.

"Right," Billetdoux said, grinning horribly.

"Well, why don't you come inside and take some pictures of our antiques? Nedda, my wife, is a collector."

Billetdoux looked at me, his face so deadpan that I almost giggled. We followed the old man along the fence to the main gate. He sent the dogs away and then let us in.

The man's wife, Nedda, showed us through the house. She was tall and elegant with fine silver hair. She looked like the female version of her husband. They could have been twins.

The house was lavishly furnished with antiques. The dry, musty smell of old money was everywhere. It rose up in the dust from the oriental carpets. It fell from the handsomely papered walls. It lived in the stately light that slanted into the rooms from the tall windows. It was a forlorn, bittersweet smell, like stale chocolate, or maybe the breath of a Pharaoh.

After the tour, we were given ham sandwiches and coffee along with coleslaw. Nedda brought in a tray of wonderfully frosted cookies and refilled our coffee cups. Then we toured the house again, the fourth floor where Nedda kept her most prized antiques. Billetdoux, still playing the journalist, snapped a dozen flash pictures. He was working with a kind of controlled panic, on the verge of breaking an avaricious sweat. His jacket clinked with dead flashbulbs.

We went downstairs, exchanged a few more pleasantries, and left. "Guess you were wrong about them," I said.

He brushed the air between us with his hand. "Petty bourgeois front, amigo. Don't kid yourself."

"What's wrong with Lona?" I asked, surprising myself.

He shrugged. "The twentieth century," he said. "It depresses her. She's very sensitive."

"Oh," I said.

"You think being depressed is a picnic?" he said, annoyed at my tone. "It's an illness, amigo, serious as cancer."

"Really," I said.

He looked at me strangely, then slapped his stomach hard. He made a barking sound.

"What's wrong?" I asked.

"I can't eat coleslaw. The bastards put out coleslaw." We were halfway to the front gate. "I can't make it, amigo. Let's head back." He turned quickly and headed back toward the front doors. The Dobermans didn't come after us, though I expected them to come sailing around the house at any second. Billetdoux, doubled over and barking, ran up the steps of the front porch. He rang the bell until the door opened.

"The journalists," said the pleasant old man.

"Please," Billetdoux grunted. "Can I use your facilities?"

"Most certainly," said the old man. "Do come in."

The old man led Billetdoux away. I waited in the foyer. Nedda saw me. "Oh, you're back," she said.

"Yes, ma'am," I said. "My boss had to use your bathroom. He can't eat coleslaw."

She touched her cheek with her fingers. "Oh dear," she said. "I'm so sorry. I hope he isn't too distressed. Would you like some candy while you're waiting?"

"Yes, ma'am," I said. So these are the Pharaohs, I thought.

She went out and came back with a box of chocolates. I studied the brown shapes, then selected one I hoped was filled with cream instead of a hard nut.

"Oh, take more," she said, holding the box closer to me. "Fill your pocket. I'm not allowed them anyway. Neither is Burton."

Billetdoux came in, smelling of expensive cologne. "Let's hit the road, amigo," he said. "We've bothered these fine people long enough."

"No bother at all," said Nedda. "We don't get much company these days. I'm glad you came. Do drop in again, when you don't have to take pictures."

Out on the street Billetdoux said, "Christ, what a pair of phonies. I thought we'd never get out of there."

"Better check your wallet," I said.

He looked at me sharply but didn't say anything. I popped a chocolate into my mouth. Mint cream. I didn't offer him one. He reached into his pocket and pulled out a small sculpture of a Chinese monk lifting a wineskin to his grinning lips.

"Look at this piece of junk," he said. "I thought it was some kind of special jade, white jade maybe, but it's only soapstone. Chances are all those antiques are phonies too." He tossed the guzzling monk into a shrub as we walked down-hill toward the car.

After my first one-hundred-dollar week, Billetdoux invited me over to celebrate my success. "You're on your way, amigo," he said, uncapping a quart of cheap vodka. He made us a pair of iceless screwdrivers and we clinked glasses before drinking. "Here's to the hotshot," he said. "Here's to the man with the charm."

We drank half a dozen screwdrivers before we ran out of frozen orange juice. Then we switched to vodka on the rocks, minus the rocks. His mood changed as we got drunk.

"Here's to the hotdog capitalist," he said, turning ugly. "Here's to J.P. Morgan Junior."

He spread the photographs of Nedda's antiques out on the table before us. "There could be some money in these items, amigo. Enough to finance my retirement. Enough to escape the twentieth century. Unless they're fakes." He looked at me then, his eyes hard and rock steady. "How about it, amigo?"

"How about what?" I said, thick-tongued.

"How about we take it. How about we pay a midnight visit to Pinnacle Drive and get us a truckload of antiques?"

My mouth was already dry from the vodka, but it went drier. "No way," I said. "I'm a photographer, not a felon."

"Photographer my suffering ass!" he said. "You just don't have the belly for it, amigo. Look at yourself. You're about to muddy your drawers." He laughed happily, poured more vodka. My stomach rumbled on cue, and he laughed again.

Dinner was a blistered pizza that was both soggy and scorched. Shyanne made it from a kit. She cut it into eight narrow slices. Billetdoux and I ate at the kitchen table. Shyanne carried a tray into Lona's bedroom, then went into the living room with her two slices of pizza to watch TV.

"I should have gotten some T-bones," Billetdoux said.

"No, this is fine," I said.

"Don't bullshit a bullshitter, amigo," he said.

To change the subject, I reminded him of some of my weirder customers. I told him about the old weight-lifting champ who posed for me in a jockstrap, holding a flowerpot in each hand to make his biceps bulge. I told him about the couple who took turns sitting in each other's lap, touching tongues. Then there was the crackpot who wore a jungle hat and spoke German at a full shout to a photograph of his dead wife.

Billetdoux wasn't amused. "You think the human condition is a form of entertainment for us less unfortunate citizens, amigo?" he said. "Remember, 'There but for the grace of God go I.'"

I thought about this for a few seconds. "Sometimes it is," I said, refusing to buckle under to his hypocritical self-righteousness. "Sometimes it's entertaining as hell."

He glowered at me, then brightened. "Hey, come out to the garage with me. I want to show you something."

I stood up, felt the floor tilt and rotate, sat back down. When the room stabilized itself, I got up again.

Outside, the air was crisp. A cold wind seemed to be falling straight down out of the sky. Billetdoux opened the garage door and switched on the lights. "Ta da!" he sang.

A long, pearl-gray car gleamed in the overhead light. "Wow," I said, honestly impressed. "What is it?"

"That is a *car*, amigo," he said. "It's a 1941 LaSalle. I got it for a song from an old lady who didn't know what she had. It's been in storage—only eleven thousand miles on it."

We got in. The interior was soft, wine-dark plush. Even the door, when it latched, sounded like money slapping money. Billetdoux started it and backed out onto his lawn.

"It's a little dusty," he said, getting out of the car. "I'm going to hose it off. Dust will murder a finish like this."

I went back into the house. I found the vodka and poured some into my glass. Noise, like a mob of crows in flight, passed through the kitchen. I looked out the kitchen window. Billetdoux was leaning against the front fender of the LaSalle. He saw me and winked. He began to undulate, as if performing sex with the car. "I think I'm in love!" he shouted.

What had sounded like a mob of raucous crows was actually Lona. She was singing in a language that might have been Egyptian. She could have been strumming her guitar with a trowel for all the music that was coming out of it. Then a tremendous crash shook the house. Glass tinkled.

Billetdoux came in. "Are they at it again?" he asked me. Glass shattered. Wood splintered. "Oh oh," he said.

Oh oh seemed like a totally failed response to the din.

Billetdoux sighed weakly. "I smell trouble," he said.

We poured ourselves some vodka. The uproar changed in character. Two voices were now harmonizing in throat-tearing screams. Now and then something made the walls shake.

"Maybe we'd better have us a look-see," he said, sipping.

I sipped too. Outside the kitchen window the perfect LaSalle gleamed like a classy rebuttal to human life.

We went to the back of the house. Lona's bedroom door was open. For a second or two I didn't understand what I was looking at. What I saw was Lona and

Shyanne kneeling face to face on the bed, combing each other's hair. A dresser was lying on its side and a mirror was on the floor cracked diagonally in half. I saw then that neither one of them had combs in their hands. Just great knots of hair. Lona was growling through her clenched teeth and Shyanne was hissing. Shyanne's mouth was very wide and the teeth were exposed past the gum line. She looked like a cheetah. Then they fell over and rolled to the floor. They rolled toward us and we stepped back, holding our drinks high. The air before us was filled with flailing legs and whipping hair. "Knock it off, okay?" Billetdoux suggested meekly. He watched them a while longer, then set his drink on the floor. "Give me a hand, will you, amigo?" he said.

He grabbed Shyanne under the armpits and lifted her off Lona. She continued to kick out at Lona as Billetdoux pulled her into the hall. I reached for a waving leg, then thought better of it. Lona got heavily to her feet. Her gray hair had shapes wrung into it. Horns, knobs, antennas. Lumps that suggested awful growths. She picked up a lamp and flung it at Shyanne, who was no longer in the room. It exploded against the wall, next to my head. "God damn you to hell," she said to me, but meaning, I think, Shyanne.

"Fat witch! Pus hole! Slop ass!" Shyanne yelled from somewhere in the house.

"Bitch whore! Scum! Strumpet!" Lona countered.

After things quieted down, Billetdoux fixed us a new round of drinks. Vodka and warm apricot nectar. "That was embarrassing, amigo," he said. "They go ape shit like that about once a month or so. Don't ask me why."

I made some kind of suave gesture indicating the futility of things in general, but it didn't come off well since I was barely eighteen and hadn't yet earned the right to such bleak notions. I pulled in my gesturing hand so that it could cover my mouth while I faked a coughing fit.

Billetdoux wasn't paying any attention to me. "The television, the guitar," he said. "This house is too small for us. They tend to get on each other's nerves. Sometimes it comes to this."

I was drunk enough to say, "How come you let your daughter treat her mother that way?"

Billetdoux looked at me. "My daughter?" he said. "What are you saying, amigo?"

"Your daughter, Shyanne, she..."

"My *daughter?* You think I'm beyond insult, amigo? You think we've reached a point in time where anything at all can be said to Price Billetdoux?" For the first time he pronounced his name in accurate French.

"She's *not* your daughter?" I said, completely numb to the hard-edged peculiarities of Billetdoux's life, but somewhat surprised anyway.

"Damn," he said glumly.

"Then Lona..."

"Lona? Lona? Jesus, amigo, what godawful thing are you going to say now?"

"I thought Lona was your wife."

"Lona," he said, measuring his words, "is my mom." His voice was dark with a dangerous reverence that adjusted my frame of mind for the rest of the evening.

Shyanne came into the kitchen. She opened the fridge and took out a bottle of Upper Ten. She made a face at Billetdoux, then at me. "Oh baby baby," Billetdoux said, his voice wounded with love.

"I think you should tell her to move out," Shyanne said.

"Oh, baby. No. You know I can't do that. It would kill her."

"How do you think *I* feel?" she said. "Maybe you want *me* to move out. Is that what you want?" Her small red lips puckered into a hard, toy-doll pout. "I'll go. I'll just *go.*"

"Don't say that, baby," Billetdoux said, miserably.

Shyanne still looked twelve years old to me. But the hard, unwavering stare she had leveled at me was not something a child was capable of. I moved her age up to sixteen or seventeen. But something older by five thousand years hung stupidly in her face.

"Say the word, daddy, I'll go pack," she said.

I went out into the living room as Billetdoux began to weep on the small breast of his teenage wife.

I switched the TV to the "Perry Como Show." I watched it all. Then I switched to "Wagon Train." I had ignored the sounds coming from the kitchen—the soft, sing-song assurances, the cooing words that dissolved into groaning embraces, the serious oath-making, the baby-talk threats, and, finally, the mindless chit-chat.

Billetdoux came in and sat on the couch next to me. He was eating a peanut butter sandwich and drinking beer. "What can I say, amigo?" he said. "Are you going to think of me now as an old cradle robber? Hell, I'm only thirty-eight. Shyanne's almost sixteen. You think that's too young?"

I shrugged. "What's a dozen years more or less," I said, my arithmetic deliberately sentimental.

He straightened up, set his sandwich and beer down on the coffee table. "My situation is not easy, amigo. I'm so crazy about Shyanne. I can't live without her. You understand? No, you don't. Maybe someday you will, if you get lucky. At the same time, I've got to think about Lona. I can't set her adrift after all she's done for me, can I?"

"No," I said, remembering to be careful.

Billetdoux was chewing his lower lip and absent-mindedly cracking his knuckles. "Mom thinks the world of me," he said. "Did I tell you that? She calls me her Honey Boy."

I went back to the kitchen to get myself an Upper Ten. My stomach felt like I had swallowed a cat. Shyanne was still at the table. She was looking at her hands, studying first the tops, then the bottoms.

"They're red," she said, without looking up. "I hate these hands. Look at them. They're not very elegant, are they."

I got my Upper Ten, opened it.

"I'm sick of my hands," she said. "I'd just as soon cut them off."

She tried to show me her hands, but I walked past them and back to the living room. Billetdoux was pacing in front of the TV. "I'm going to Carnuba the LaSalle," he said. "It's been on my mind." He stalked out, like a man with pressing business.

I sipped my pop. Some kind of detective show was on now. After a while, Shyanne came in and sat next to me. Lona was strumming her guitar again and singing in Egyptian. "Are you going to take me fishing or not?" Shyanne said, her lips brushing my ear. Her tone of voice made me feel as though I'd broken every promise I'd ever made.

"Did I say I would?" I said.

"No one's taken me fishing since we came to this dumb town."

I noticed she was sitting on her hands.

"I know what you're thinking," she said, turning her face sidelong to mine, her small teeth catching the TV's gray light. "I know *exactly* what you're thinking."

I got up and went outside. Billetdoux was out on the lawn rubbing wax into the gleaming LaSalle. He was holding a flashlight in one hand and buffing with the other. "Amigo," he said. "Loan me twenty before you go, okay? I'm in a bit of a jam."

I gave him twenty without comment and walked away. I felt, then, that I'd seen enough of the Billetdoux family and that I wouldn't be back, ever.

But half an hour later I was in his kitchen again for no reason other than a vaguely erotic curiosity. I made myself another vodka and nectar and took it out to the backyard. It was a clear, moonless night. *The moon,* I thought, *is in Egypt.*

I sat on the dead grass and drank until I got sick. The sickness was sudden and total and my stomach emptied itself colossally into the lawn. When I was able to sit up again, I saw Lona. She was standing before the open bedroom window, naked, her strangely tranquil face upturned to the sky. Her eyes were closed and she was holding her arms out in front of her, palms up, in a gesture that reminded me of ancient priestesses. Her big silver breasts gleamed in the chilly starlight.

"Honey Boy," she said, her eyes still closed, her face still raised to the delicate radiations of the night. "Honey Boy, come here."

I got up heavily. I thoroughly believed in that moment that I had once again decided to leave. But I found myself walking trancelike to Lona. Like an inductee to a great and lofty sect, having passed my preliminary ordeal, I moved, awestruck, as if toward the sphinx.

D ig in!" I'd say, and the silverware would fly! Those were the days. If we saw a nibbler we would always be sure to let him see us unload our heaping forks. Our cheeks would balloon, our nostrils flare, and our eyes would roll with the sheer ecstasy of eating. The nibbler would usually dab his pinched-up mouth with his napkin and wash down his pellet of food with quick sips of water. A sickening tribe of birds, are they not? They make me gag.

We traveled a lot. The first thing we would do in a new town would be to scout the restaurants. And I mean *restaurants*. I do not mean the fast-food slop houses, the so-called "coffee shoppes," or the little neighborhood diners, where you eat at considerable risk. Ptomaine, I mean. We gave them grades. A for best, F for dismal failure. Quality and *quantity* first, service second. Atmosphere a distant third. We do not eat the atmosphere.

Now hear this: are you nervous? Are you thin? Then *eat!* What do you want to be like that for? Eat, sleep, and move your bowels. This is basic. This is life. I have seen too many human skeletons, *nibblers,* nervous as cats, eating that ghastly Jell-o on lettuce. Their reward? Stubborn stool dry as birdshot, and they sleep in fits.

Life Between Meals

I speak from experience. I was there. We were thin. "Doctor's orders." Antoinette was down to one hundred and forty pounds, and I teetered at two-twenty. We were a pair of rails. I looked somehow fraudulent in my uniform—no bearing, no authority, no style. A year before I'd been up to three-sixteen and Antoinette was a succulent two-oh-nine. We were a hefty duo, and happy. The famous internist said, "You lose one hundred pounds of that lard, Commodore, or you're sunk. Your heart will not bear the strain." And I believed his claptrap.

Broiled slivers of freshwater fish, naked green salads, fruit cocktails sweetened with something made out of coal tar, unsalted wafers, zwieback, fingers of asparagus without a nice blanket of buttery hollandaise, and, of course, the ever-present Jell-o on lettuce. We went through hell. We suffered. And for what, I ask.

Our health did not noticeably improve. Personally, I felt worse. I believed my death was imminent. I said, "Antoinette, my love, what is life *for*? Answer me that?"

She just cupped her shrinking breasts and laughed, rather thinly I thought. She called me her "enormous whale baby." But there was a hungry glint sharking the blue waters of her eyes. I whispered heavily into her ear, "Banana nut bread, my darling." I let the syllables roll off my tongue like buttered peas. "Chicken Supreme," I said. "Braised Rabbit à la Provence. Shrimp Mull. Creamed Cod Halifax. Marzipan. Fondant. Marshmallow Mint Bonbons." These were some of her favorites.

I wore her down. "My darling," I said. "I could eat raw and rotting squaw fish, I am so very hungry." But Antoinette wanted to remain faithful to the famous internist. She said, "You are forgetting your promise to doctor, Gabe." And I replied, "I do not care about doctor, Antoinette! I am going to die of misery! This is no way to live!" Eventually I won her over. We gave up on the diet and went back to real food. "We are going to be happy again, darling, I promise you." And for a while it was true.

Now hear this: I am hungry all the time. You may choose not to believe that. You might find such a statement a trifle on the bizarre side. But it is true. I simply do not stay full. I convert food to energy and bulk very quickly. I might go through a platter of oysters on the half shell, a tureen of minestrone, a tub of Texas hash, a loaf of Irish soda bread, three or four slabs of black bottom pie, ten cups of thick coffee, and do it all over again in a couple of hours, believe what you will.

We were cruising around a pretty little inland town checking out Mexican restaurants. We'd found a lovely little place. But Antoinette had the blues. She said, "God, I just don't know anymore, Commodore." Sometimes she called me Commodore. I found it pleasurable.

Something was eating her. She'd been depressed lately. Chewing, her face would sour. She'd put down her fork. "What is it, my darling?" I'd ask. "The meat not done well enough? The sauce flat? Light? Too sweet? Too tart? No character? No spunk?" She would shake her head, run her tongue over her teeth, lift her large breasts off her stomach as if trying to ease her breathing. "Oh, I don't know, Gabe. It's just me, I think." But this was not a satisfactory explanation.

And now, in Guzman's Authentic Sonoran Cuisine, she was balking at the menu. I ordered for her, which was something I hesitated to do. Ordering, after all, is half the *fun*.

"*Matambre, por favor,*" I said to the waiter.

"*Matambre,*" said Antoinette, "is not Sonoran."

I looked at the waiter, a blond boy with large pimples on his neck, his nose ring outlined with threads of acne. "She is right, you know," I said.

He shrugged. "Get the chicken enchiladas," he said. "It's the best thing on the menu."

"We can get chicken enchiladas anywhere," I said. "No, we'll try the *matambre.*"

In fact, it was wonderful *matambre.* My appetite increased. I ordered the *tostadas estilo,* which were made with pig's feet and beans. Antoinette ate as much as I did, but without evident relish.

We drove down to our condominium on San Diego Bay. I like the view, the great naval fleet, the fine tuna seiners, the pleasure craft. Sitting on our balcony, ten floors above the waterfront, I said, "Come on, Antoinette. Out with it. What's wrong, darling?"

There was a platter of cold tongue slices garnished with pimento olives and sweet gherkins between us. The boy had brought them. Antoinette was playing nervously with her diamonds. I tossed a piece of tongue into the air and caught it in my teeth. A small aircraft carrier was easing into the bay. I picked up the glasses to observe it.

"A," she said, "I have no friends. And, B, life between meals is empty."

I put down the glasses and handed her a cool slice of meat. "We have each other," I suggested. In retrospect, I imagine my tone was peevish.

She took a thoughtful bite of the tongue, but would not meet my eyes. The sun was warm on our large bodies. We liked to sit without our clothing on our little terrace, watching the boats. The boy, Wing, was as discreet as only the Chinese can be.

That night, Antoinette woke up in a thrashing sweat. I turned on the lights. "Feel my heart," she said. I pressed my ear to her sweat-filmed breast. Something wild was walloping around in there.

"Take it easy, darling," I said, ringing for the boy. "Try to relax. Was it a dream?"

I had Wing fix a plate of leftover cold cuts for us. It was 3:00 a.m. I opened a quart of Pilsner. I covered two slices of rye with a nice hot mustard and then laid in the meat.

I heard her gagging in the bathroom. She stayed in there for quite a while. Then she came into the kitchen and sat at the table. Her eyes were red and she smelled sour. "Fix me one of those," she said, looking at me with those direct, blue, challenging eyes that first attracted me to her four years ago.

"With or without," I said, holding up a jar of *Weinkraut.*

"With," she said defiantly.

I breathed a sigh of relief. Whatever had troubled her sleep had passed. Or so I believed.

That summer I reached a happy three hundred. I felt good. Antoinette was only one-ninety, but she was coming along fine. When she hits two hundred, I told myself, look out! Her stomach blows out in front, shoving her loaf-like breasts up high and handsome, the nipples spreading wide like brown saucers, and a gossamer rump so soft and creamy it could melt your heart and bring water to your mouth.

"Come over here, you lovely dumpling!" I'd command, and the walls of our condo would shake. I'd imagine the floor joists sagging, the wall studs splintering, the sheetrock crumbling, the roof tiles slipping off and crashing into the streets below.

By fall I made three-twenty and Antoinette reached two-oh-nine, equaling her previous high. We were never happier. We cavorted like honeymooners and ate like young whales. Dig in! Dig in!

We'd go to one of those smorgasbord places just for the fun of it, the ones that advertise, "All You Can Eat For Ten Dollars!" We loved to watch the manager's face sag as we lined up for seconds and thirds and fourths, on and on.

"Fifteen trips, Antoinette," I'd say, a friendly challenge, and she would sweetly reply, "You are on, Commodore!" And we'd fill and empty our trays fifteen times, *heaped,* while the manager would whimper to his girls and shake his head. Once we cleaned out an establishment's entire supply of veal-stuffed zucchini, which was supposed to be the specialty of the house. The manager was a skinny twerp who kept snapping a towel at flies. He didn't bother us.

Now hear this: Skinny people can't be trusted. A man who can get along on cottage cheese, pears on lettuce, or chicken salad sans mayo, bears watching. A man who keeps a girl's waistline is probably *sly.* I wouldn't touch one of those female skeletons you see in the ads. Like bedding down with Tinkertoys. I'd crush her dainty innards, her bones would go like twigs. All of them, the thin ones who are thin by choice, are *nibblers.* We once elected a tribe of fancy nibblers to high office and look where it got us. They make me gag.

Steak and potatoes, hot rolls and butter, cheese sauce and broccoli, stuffed eggplant, black bean soup, honey-glazed ham, Bavarian cream, chocolate butter sponge cake, jelly rolls, doughnuts, cookies, ice cream! Eat, eat, enjoy! Make that table groan. What do you have a mouth with teeth in it for? Whistling and smiling?

Our national flag should be a steaming dressed-out turkey with stuffing oozing out onto a garnished platter.

We were in a nice restaurant up north. Antoinette had been feeling a little moody again and I thought a change of scene would do her good. She was up to two-twenty, an all-time high, and she never looked better. I was holding steady at three-forty-nine. Everyone has an upper limit, unless there's a problem and your glands explode on you. Then you get the six-hundred-pound abnormals, the half-ton shut-ins.

Steak and kidney pie was the specialty of the house. The servings were generous enough, but we ordered, as usual, seconds and thirds. Now, the thing is, we were very serious about eating. We would tuck our napkins in and we would *eat.* No small talk. No stopping for cigarettes. If we spoke at all, it was to get the salt, the pepper, butter, soy sauce, and so on. Later, over coffee, we might talk.

We would get down, close to the plate, and we would keep the silverware moving. Lift dip, lift dip, lift dip. The object is to get the food into the stomach.

So I did not hear him when he first said it because I was occupied in the manner described. Then, when he raised his voice, I said, "Are you addressing me, sir?" He said he was. I dried off my mouth with my napkin and looked at him. I do not like to be interrupted when at table.

"You disgusting goddamn pigs," he said.

He was tall and skinny and had a cowboy-thin face that jutted out with years of lean living. I did not like his looks.

"You people look like you got greased life rafts tied around your necks, you're so goddamn sinful fat and slobbery."

Antoinette was still eating but her fork had slowed considerably.

"You supposed to be some kind of fucken sailor?" said the cowboy, sneering at me now and looking back to his table for approval. I sat erect in my chair, removed my napkin from my lap, and gazed coolly at him. "You got near everyone in this restaurant ready to blow chunks, the way you pig down that food, admiral," he said.

"That will be quite enough," I said.

He laughed at me and did something obscene. He threw his cigarette on my plate. Then he went back to his table, which greeted him heartily, like a returning hero.

"Now hear this, Antoinette," I said. "We will not stand for this impudence. We have our dignity." Antoinette was white as her napkin and her eyes were teary. She had put her fork down. Her lip was trembling. She touched the sides of her neck with her careful fingertips.

"Life rafts?" she said.

I pushed away from the table and stood up. The skinny cowboy saw me coming but he turned his back deliberately as if I was not someone he should be concerned about. No one takes the fat man seriously.

"I believe this is yours, sir," I said.

I had my plate with me, complete with his dirty cigarette sticking out of my mashed potatoes. He turned slowly and looked at me in an offhanded way. Even his mouth was skinny, the lips like blades.

"What's that, pig face?" he said. The two skinny women and the skinny man who were at his table laughed. They were eating breaded fingerlings of some kind and crackers.

I took the back of his head in my left hand and with my right hand I shoved that plate full of ruined food into his face. His mouth yawned open for air under a smothering gray slick of potatoes and gravy. He was quite surprised by my action. Fat men are not generally regarded as quick, strong, or willing to retaliate. This is a common error. At twohundred pounds I can barely lift a kitten. At three-forty-nine, I am strong as a bear and quick enough. And, I am more than willing to demand satisfaction from the likes of the skinny cowboy.

He jumped to his feet and began throwing punches at me. But he was wild, hitting only my shoulders and chest, which met his fists like sofa cushions. I pushed him off balance and kept pushing him until he was against a wall. Then I leaned, belly first, and the air whistled out of him. Antoinette came over then and pinched his cheek so hard that a welt appeared. He tried to kick me but his legs were about as dangerous as pencils. Behind us, his table was laughing and singing *Anchors Aweigh.*

I took Antoinette on a clothes-buying expedition to cheer her up. That ugly incident had made her blues return stronger than ever. At night she would wake up, filled with gas and sour dreams, gagging.

"These dresses," she said, holding several of the new items up. "They are *circus* tents." We'd bought them at the *Wide Pride* outlets, the only clothing emporiums that carry Mega X sizes. We were in our bedroom. I was in bed watching the morning news. The navy, I was sad to learn, was in full retreat before the budget-cutting demands of several skinny congressmen. They were denying the return of the beautiful battlewagons, calling them "fat missile targets." I made up my mind then and there to send telegrams to our legislators, urging them to bring the great wide-beam navy back. Stop this mindless downsizing. Then a commercial came on, diverting my thoughts. Ham and eggs in a sunny kitchen, whole wheat muffins stacked like shingles, prune Danish, fritters, and the lovely girl was taking potato pancakes out of the pan and carrying them to her smiling husband, a good-sized man of healthy appetite. My mouth watered.

Antoinette threw her new dresses aside and stood before her mirror. "Elephant," she said. She made her reflection jiggle and blur by rising up on her toes and letting her weight come down hard on her heels. The room vibrated. Then she began to prance. But it wasn't for fun. She was mocking herself. "Look at me!" she shouted with false merriment. "The elephant is dancing! Come one, come all!"

I thought she looked good. Lovelier than ever. Her rain-barrel thighs roared across my field of vision. Her meal-sack breasts swung. Her dimpled rump seemed to fill the room. I was, quite frankly, aroused. I caught her by the wrist.

"Oh no you don't!" she said. But I pulled her anyway. She came down, off-balance, and the wood slats of the bed cracked. Bang, and the bed came down. The room quaked, and I imagined plaster dust graining the air of the room below. "No, Commodore!" she said. "I told you *no!*"

But the Commodore cannot be denied. "Jumbo lover," I whispered hoarsely into her tangled hair. I pinned her and our tonnage moved the seismographs of Spain.

She poked at her breakfast. I didn't like to see that. "Come, come, cupcake," I said. "What's wrong now?"

She looked at me across the laden table, her keen blue eyes gone soft and waxy. She touched her neck, an unconscious habit which began in the restaurant where I had been forced to discipline the skinny cowboy. I folded a piece of ham in half and speared it. She stabbed a fritter but she did not lift it to her lips. I chewed slowly, waiting. My patience, I confess, was wearing thin. Finally she put down her fork. I put down mine.

"My darling," I began. "Everything is either inside or it is outside. Make no mistake. If it is inside, it is being eaten. If it is outside, then it is either eating or waiting to eat. That is all anyone can say about it. The rest is manure. Things on the outside sooner or later find themselves in the inside. For, you see, everything gets its chance at being on the outside *eating,* or in the inside getting *eaten.*

My darling, everything in the wide world is food. Us included. It is so very simple. I don't understand your confusion. We are lucky eaters now, but someday that will change. Dig in, my darling. It is the skinny people of the world who are stuffed to their eyes with illusions."

"We're freaks," she said. She left the table and went into the bathroom, where she retched.

I followed her and stood outside the door. "Are you making yourself vomit deliberately, Antoinette?" I asked. She did not reply. "I cannot sanction that, my darling. I can never sanction that." Still she did not reply. Then I humbled myself. I knelt on both knees before the sullen door. "Ah, love, we *must* be true to one another," I said. "We have nothing else, don't you see?" But she would not answer.

Now hear this: Like most large men I'm tolerant and easy to get along with. But there is a line. If you are a skinny man you may not understand what I am saying here. Suppose, then, that you are a skinny dancer and you have married a skinny woman who is also fond of dancing. Then she decides, without consulting you, that she's tired of dancing and would rather sit down and eat. Soon she blossoms out to a healthy size eighteen or twenty and will not roll back the carpet when the Lawrence Welk rerun comes on TV. You soon begin to feel stupid foxtrotting around your rumpus room with a barstool in your arms while the little woman has her face parked in the Kelvinator. Where is the little girl I married, the girl with the twinkling feet? you ask yourself. I shall tell you where she is. She has shipped out. That size eighteen or twenty with the drumstick in her hand is someone else. You have begun to sense this yourself and have taken to calling her the USS *Tennessee* or some such appellation meant to discourage her. But she is not discouraged. She has, perhaps, found herself a new companion, fat as herself, and you find them together laughing wonderfully between mouthfuls of guacamole dip and tortilla chips. You're beginning to feel left out. You are disgusted by her. You are angry. Bitterness taints every bite of food you take and you grow skinnier and thus even farther away from her than ever. She asks, so innocently, what's wrong with you lately, and you can only stare at her as if she is the last person in the world who has the right to ask that question. But you won't say a word because you are afraid, at this point, of what might happen if you open your mouth and let loose what's really troubling you. You have been *betrayed,* skinny, but you cannot say a word because that kind of betrayal is not punishable by God's law or by court martial.

A betrayer needs an ally. Our condominium had a number of candidates. Skinny food-haters, dozens of them. Fifty-year-old business executives with the bodies of schoolboys. Suntanned grandmothers in string bikinis. You never see them with food in their mouths. They live on vitamin supplements and protein tablets. One of these food-haters, Bessie Carr, gave Antoinette a subversive menu guaranteed to burn away her fat in a matter of weeks.

Antoinette refused to sit down with me and discuss it. "My darling, such diets are dangerous," I said. She looked at me with that challenge in her eyes, but it wasn't the same. There was no promise of fun in this new defiance. I felt sick at heart.

"You are the one, Gabe, who is digging his grave," she said. "And you are digging it with your mouth."

It was the realization of my worst fears. It had happened to me before, with the others. *Am I cursed?* I asked myself. A trichinosis of self-doubt undermined the shank and brisket of my soul.

"Come, my darling," I said one morning, hoping to retrieve something of our former happiness, "let us do a Roly-Poly." But she looked at me with icy disgust. We hadn't done a Roly-Poly since our honeymoon and the two or three months of high excitement that followed. Yes, it is the pinnacle of frivolity, but I was desperate. My life, once again, was listing severely and threatening to capsize.

"Don't be vulgar," she said.

We used to do it in the hot tub. It was a game. We'd get about seven hundred tins of liverwurst and Wing would open them on the electric opener. Then we would cover ourselves with the tasty paste. We would roll and slide in the drained tub, nibbling liverwurst from each other until it was gone. It was the appetizer to afternoons filled with a smorgasbord of delights. I can remember Antoinette rolling like a dolphin and murmuring, "Yummers." Once we tried deviled ham, but it did not hold well to the skin. Those were the days. We were hot pink whales in a soupy bay.

But now her fat was going like lard in a skillet.

I began to eat for both of us, as if I could maintain her bulk by doubling my intake. By the time she dropped to one-fifty, I had climbed to three-eighty. I had passed my upper limit and the difference made me nervous and gassy.

Bessie Carr used to be fat herself. She brought over an album of snapshots showing her progress from a size twenty-two to a size nine. They were at the kitchen table, poring over the pictures. I said, leaning over them, "Now hear this: *there* is a woman after my own heart." I pointed to a picture of Bessie lying in a child's wading pool. Arms and thighs, like great roasts, fell over the sides of the inadequate pool. Her breasts expanded in the buoyancy of water. They looked like fine wheels of white cheese. The pale hummock of her belly was a vast, North African kingdom. She turned the pages, however, until she found herself thin. There she was in a bikini, daylight blaring between her thighs even though she was standing in a normal way. So much daylight, quite frankly, that you could have placed an entire chicken between her upper thighs and it would have fallen to her feet without touching her! It was horrible, enough to make a leper queasy. I sighed regretfully and they both looked at me with undisguised scorn, and then pity.

"Adipose Tissue and Its Spiritual Implications," said the brochure I happened to find on Antoinette's vanity. I thumbed through it. There was a good deal of nonsense about something called, "The Great Need." It seemed that we were very hungry, but not for food.

I went into the living room to point out the foolishness of such claims to her. She was sitting on the floor, before a black man with thickly lidded eyes. The black man was on the TV set, speaking in low tones. He was wearing a turban of some kind.

"Antoinette," I said. "May I have a word with you?"

"Shh," she said.

"Please, my darling, we must discuss this thing."

She turned to me then, annoyed. "I am listening to Sri Raj," she said sharply.

"I would rather that you listened to *me* for a moment," I said, somewhat offended.

"No," she said. "I'm learning about it."

"It?" I asked, glancing at the black man, who seemed on the verge of nodding off to sleep.

"Life, Gabe," she said. "I'm learning how to flower. The spiritual garden within is starving, according to Sri Raj."

I dropped the brochure. It fluttered to the floor beside her. "I'm going to have lunch," I said. "I'd like you to join me, Antoinette." I snapped off the TV set.

This angered her. "Don't call me Antoinette anymore!" she said. "My name is Debbie! I've always *hated* that name Antoinette!"

"Have you now," I said.

"Yes, I have! It's a pig's name! Farmers give their eight-hundred-pound sows names like Antoinette and Veronica and... and... *Emmeline!*"

"Do they," I said.

She turned the TV back on and the black man rolled into the screen. "Be joyful, then, as the little birds," he said.

I lunched alone. Wing, sensitive as ever to crisis, had made a wonderful Viennese *linzertorte,* one thousand calories per serving!

"Wing, old son," I said, affectionately. "Pack up my uniforms. I am afraid it's time to ship out."

And ship out I did. I am not such a fool as one who will humiliate himself before the inevitable. I bought into another condominium up the bay toward the city. Of course, I missed her terribly. I always miss them terribly. And why shouldn't I? It is no great pleasure to take your meals alone, is it? And what of the great restaurant hunts? The round-robin eating binges? The king-size bed with double-strength frame? Such a bed needs a great and ample queen.

Faithful Wing drove me about the city, looking for a new companion. Wing's careful manner at the wheel tended to hold my eagerness in check. The way he held to the speed limits, the sober way he lifted the gear lever, the delicate gloved hand on the wheel—all these things served as an example to my hasty mind. Haste, in such a weighty enterprise, can serve no good purpose. Had I taken more time to observe Antoinette four years ago, I might have detected the worm of discontent that eventually fouled our pleasant arrangement.

"I think we should look for a younger one this time, Wing," I said. "One with a simpler, more reliable outlook."

Wing understood immediately and turned the car toward the beach areas where the cheap, fast-food restaurants thrive. We cruised the neon boulevards, scanning.

"Starboard bow, Wing," I said, pointing to a place called *Holy Cow!* It was a hamburger house shaped like Borden's Elsie. Sitting alone on the patio, a tray of giant cheeseburgers before her, was a likely prospect, a hefty redhead of eighteen or so. Her complexion was unfortunate, perhaps, but a year of clean, expensive food properly prepared would clear it up just fine. There were other young people there, but they sat tables away, avoiding her as though she had a dreaded disease.

We sat in the parking lot for half an hour, simply observing her. Wing had the video camera going and I was making copious notes. Even though I was wearing my elegant "King Edward" naval uniform, and would have made a smashing impression on her, we needed to exercise some empirical caution this time. But all the signs looked very good.

The longer I watched her lift those cheeseburgers to her lonely but shameless jaws, the more convinced I was that we were meant for each other. Her name was probably Kathy, Wendy, Jean, or Pam—something that did not give credit to her true nature. I thought about it for a while, then snapped my fingers, making Wing jump.

"Roxanne!" I said. "We shall call her Roxanne!"

Dobb knows the cooped housewives need him. A new breed of degenerate (de-gents, Cobb calls them) has been making the headlines. A door-to-door salesman with a sharp yen for the average, haggard, wide-beam housewife. Cobb saw it in the Times yesterday morning. This de-gent peddling a glass knife guaranteed to slice overripe tomatoes. College-educated guy at that. Nice, trim, clean-cut, good suit from Bullock's or Macy's, and this normally cautious housewife lets him in. He demonstrated his glass knife on her. Sliced her, diced her, iced her. Then went out to his Volvo to jerk off. Bad news. The bad old world is full of it, but Cobb's product promises freedom from such bad dreams. He holds the three-inch chrome-plated cylinder up to the cracked (but still chained) door so that the lady can see it clearly. His blond, unlined face looks harmless and sincere and deeply concerned about Home Security. It's his business, and Cobb has been working the hot neighborhoods of West L.A. all morning this burning day in early August.

The Smile of a Turtle

"You need this device, ma'am," Cobb says, sincere as the Eagle Scout he once was. "Every housewife in L.A. needs it. A simple demonstration will make this abundantly clear. The de-gents, ma'am, are everywhere." He says "ma'am" in the soft southern way to slow her trotting heart. But the gadget sells itself. And it's a bargain at five dollars. Ten would be fair and most would pay twenty, but all he wants is the price of a movie ticket. Isn't Home Security worth at least that much—the price, say, of *Friday the 13th, Part Three* or *Dressed to Kill*?

She opens the door a hair wider, hooked. Cobb looks like her kid brother, or her old high school boyfriend, or maybe the nice boy who delivers the paper. All American Clean-cut. He looks harmless as a puppy. There's even something cuddly about him, something you could pet. A dancing prickle of heat glides across the nape of her neck and into her hair line.

Cobb is working on projecting these positive vibes. He feels that he's able, now, to radiate serious alpha waves. His boss, Jake the Distributor, has this theory. He thinks every man and woman is an animal at heart. We respond, he says, to the animal in each other. We see it in our little unconscious moves and gestures. We see it in our eyes. The trick, says Jake the Distributor, is to identify *your* personal animal and let the pure alpha waves flow out of it. This is how you become a world-class salesman. Jake the Distributor has studied the subject in depth. "You," he said to Cobb, "are obviously a turtle." He said this at a big sales meeting and everyone laughed. Turtle, what good is a turtle, Cobb thought, humiliated, and, as if answering his thoughts, someone hollered, "Soup! Soup!" and they all laughed at him and among the laughers he identified the barking hyenas and dogs, the hooting chimps and gibbons, and the softly hissing turtles.

Cobb bought Jake the Distributor's theory. He made a study of turtles. The Chinese had some definite ideas about them, for instance. On the plus side, turtles are careful and shy, fond of warm mud, and ready to leave a bad scene at the first sign of trouble. On the minus side, they are shifty, shiftless, and dirty-minded. They think about getting it morning, noon, and night. They are built for getting it. Even their tails help out. The turtle tail is prehensile during the act. It holds the female close and tight and there's no way she can detach herself once things get under way. Turtles can screw ten, fifteen times a day and not lose interest.

But Jake the Distributor says, Emphasize the positive and you will make your fortune. Keep your fingernails clean and clipped. Wash up several times a day—you can develop a bad stink walking the neighborhoods all day long. Change your shorts. Use a strong underarm spray. Don't touch yourself out of habit in the area of your privates while in the process of making a pitch. Keep a good shine on your shoes. Keep your nap up. Hair trimmed and combed. Teeth white, breath sweet, pits dry. Groom, groom, groom.

It's the brace-and-bit, though, that tends to do major harm to his first good impression. This can't be helped—tools of the trade. Cobb tries to hold it down behind his leg. But she's seen it and is holding her breath. So he starts his pitch, talking fast. "It's called Cyclops, ma'am," he says. (Southern, says Jake the Distributor, don't forget to sound southern. They *trust* southern. Sound New York and you are dead meat in the street. Sound L.A. and you get no pay. Think genteel, southern Mississippi. Think graceful Georgia. But do not think Okie. Talk Okie and they will pee their drawers. Bike gangs are Okie. Bible salesmen are weirdo Okie. Think magnolia blossoms and buggy whips and mint juleps. Think *Gone With the Wind.* Make them think they are Scarlett O'Hara.) "The *Farrago* Cyclops, ma'am," Cobb explains. "Charles V. Farrago being the name of the gentleman who invented it and who currently holds the exclusive manufacturing rights. Yes, there are many cheap imitations, ma'am, but there is only one Farrago Cyclops!"

She stands there blinking in the crack of the chained door. She's a *mouse,* Cobb begins to realize. Thirty-five to forty, afraid of sudden moves and noise, bright outdoor light always a threat, for there are hawks, there are cats. Her house is dark inside, like a nest chewed into wood by quick, small teeth. She is wearing a gray housecoat and she is nibbling something—a piece of cheese!— and Cobb almost grins in her face, pleased that he's identified her secret animal so perfectly.

He fights back his knowing smile, for the smile of a turtle is a philosophical thing. It tends to put things into long-term perspective. It makes the recipient think: there's more to this situation than I presently understand. It will give the recipient a chill. A mouse will run from such a smile, though in nature mice and turtles are not enemies. But, Cobb thinks, we are not in nature. This is L.A., this is the world. He masters the smile and muscles it back to where it came from.

"Here you go, ma'am," he says. "Take it. Try it." She receives it gingerly, as if it were a loaded gun with a hair trigger. *Microtus pennsylvanicus,* Cobb thinks, mouse, and that is what she surely was meant to be, down to the cream-cheese marrow of her small bones. He begins to think of her as "Minnie."

Cobb kneels down suddenly on her welcome mat. Stitched into the sisal mat are the letters of a Spanish word, *bienvenido.* He crouches down as low as he can get. Neighborhood children freeze with curiosity on their skateboards. The heat leans down through the perpetually grainy sky. In the north, the annual arsonists have set fire to the brushy hills. In the east, flash floods. Rapists, stranglers, and slashers roam the jammed tract-house valleys. Santa Ana wind, moaning in the TV antennas, spills over the mountains from the desert, electrifying the air. The ionized air lays a charge on the surface of his skin, the hair of his arms stands up stiff and surly, as if muscled, and his brain feels tacked into its casing. His back is soaked with sweat and his pits are swamps.

"Sometimes these de-gents will ring your bell, ma'am," he says, "and then drop down to all fours like this hoping that the lady occupant, such as yourself, will make the fatal mistake of opening the door to see what's going on even though she didn't see anybody in the peephole. Some of these de-gents are real weasels, take my word for it. But the Farrago Cyclops will expose them, due to the fish-eye lens system." And he can see now that she is suddenly gripped by the idea of the sort of weasel who would ring her bell and then hide on her doorstep, waiting to spring.

"The worst is sure to happen, ma'am" he say, gravely, "sooner or later, because of the nature of the perverted mind in today's world. This is a proven statistical fact, known to most as Murphy's Law." Cobb makes a movement with his wrist, suggesting a weapon. Sledge, ax, awl, ice pick, the rapist's long razor, the slasher's stiletto. He shows her some crotch bulge, the possible avenger in there, coiled to strike. "You *can* see me, ma'am?" he asks. She gives one nod, her face crimped up as she peers into the Cyclops. "That's it, ma'am," says Cobb, doing Georgia, doing 'Bama. "Hold it level to the ground, as if was already in place in your door."

"You look sort of funny," she says. "Oblong. Or top-heavy."

"It's the lens, ma'am. Fish-eye. It puts a bend in the world, but you get to see more of it that way."

Cobb stands up and makes a quick pencil mark on the door. "Right about here, I guess. What are you, ma'am, about five foot one?" She nods. "Husband gone most of the day? His work take him out of town a lot? You spend a lot of time alone?" She looks like a fading photograph of herself. Cobb stops his grin before it crawls into his lips. He raises the brace-and-bit, pauses just long enough to get her consent, which she gives by stepping backward a few inches and turning her head slightly to one side, a gesture of acquiescence, and Cobb scores the flimsy laminated wood with the tip of the bit and starts the hole, one inch in diameter, right on the pencil mark, level with her wide-open eyes. He leans on the brace and cranks. The wood is tract-house cheap, false-grain oak, hollow, so thin a child could kick a hole in it.

To see how fast her door can be penetrated unsettles her and so Cobb tries to calm her down with a brief outline of the Charles V. Farrago success story. Rags to riches in the Home Security field. From shop mechanic to multimillionaire. From Cedar Rapids to Carmel By The Sea. The undisputed king of home surveillance devices. A genius by any standard. Cobb carries a photograph of Charles V. Farrago and promises to show it to the woman as soon as he drills out her door. In the photograph, taken some twenty or thirty years ago, Farrago has a big round head and a smile that goes two hands across with more teeth in it than seem possible. He has shrewd little eyes that preside above the smile like twin watchdogs.

Cobb tells the woman other stories. He tells her about the woman, housewife like herself, who had oil of vitriol pumped up her nose through one of those old-fashioned door-peepers. Knock knock, and she opened the little peeper to see who was there and it was a de-gent. Splat. Blinded for life and horribly disfigured all for the want of a proper doorstep surveillance device. Blue crater where once was her nose, upper lip a leather flap, eyes milky clouds. The reason? No *reason.* There never is a reason. It was a prank. The de-gent chemistry student had seen Phantom of the Opera on TV. It was Halloween in Denver or Salt Lake or Omaha. A few years ago. He told the police: "I just had this big urge to melt a face, you know?"

Cobb tells her the one about the naked de-gent who knocked on a peeperless door and said, "Parcel Post!" He made love to his victim with a gardening tool right in front of her little kids. He left a red hoofprint on her shag carpet and that's how the cops caught him: his right foot had only two toes and the print looked cloven, like it had been left by a goat. The *Times* called him "The Goatfoot Gasher."

The grumbling bit chews through the last laminations of veneer and Cobb reaches around the still-chained door to catch the curls of blond wood, which he puts into his shirt pocket. Do not leave an unsightly mess, says Jake the Distributor. Be neat as a pin. Cobb inserts the Cyclops gently and with a little sigh into the tight hole, then screws on the locking flange. "Let's give it a try, ma'am," he says.

She closes the door and Cobb goes out to the sidewalk. He stands still long enough for her to get used to the odd shapes the fish-eye lens produces, then starts to move down the sidewalk in big sidesteps to the other extreme of her vision. He approaches the house on the oblique, crossing the lawn, dropping behind a shrub, reemerging on hands and knees, moving swiftly now like a Dirty Dozen commando toward the welcome mat. He knows what she is seeing, knows how the lens makes him look heavy through the middle, pin-headed, legs stubby, his shined shoes fat as seals, the mean unsmiling lips, the stumpy bulge at the apex of his fat thighs, the neighborhood curving around him like a psychopathic smirk.

"It really *works,*" she says, showing as much enthusiasm as she feels she can afford when Cobb reappears at the door, brushing off his knees and smiling like a helpful Scout. She slips a five-dollar bill through the cracked door and Cobb notices that it has been folded into a perfect square the size of a stamp.

"Satisfaction fully guaranteed, ma'am," he says, unfolding, meticulously, the bill. A fragrance, trapped in the bill for possibly years, makes his nostrils flare.

Cobb winks and the woman allows herself a coo of gratitude. Turtle and mouse rapport, Cobb thinks, pleased. This is what you strive for, says Jake the Distributor. Cross the species lines. This is the hallmark of the true salesman. Make them think you are just like them, practically *kin,* though we know that this is basically laughable.

This is Cobb's tenth sale this morning. He keeps one dollar and fifteen cents out of every five. On good days he'll sell fifty. But today won't be a good day— for sales, at least. Too hot. He feels as if there's this big unfair hand in the sky that's been lowering all morning, pushing him down. He needs a break. He needs to cool off, wash up—a nice shower would do it—he needs to get out of his swampy shirt, air his pits and the steaming crotch of his slacks. He wants to use her john, but he knows her mouse heart will panic if he asks. Instead, he asks if he can use her phone. "Need to check in," he explains, his voice decent, a fellow human being making a reasonable request, a finely honed act. She fades a bit, but she is not a swift thinker and can't find a way to say no pleasantly. Cobb has his Eagle Scout glow turned up full blast. His boylike vulnerability is apparent in the bend of his spine, put there by the unfair bone-warping hand that presses down on him from the dirty sky, trying to make him crawl again, but he is through crawling today and is ready to lay claim to the small things of this world that should be his, but are not. The woman slides the chained bolt out of its slot and opens the door wide in jerky, indecisive increments.

"Oh, lady," he says, his voice relaxing now into its natural cadence. "You're the angel of mercy in the flesh. Really." Cobb, hard thin lips flexed in a triumphant V, walks in.

A black helicopter flapped out of the morning sun and dumped its sweet orange mist on our land instead of the Parley farm where it was intended. It was weedkiller, something strong enough to wipe out leafy spurge, knapweed, and Canadian thistle, but it made us sick.

My father had a fatal stroke a week after that first spraying. I couldn't hold down solid food for nearly a month and went from 200 pounds to 170 in that time. Mama went to bed and slept for two days, and when she woke up she was not the same. She'd lost something of herself in that long sleep, and something that wasn't herself had replaced it.

Then it hit the animals. We didn't have much in the way of animals, but one by one they dropped. The chickens, the geese, the two old mules—Doc and Rex—and last of all, our only cow, Miss Milky, who was more or less the family pet.

Weeds

Miss Milky was the only animal that didn't outright up and die. She just got sick. There was blood in her milk and her milk was thin. Her teats got so tender and brittle that she would try to mash me against the milk stall wall when I pulled at them. The white part of her eyes looked like fresh meat. Her piss was so strong that the green grass wherever she stood died off. She got so bound up that when she'd lift her tail and bend with strain, only one black apple would drop. Her breath took on a burning sulfurous stink that would make you step back.

She also went crazy. She'd stare at me like she all at once had a desperate human mind and had never seen me before. Then she'd act as if she wanted to slip a horn under my ribs and peg me to the barn. She would drop her head and charge, blowing like a randy bull, and I would have to scramble out of the way. Several times I saw her gnaw on her hooves or stand stock-still in water up to her blistered teats. Or she would walk backward all day long, mewling like a lost cat that had been dropped off in a strange place. That mewling was enough to make you want to clap a set of noise dampers on your ears. The awful sound led Mama to say this: "It's the death song of the land, mark my words."

Mama never talked like that before in her life. She'd always been a cheerful woman who could never see the bad part of anything that was at least fifty percent good. But now she was dark and careful as a gypsy. She would have spells of derangement during which she'd make noises like a wild animal, or she'd play the part of another person—the sort of person she'd normally have nothing to do with at all. At Daddy's funeral she got dressed up in an old and tattered evening gown the color of beet juice, her face painted and powdered like that of a barfly. And while the preacher told the onlookers what a fine man Daddy had been, Mama cupped her hands under her breasts and lifted them high, as if offering to appease a dangerous stranger. Then, ducking her head, she chortled, "Loo, loo, loo," her scared eyes scanning the trees for owls.

42

I was twenty-eight years old and my life had come to nothing. I'd had a girl but I'd lost her through neglect and a careless attitude that had spilled over into my personal life, souring it. I had no ambition to make something worthwhile of myself and it nettled her. Toward the end she began to parrot her mother: "You need to get yourself *established,* Jack," she would say. But I didn't want to get myself established. I was getting poorer and more aimless day by day. I supposed she believed that "getting established" would put a stop to my downhill slide but I had no desire to do whatever it took to accomplish that.

Shortly after Daddy died, the tax man came to our door with a paper in his hand. "Inheritance tax," he said, handing me the paper.

"What do you mean?" I asked.

"It's the law," he said. "Your father died, you see. And that's going to cost you some. You should have made better plans." He tapped his forehead with his finger and winked. He had a way of expressing himself that made me think he was country born and raised but wanted to seem citified. Or maybe it was the other way around.

"I don't understand this," I mumbled. I felt the weight of a world I'd so far been able to avoid. It was out there, tight-assed and squinty-eyed, and it knew to the dollar and dime what it needed to keep itself in business.

"Simple," he said. "Pay or move off. The government is the government and it can't bend a rule to accommodate the confused. It's your decision. Pay, or the next step is litigation."

He smiled when he said good-bye. I closed the door against the weight of his smile, which was the weight of the world. I went to a window and watched him head back to his government green car. The window was open and I could hear him. He was singing loudly in a fine tenor voice. He raised his right hand to hush an invisible audience that had broken into uncontrolled applause. I could still hear him singing as he slipped the car into gear and idled away. He was singing "Red River Valley."

Even though the farm was all ours, paid up in full, we had to give the government $7,000 for the right to stay on it. The singing tax man said we had inherited the land from my father, and the law was sharp on the subject.

I didn't know where the money was going to come from. I didn't talk it over with Mama because even in her better moments she would talk in riddles. To a simple question such as, "Should I paint the barns this year, Mama?" she might answer, "I've no eyes for glitter, nor ears for their ridicule."

One day I decided to load Miss Milky into the stock trailer and haul her into Saddle Butte, where the vet, Doc Nevers, had his office. Normally, Doc Nevers would come out to your place but he'd heard about the spraying that was going on and said he wouldn't come within three miles of our property until they were done.

The Parley farm was being sprayed regularly, for they grew an awful lot of wheat and almost as much corn and they had the biggest haying operation in the county. Often the helicopters they used were upwind from us and we were sprayed too. ("Don't complain," said Big Pete Parley when I called him up about it. "Think of it this way—you're getting your place weeded for free!" When I said I might have to dynamite some stumps on the property line and that he might get a barn or two blown away for free, he just laughed like hell, as if I had told one of the funniest jokes he'd ever heard.)

There was a good windbreak between our places, a thick grove of lombardy poplars, but the orange mist, sweet as a flower garden in spring bloom, sifted through the trees and settled on our field. Soon the poplars were mottled and dying. Some branches curled in an upward twist, as if flexed in pain, and others became soft and fibrous as if the wood were trying to turn itself into sponge.

With Miss Milky in the trailer, I sat in the truck sipping on a pint of Lewis and Clark bourbon and looking out across our unplanted fields. It was late—almost too late—to plant anything. Mama, in the state she was in, hadn't even noticed.

In the low hills on the north side of the property, some ugly-looking things were growing. From the truck they looked like white pimples on the smooth brown hill. Up close they were big as melons. They were some kind of fungus and they pushed up through the ground like the bald heads of fat babies. They gave off a rotten meat stink. I would get chillbumps just looking at them and if I touched one my stomach would rise. The bulbous heads had purple streaks on them that looked like blood vessels. I half expected to one day see human eyes clear the dirt and open. Big pale eyes that would see me and carry my image down to their deepest root. I was glad they seemed to prefer the hillside and bench and not the bottom land.

Justified or not, I blamed the growth of this fungus on the poison spray, just as I blamed it for the death of my father, the loss of our animals, and the strangeness of my mother. Now the land itself was becoming strange. And I thought, what about me? How am I being rearranged by that weedkiller?

I guess I should have gotten mad, but I didn't. Maybe I *had* been changed by the spray. Where once I had been a quick-to-take-offense hothead, I was now docile and thoughtful. I could sit on a stump and think for hours, enjoying the slow and complicated intertwinings of my own thoughts. Even though I felt sure the cause of all our troubles had fallen out of the sky, I would hold arguments with myself, as if there were always two sides to every question. If I said to myself, "Big Pete Parley has poisoned my family and farm and my father is dead because of it," I would follow it up with, "But Daddy was old anyway, past seventy-five and he always had high blood pressure. Anything could have touched off his stroke, from a wasp bite to a sonic boom."

"And what about Mama?" I would ask. "Senile with grief," came the quick answer. "Furthermore, Daddy himself used poison in his time. Cyanide traps for coyotes, DDT for mosquito larvae, arsenic for rats."

My mind was always doubling back on itself in this way and it would often leave me standing motionless in a field for hours, paralyzed with indecision, sighing like a moonstruck girl of twelve. I imagined myself mistaken by passers-by for a scarecrow.

Sometimes I saw myself as a human weed, useless to other people in general and maybe harmful in some weedy way. The notion wasn't entirely unpleasant. Jack Hucklebone: a weed among the well-established money crops of life.

On my way to town with Miss Milky, I crossed over the irrigation ditch my father had fallen into with the stroke that killed him. I pulled over onto the shoulder and switched off the engine. It was a warm, insect-loud day in early June. A spray of grasshoppers clattered over the hood of the truck. June bugs ticked past the windows like little flying clocks. The thirteen-year locusts were back and raising a whirring hell. I was fifteen the last time they came but I didn't remember them arriving in such numbers. I expected more helicopters to come flapping over with special sprays meant just for them, even though they would be around for only a few weeks and the damage they would do is not much more than measurable. But anything that looks like it might have an appetite for a money crop brings down the spraying choppers. I climbed out of the truck and looked up into the bright air. A lone jet, eastbound, too high to see or hear, left its neat chalk line across the top of the sky. The sky itself was hot blue wax, north to south. A fat hammerhead squatted on the west horizon. It looked like a creamy oblong planet that had slipped its orbit and was now endangering the earth.

There's where Daddy died. Up the ditch about fifty yards from here. I found him, buckled, white as paper, half under water. His one good eye, his right (he'd lost the left one thirty years ago when a tractor tire blew up in his face as he was filling it), was above water and wide open, staring at his hand as if it could focus on the thing it gripped. He was holding on to a root. He had big hands, strong, with fingers like thick hardwood dowels, but now they were soft and puffy, like the hands of a giant baby. Water bugs raced against the current toward him. His body blocked the ditch and little eddies swirled around it. The water bugs skated into the eddies and, fighting to hold themselves still in the roiling current, touched his face. They held still long enough to satisfy their curiosity, then slid back into the circular flow as if bemused by the strangeness of dead human flesh.

I started to cry, remembering it, thinking about him in the water, he had been so sure and strong, but then—true to my changed nature—I began to laugh at the memory, for his wide blue eye had had a puzzled cast to it, as if it had never before seen such an oddity as the ordinary root in his forceless hand. It was an expression he never wore in life.

"It was only a weed, Daddy," I said, wiping the tears from my face.

The amazed puzzlement stayed in his eye until I brushed down the lid.

Of course he had been dead beyond all talk and puzzlement. Dead when I found him, dead for hours, bloated dead. And this is how *I've* come to be— blame the spray or don't: the chores don't get done on time, the unplanted fields wait, Mama wanders in her mind, and yet I'll sit in the shade of my truck sipping on Lewis and Clark bourbon, inventing the thoughts of a dead man.

Time bent away from me like a tail-dancing rainbow. It was about to slip the hook. I wasn't trying to hold it. Try to hold it and it gets all the more slippery. Try to let it go and it sticks like a cocklebur to cotton. I was drifting somewhere between the two kinds of not trying: not trying to hold anything, not trying to let anything go.

Then he sat down next to me. The old man.

"You got something for me?" he said.

He was easily the homeliest man I had ever seen. His bald head was bullet-shaped and his lumpy nose was warty as a crookneck squash. His little, close-set eyes sat on either side of that nose like hard black beans. He had shaggy eyebrows that climbed upward in a white and wiry tangle. There was a blue lump in the middle of his forehead the size of a pullet's egg, and his hairy earlobes touched his grimy collar. He was mumbling something, but it could have been the noise of the ditch water as it sluiced through the culvert under the road.

He stank of whiskey and dung, and looked like he'd been sleeping behind barns for weeks. His clothes were rags and he was caked with dirt from fingernail to jaw. His shoes were held together with strips of burlap. He untied some of these strips and took off his shoes. Then he slid his gnarled, corn-crusted feet into the water. His eyes fluttered shut and he let out a hissing moan of pleasure. His toes were long and twisted, the arthritic knuckles painfully bright. They reminded me of the surface roots of a stunted oak that had been trying to grow in hardpan. Though he was only about five feet tall, his feet were huge. Easy size twelves, wide as paddles.

He quit mumbling, cleared his throat, spit. "You got anything for me?" he said.

I handed him my pint. He took it, held it up to the sunlight, looked through the rusty booze as if testing for its quality.

"If it won't do," I said, "I could run into town to get something a little smoother for you. Maybe you'd like some Canadian Club or some twelve-year-old Scotch. I could run into town and be back in less than an hour. Maybe you'd like me to bring back a couple of fried chickens and a sack of buttered rolls." This was my old self talking, the hothead. But I didn't feel mad at him and was just being mouthy out of habit.

"No need to do that," he said, as if my offer had been made in seriousness. He took a long pull off my pint. "This snake piss is just fine by me, son." He raised the bottle to the sunlight again, squinted through it.

I wandered down the ditch again to the place where Daddy died. There was nothing there to suggest a recent dead man had blocked the current. Everything was as it always was. The water surged, the quick water bugs skated up and down inspecting brown clumps of algae along the banks, underwater weeds waved like slim snakes whose tails had been staked to the mud. I looked for the thistle he'd grabbed on to. I guess he thought that he was going to save himself from drowning by hanging on to its root, not realizing that the killing flood was *inside* his head. But there were many roots along the bank and none of them seemed more special than any other.

Something silver glinted at me. It was a coin. I picked it out of the slime and polished it against my pants. It was a silver dollar, a real one. It could have been his. He carried a few of the old cartwheels around with him for luck. The heft and gleam of the old silver coin choked me up.

I walked back to the old man. He had stuffed his bundle under his head for a pillow and had dozed off. I uncapped the pint and finished it, then flipped it into the weeds. It hit a rock and popped. The old man grunted and his eyes snapped open. He let out a barking snort and his black eyes darted around fiercely, like the eyes of a burrow animal caught in a daylight trap. Then, remembering where he was, he calmed down.

"You got something for me?" he asked. He pushed himself up to a sitting position. It was a struggle for him.

"Not anymore," I said. I sat down next to him. Then, from behind us, a deep groan cut loose. It sounded like siding being pried off a barn with a crowbar. We both turned to look at whatever had complained so mightily.

It was Miss Milky, up in the trailer, venting her misery. I'd forgotten about her. Horseflies were biting her. Black belts of them girdled her teats. Her red eyes peered sadly out at us through the bars. The corners of her eyes were swollen, giving her a Chinese look.

With no warning at all, a snapping hail fell on us. Only it wasn't hail. It was a moving cloud of thirteen-year locusts. They darkened the sky and they covered us. The noise was like static on the radio, miles of static across the bug-peppered sky, static that could drown out all important talk and idle music no matter how powerful the station.

The old man's face was covered with the bugs and he was saying something to me but I couldn't make out what it was. His mouth opened and closed, opened and closed. When it opened he'd have to brush away the locusts from his lips. They were like ordinary grasshoppers, only smaller, and they had big red eyes that seemed to glow with their own hellish light. Then, as fast as they had come, they were gone, scattered back into the fields. A few hopped here and there, but the main cloud had broken up.

I just sat there brushing at the lingering feel of them on my skin and trying to readjust myself to uncluttered air, but my ears were still crackling with their racket.

The old man pulled at my sleeve, breaking me out of my daydream or trance. "You got something for me?" he asked.

I felt blue. Worse than blue. Sick. I felt incurable—ridden with the pointlessness of just about everything you could name. The farm struck me as a pointless wonder and I found the idea depressing and fearsome. Pointless bugs lay waiting in the fields for the pointless crops as the pointless days and seasons ran on and on into the pointless forever.

"Shit," I said.

"I'll take that worthless cow off your hands, then," said the old man. "She's done for. All you have to do is look at her."

He didn't seem so old or so wrecked to me now. He was younger and bigger somehow, as if all his clocks had started running backwards, triggered by the locust cloud. He stood up. He looked thick across the shoulders like he'd done hard work all his life and could still do it. He showed me his right hand. It was yellow with hard calluses. His beady black eyes were quick and lively in their shallow sockets. The blue lump on his forehead glinted in the sun. It seemed deliberately polished as if it were an ornament. He took a little silver bell out of his pocket and rang it for no reason at all.

"Let me have her," he said.

"You want Miss Milky?" I asked. I felt weak and childish. Maybe I was drunk. My scalp itched and I scratched it hard. He rang his little silver bell again. I wanted to have it but he put it back into his pocket. Then he knelt down and opened his bundle. He took out a paper sack.

I looked inside. It was packed with seeds of some kind. I ran my fingers through them and did not feel foolish. I heard a helicopter putt-putting in the distance. I'll say this in defense of what I did: I knew Miss Milky was done for. Doc Nevers would have told me to shoot her. I don't think she was even good for hamburger. Old cow meat can sometimes make good hamburger, but Miss Milky looked wormy and lean. And I wouldn't have trusted her bones for soup. The poison that had wasted her flesh and ruined her udder had probably settled in her marrow.

And so I unloaded my dying cow. He took out his silver bell again and tied it to a piece of string. He tied the string around Miss Milky's neck. Then he led her away. She was docile and easy as though this was exactly the way things were supposed to turn out.

My throat was dry. I felt too tired to move. I watched their slow progress down the path that ran along the ditch. They got smaller and smaller until, against a dark hedge of box elders, they disappeared. I strained to see after them, but it was as if the earth had given them refuge, swallowing them into its deep, loamy, composting interior. The only sign that they still existed in the world was the tinkling of the silver bell he had tied around Miss Milky's neck. It was a pure sound, naked on the air.

Then a breeze opened a gap in the box elders and a long blade of sunlight pierced through them, illuminating and magnifying the old man and his cow, as if the air between us had formed itself into a giant lens. The breeze let up and the box elders shut off the sun again and I couldn't see anything but a dense quiltwork of black and green shadows out of which a raven big as an eagle flapped. It cawed in raucous good humor as it veered over my head.

I went on into town anyway, cow or no cow, and hit some bars. I met a girl from the East in the Hobble who thought I was a cowboy, and I didn't try to correct her mistaken impression, for it proved a free pass to good times.

When I got home, Mama had company. She was dressed up in her beet-juice gown and her face was powdered white. Her dark lips looked like a wine stain in snow, but her clear blue eyes were direct and calm. There was no distraction in them.

"Hi, boy," said the visitor. It was Big Pete Parley. He was wearing a blue suit, new boots, a gray felt Stetson. He had a toothy grin on his fat red face.

I looked at Mama. "What's *he* want?" I asked. Something was wrong. I could feel it but I couldn't see it. It was Mama, the way she had composed herself maybe, or the look in her eyes, or her whitened skin. Maybe she had gone all the way insane. She went over to Parley and sat next to him on the davenport. She had slit her gown and it fell away from her thigh, revealing the veiny flesh.

"We're going to be married," she said. "Pete's tired of being a widower. He wants a warm bed."

As if to confirm it was no fantasy dreamed up by her senile mind, Big Pete slid his hand into the slit dress and squeezed her thigh. He clicked his teeth and winked at me.

"Pete knows how to run a farm," said Mama. "And you do not, Jackie." She didn't intend for it to sound mean or critical. It was just a statement of the way things were. I couldn't argue with her.

I went into the kitchen. Mama followed me in. I opened a beer. "I don't mean to hurt your feelings, Jackie," she said.

"He's scheming to get our land," I said. "He owns half the county, but that isn't enough."

"No," she said. "I'm the one who's scheming. I'm scheming for my boy who does not grasp the rudiments of the world."

I had the sack of seeds with me. I realized that I'd been rattling them nervously.

"What do you have there?" she asked, narrowing her eyes.

"Seeds," I said.

"Seeds? What seeds? Who gave you seeds? Where did you get them?"

I thought it best not to mention where I'd gotten them. "Big Pete Parley doesn't want to marry *you*," I said. It was a mean thing to say and I wanted to say it.

Mama sighed. "It doesn't matter what he wants, Jack. I'm dead anyway." She took the bag of seeds from me, picked some up, squinted at them.

"What is that supposed to mean?" I said sarcastically.

She went to the window above the sink and stared out into the dark. Under the folds of her evening gown I could see the ruined shape of her old body. "Dead, Jack," she said. "I've been dead for a while now. Maybe you didn't notice."

"No," I said. "I didn't."

"Well, you should have. I went to sleep shortly after your Daddy died and I had a dream. The dream got stronger and stronger as it went on until it was as vivid as real life itself. More vivid. When I woke up I knew that I had died. I also knew that nothing in the world would ever be as real to me as that dream."

I almost asked her what the dream was about but I didn't, out of meanness. In the living room Big Pete Parley was whistling impatiently. The davenport was squeaking under his nervous weight.

"So you see, Jackie," said Mama. "It doesn't matter if I marry Pete Parley or what his motives are in the matter. You are all that counts now. He will ensure your success in the world."

"I don't want to be a success, Mama," I said.

"Well, you have no choice. You cannot gainsay the dead."

She opened the window over the kitchen sink and dumped out the sack of seeds. Then Big Pete Parley came into the kitchen. "Let's go for a walk," he said. "It's too blame hot in this house."

They left by the kitchen door. I watched them walk across the yard and into the dark, unplanted field. Big Pete had his arm around Mama's shoulder. I wondered if he knew, or cared, that he was marrying a dead woman. Light from the half-moon painted their silhouettes for a while. Then the dark field absorbed them.

I went to bed and slept for what might have been days. In my long sleep I had a dream. I was canoeing down a whitewater river that ran sharply uphill. The farther up I got, the rougher the water became. Finally, I had to beach the canoe. I proceeded on foot until I came to a large gray house that had been built in a wilderness forest. The house was empty and quiet. I went in. It was clean and beautifully furnished. Nobody was home. I called out a few times before I understood that silence was a rule. I went from room to room, going deeper and deeper toward some dark interior place. I understood that I was involved in a search. The longer I searched, the more vivid the dream became.

When I woke up I was stiff and weak. Mama wasn't in the house. I made a pot of coffee and took a cup outside. Under the kitchen window there was a patch of green shoots that had not been there before. "You got something for me?" I said.

A week later that patch of green shoots had grown and spread. They were weeds. The worst kind of weeds I had ever seen. Thick, spiny weeds with broad green leaves tough as leather. They rolled away from the house, out across the field, in a viny carpet. Mean, deep-rooted weeds, too mean to uproot by hand. When I tried, I came away with a palm full of cuts.

In another week they were tall as corn. They were fast growers and I could not see where they ended. They covered everything in sight. A smothering blanket of deep green sucked the life out of every other growing thing. They crossed fences, irrigation ditches, and when they reached the trees of a windbreak, they became ropy crawlers that wrapped themselves around trunks and limbs.

When they reached the Parley farm, over which my dead mother now presided, they were attacked by squadrons of helicopters which drenched them in poisons, the best poisons chemical science knew how to brew. But the poisons only seemed to make the weeds grow faster, and after a spraying the new growths were tougher, thornier, and more determined than ever to dominate the land.

Some of the weeds sent up long woody stalks. On top of these stalks were heavy seedpods, fat as melons. The strong stalks pushed the pods high into the air.

The day the pods cracked a heavy wind came up. The wind raised black clouds of seed in grainy spirals that reached the top of the sky, then scattered them, far and wide, across the entire nation.

From **THE COMING TRIUMPH OF THE FREE WORLD**
(1988)

E very morning at 3 a.m. a dog would sit in front of our house and bark. It was a big dog, a wolfhound of some kind—Irish or Russian—and its bark broke into our sleep like a shout from God. More than loud, it was eerie. The barks came up from the street with an urgency meant to induce panic. The Huns were at the gate, the tidal wave was almost here, the volcano was about to blow. Every night I fell out of bed in a running crouch, my heart looking for a way out of its cage.

Then I'd get back into bed and pull the pillow over my head. But Raquel, stiff with rage, wouldn't let me have this easy escape. She would sit up in bed, turn on the weak lamp, and light a cigarette. "I am losing my mind," she said. "How can you expect me to go to work every morning without sleep?"

Finally, after the tenth night of the punctual dog, Raquel said, "I want you to buy a gun."

Her face was a spooky, hovering oval in the lamp's yellow glow. Her eyes were fixed on a resolute vision. I'd seen her pass through some alarming changes since I had lost my job and she had become chief breadwinner, but this tightly focused rage made me believe significant trouble was on the way.

The Handgun

"We can't afford a gun," I said. Which was true. We were barely making our house payments on her secretarial wages. "Not a good gun, anyway. A good rifle with a scope runs four or five hundred."

"My hunter," she said, a sneer curling her lips. "I am not talking about a rifle. I want you to get a pistol. Just a .22 target pistol. They sell them even in drugstores."

I knew it would grate on her but I tried a patronizing chuckle anyway, hoping to deflect her anger to me and thereby leave this gun business far behind. "You can't go out on the street and shoot animals. This is a neighborhood. People will get upset."

She turned to me—mechanically, I thought. Her smile would have done credit to the Borgia family. The warmth of the bed was dissipating noticeably. "I thought of that," she said. "But it's almost the Fourth of July. The neighbors will think it's only boys who could not wait to blow up their firecrackers. No one will get out of bed to investigate."

"You've been thinking about this for some time," I observed, mostly to myself.

"Yes. I have. And we won't go into the street. We will shoot from the window, behind the curtains. We will put Kleenex over the barrel so that the flash will not be seen."

"You'd be murdering someone's companion, a pet..."

She gave me a lingering, abstracted look, the look she might give a complete stranger who had offered a demented opinion. "You," she said, "suffocate me."

The distance between us enlarged. Madness does that. It seemed like a trend. Her response to straightforward remarks might come from left field or from outside the park. I thought she might be in the early stages of a breakdown. The thought depressed me. I got up and went into the bathroom, where I took an Elavil.

I didn't want a gun in the house. I'd recently read a sobering statistic: of all handgun deaths in private homes, only a tiny percentage involved intruders. The majority of victims were members of the gun owner's immediate family. The usual motive was suicide. And sometimes, but not rarely, murder *and* suicide. I thought: *Baloney.* Then I saw that it made perfect sense. I couldn't count the number of times I'd raised my finger to my head and said "Bang" after reading, say, a turn-off notice from the power company, or a credit-threatening letter from Penney's or Sears. A finger to the temple and the sadly muttered "Bang" is a clown's gesture, wistful at best, but signifying the ever-present wish to put out one's lights.

"Go to Mel's Pawnshop tomorrow," Raquel, or the person Raquel was in the process of becoming, said when I came back to the bedroom. "They sell fine guns there for under one hundred dollars."

She'd turned out the lamp and was sitting naked next to the window, looking down on the dog. It had quit barking and was just staring, like a rejected lover, at the cold beauty of Raquel's unforgiving silhouette.

"It's against the *law* to shoot fine guns in the city," I said, mocking her lambent Hispanic fire and lilt. "It's a felony."

"I am not interested in your *putrefacto* laws," she said.

"What do you know about Mel's Pawnshop, anyway?" I said. I stepped behind her and put my hands on her moon-dusty shoulders. The moon was nearly full and she was incandescent with a chalky light. Given the state of our lives, 3 a.m. sex was unlikely, but this crazy moonlit woman in the window broke the spell hard times put on flesh. I slipped my hands down to her breasts like a repossessor.

She hunched away from me. "I want to put a bullet in that dog's throat," she said.

I went back to bed as the dog resumed its pointless assault on our lives. "I am not going to Mel's," I said.

"Fine, St. Francis," she said. "I'll go."

But she didn't go. She was afraid to. The pawnshop area of town was full of aimless psychotics. Now and then one of them would be picked up for a crime committed in another part of the state or country. In fact, a serial murderer had been arrested in Mel's a year ago as he was trying to trade a necklace made of human kneecaps for a machete.

The next night a weather front moved in and the air was stifling. The changed atmospherics improved the acoustics of the neighborhood. The dog, it seemed, was in bed with us.

"I can't stand it!" Raquel screamed. "You have to do something!" She pulled the pillow off my head and threw it across the bedroom.

I got up and opened the window. "Shut up, dog!" I yelled, but I might as well have been arguing with a magpie. We were not on the same wavelength. The odd timbre of the dog's bark gave it an almost human quality. I could nearly make myself believe I was hearing a kind of garbled English. "What what *what*?" or "Hot, hot, what?" But there was also a forlorn tone that was not translatable. A canine refusal to accept some wrenching loss. I went back to bed.

"I've got this feeling, hon," I said. "Like that dog is in mourning for its lost mate." We'd called the Animal Control cop days ago and his white van toured the neighborhood, picking up strays. Maybe the big dog lost his ladylove in that sweep.

Raquel turned on the bed lamp and studied my face for signs of mockery or perhaps derangement. "Are you *crazy*?" she asked. "Dogs don't mate for life like *swans*. They screw any bitch in heat. Don't try to turn that monster into a brokenhearted family man."

Then she said the thing that forced the issue. "Look, *hon*," she mocked. "Either you get that gun or I am going to find somewhere else to sleep at night."

My joblessness, and now my refusal to take action in an emergency, had turned her against me. "All right," I said. "I'll get the gun."

The next day, after I had made breakfast and Raquel had gone to work, I walked through the neighborhood looking for the dog. I'd already done this several times, but now I knocked on doors and asked questions. No one would admit to owning such a dog, not on our street or on the several adjacent streets. But even more curious than this, no one admitted to having heard the dog bark. Evidently its tirades were sharply directional, like the beam from a radar antenna, hitting only the thing it aimed at.

"Did you get it?" Raquel asked me when she got home from work.

I stalled. "Bindle-stiff chicken tonight, darling," I said. "Plus asparagus à la Milwaukee vinaigrette." These were recipes I had invented. I was proud of them. They were Raquel's favorites.

"You didn't get it," she said.

"All Mel had were big-caliber revolvers—.357s and .44s. Nothing we could use comfortably. We'd wreck the neighborhood with those cannons."

"You didn't go," she said.

I stuttered, a dead giveaway, then faced a wall of spiting silence the rest of the evening. She didn't touch my wonderful dinner.

The following morning at nine-thirty I saw Dr. Selbiades, my shrink. I told him all about the dog, the gun, and Raquel's threat. I had not called him up about this crisis, and I could tell that it miffed him a bit.

"So," he said, in that loftily humble, arrogant, self-effacing way of his. "Your wife wants you to get a... *gun.*"

Selbiades is not a Freudian, so this was only a joke—meant, no doubt, to get even with me for keeping secrets.

"I've decided to get one this afternoon."

"Just like that?" he said, rocking back in his five-hundred-dollar leather-covered swivel chair.

"Yes. A .22 automatic."

"It would be a mistake, my friend," he said.

"Probably. But I don't see that I have a choice."

He stood up and flexed his hairy arms over his head and yawned. His yawn was as healthy and as uninhibited as a lion's. He scratched his ribs vigorously, then sat down again. He was wearing a T-shirt and Levi's and running shoes. He never wore anything else, at least in his office. "Christ, man," he said at last, his thick neck corded, it seemed, with redundant veins and arteries. "Of course you have a choice! Unless..."

I bit. "Unless?"

"Unless you hate her."

"*Hate* her? I love her! What do you mean, *hate*?"

"It just sounds like some classic passive-aggressive bullshit, my friend. You're giving her enough rope to hang herself with."

"I am terrified of losing her," I said, my voice ragged.

Selbiades swiveled his chair around abruptly, so that he now faced the window behind his desk. "There is, of course, a level on which what you say is true," he said, his tone suggesting a far too intimate knowledge of mankind. His window gave out on a view of fields, freshly scraped down to naked earth in preparation for a town-house development called Vista Buena Bonanza. He clasped his hairy hands behind his head and contemplated this field. He owned it and was a partner in the new development. I envied him: he was the happiest man I knew.

"What about bullets?" Raquel asked that evening. I gave her the small paper bag that had four boxes of .22 ammo in it. She snatched the bag from me and inspected each box.

"No blanks," I said, thinking that blanks would have been fine. I was sure all she wanted to do was scare the dog off, not actually wound it.

She looked haggard sitting at the kitchen table, holding the pistol in one hand and sorting through bullets with the other. Then she put the gun and bullets in one messy pile and shoved them to the center of the table. She stood up and hugged me. "I am so proud of you at this moment," she said.

But it was a soldierly embrace. French or Russian, it would have involved tight-lipped kisses on both cheeks. A distinct warpage had entered our lives.

While I did a stir-fry, she paced around the kitchen smoking cigarettes, lost in strategy. She had been putting on weight and her heavy stride made the wok shimmy. I guessed that she'd put on twenty or thirty pounds since she'd taken the job at the courthouse. I hated to see that. In spite of our quick lip service to the contrary, physical attraction is the first thing that draws men to women, and vice versa. Time and mileage do their damage, but Raquel was too young to lose her figure. She had the long-muscled legs of a Zulu princess, along with the high-rising arch of spirited buttocks. Her torso was wide and ribby, the breasts not large but dominant and forthright. But now that rare geometry had been put in danger by the endless goodies office workers have to contend with every day. The county office in which she processed words seemed more like a giant deli than an arm of government. Often she would bring me pastries oozing lemon curd or brandied compote, or giant sandwiches on kaiser buns thick with ham or beef, and on special occasions such as office parties, entire boxes of sour cream chocolate cookies, brownies, or Bismarcks. She wouldn't step on the scale. When I suggested it, she snapped, "I know, I know, I've put on a couple of pounds. I don't need to have it shoved in my face."

But it was more than her waistline that was changing. She began to embrace opinions that seemed alien to her nature. She'd sit on the sofa in front of the evening news with watchdog attentiveness. ("See how Rather works in the knee-jerk liberal point of view?" "Look at the expression on Brokaw's face when he mentions the Contras. Looks like he wants to spit.") In the past she had no coherent politics. She was resolutely apolitical, in fact. But now she was listing sharply to the no-nonsense Right.

"The people are going to take law and order into their own hands if the courts keep turning loose the rapists and killers," she once said.

"That's how a society destroys itself," I suggested, fatuously, I admit.

Raquel scoffed. It was the first time in our eight-year marriage that she had shown outright contempt for me. It stung. The scar is still warm. "That is how a society *saves* itself," she said.

And, on another occasion, she said that the bureaucrats didn't care a bit about the common man. "All they care about is raising taxes so they can keep their soft jobs." She had good evidence for this, having spent the last six months working for the Department of Streets.

That first night of the gun was electric with adrenaline. We couldn't sleep at all. We watched TV until 2 a.m., then went up to the bedroom. We got undressed— no pajamas or nightgown, as it was another hot, humid night—and got in bed. Raquel was giddy with high excitement. I was tense, and not looking forward to the dog's appointed hour. I wished now that my passive-aggressive bullshit had not expressed itself so classically.

The bed got swampy with body steam. Raquel threw off the sheet and thin blanket and sat up. She took the gun off the night table and couched it on her belly. Goosebumps, triggered by the cold steel, radiated upwards to her breasts, stiffening the nipples, and downwards to her thighs, making them twitch. The moon was on the wane but still bright. A thin film of sweat made her body glow metallic. *Oh rarest of metals*! I thought, choking back a desperate love. The gun muzzle slipped down into the dark delta at the vertex of her thighs. Perversions of wild variety and orientation presented themselves to me.

"Forget it," Raquel said, sensing my state of mind. "He might start any minute now."

"It's not three yet. It's only two-thirty."

I was pleading. I hated myself, a beggar in my own bed.

"Afterwards," she said, her voice oddly abstract in the abstract light of the moon. "It will be *better* afterwards."

I couldn't see her eyes, just the black skull-holes that held them. She was smiling.

I snapped on the bed lamp, but didn't look at her. I wanted to avoid her, to organize my thoughts; I wanted to hold back the clock. I picked up a *Newsweek* from the magazine rack under the night table and flipped it open. I read about a woman in Pennsylvania who boiled her baby and sent the parts of the cooked body to a newspaper editor who had denounced abortion. Another article suggested that eighty percent of all children under the age of twelve will one day be the victims of a violent crime. I switched to the opinion columns, but those genteel, sharp-witted souls seemed to be writing about a world in which sanity was a possibility.

Then it was three o'clock. "How do you shoot this thing?" Raquel asked, looking at the gun as if for the first time.

"You aim and pull the trigger. It's easy," I said. I heard my passive-aggressive bullshit sprocketing these words out of my lungs.

"Isn't there something here called the safety?" she asked. It made me happy that the enormity of the coming violence had made her a bit timid.

"That little lever, up on the handle, I think." Actually my knowledge of guns was not much better than hers.

"*Where*?"

"Push it up, or maybe down. I don't know."

The gun, wobbling around in her hand, gradually aimed itself at her throat as she fiddled with its levers and knobs.

"Jesus Christ!" I said, grabbing the gun away from her. It went off. It shot a Currier and Ives print off the wall. It was an original, given to me by my grandmother. *Fast Trotters in Harlem Lane, N.Y.* Men in silk hats driving fine teams of horses down the dirt roads of nineteenth-century Harlem.

Raquel burst into tears. It shocked me. Not the tears but the realization that I could not remember the last time she had cried. I put my arms around her, half expecting her to shove me away. She didn't.

Then something else happened. Or failed to happen. It was three-fifteen and there was no dog in the street calling to us. "Listen, honey," I said.

But her sobs had been on hold too long to be put off. She cried for another five minutes. Then I said it again, as gently as I could. "Listen, Raquel. No *dog.*"

We both went to the window. The street was empty. Whatever the big dog had wanted to get off his chest was gone. He had exorcised himself, or at least that's what I hoped. There was the possibility that he'd taken a night off and would come back. But I didn't have to think about that now. Thinking about that, and what I would have to do about it, could wait.

I went downstairs and made a pot of hot chocolate. I brought two big mugs of it back to the bedroom. But Raquel was already asleep. I was too rattled to sleep. I went back down and drank hot chocolate until 5 a.m. The dog never showed up.

When I went back upstairs, the sun was flooding the bedroom with its good-hearted light. It was the same good-hearted light that fell on the heads of baby boilers and saints alike, unconditionally.

The last thing I saw before dropping off to sleep that morning was the gun, shining on the night table like a blue wish. I had one of those half-waking dreams that give you the feeling that you've understood something. I understood that the barking dog had been a sponsor for the gun. The gun had sought us out, and found us, with the assistance of the dog. *Go to sleep, you fool*, Raquel said. But that was the dream, too, and I realized that the gun had summoned, again with the aid of the dog, real changes in Raquel.

Morning dreams always wake me up, insisting that I register their fake significance. I got out of bed and went to the bathroom. I took a long look at my face. It had more mileage on it than my life justified. I rummaged through the stock of pills in the medicine cabinet, then went back to bed armed with Seconal against smart-ass dreams. The gun caught my eye again. It had a tight, self-satisfied sheen, like a deceptively well-groomed relative from a disgraced branch of the family who'd come to claim a permanent place in our home.

P ixel. A small word, filling a few bytes of memory at most, but it sat in Albert Court's mind like a huge bird of prey. No other words could get past pixel. He was blocked again. The brain could store millions of megabytes of information, and yet here was pixel in ten-foot-high neon letters declaring itself supreme, the only word in the world.

Albert looked at his damaged son, trying to force the stopper out of his mind, hoping for simple fluency. "Tommy," he said, but the obstinate *pixel* shoved the next word aside.

Tommy Court regarded his sweating father. *My sire*, he thought, amused.

Albert touched his son's lips with a Kleenex. The sedative, tranquilizer, antidepressant, or whatever it was they'd given him caused the boy to salivate heavily. Tommy turned away, refusing his father's attentions.

Then, mercifully, *pixel* opened its wings and sailed out of Albert's mind. Wiping his forehead with another Kleenex, he said, cheerful with relief, "Well, Tomaso, isn't this one grade-A hell of a fix?" He laughed, jovial at the sudden release of language.

disneyland

Tommy was being kept in the hospital for psychiatric observation because of what he'd done to himself. The family physician, Dr. Bud Rossetti, thought it best. It wasn't a private room—Albert's Health Maintenance Organization didn't permit private rooms—and the fat man in the other bed flooded the small room with the steady rasp of difficult breathing. The man was sitting up in bed, bent over a crossword puzzle. "What's a four-letter word for 'think tank'?" he asked.

"Rand," Tommy said, holding his bandaged arms over his head, like a referee's signal for "touchdown."

"Come again?" the fat man said, staring dubiously at Tommy over his half-moon reading glasses.

"Rand," Tommy repeated. "The Rand Corporation."

"Oh, Christ. Of course." The fat man leaned into his puzzle, wheezing.

"Tommy," Albert said, his voice hushed discreetly. "Sylvia's a wreck. Look, you're her only child. You know how she feels about you. What you've done to her... No, scratch that, Tomaso. I meant, what happened—" He stopped himself, realizing too late his blunder.

Tommy wouldn't let his father off the hook. "*Go* for it, Pops. *Say* it."

"No, son. You know that's not what I meant to say."

"Sure it was. You wanted to say that what I did to myself was actually meant for puddly old Sylvia's benefit. Every fucking thing that sends her up the walls is old Tomaso's fault, like she had a full deck before I started screwing up my life. Right?"

Albert glanced nervously at the fat man, but the fat man was engrossed in his puzzle, or at least was civil enough to be faking it. "Seven letters," he murmured to himself, "meaning 'danger for the unwary.'"

Albert picked up the water pitcher and filled the glass on Tommy's night table. He drank all of the water, then refilled the glass.

Wriggle, wriggle, Tommy thought, smiling faintly.

Words: in the best of times they were difficult for Albert. They were nearly impossible when he had to deal with crisis situations. Sometimes he believed he was dysphasic, and at other, more despairing moments, he thought he had a form of Parkinson's disease, a radical decay of the area of the brain responsible for speech.

He had to dredge for words, even when the stakes were light, and the dredging made him sweat. And yet he was a crack salesman for Funtron, Inc., a manufacturer of recreational software for personal computers. His colleagues on the sales team decided that this simple incongruity was responsible for Albert's success. People in the trade, they reasoned, were probably fed up with the slick, hotshot, silver-tongued types that dominated the early years of the business. They no doubt found a quiet man's struggle for words downright refreshing, even *touching*. The theory was hard to believe, but no one could advance a second explanation.

Tommy swung his pajamaed legs out of the bed and walked around the fat man's bed to the room's single window. A work crew was demolishing an old building across from the hospital. There was a message scrawled in spray paint on the remaining upright wall of the old building: HANG UP THE PIN, WILMA. The building was an old flophouse, the city's last blemish. The old flophouse had been a refuge for winos and homeless psychotics. A city councilman had announced, "We intend to enter the twenty-first century with a clean slate. These reminders of defeat and degradation must be erased from the public memory."

Tommy thought: *I'll get on the pin, like pissy old Wilma, heavy into scag. I'll get totaled on smack, crack, and what-you-got-Jack. I will free-base among the kamikaze zombies and go down in flames.*

When Tommy came back to his bed, Albert said, "Mother-board." The new stopper had waddled into his mind unnoticed and tricked him into verbalizing it. And now it sat, wide and sleek as a hippo or beached whale, jamming up the little speech Albert had prepared to defuse the situation. Sweat rolled down from his hairline into his eyebrows and down his cheeks. He drank more water, praying wordlessly for release.

"I don't think we're on the same page, Pop," Tommy said.

"*Pit*fall," the fat man said, triumphant.

Albert drove home. His wife, Sylvia, was under sedation. A nurse was in the house, sent over, he guessed, by Dr. Rossetti. Albert hadn't asked for a nurse, but was relieved to find a trained professional there. It was a good idea, although he wasn't sure his HMO would pay for it. No matter, he'd had an excellent year. Funtron, Inc., had come up with six innovative games, interactive fictions, and all of them were hot sellers. *Gaslight*, a Victorian romance, had stunned the industry with its success. Twelve retail outlets in his territory had the software on back order. No one thought *Gaslight* would become a mainstay of the Funtron line, but the public, so far at least, couldn't get enough of it. Letters from ecstatic customers came in daily. They loved how the program allowed Jack the Ripper a wide range of character traits, from remorseless, deadpan sadism to the engaging wit of a Lothario. They loved how they could program Prince Edward, Lloyd George, and young Winston Churchill to become players in labyrinthine love affairs that were consummated in the most glamorous cities in Europe.

The nurse was sitting on the sofa watching a soap opera. Albert stepped in front of the TV set. "How is she?" he asked.

The nurse, after trying to look past Albert's legs, said irritably, "You know. Breathing in, then breathing out. Would you scoot over, please? I think Inez is getting ready to give in to that bastard Ronnie Powers."

"Is she... can I see her?" he asked.

"Up to you. She's sort of asleep, though."

Albert went into the kitchen and opened the fridge. He wasn't hungry, but knew he hadn't eaten since Tommy tried to kill himself. He took out some sliced cheese, pastrami, the pickles, mayonnaise, and a can of Diet Sprite. He made a sandwich and carried it into the living room. He sat in his recliner and watched the soap opera. A woman—Inez, he imagined—was trying to light a cigarette while lying across a bed. She was wearing black bikini panties and bra. "Damn you," she said to her lighter as the scene dissolved to a man crouched in a stairwell.

Albert glanced at the nurse. She was young and exotic-looking. Possibly Asian. Possibly Martian. She had smooth amber akin and streaked, triple-toned hair. Her name tag said LEEANN. Her hair was auburn, yellow, and black. It furled tightly out from her head like a frozen banner. She looked competent. She had a beautiful figure under a crisp, light-blue uniform.

"Go for a sandwich?" Albert said, holding up the remains of his.

The nurse held up her hand to quiet him. "Wait," she said. "Here it comes. This really gives me the blues. I wish she'd kick that jerkoff Ronnie Powers out."

Inez had given up trying to light her cigarette. She was facedown on the bed now, sobbing. Ronnie Powers, a dark, wavy-haired man, sneered at Inez from a doorway. He threw some money on the floor. "You're trash," he said. "You'll always be trash."

The nurse lit a cigarette and blew smoke at the TV set. "I *mean*," she said, rolling her eyes dramatically, "this Ronnie Powers guy is *such* a dick."

Albert went upstairs. Sylvia was curled up under the electric blanket. Her face had the transparent look of white wax. The room smelled of wet eucalyptus leaves. Albert sat down on the bed. Sylvia didn't open her eyes or change position but reached out for him very slowly and sought his hand. He took her hand and kissed it, then squeezed it tightly. "Old Tomaso," he said, his voice hoarse. "He's going to be okay."

Sylvia's eyes fluttered, then opened. They looked dreamy and carefree. Except for her color and the stringy condition of her hair, Albert could almost believe she was well.

"It's true, darling. You should see him. Oh, he's mad as hell... at him*self*... for doing such a thing. But that's understandable. He's quite a Tomaso, that kid."

Sylvia gradually brought her husband into focus. Then she frowned. "Why?" she said.

Rows of modems tractored through his mind. He took a deep breath. *Modem, modem*, like heartbeats, scattered his thoughts. He shrugged. "Girl," he finally managed. "Fickle girl..." He felt dizzy; a roaring in his ears made him steady himself on the bed.

His wife looked away. The lids of her eyes were thick as crepe. "Girl," she murmured, her drug-swollen tongue unable to flex properly around the syllable.

Albert patted her hand.

"What's wrong with you?" his wife said, her voice suddenly alert.

Albert's heart knocked against his ribs. "What? Me? Nothing." He hesitated. "I feel sort of... unplugged from my database," he said, chuckling nervously.

"You sound—" she began, but the drug asserted itself again and the thought dwindled away until it became the sound of her own breath as it labored through her nostrils.

Dr. Rossetti had culled the story from Tommy. Then, in the privacy of his office, he told it to Albert, not sparing the details. The girl, Barbara Sunderlin, had decided that she needed a more educational range of experience. She and Tommy had been going steady, but she felt that their relationship was becoming too confining and that it would ultimately be a sounder relationship if it were more "open." Besides, she was a freshman at State College and he was a senior in high school. She was not especially pretty, but she had no trouble getting other dates. She told Tommy about them. When things went badly for her, she'd cry on Tommy's shoulder and tell him what had happened in vivid detail. She told Tommy that she needed him, that he was the strong, silent, clean-cut type.

Some of those fraternity boys were degenerate beasts, she said. They were soul-less harbingers of a mechanistic future. Tommy was a refreshing throw j66 back, without the pregenital neuroses that characterized the perverts she was seeing regularly now. It is beyond your imagination, Tommy, she told him, what those fraternity boys make me do. Dr. Rossetti had tried to put this part of the story into clinical terms, but, even so, Albert was still embarrassed at the anato-my of the sexual imagination.

Tommy had raged. He was a strong boy, a weight lifter and member of the high school wrestling team. He wanted to twist the heads off those fraternity creeps, he said. But Barbara wouldn't give him the name of the fraternity. It was for his sake, she said, that the name must be kept secret. She would blame her-self if something happened. She told him she loved him and would always love him. He believed her. He told her he would always love her, too. They exchanged rings. These rings symbolize the eternal, *spiritual* nature of our rela-tionship, she said. Our love is sane and simple and shall always remain so, she said. You are my sunny knight in bright armor, Tommy, you are my clean ray of optimism and decency in a toxic-waste-dump world. Tommy wanted to go steady again, even get engaged, but Barbara said she intended to become a seri-ous poet and needed the kind of wide-spectrum experience she was now begin-ning to acquire. I must descend into the mire, she said. I am an erotic explorer entering the dark jungles of desire. I intend to encounter the beasts who live in that jungle and thus, step by step, gain an understanding of the human animal himself. It's the only way. Academic psychologists, even clinical therapists, do not have access to the beast on an eye-to-eye basis. They remain antiseptically aloof.

But Tommy couldn't accept her behavior. Her exploration of the dark jun-gles of desire distressed him. The types of things she was doing with the frater-nity boys were absolutely beyond belief. He insisted she stop. It isn't possible for me to stop, she said. Don't be a child, Tommy, she said. Try to grasp the ele-mental nature of my quest. On one occasion, Tommy, in a tearful rage, slapped her face.

Their relationship began to change. Barbara became abusive. She began to ridicule his naiveté. She sent him a poem that pointed out his self-delusions. Finally, she sent him a collection of Polaroids of herself and several others. That night, after drinking a pint of vodka, Tommy hacked at his wrists and arms. The cuts were serious but the main arteries were not involved.

Albert had called Barbara's father. His rage and embarrassment flooded his mind with thought-blocking nonsense words. Mr. Sunderlin was mystified by the call. He had no idea what his daughter and Albert's son had been up to. He was a pleasant, soft-spoken man, a civil engineer with the county. Albert was able, eventually, to give the man a few clues, and the man filled the awkward silence with some platitudes about the generation gap. He recommended a book called

How to Deal Effectively with Your Problem Teen. Albert choked out the word *microstuffer*, and another long silence ensued. Then, when the stopper drifted out of his mind, he said, quickly, "My son tried to take his own life."

"Oh, good Lord," said Mr. Sunderlin. "I had no idea."

The nurse, LeeAnn, went to the guest room after *Dynasty.* She came out a few minutes later in a bathrobe. There was a flowery shower cap on her head and a transparent gel on her face. "You can call me if she wants something," she told Albert.

She seemed friendlier now. Her robe was partially open, and her fine, tawny skin gleamed between her breasts. Albert started to say something, but she smiled and put her finger to her lips.

"I sleep real light," she said, "don't worry."

Albert watched TV for a while, but the jokes on the Letterman show were exceptionally snide and the response from the audience seemed eagerly cruel. Albert switched off the set and went out into the garage. He had a fully equipped workshop there. Against one wall were several woodworking machines, but he had never really used any of them. Sylvia and Tommy had surprised him a few Christmases ago with a complete Home Craftsman set. Albert often complained about not having a hobby, something to do with his hands. His work at Funtron was mainly mental. He ran on nervous, caffeine-enhanced energy and was exhausted most of the time. A workshop with good tools seemed just the thing. But he never got around to learning how to use them. He'd gotten as far as buying some quality pine and alder, but had only cut some boards up to see how the saws worked. He liked the sound of the saws. He liked the deep thrum of the strong electrical motors, and the whine of the spinning blades made him feel relaxed. His mind, filled with the whine and thrum of the machinery, would be cleared of its useless clutter.

He turned on the table saw and sat on his stool. The table saw had the most satisfying sound of all the tools. Its motor was the largest, and the big, savage-looking blade made a breathy whir. He went back into the kitchen and fixed himself a large Scotch and soda, then returned to the garage and the moving saw. He stayed there an hour, nothing in his mind but a ten-inch circle of steel with razor-sharp teeth spinning at thousands of RPMs.

He carried another drink to Tommy's room. He sat on the bed and looked at the elaborately decorated walls. Pennants, comical signs (CLOSE TOILET BEFORE FLUSHING, NO PEDDLERS, BEWARE OF VICIOUS TUR-TLE, SPEED BUMPS). There were posters of rock stars—all with the same annoying expression on their pocked, ghost-white faces.

He turned on Tommy's Macintosh and was surprised to see that he had *Gaslight* already loaded in. Albert clicked on an icon and a question appeared on the screen: "Who is Jack the Ripper?" Albert, feeling a little drunk, typed "I am," but the program wouldn't accept that response. It scolded him and asked that he answer the question within "game parameters." Albert switched the machine off.

He looked at Tommy's barbell shoved up against the closet door. He went over to it and set his drink down on the floor. He gripped the weight with both hands and tried to lift it. The barbell didn't move. He picked up his drink and sipped at it. Then he saw the poems. They were on Tommy's desk, next to the Mac, under a half-eaten doughnut. He knew they were poems because the words were scattered on the pages. Each poem was signed by Barbara Sunderlin. The signature was large and childishly elaborate.

This is not prying, he told himself. The poems were out in the open. Removing a doughnut doesn't count. He slid a poem out from the stack and read it:

my bittersweet rose
burns
with a fire
of tongues

He took another poem from deeper in the stack:

night thoughts of bulls
thunder
in my field
O how I moo
at the boney moon

The next poem was no poem at all:

in it
in it
in it
in it
in it

There was a poem called "Quixote in Blue Denim." It was dedicated to Tommy Court:

Grab your section
Sunny Jim, while
I tell you a tale
Of animal connection

Albert was unable to read the rest.

He sat in his car for several minutes in front of the Sunderlin home, thinking. He had to have better reasons for coming here than curiosity and anger. But nothing else occurred to him. He went to the door, poems in hand. A woman answered. She was a tall, striking blonde, elegantly dressed. The Sunderlins were evidently going out for the evening. This immediately threw his planned speech into a disarray of broken phrases. He felt foolish. The woman was smoking a long cigarette.

"Albert Court," he sai, at last.

The woman raised a penciled eyebrow and blew a thread of smoke out one side of her mouth. "Oh, of course," she said. "You're the boy's father."

Mr. Sunderlin, wearing a chocolate-brown tux, stepped up behind his wife. "Come in, Mr. Court," he said, sliding back his sleeve to glance at his watch. "We have a few minutes."

Barbara Sunderlin was sitting in a high-back chair reading a thin volume of poetry.

"Babsie, honey," Mr. Sunderlin said. "Mr. Court is here."

The girl looked up from her book. She was wearing glasses. The lenses were narrow rectangles, smoke-tinted. She looked over them at Albert with a flat, analytical gaze. She was not attractive. She had a high, round forehead and she wore her hair swept back into an old-fashioned bun. Her nose was long and thin, the nostrils pinched asthmatically. Her lips were dark and full and frozen in a pout. Albert could not believe she was a nineteen-year-old girl. She looked thirty-five.

She closed her book and stood up. She was tall and slender, but her breasts were sharply conical in her dark red cardigan.

"Oh, Mr. Court!" she said, suddenly distraught. She went to him and threw her arms around his neck. She put her head on his shoulder and moaned. Albert was stunned. Her loud, wet sobs were muffled in the cloth of his jacket. He felt her thin body shuddering against him.

Albert didn't know what to do. He'd walked into this house, prepared to tell them what had happened to Tommy, whose fault it was, and to demand some sort of reparation, but now he was helpless as the sobbing girl clung to him as if he were her sole emotional support in this crisis.

He was still holding the poems. He looked over Barbara's quaking shoulder at Mr. and Mrs. Sunderlin, hoping for rescue. The Sunderlins were attractive, sophisticated people, and Albert began to lose his nerve before their stylish self-confidence. They were the kind of people he had always envied, even though they were not economically better off than he was. He raised his hands stiffly and patted Barbara on the back in a clumsy attempt to console her. The poems rattled, calling attention to themselves. Mrs. Sunderlin looked faintly amused, but her amusement faded quickly to boredom. Her perfect eyebrows were arched and she was squinting through a screen of blue smoke.

"I'm intruding," Albert said, trying to pull away from the sobbing girl. He wanted to leave now, but could not make himself utter the words that would allow him to do this without appearing a complete fool. The splendid calm of the Sunderlins had somehow canceled his right to speak to them on equal terms. The complaint he had intended to make them listen to was gone; he couldn't even recall who it had been intended for, the girl or her parents. A storm of self-hatred scattered his thoughts. He felt guilty and shy. Barbara, as if sensing his extreme discomfort, tightened her embrace. Her small sobs warmed his neck. Albert kept patting her on the back, and the rattling sheaf of poems grew perversely loud.

"So, you're into software," Mr. Sunderlin said.

"Just sales," Albert said.

"Don't knock sales. The world turns on sales. Eleanor—my wife, Eleanor—she's into real estate."

The woman's faint smile seemed to summon up a stopper. *Parser* slipped into Albert's mind, a vivid python, and began to uncoil. "Parser," he said, blushing instantly.

Mr. Sunderlin chuckled suavely. "Babsie, why don't you let the poor gentleman go? I think he under*stands* your feelings."

Barbara stepped away from Albert and leveled a vicious look at her father.

Sylvia's condition became worse. Dr. Bud Rossetti prescribed a more potent tranquilizer. "It's time to upscale the chemistry, Albert," he said. "I think it's time to move up to the phenothiazines."

Albert had mentioned Sylvia's dreams. They threw her into terrible panics. She screamed on waking. Sometimes she wasn't sure she'd been asleep. And when she was awake, she sometimes believed she was still sleeping. In one dream there had been a basket of bleeding fruit on the breakfast table. Tommy would not eat. She tried to give him a bloody apple but he turned his face away. A butterfly big as a cat sat on top of the fruit basket. It turned to her and opened its jaws. Sylvia had thought that the butterfly was trying to speak to her. She got the idea it wanted to say her name. "I couldn't," Albert said, "make her stop. Screaming, I mean."

Dr. Rossetti wrote two prescriptions in a hasty scrawl. He shook his big dark head back and forth as he wrote. "Grim city, Albert," he said. "All we can do is pray that it passes. The human organism is amazingly resilient. Think of it as weather, Albert. Good air will eventually blow the bad air out."

"No, it won't," Albert said.

Dr. Rossetti took Albert in his big arms. "You have my personal guarantee," he said.

Albert pushed the big doctor away. "Thanks," he said.

"'You're a quality guy, Albert," Dr. Rossetti said.

Albert left Sylvia in the care of LeeAnn and drove out to the hospital. Tommy was having his wrists and arms rebandaged and after that a psychologist was going to give him another test. He couldn't have visitors for a couple of hours.

Albert decided to spend the time in the waiting room. He didn't want to go back home, even though it was only a ten-minute drive.

"Well, hi there, Mr. Court," someone said.

Albert looked up from the copy of *Time* he'd been reading. The harsh white light of the waiting room made his eyes blur.

"It's me. It is I. You know. Barbara Sunderlin."

She had been sitting across from him, not more than twelve feet away. How long had she been there? The feeling that she had just materialized, unbeckoned, struck him. His heart tripped on the idea, then began to beat noticeably. The mind was a magic crystal: things appeared in it out of nowhere. His whole life seemed to him like a series of abrupt manifestations, things and events without antecedents. Everything discrete, self-sufficient, like the binary digits of a computer program. Nothing had the old continuity of the analog model of reality. *Multiplexor* slipped into his mind, then a quick series of flip-flops between *and-gate, or-gate*, and *zero-wait-state*.

Barbara came over and sat in the chair next to him. "Mr. Court, I can't tell you how *awful* I feel," she said, her voice rising. The receptionist looked up from her desk. "Look," Barbara said. "I was going to give this to Tommy!" She held up a small gift-wrapped package. "It's a new wallet. Alligator. A get-well present." Her voice thickened with self-loathing. Other people in the waiting room were looking at them. The receptionist frowned at Albert. "What kind of rotten *creep* would give a boy who tried to kill himself a fucking alligator *wallet*?" She began to cry.

"Maybe we should talk outside," Albert said.

They went out to the parking lot and sat in Albert's car. Barbara was now weeping uncontrollably. She put her head on Albert's chest. She didn't seem thirty-five years old to Albert now. She seemed twelve. He was grateful for the anonymity of the parking lot.

"Drive me someplace," Barbara said, lifting her face from his chest.

She was calmer now, and Albert was grateful for that. "Sure," he said. "Where do you want to go?"

"Anywhere. I always drive around whenever I feel too shitty for words."

"I'll take you home," he said.

"No. Not there. Not home."

Albert drove aimlessly for a while, allowing himself to be drawn into this lane or that turn by the random pressures of traffic. He, too, found that driving around casually was a soothing experience. It was a California thing, he decided, it's what we do. And now that the access ramps were computer-controlled, it made the whole process a lot easier.

He merged into the fast traffic on the Santa Ana freeway. Barbara was slumped against the door, the side of her face pressed against the window. Her expression was calm and vacant. She stared straight down the freeway, eyes relaxed on distance.

"Listen, Mr. Court," she said abstractedly. "I've been thinking. I've got this great idea."

"I'd better be getting home," he said.

"Beautiful," she said. "Just fucking beautiful."

They drove without speaking. To the right of the freeway, the Alps of Disneyland loomed against the grainy sky. The spires and towers of Fantasyland leaped up at them like a forgotten childhood dream returning, colossal and strange, as if it had been growing cancerously in some dark corner of the mind.

"My father is an intellectual snob," Barbara said. "You know the kind—reads Aldous Huxley and Ayn Rand, always quoting them. He never once took me to Disneyland. Even when I was in grade school and couldn't have understood what he meant, he made cutting remarks about this place. Hell, maybe he was right. I don't know. But I've always wanted to come here. It's as though there's this denied child within me, and this has been her secret ambition forever."

"*Okay*," Albert said, flipping on his turn signal.

Albert bought two multiple-ride coupon books. The crowd was relatively small. Albert and Barbara were the only couple on the trip to the moon. There were only four other passengers on the submarine voyage. There were more people on the flatboat trip through the jungle, but it was a quiet crowd. They seemed unaware of the festive nature of the giant amusement park. Barbara called them Russians. In fact, they did look like foreigners—East Europeans, possibly Russians. The men were wearing dark, bulky suits and the women were stocky matrons in low heels. There were no children with them. It was a solemn crowd that looked somehow displaced, and the entire trip through the jungle seemed more like a forced trek to some grim place of exile than an amusement. The crowd at the Haunted House, to Albert's relief, seemed more typical.

"I just *love* it," Barbara said gaily. "Don't you, Mr. Court?" They were out on a mall, strolling among human-sized mice.

He wanted to answer her, he wanted to say, Yes, I love it, but he frowned and looked at his watch instead. "Almost four," he said.

A very tall man wearing only Jockey shorts stepped into their path. He'd been hiding behind a closed information kiosk. "Nay!" he shouted. He was at least six feet ten inches tall and his coarse gray hair fell past his shoulders, stiff with grime. Black hearts the size of dimes were tattooed across his chest. Little red arrows, the tips dripping blood, pierced the black hearts. "Nay!" he repeated, his voice cracking with either emotion or the chronic strain of his existence.

Barbara took Albert's hand and tried to pull him to one side, but Albert froze before the giant. The giant stepped closer to Albert and glared down at him. An extreme truth danced lightly in his wide, pale eyes. Other people passed by swiftly, hoping to escape unnoticed. But the giant man in Jockey shorts seemed interested only in Albert and Barbara.

"I am the god Cupid," the man said. He placed his hands on top of Albert's and Barbara's heads. "Kneel before me, my children." His voice was now rich and sonorous, a melodious basso, vibrant with self-confidence.

"Do it," Barbara whispered. "He's nuts."

Albert saw the security guards running towards them. The guards were heavy, slow men. Albert sank to his knee.

"Thus do I bind thee together in the eternal bower," the giant said. The powerful hands of the giant brought Albert's and Barbara's heads together gently. Barbara's face felt cold against his. Albert noticed that the giant's feet were bleeding, as though he'd been walking through broken glass. Barbara squeezed Albert's hand as the giant rotated their heads slowly until they were face to face, lips against lips. "Blessed are they who loveth," he pronounced. Then the security guards arrived and dragged the man away.

"Well, we have one more ride left," Barbara said, dusting off her skirt.

"I don't know," Albert said, his voice shaky. "I don't think I'm up to it."

"Sure you are. He was just a harmless old nut. They thrive around here. The setting appeals to them."

There was a long line in front of Pirates of the Caribbean, but Barbara insisted they get in it. "It moves fast, you'll see," she said.

When it was their turn, they boarded a small, two-person boat that was launched down a dark tunnel. Soon they were out on a subterranean river. Crazed buccaneers leaped out at them from dark crevices, cutlasses brandished high. These were crude robots, their movements too stiff to be believable. Even so, Barbara cringed away from them. Across the water a galleon burst into flames as cannons boomed. Their boat rocked in the churning water. Tongues of real fire licked out at them. Explosions rumbled through the caverns. Bloodthirsty laughter avalanched down from a black, starless sky. Islands of booty glittered in the amber light of torches. The screams of a Spanish princess locked in the brutal arms of a hairy corsair rose above the din. "¡*Ayúdame!*" she called. "¡*Por favor! ¡Ayúdame!*"

Sudden high seas made their boat lurch. A hurricane warning sounded. Barbara fell across Albert's lap. Albert caught her by the shoulders and tried to lift her off, but she didn't move. He watched helplessly as her thin shoulders quaked.

"Barbara?" he said. "Are you crying?"

She lifted her head slightly. Albert saw that her face was wet, that her tears were real and abundant. "I'm *trying* to have fun," she sobbed, miserably. "Honest to Christ, Mr. Court, I am *trying*."

It's *okay*, Barbara," he said, as the people in the boat ahead of them turned to see what the trouble was.

"It's *not* okay!" Barbara shouted. "God damn you people, can't you understand that it's *not* okay?"

A breeze from the approaching exit cooled Albert's face. "No one holds you responsible, Barbara," he said, surprising himself.

Barbara raised herself and looked at him. "What are you talking about, Mr. Court?"

"Tommy. You couldn't have known, could you? I mean, known what he was going to do. I don't condone what you—"

"Jesus H. Christ on a skateboard," she said.

Albert wiped her face with his handkerchief. He was thinking that her life was probably not as easy as it looked, not nearly as privileged. Those parents of hers, cold as ice and on the climb, socially. "Don't—you shouldn't, Barbara—punish yourself." A tear he had missed sparkled on her chin. He dabbed it away with his handkerchief.

She laughed suddenly and he was shocked by its metallic brilliance. It was an eerily beguiling laugh. It made his scalp tingle. "You silly person," she scolded." "It's *you* I'm crying for, Albert. And me. It's you and me, that's who I'm crying for," she said.

It was dark when they left. In the parking lot, Barbara kissed Albert. He'd been unlocking the car when she slid between him and the door. He tried to back away from her, but her hands locked at the back of his head. He put his hands on her shoulders to force her away, but she yielded so dramatically that he couldn't bring himself to be rough with her. Then her tongue, hard and minty, slid past his lips. He made a sound in his throat, but it didn't deter her. His thick, bewildered tongue met the cool, flexing sweetness of hers hesitantly. She was able to do things with her tongue that had the intricacy of ritual. Then, by strong suction, she pulled his tongue into her mouth. he moved it dumbly, without skill. It was like laboring for speech, and he began to sweat. In the car, he said, "I'm sorry. I should *not* have done that." His voice was small but passionate with shame.

"Don't be a goof," she said. "We're friends, aren't we?"

Albert bought Tommy a new set of steel-belted radials for his car as a welcome-home present. They stood in the garage looking at the new tires. Tommy was feeling much better. He was a good-looking boy, a fine athlete, and he was intensely humiliated by what he had done to himself. *That slime hole*, he thought. He couldn't believe he'd let a punchboard like Barbara Sunderlin get to him. *That crab farm*, he thought. *That pus pit. That walking slit trench.* He ran his hand over the bold tread of the tires. *Fucking Pirellis*, he thought, jubilant. He pictured himself banking into a hairpin curve up in the Sierras, power on, engine winding out, downshifting dramatically to third, the road treacherous with rain, a semi jackknifed across the road ahead, then barreling into the ditch and powering through it, and up the embankment around the trailer, back onto the pavement, *control* a beautiful dream come true, and there, ahead—*check it out*—a lovely woman behind the wheel of a stalled BMW, her hopeful eyes meeting his...

Albert, though he loved his son's obvious enthusiasm for the tires, wasn't feeling very well. Guilt and lust had grown in him like twin tumors. He had tried to bury himself with work. He stayed late at the office, studying new software proposals, new marketing areas. He attended engineering meetings that were over his head, sales meetings that didn't concern his territory. But nothing helped. A physical memory of Barbara's busy tongue in the Disneyland parking lot broke his concentration. And to make things worse, to complicate things further, they made plans to see each other again. *What in the hell am I trying to do?* he thought. *Wreck what's left?*

He met her in public places. Beaches, amusement parks, cafés, McDonald's, movie theaters, and Disneyland. They went to Disneyland often and once made love in the back of the submarine when they were the only passengers. He half expected to see the psychotic giant who called himself Cupid, and kept a wary eye whenever they went to the huge amusement park. He could still feel, when he thought about it, the giant's powerful fingers on his skull, forcing his face into Barbara's.

Barbara wrote poems dedicated to him. She mailed them boldly to his house, the envelopes addressed to Alberto Cortazuma. He hid the poems in his workshop and read them at night with the table saw running. The things they did together were gathered in farfetched metaphor and simile.

They exchanged small presents. He bought her a gold bracelet. She bought him garish, hand-painted neckties. She even had herself tattooed for him: flaming lips uttering, by means of a comic-strip balloon, his name.

Pretending to be serious, they discussed eloping to Mexico. In bed, late at night, listening to Sylvia's tranquilized breathing, he would convince himself that they *were* serious, and he would try to visualize the uncomplicated air of the lower Baja.

But he had obligations, duties. *My son, for instance*, he reminded himself. What would Tommy think? How could he expect Tommy not to react with scorn and rage? And then, how could he possibly sleep easy in Mexico knowing the total wreckage he'd left behind? He looked at his son. Tommy was hefting a Pirelli. His tanned biceps were round and hard as apples. Albert loved him. He would give his life for the boy without thinking, without even a sense of martyrdom. A gesture as automatic as a leaf falling in October.

"Tomaso," he said, hoping that speech would not fail him this time.

"Yes, Dad?" Tommy said, glancing at his father quickly, then, just as quickly, looking away. *It's Father-and-Son Time*, he thought, peevish.

Albert wanted to make sure that Barbara was out of the boy's mind, but he wasn't sure how to open the touchy subject "Deep wounds," he said at last, "sometimes don't heal completely."

Tommy turned his face away from his father so that his smile would not be seen. He picked up another tire, pretended to inspect the tread. "Don't sweat it, Pops," he said. "Old Shit-for-Brains has learned his lesson the hard way."

Albert began to labor. He arched his back and breathed deeply. Tommy looked at him then. "What I mean, Tomaso," Albert said. "What I'm trying to *get* at is, will she—"

"*She?*"

"Don't be annoyed, son. I mean Barbara. Barbara Sunderlin. Will Barbara—"

"Bum me out again? *That* blowjob?"

Albert chewed the inside of his cheek as a stopper moved into his mind. *Rom, rom, rom*, like an audible, high-blood-pressure pulse, richly liquid, staggered him. Then he realized that it *was* his pulse, and that he felt wobbly with vertigo, and the palms of his hands were damp. "Let's get those tires on, Tommy," he said.

Albert dreamed he had fallen out of a hot-air balloon. A rope wrapped itself around his thigh, saving him. But as the supple rope tightened, it made a noose around his genitals. He was hanging from a balloon, high above Disneyland, by his genitals. The pain was spectacular. A crowd of solemn Russians looked up, attracted by his screams.

He woke to find Sylvia pulling his genitals. She had a white-knuckled grip on them. She seemed to be asleep, but her eyes were partly open. She wasn't making a sound other than the slow, deep breathing of a sleeper. He took her by the wrist and tried to remove her hand from him, but she would not release her hold. The pain was severe. He slapped her face as hard as he could from his awkward position, and kept slapping her until she raised her hands to protect herself. Albert got up and went into the bathroom.

After his pain subsided a bit, he found her pills. "Is it one from the blue bottle and two from the red, or vice versa?" he called, but Sylvia didn't answer. He carried the bottles of pills and a glass of water into the bedroom. Sylvia was sitting on the bed with her knees drawn up to her chin. Her eyes were fiercely distrustful.

He put the glass of water and the pills on the night table on her side of the bed. Sylvia's eyes, watchful and bright, like the eyes of a cornered animal, studied his every move, unblinking. Albert put on his bathrobe and Sylvia's eyes darted to each small movement of his hands as he looped and cinched the belt. He glanced at their twenty-three-year-old wedding picture on the dresser. It startled him. Then he went down to his workshop to listen to the saws.

Barbara wanted to go to Palm Springs for the weekend. Albert told LeeAnn, the nurse, that he had to go north on a business trip. Sylvia accepted the story without comment. Dr. Bud Rossetti had changed prescriptions once again, but Sylvia had not improved noticeably. Tommy's return from the hospital did not have the salutary effect Dr. Rossetti was hoping for, either.

"I don't understand it," Albert had told Dr. Rossetti.

"No one does," the doctor admitted, shaking his dark, mournful head slowly. "Christ, Albert, we don't even understand *aspirin*. How can we be expected to grasp acetophenazine maleate?"

"Her breasts have gotten larger."

"A possible side effect."

Albert smiled; the doctor misunderstood it and winked.

"No," Albert said. "I was just thinking. In a sales meeting the other day... I sort of went blank. Then someone was tugging at my sleeve. They said that I repeated the words 'motherboard of the mainframe' a couple of dozen times, like a broken record."

"That isn't funny, Albert. It sounds like a symptom, if you want an off-the-cuff opinion."

"Symptom of what?"

"I don't know. Could be a form of Gilles de la Tourette's syndrome. Who can say? It keeps up, you might be a candidate for haloperidol."

"Well, sure, of course," Albert said, his mind elsewhere.

"A sea of troubles," Dr. Rossetti said, sighing massively. He slung his heavy arm around Albert's shoulder. "Look, Albert. Why don't you get Sylvia a nice little dog?"

"Dog?"

"Well, hell! Why not? Do you both good. You never know. A little thing like that might be the missing factor. A lapdog, cuddlesome. A cockapoo, say. One of those little crappy yappers who give you all their love."

Albert stood bewildered before the big, jovial doctor.

Reading Albert's confusion as skepticism, Dr. Rossetti said, "Jesus, Albert, chemistry isn't everything. We're flesh and blood, after all. We're only human. The next logical step is commitment. That's why I brought up the dog. A god-damned dog might just be the ticket. I've heard of stranger things."

"No dog," Albert said. "Sylvia hates dogs."

The desk clerk was smiling and he wasn't smiling. The smile was in the darkness behind his neutral eyes, not in his face. It was an unassailable smile. Albert, even so, was enraged by it, wherever it was. It was in the clerk's shoulders, his hands, his fastidious movements behind the hotel desk. Albert felt stung by the clerk's abstract smile. *He thinks I'm a forty-nine-year-old man shacking up with a girl young enough to be my daughter*, Albert thought.

In their room, Barbara took her clothes off immediately and went out on the private balcony that overlooked the desert. Albert sat on the bed, watching her move. She was doing a little dance step, a half-unconscious movement generated by a distant radio playing rock. Albert was still mad at the desk clerk. Impudence. As he approached fifty, he saw it everywhere. Barbara stopped her little hip-hiking movement and held her arms up to the black desert sky in a gesture that looked like both indecent exposure and worship.

"*Is* it a starry dynamo," she said, "or just a pretty nonsense?"

"What?" Albert said.

She came back into the room, dancing again. The nipples of her breasts were stiff with chill. She stood in front of him, legs apart, hands on the bony shelves of her hips. "Ginsberg," she said. She quoted, "'...hundreds of suitcases full of tragedy rocking back and forth waiting to be opened.'"

Albert gave her a wincing smile. "I'm sorry... *who*?"

"The old beatnik. *Your* generation, Albert. You ought to remember."

She straddled his lap and forced him backward down on the bed. "Interface ports," he said.

"You got it, handsome," she said.

Later, Albert went into the bathroom and poured Scotch into two plastic cups. Barbara ran down the hall for ice, wrapped in a bed sheet. They sat together on the balcony and sipped their drinks. The stars in the jet-black sky were bright and steady. They made Albert think of a matrix of solder joints on the underside of a circuit board. He laughed a little, then said, "I've been thinking about eloping."

"Eloping?"

"You know. Mexico. We talked about it."

"Quaint," she said, smiling into her drink.

"You're making fun of me," he said.

"No. It *is* quaint. Quaint things turn me on. Like going to a priest and saying *padre*. Or honeymoons. Words like *spellbound* and *womanize*. Gravy is quaint. Pizza. Sock hops and slumber parties. Athletic sweaters. Extramarital affairs. Communists. Vasectomies. The Sears catalog, the Royal Couple, a liberal education. I could go on and on."

"You are really something," Albert said.

Sometime before dawn Barbara whispered into Albert's ear, "How do you think Tommy is going to take this? You and me, I mean."

"Don't make these cruel jokes, Barbara," Albert said.

"Who says I'm joking? I think he should know all about us. I hate deception. It's tacky."

"I said. I said don't."

"Have it your way, Daddy," she said. "But you should know something.

Papa's got a bigger crank than his bouncing baby boy, although the kid's got more staying power. It evens out, I guess."

He realized, then, that she *was* just teasing him. "You little *brat*," he said, slapping her thigh gently.

Albert couldn't sleep. He went into the bathroom and made himself another drink. He turned on the ceiling vent. He sat on the edge of the tub and listened to the fan's weak hum. Then he went back into the bedroom.

Barbara was asleep. A shaft of light from the bathroom fell across her neck. Albert knelt beside the bed to kiss her and saw the quick pulse define the artery that ran along her narrow throat. It moved him, and he said her name. Her eyes opened wide. Her face looked very young and frightened. "I'll go anywhere with you, Albert," she said, her voice high and childlike. "I'll do anything you want me to do."

"Maybe," he said. "Maybe you will."

A mass of hot, dry air had moved in from the desert. Tommy couldn't sleep. He got out of bed and loaded *Gaslight* into the disk drive of his Mac. He began the interactive fiction after the fifth unsolved murder. Things were going badly for Scotland Yard. The press was relentlessly critical, and the Queen had called for an internal investigation. Jack the Ripper, whoever he was, had mocked the Yard by sending contemptuous letters to the *Times*. The letters were articulate, witty, and seemed to hold clues that tipped off his future plans. The story switched then, at Tommy's bidding, to a rundown hotel room in Soho. A man and a woman were sitting on a rickety bed. "I knew the instant I saw you that you were not the commonplace slattern," the man said, kissing the woman's hand. While the man's head was bent for the kiss, the woman looked at the ceiling and smiled. Tommy typed in the command for "pause" and asked the program to insert Jack the Ripper's third identity, and to substitute him for the man on the bed. Jack the Ripper's third identity was Dr. Florian Foxglove, respected surgeon. The man on the bed, tubby now and bald, reached into his coat pocket and removed a scalpel.

Sylvia came in carrying a glass of milk. "Oh, good," she said. "I *thought* you were awake. This heat is terrible." She was in her nightgown. "I couldn't sleep, either."

Tommy watched the Ripper cut a neat red smile in the woman's throat, then switched off the machine. "Could I have some of that, Sylvia?" he asked.

Sylvia gave him the glass of milk and Tommy drained it. He wiped his mouth on his pajama sleeve and handed the glass back to his mother.

Sylvia touched his shoulder and squeezed. "I'm so glad you're out of that hospital," she said.

"So am I, Mom," Tommy said. "Did I tell you about the fat guy in the bed next to mine?"

"Do you want some more milk, honey?" she said.

"Sure. But this humongous guy next to me, he *died*. He was a big fat slobbo, always working a crossword puzzle. He died while he was working on one, in fact."

"Oh, no, Tommy, how *awful* for you," she said, leaning down to kiss his hair.

"More like *weird* than awful. He was stuck on a word meaning 'sudden reversal of polarity.' I knew the answer but figured that I'd already spoiled enough of his dumb puzzles by giving him answers. He died straining for the word. I heard his heart *explode*, Sylvia. It sounded like a wet fart, muffled under his blanket and all. It must have lasted about thirty seconds, *fwuup*. I mean, it was *totally* weird."

Sylvia shuddered. "I wish you hadn't seen such things, honey," she said. Though she was pale, and there were dark hollows under her eyes, she was feeling much better. Dr. Rossetti's latest prescription had worked wonders. Her sense of well-being was nearly constant now and could be depended on. The side effects were hardly noticeable. She didn't care at all about the side effects. She was back on her feet and feeling good about things in general, and that was all that mattered. It didn't even bother her that Albert had apparently left home for good. In fact, his unannounced departure made her feel lighthearted and giddy. This reaction puzzled her, but Dr. Rossetti's wonderful chemicals wouldn't let her puzzlement become unmanageable. The future looked bright.

She kissed Tommy's hair again, loving its clean smell and springy strength. She had a wonderful son, a fine, intelligent, handsome son. "I'll get us some more milk," she whispered.

Tommy switched on his computer again. The surgeon, having completed his lethal stroke, held the scalpel gracefully out to one side, at arm's length, the way a conductor of an orchestra would hold his baton to draw out and savor the last sweet outswelling of a symphony.

I f this was not meant to be, then nothing was meant to be. Sometimes when two strangers meet they feel they've known each other forever. The tall man in cowboy regalia was such a person to Marianna. She quivered involuntarily, like the delicate needle of a compass, before the quiet magnetism of his masculine presence. A sleeping passion stirred restlessly in her neglected loins. Was he the man she'd envisioned years ago in the hazy longing of adolescent daydreams—a vision dismissed a few years later as the pubescent fantasy of an imaginative child? More to the point, was he her type? But what was one's "type"? Of this she had no idea. Years of carefully managed emotions had dulled her judgment in these matters. For to know one's type is to know one's needs. Marianna Kensington was a desert of unknown needs that any random flood might violate into bloom.

Romance: A Prose Villanelle

After years of indifferent love from a man she'd lost all respect for, Marianna had ventured west to begin her life anew. As she deplaned at the Albuquerque airport and entered the terminal, a chill of anticipation had made her shiver despite the horizon-warping heat of the southwestern desert. Though she was forty now, she had lost nothing of her superbly svelte yet roundly voluptuous figure, which her husband, Kenneth, had nagged her to conceal, even though he no longer responded to it. And conceal it she did—in bulky knit sweaters with high necks, in voluminous stretch pants designed to hide matronly thighs and backsides, and in unfashionable but "sensible" shoes with good supports. Kenneth wanted, above all, for Marianna to project the image of the efficient housewife, the dedicated mother, the resourceful community volunteer. It was important to his self-image that she be regarded as a paragon of domestic reliability and propriety. For her part, Marianna was compliant as potter's clay. She had allowed Kenneth to mold her with his hectoring demands, making her fit each image he believed enhanced his career as deputy advisory to the assistant mayor.

She'd walked away from a twenty-year marriage without regret. The children were grown and gone. She still had time, she felt, to find out who Marianna Kensington was. Perhaps she was no one. How frightening! But how much more frightening to deceive yourself into thinking you were complete when in fact you were nothing but a blank page waiting to be filled in! The suburbs were crowded with safe and comfortable women who were essentially blank pages waiting for a violating pen. Silence was their chief enemy. For silence could let the inner emptiness rise to the surface, like a submerged but featureless continent. And so they filled each waking hour with gossip and chat, with shopping, and with the tedium of domestic chores. The resented demands of children were, in fact, a necessary barrier reef that prevented the intrusion of that dangerous silence. The famous "empty-nest syndrome" was but a high-toned euphemism that denoted the terrifying enemy, Silence, who, given a small opportunity, would enter the house and sit down like a bold intruder. The intruder smiles with his superior knowledge of the little dark mechanisms of your heart. Ignoring him, you pick up the latest Silhouette or Harlequin Romance and try to read, but the words blur together, passion links arms with despair—jealousy, anger, spite, kink up like a bicycle chain that throws itself loose from its sprocket and the whole enterprise coasts to a dismal stop halfway to nowhere. You skip ahead to the forlorn sobs of the heroine as the handsome but brutal horseman rips her blouse to the waist, or takes her roughly in an autumn copse, or more gently but with degrading insouciance in the elegantly appointed drawing room of his antebellum mansion. It doesn't help. The silence you have contrived successfully all your life to hold at bay slips in between the lines of bloated prose, it invades each preposterous scene or trumped-up emotion, it collects in the gaps between chapters. And it is there, waiting for you at the end, in the gritty dead-white paper, rustling patiently with the last word.

"My name is Jeff Granger," the tall cowboy said. "I'm foreman out at the Y Bar Y. You'll be cooking for my crew." She put down her valise and extended her hand. He took it in his and something like an electrical current passed between them in a hard, shocking vibration. She wondered if he felt it. It embarrassed her, and when he released her hand, a wave of dizziness almost overcame her. His hand had been hard and callused, its great strength had been apparent, and yet it had been gentle and warm. "Jorge Méndez here will be your assistant," he continued, his voice edged now with a wariness and Marianna knew that he, too, had felt the vibrant current pass between them. A short heavyset man of mixed blood who had been standing behind Jeff and off to one side stepped forward holding his wide-brim straw hat in his brown hands. "*Buenos días, señora*," he said, with an almost courtly deference, but in his Indian-black eyes Marianna thought she saw a flicker of icy resentment.

Marianna had answered an ad that for some reason had been placed in the *Boston Globe*: "Wanted, Ranch Cook. Hard work. Fair pay. Some benefits. Healthiest life-style going." Her marriage to Kenneth was finished as far as she was concerned. Kenneth had raged and threatened, but she had met this display with unruffled calm, and all his fury came to nothing, like a dry summer storm that begins with the promise of deluge but offers only a few strokes of lightning and an afternoon of darkened skies. When his rage turned to abject pleading, her cold resolve became colder and more resolute. She realized then that there had never been anything to love in this man. What she'd once believed was strength she now saw as head strong infantile petulance. What she'd taken as love was only his bottomless need for constant reassurance and praise. What she once saw as his intelligent commitment to honorable ideals she now saw as commonplace ambition. In midlife she had been given the ability to see things for what they were. Her two children, Annie and Ken Junior, were away at college. There was no reason to stay and every reason to go. A ranch in New Mexico seemed as good a place as any to start a brand-new life. She climbed into Jeff Granger's beat-up Ford Bronco with a clear sense of leaving her old life and starting her new one. Jeff knocked his dusty Stetson back on his head, revealing a rich shock of wavy chestnut hair, a few strands of which were pressed to his forehead with honest sweat. He smiled at her as she settled into the seat beside him, and Marianna's heart suddenly felt too big for her chest.

If this was not meant to be, then nothing was meant to be. Sometimes when two strangers meet they feel they've known each other forever. Jeff Granger was such a man to Marianna. She quivered before the quiet magnetism of his masculine presence. A sleeping passion stirred restlessly in her neglected loins. Was he the man she'd envisioned years ago? More to the point, was he her type? What *was* one's type? She had no idea. Years of careful emotions had dulled her judgment. For to know one's type is to know one's needs. Marianna was a desert of unknown needs that any random flood might violate into bloom.

The ride out to the Y Bar Y was bone-jolting rough. Jeff drove with one careless hand on the wheel at high speed, heedless of the rutted road. Marianna held on to the door handle and more than once had to steady herself by grabbing his shoulder. "What's the hurry?" she'd wanted to say, but didn't. She was now an employee of a large cattle ranch and not in a position to criticize the foreman. In the back of the Bronco, Jorge Méndez dozed. Jeff played country and western tunes on the tape deck at high volume. It occurred to Marianna that this was a rude thing to do since it preempted any attempt at civil conversation. It was as if Jeff were saying, *I don't want to talk to you, what you have to say doesn't interest me.* She tried to shout a question about the countryside, but either he didn't hear her or he pretended not to. *He doesn't approve of me*, she thought. She concluded it had not been his idea to run the ad for a ranch cook in the *Boston Globe* . But if it hadn't been Jeff's idea, whose *had* it been? The question burned in her mind as the truck plummeted toward a mirage of outbuildings that seemed to float in a lake of heat.

When Jeff pulled the Bronco into the circular driveway in front of a huge ranch house—a magnificent structure of rough-hewn logs and fieldstone—he said, "Mrs. Kensington, I have to ask you something. Have you ever cooked for forty workingmen before?" She answered that she had, in fact, cooked for large groups of people on various occasions—church camp once and several times for her daughter's Girl Scout troop. Then there were the political dinners Kenneth hosted... Jeff Granger laughed abruptly. "This is not suburban Massachusetts, Mrs. Kensington," he said. She didn't care for his tone. Surely she had been mistaken about the "magnetic" attraction she had experienced back at the airport. It must have been the heat, the unfamiliar surroundings, the strain of travel, and her exaggerated sense of high expectations no doubt induced by fatigue. What a fool she'd been! A sudden deflation of spirit overwhelmed her. Perhaps she'd made a terrible mistake in coming here to this godforsaken place. What had made her think, after all, that her life as the accommodating wife of a minor political functionary was something to *scorn*? What had made her think that she was unusual, that she deserved something better than ninety percent of the women she knew? Why had she aspired to some lofty goal that even now she could not fully define? Jeff Granger had laughed at her, and now she laughed at herself. What had made her believe she had been given the ability to see things for what they were? She wanted to tell Jeff to turn the Bronco around, take her back to the airport. But then, where could she go? She'd burned her bridges rather thoroughly. Even if she had the capacity to humble herself before Kenneth, why should he take her back after the devastating things she'd said to him? In a cold, analytical way, she'd told him how she'd come to scorn him as a man, in his public life and in his private life as husband, father, and lover. "Christ, you even take an opinion poll in bed!" she'd told him. No, there was no way she could return to Kenneth. She'd take this job at the Y Bar Y and she'd *succeed*. If there was one virtue she possessed, it was determination. Even though Jeff Granger evidently thought very little of her, cooking for forty workingmen could not be all that different from cooking for a Girl Scout troop or for a house full of greedy politicos. It would be hard at first, even scary, but everything worthwhile in life required risk. Safety and comfort were highly overrated as far as Marianna was concerned.

She'd walked away from a twenty-year marriage without regret. The children were grown and gone. She still had time to find out who Marianna Kensington was. Perhaps she was no one. How frightening! But how much more frightening to deceive yourself into thinking you were complete when in fact you were nothing but a blank page waiting to be filled in! The suburbs were crowded with safe and comfortable women who were essentially blank pages waiting for a violating pen. Silence was their chief enemy. For silence could let the inner emptiness rise to the surface, like a submerged but featureless continent. Given an opportunity, silence would enter the house and sit down like a bold intruder. The intruder smiles with his superior knowledge of the little dark mechanisms of your heart. You pick up the latest Silhouette or Harlequin and try to read, but the words blur together, passion links arms with despair—jealousy, anger, spite, kink up like a bicycle chain that throws itself loose from its sprocket and the whole enterprise coasts to a dismal stop halfway to nowhere. You skip ahead. It doesn't help. Silence slips into the bloated prose. It invades each trumped-up scene. It collects in the gaps between chapters. It waits for you at the end in the gritty dead-white paper, rustling patiently with the last word.

The Y Bar Y was all she expected and more. From the center of the huge house a stone chimney rose massive and tall. The house itself seemed anchored to the world by the girth and heft of this proud tower. Marianna knew, then, that her decision to stay had been correct after all. There was a "rightness" in the scene that defied rational expression. Some things you know only in your heart of hearts. No logic can deny such knowledge. She was shown to her quarters—a spacious second-story room with a view of the magnificent Sangre de Cristo mountains, whose snow-capped eminence seemed Tibetan. Yes, yes, she *had* come to the right place at the right time in her life. She knew it now as well as she knew anything. It was here she would make her stand. It was here that she would reestablish herself in the world. She shuddered, not in trepidation but in joyful anticipation.

When she had finished unpacking, there was a knock on the door. It was Jeff Granger. Though she had opened the door wide, inviting him in, he remained beyond the threshold. "Please come in." She laughe,. "I don't bite, honestly!" Jeff filled the entire doorway. Both his shoulders grazed the frame, and his head almost touched the top. She hadn't realized before how really large Jeff was. He smiled—shyly, Marianna thought—and once again she felt her heart surge with strange voltage. His smile, set against an angular suntanned face, sent ripples of nervous spasms along her thighs and stomach. She folded her arms across her breasts to prevent herself from shaking visibly. She felt giddy. She didn't trust herself to speak. "I just came by to tell you that we get off to a pretty early start, Mrs. Kensington. So, I reckon—" Marianna interrupted him. "Please," she said, "call me Marianna. Mrs. Kensington is someone I am trying desperately to forget." Jeff looked at her for a long moment. Then he said, "Marianna," as if tasting the syllable. "I like that. My mother's name is Marianne." He cleared his throat self-consciously, as though he'd revealed something a bit too personal about himself. "Anyway, Mrs. Ken—I mean, Marianna, the kitchen crew starts at three-thirty a.m. The men eat at five o'clock sharp. Not a minute later. So you'd better turn in pretty early tonight." He turned to leave, then stopped. "One other thing, Marianna," he said, his back still turned to her. "The kitchen here looks more like a boiler factory than any kitchen you're used to. I suggest you let Jorge give you a run-through this evening sometime." Marianna thought, once again, that she detected a coolness in his tone. No, she told herself, it had not been Jeff Granger's idea to hire a woman from the East to run the kitchen of the Y Bar Y.

Before he left her room, she said, "Jeff—be honest. Just whose idea was it to hire me, anyway? It wasn't yours, was it?" He turned to look at her then. She saw something in his eyes that disturbed her. Sadness? Resentment? "No," he said slowly. "It wasn't my idea. It was my brother Thorne's idea. Thorne thought bringing in a woman from the East would give the place some... *class*, I think he called it." He left then, his boots echoing through the hallway and stairwell, leaving Marianna to stare at the large space he'd filled. She hadn't liked the emphasis he'd placed on "class," and yet she couldn't help but feel that Jeff Granger liked her, in spite of his obvious prejudice...

...for if this was not meant to be, then nothing was meant to be. Sometimes strangers feel they've known each other forever. Jeff was such a man to Marianna. She quivered. Passion stirred her neglected loins. Was he the man she'd envisioned? Was he her type? What was one's "type"? She had no idea. Years of careful emotions had dulled her. To know one's type is to know one's needs. Marianna was a desert of unknown needs that any random flood might violate into bloom...

The huge ranch-house kitchen should have been a bedlam of activity. It wasn't. The bedlam was in her mind only. There were twelve dozen eggs and eighteen pounds of bacon to fry! There were loaves and loaves of bread to toast! Gallons of coffee to make! Tubs of hash browns! Hot gravy from last night's ham drippings needed to be prepared! Marianna had help, of course, but the kitchen workers seemed reluctant to do anything without explicit instructions from her. They stood waiting—sullenly, she thought—for her to give commands. And yet they knew what they had to do—they'd been doing it all along! Clearly, she was resented here and the kitchen crew was letting her know it. Jorge Méndez, somehow, was at the root of the problem. He was her assistant, second in command, and yet he seemed as reluctant to help her as any of the underlings. She would ask him a question and he would stare at her as if it were the stupidest thing he'd ever heard. Then he'd answer slowly, enunciating the syllables as if he were speaking to a mental defective. The previous evening, when he'd given her a tour of the kitchen, he had glossed over the details of equipment operation, scheduling, duty assignments, and so on, so that she had had to ask the same questions several times before she understood the answers. It was infuriating, and yet she did not show her impatience. She was determined to win Jorge Méndez over to her side, to prove to him that she was going to be a fair and loyal supervisor, and that as far as she was concerned, his job was secure at the Y Bar Y. Marianna was a quick learner, however, and despite these roadblocks she managed to get breakfast served right on time, at 5 a.m. sharp. Even though some of the eggs were fried too hard, or some rashers of bacon too crisp, the food was more than just edible. Lunch was no problem, since it was the function of the chuck-wagon crew. The chuck wagon was a Mercedes-Benz diesel bus that had been converted to hold a portable kitchen. A separate crew ran the chuck wagon. Marianna's only responsibility regarding the lunch crew was to make sure there were enough supplies on hand to stock the chuck wagon's refrigerators. But the evening meal—supper—was an out-and-out disaster. At 4 p.m. Jorge Méndez wheeled a side of beef out of the cold locker and, with the help of two kitchen boys, hoisted it onto a massive butcher-block table. "What am I supposed to do with this?" Marianna asked. The huge, purplish-red carcass disgusted her. "Take the rib steaks and the T-bones, *señora*," Jorge said. "Leave the sirloin for Sunday." He handed her a meat cleaver that must have weighed six or seven pounds. "Make sure, *señora*, that the cuts are even—twelve to four-teen ounces each—the *vaqueros* don't like to see a bigger piece of meat on the plate next to them. They like it even Steven." He left her then with the half-beef, a mountain of flesh that probably weighed two or three hundred pounds. Marianna had two hours to hack it into perfect steaks! In desperation she attacked the animal with the heavy cleaver. But she struck it a glancing blow that only gouged a wedge of fat and gristle from it. She tried again, harder, but she hit it another off-line blow and a shrapnel of bone bits sprayed across the kitchen. She thought she saw one of the kitchen boys smile briefly, then turn his laughing face away from her. Jorge Méndez returned with a big meat saw. "Perhaps if you cut away from the shoulder back to the center loin, then with a knife you could take it from the brisket and flank. After that it will be easy to make your cuts. Then from the sirloin you can take flat-bone cuts and wedge-bone cuts." His instructions meant nothing to her! She made him repeat it care-fully, but now she had begun to panic and it made even less sense to her! After a half hour of sawing and hacking, the intransigent beef retained its steaks. Marianna began to cry. In that huge mass of animal flesh, there were dozens of steaks—rib-eye steaks, porterhouse steaks, club steaks, sirloins—but they would not yield themselves to her amateurish hacking. Finally, after nearly two hours of futile mutilation, she managed to produce lumps of meat that looked somewhat like beefsteaks. But there were only enough for half the men. She cut what she had into pieces the size of a large man's thumbs. These she fried on the big griddle in heavy grease. Then she ordered—too sharply, to her dismay! — one of the Mexican kitchen boys to slice twenty pounds of potatoes. The boy's eyes widened, as if she'd slapped his face, and she immediately apologized to him. He said something in Spanish and she realized that he could not under-stand her! New tears streamed down her face as she showed him what she want-ed in a jerkily hysterical sign language. The boy cut the potatoes too thin and when she fried them in the hot grease they immediately blackened. For a veg-etable she opened twenty-seven cans of asparagus and heated them to pulp in a big kettle of boiling water . When the meal was served, the cowboys would not eat it. Trays of untouched food were returned to the kitchen. "They will not eat," Jorge Méndez said, the light in his inscrutable eyes clearly triumphant. Marianna threw off her apron and ran out of the kitchen, sobbing. She ran away from the ranch house, through a grove of scrub pine, down a hill and to the grassy bank of a river. It was the worst moment in her life.

A lone rider followed her, though she was not aware of it. Under a sky the color and texture of hammered aluminum, she wept. The horseman walked his palomino to a point just above her on the river's edge. He looked down on her, a tight smile on his thin lips. He tied his horse to a stunted pine and approached her. She still was unconscious of his presence, her mind occupied, as it were, with the immediate disaster that threatened to turn her life toward a bleak future. She was thinking how worthless she was, and how stupidly arrogant she'd been to have believed that she could take over the kitchen duties at a serious cattle ranch! In a sudden fit of self-hatred, she pounded her fists into the loamy bank of the river. The rider knelt down beside her. "I sense you've had a bad day, Mrs. Kensington," he said. Marianna gasped in surprise. She looked up through tear-blurred eyes at a tall, dark man smiling down at her. She wiped the tears away with the back of her hand like a child and tried to compose herself, even though she could not immediately stop whimpering. The tall man looked remarkably like Jeff Granger, except that he was darker and had a thin mustache. His eyes, too, were different. They had a hard glint to them, and were set deeper in his head, making them seem shadowed with enigmatic musings. Like Jeff, this man was terribly handsome, but unlike Jeff, his chiseled features were dominated by a wry, disdainful loftiness of spirit that rose from a jaded cynicism. He had the look of a man who had seen just about everything the world had to offer and had found it wanting. A shiver of apprehension passed through Marianna so powerfully that the man noticed it. He sat down on the loam next to her and put his hand on hers. His hand was not hard and calloused like Jeff's but was soft, almost as soft as a woman's. He removed his hat, a black Stetson, and offered Marianna a cigarette, which she refused. "I am Thorne Granger," the man said. "Jeff's big brother. I'm sorry you had a rough afternoon. But, listen, it wasn't your fault, Marianna." She looked at him questioningly, wondering if he was only trying to boost her morale or if he actually meant what he said. Seeing the question in her eyes, Thorne insisted, "No, really, it *wasn't* your fault. Jorge was supposed to cut the beef. He's terribly offended, you know, that I hired you over him. He was expecting to take over as chief cook when Frank Delaney—our cook for twenty-eight years—died of acute cirrhosis. Jorge's good, but I wanted a woman's touch in the kitchen for a change. You can understand what I mean, can't you?" Marianna nodded, but his strangely mocking smile made her wonder just what it was she was assenting to. "In any case, I've disciplined Jorge. From now on he'll see to the meat cutting and any other work that requires a man's strength. I didn't hire you on as a stevedore. Your job, Marianna, is strictly supervisory. I want you to oversee food preparation only—to give it that woman's touch you just don't get with ordinary ranch cooks." He put his hand on her shoulder and squeezed it gently, as if to encourage her, but the pressure of his fingers promptly aroused a cautionary hesitation in her heart She looked into his hooded eyes but could not divine his intentions at all. At that moment lightning fractured the sky and hailstones began to drum the ground. Thorne Granger leaped to his feet and untied his horse. He mounted gracefully and pulled Marianna up behind him. She felt nearly weightless in his powerful grasp. Then he trotted the horse into the shelter of a copse of quaking aspen. He swung her down from the horse as though she were a rag doll. When he dismounted, he took her roughly in his arms. He pulled her close, so close that the air was crushed out of her lungs. He kissed her then, smothering her weak protest under the bristles of his mustache. She felt the same surge of electrical current she had experienced at Jeff's more gentle touch, only now the power of it was magnified a thousand times. "You are indeed very beautiful, Marianna," he said, hoarse with contained passion. "Beauty is the only thing in the world I have respect for any longer. The rest of it can burn in Hades!" She wanted to tell him that this was no way to show respect for a lady, but his savage mouth was on hers again and he forced her backwards and down until they were lying on the soft duff beneath the blowing trees. Thorne Granger's urgent manhood throbbed primitively against her helpless thighs. "No!" she screamed at last, twisting away from him. But he caught her face in his powerful hand and kissed her once again. Then he rose away from her momentarily, regarding her with eyes that seemed both innocent and insane. Marianna was terrified—too terrified to move. He put his hands on her blouse and opened it to the waist, heedless of the flying buttons. "Good Christ Almighty!" he said, his voice hushed and trembly with the sort of reverence only the damned can feel. "They are so *exquisite*, my dear!" he managed. His tortured eyes, smoldering in their sockets like coals, slaked themselves with the beauty of her breasts as a nearby flash of lightning turned them violet in the thrashing air. In spite of herself, Marianna remembered Kenneth's torpid desire, his perfunctory lust so quickly and dispassionately spent, and she felt herself loosening under the overwhelming need of Thorne Granger. Then, as if the thunder itself had become articulate, a voice shouted, "Take your rotten hands off her, Thorne!" It was Jeff, dismounting from a roan stallion, running toward them, his face mottled with rage. Thorne got up to meet his brother's charge, but Jeff struck him on the jaw before Thorne had a chance to defend himself. Thorne got up, wobbling noticeably from the force of his brother's punch. He tried to deliver a blow, but Jeff ducked it neatly and floored Thorne once again. "Get back to the house, Thorne," Jeff said. "You've blown it for sure, this time." With that, Thorne Granger, visibly diminished, got up and left. "I can't tell you how sorry I am this happened, Marianna," Jeff said. Marianna pulled her shredded blouse around her exposed breasts as best she could. "He almost raped me," she said. "It's his way," Jeff replied helplessly. "Thank you," she said, "for coming when you did. I... didn't—" She couldn't finish. A weakness swept over her and she staggered. Jeff caught her before she fell. "I'm going to take you back to the house, Marianna," he said, picking her up in his powerful arms. "You've been through quite an ordeal. I only hope you can forgive us."

("Dear Diary: I walked away from a twenty-year marriage without regret. My kids were grown up by then and gone. I felt, and *still* feel, I had time to find out just who Marianna Kensington is. Maybe I am no one! SCARY! But how much scarier to trick yourself into thinking you are perfectly fine... a complete human being! Where I came from, everyone thinks they are just fine. No problems. But they are just blank pages waiting for somebody to write on them. You know what they hate most? A quiet afternoon by themselves. Because the quiet hurts, I mean, the quiet is dangerous. Like a burglar is dangerous. Or like a rapist. It is there suddenly in your living room and there's no help to be found. It gets you. It has eyes and ears. It knows a lot about you. What a complete and stupid lie your life has been up to now. Squirm, squirm. It feels like uneasiness. Maybe you go to the medicine cabinet to try some more Tranxenes. Or you pick up one of those trashy novels about this woman like yourself who goes out into the world to escape from her life and gets herself into one scrape after another until Mister Right gets into her pants. Jesus, I'd rather eat bloated trash fish dredged up from Boston Harbor! It would be less poisonous to the soul. And it doesn't hold back the quiet afternoon. The quiet is there in the stupid love scenes. The quiet is there, untouched, cover to cover.")

"I only hope you can forgive us," Jeff repeated. But it wasn't really a matter of forgiveness. Marianna didn't know if she could trust Thorne Granger ever again, much less forgive him. And the most important consideration was not even Thorne Granger, but her job and her new life. What was to become of her now? She could turn tail and run back to the safety of the East, or she could grit her teeth and stick this job out. She could fight for the respect of the kitchen crew and especially for the respect of Jorge Méndez. She could do everything in her power to see that Jorge was recognized as her equal in the kitchen. And if Thorne Granger ever touched her again, or so much as looked at her offensive-ly, she could threaten him with legal action. Women these days did not have to put up with that sort of sexual intimidation from their employers. More than anything, she did not want to fail! She wanted badly to become a first-rate pro-fessional ranch cook. *That*, she knew, was how one found oneself in this life. *That* was how one filled in the awful blanks of a blank existence. You did a job, any job, and you did it with dedication and to the best of your ability. You com-mitted yourself. Talent was not a factor. You found the thing you did best and you did it as best you could. No job was menial or less important than any other job. Only the quality of workmanship could be assigned these arbitrary values. An inferior neurosurgeon was a "menial" compared with a prideful auto mechanic or legal secretary. She had never before grasped the simple truth of this universal fact of life. Later that evening she made a crude sign with notepaper and an India ink marking pen: I AM WHAT I DO. NO MAN CAN PROVIDE MY IDENTITY. She slept well that night, knowing that in the morning she would wake to that sign, taped to her wall, and that its wisdom would let her approach the new day with self-confidence and courage. Jorge Méndez, whether he knew it or not, had himself a damned good kitchen boss.

Before the month was out, Marianna had the kitchen under control. She'd talked to Jorge several times to clarify their relationship and to assure him that, as far as she was concerned, he was every bit as important as she was. "You will be the *corazón* of this kitchen, Jorge," she'd said, "and I will be its *alma*." This delighted Jorge. The "heart" and the "soul" of the kitchen would work together in preparing the best ranch cuisine in the West! Marianna studied Spanish every night for an hour in her room and soon was able to utter phrases in dialect that shocked the kitchen boys into gales of approving laughter. "¡*Qué la chingada*!" She would shout at minor accidents and setbacks, and the boys would whoop in delight at the immense obscenity. Jorge, as he grew to trust and respect Marianna, became her good friend. Sometimes, in moments of slack activity, they would take their coffee out to the back patio and share opinions about ranch life and life in general. She discovered that Jorge was a man of subtle intelligence and strong feelings. He had been devastated by Thorne Granger's thoughtless, even perverse, hiring of a woman with essentially no experience to supervise the kitchen. But Marianna was not about to let the injustice continue or to allow the prejudice against a *gringa* go unchallenged. She saw to it that everything done in the kitchen required Jorge's approval. And, in accepting this responsibility, Jorge became a force to contend with. His demeanor became casual and self-confident; his courtly deference was replaced by a polite assertiveness that sometimes—to Marianna's delight—furrowed the brow of Thorne Granger with confusion and, possibly, *fear*. Once, when Thorne had entered the kitchen on what was ostensibly an inspection tour, he found Jorge sitting at a table reading *The Wall Street Journal* while Marianna mixed piecrusts. Thorne had stared speechless at Jorge, but Jorge merely looked up from his paper and said, "Beef futures opened very high today, Boss." Thorne turned pale but could only say, "Really." Marianna laughed, remembering the incident. She was in her room, studying her Spanish text. "(*Qué es un romance?*" she read aloud, as someone tapped lightly on her door. It was Jeff Granger, tall in the doorway. She called him into her room. He entered, almost reluctantly, she thought. Out on the patio, some of the cowboys were playing guitars and singing. The desert was in bloom. The air was fragrant. "Thorne's left the Y Bar Y," Jeff said. "He's going to start a new life in a San Francisco brokerage firm." Marianna didn't try to conceal her feelings. "I can't say I'm unhappy," she said. But it soon became clear to Marianna that there was more on Jeff's mind than the departure of his brother. "Marianna," he said, taking her hand, "I think I've fallen in love with you." She let him kiss her, anticipating the electrical surge, but it did not come. She ushered him to the door. "We'll talk about it, Jeff. Right now I've got to do my lesson." A few minutes later, Jorge Méndez came by. Marianna let him in and closed the door. "*Alma*," he said, kissing her hand. "*Corazón*," she replied, her heart suddenly racing as she felt not electricity or magnetism in his touch but *heat*, the simple and generous heat of kitchens. The melodious *gringo* guitars drew them together in a long and tender embrace, and as some cowboy sang "Blue Eyes Crying in the Rain," Marianna led Jorge to her bed.

Nothing was meant to be. Sometimes when two strangers meet, their mutual strangeness seems unbridgeable. The stocky brown man of mixed blood in her arms had initially seemed unapproachably alien to Marianna. She quivered at the bizarre unpredictability of life. Passion, long dead, rioted in her loins. No, this was definitely *not* the man she'd envisioned years ago in her adolescent daydreams! He was certainly not her *type*. But what was one's "type"? Of that, more than ever, she had no idea. Years of careful emotions had dulled her judgment. For to know one's type is to know one's needs. Marianna was a desert of unknown needs this random flood was violating, with tender but strongly fluid tillage, into bloom.

She had no regrets. The children were gone. And at least she was getting to know who Marianna Kensington was. She'd been no one, she was sure of that now. How frightening! But how much more frightening to deceive yourself into thinking you were complete when in fact you were a blank page waiting to be filled in! The suburbs were crowded with safe and comfortable women who were essentially blank pages waiting for a violating pen. Silence was their enemy. Silence let the emptiness rise to the surface like a submerged but featureless continent. Silence, given a small opportunity, would enter the house and sit down like a bold intruder. The intruder smiles with his superior knowledge of the little dark mechanisms of your heart. Ignoring him, you pick up the latest Silhouette or Harlequin Romance and try to read, but the words blur together, passion links arms with despair—jealousy, anger, spite kink up like a bicycle chain that throws itself loose from its sprocket and the whole enterprise coasts to a dismal stop halfway to nowhere. You try the good parts— it doesn't help. Silence slips into the bloated prose. It invades each trumped-up scene. It collects. It is there, smirking, when you begin, there in the middle, showing a wider grin, and it waits for you at the dead end—a *surprise* ending of dead paper, rustling with the last word.

This story happened early in the history of the human race, a few years from now. It is your story, though you may have some quibbles. It's the writer's story too, but he wants to camouflage it. (The form he's chosen confirms this.) Look at it this way: he offers a parable of a parable, nut and shell, easily cracked and eaten. But the question is, will it nourish or poison or just lie suspended in the gut like a stone? It points no finger of blame, pats no one on the back, gives no guarantees beyond asserting the commonality of its long-lost roots, which are transplantable anywhere. To make matters worse, the writer (never applauded for his penetrating insights and infamous for his lack of convictions) probably won't get it right. He'll need your open-minded help to fill in the blanks or to blank out the excesses. Excess is his forte. He's made a tidy little career of it. Actually, he'll need more than your help, but nothing can be done about *that*. The narcissistic dissembler is on his own:

There once were a husband and wife who were so simple that they had no control over their lives or the lives of their children. Worse, they had no control over what they

Your Story

said. Words gushed out of her mouth like blood from a bad gash—hot, pure, terrible to behold. From his mouth they were like the dark, sour smoke from a doused fire. The two of them were reasonably civilized. They were respected in their community. Their names were ordinary: Gene and Amy Underhill. Names like these do not arouse suspicion or resentment.

One evening, at the dinner table, Amy said to Gene, "Honey, I want to get rid of the children. I've had enough of them. I want to get rid of them tomorrow."

This wasn't the first time Amy had expressed this wish. She was not one to mince words, but this was the first time she'd set a deadline.

"Well, they *are* shits," Gene agreed affably. Gene Underhill was a decent, mild-mannered man who worked as a lab technician for a company that produced titanium-alloy butterfly valves for a secret defense project rumored to be linked to the "Star Wars" program. He spoke his mind freely too, but with far less heat than his wife. He was by nature a cautious, reflective man. His wife's forthright manner kept him off balance. He was no match for her, and knew it. "I don't think I'd be able to actually *harm* them, dear," he said.

Amy, whose anger was so reliable a stone church could lean against it and not topple, said, "You incredible wimp."

Gene knew there would be no lovemaking that night, or, if there was, it would be rancorous. Which in itself could be interesting. If the rancor could be harnessed and guided into some infrequently traveled byways. Images of Gortex straps with Velcro fasteners, spandex collars, electrified quirts, suppositories dipped in nonprescription euphorics, Suggesto-Vision videotapes from the Exotica/Erotica section of the neighborhood 7-Eleven store, and so on, occurred to him.

"I read you like a book," Amy said, noticing the sweat beads forming on Gene's upper lip. "But you can put fun and games out of your mind until we get this business settled once and for all. *Then* we'll party."

Gene and Amy were eating a dinner of half-warm Big Macs and fries. The children, Buddy and Jill, had been put to bed earlier.

"We could send them away to boarding school," Gene said hopefully. He dipped his last fry into a kidney-shaped pool of catsup. He made a project out of it to avoid Amy's eyes.

"Wonderful," Amy said. "We'll send them to school in England and you and I will live in a villa on the Côte d'Azur and read French poetry and paint neo-cubist nudes. Jesus, Gene, grow *up*, will you?"

Gene and Amy were not bad people. They were beleaguered by debts they had foolishly allowed to accumulate until, at twenty-two percent interest, the debts took on an unearthly life of their own and became a fiscal Frankenstein monster that sought to destroy its creators. Gene and Amy were harassed daily by the thousand large and small demands of an underfunded, barely marginal, middle-class lifestyle. Every night they were afflicted by televised world events whose increasingly inventive perversities left them confused, angry, and spiritually at sea. The children, typically, were whiny ingrates who rarely rewarded their parents with a hint of promise, academic or otherwise. "You are a slob, just like your father," Amy once said to Buddy, in a fit of rage. Jill, on the other hand, filled Amy with silent dread. Her daughter was a miniature of herself, a brooding waxen doll. Sometimes she would catch Jill studying her with eyes that were too knowledgeable. Those dark eyes always seemed judgmental and full of sad reproach. She felt accused of some nameless crime by those eyes and was moved, frequently, to defend herself to her own daughter. It didn't make sense, but there it was, the heavy load of guilt. Amy once screamed, "I don't *deserve* this! I haven't done anything to you!" but knew, instinctively, it sounded not only crazy but *false*."

"All right," Gene said at last. "We'll do it." He felt old and heavy. He was prematurely gray and the smile lines around his eyes and mouth had hardened into permanent fissures that gave him the appearance of constant flinching. He was surprised daily by this face of his in the shaving mirror. He was only forty but he looked sixty. And yet he felt no different than he did when he was twenty. The mental picture he carried of himself was of a dark-haired, smooth-skinned boy with a good-natured smile. How had this happened? The last french fry he'd eaten had lodged itself in his chest, under his breastbone, where it scratched at him like a greasy, long-nailed finger. "We'll do it tomorrow," he said. "First thing after breakfast."

Amy got up and kissed him. "I'm so relieved, darling," she said.

Which means... Gene remarked hopefully to himself, new sweat beads glazing his lip...

"I'm in the moo-ood," Amy crooned, completing his thought.

They went up to bed. Amy was happy now. Soon, she felt, her problems would be solved. Soon, their priorities would be reordered and they would be able to concentrate on getting out of debt. Amy was only thirty-three years old and had seen enough of empty cupboards and overdrawn checking accounts and her daughter's accusing eyes. She wanted a secure, predictable life. She wanted to devote most of her time to income management, the search for safe investments, and to the establishment of a first-rate Individual Retirement Account. And she wanted to do this without *guilt*, or any other distraction.

Amy undressed slowly in the dim bedroom, revealing in tantalizing increments her still lovely body to her eager husband. Gene was already in bed, the chalk of liquid Maalox caking his lips. "Gortex straps," he suggested, hoarse with emotion.

"All right," Amy agreed. "Since you've decided to face reality like a grown-up, for once."

I turned my back on them at this point and left them to their constrained pleasures. I went to see the children. I danced my way down the creaky hall to their room. Left foot over right, hop and skip, right foot over left, turn and turn. Among other things, I am a dancer.

The children, never quite as stupid or indifferent as their parents believe, had heard it all. They were frightened, but not especially surprised.

"What will we *do*?" Jill asked her brother, Buddy.

"Play it dumb, like always," Buddy said.

Jill was nine and Buddy was going on twelve. They were beautiful children, blond as late summer wheat. They were tucked in their beds, the girl on one side of the room, the boy on the other. I kissed the girl and then the boy. The pages of the boy's comic book were riffled, as if by wind. I turned in slow, elegant circles between their sweet beds, but they saw only the shadows of their dreams.

The next day was Sunday. The family set out for the woods ostensibly to gather firewood for the coming fall. The children rode in the back of the pickup truck along with the chain saws and gas cans. It was a beautiful morning, cool and clear.

After Gene had turned off the main highway and had entered a narrow dirt road that led to the wooded foothills, Amy said, "Once we get into the trees, get off the road."

Gene slipped the Toyota into four-wheel drive, anticipating a rough climb. He leaned his head out the window and yelled back to the kids. "Hang on tight," he said. "Don't try to stand up or anything."

The engine labored as the truck struggled against the steep, loamy ground of the forest. "Keep switching back and forth," Amy said. "I want them to lose all sense of direction."

They traveled this way for nearly an hour. Gene, holding the wheel so tight-ly his hands were cramped and white, was sweating profusely. He was relieved when he found a dry creek bed that led out into a meadow. He accelerated through the wide field, which glowed almost unnaturally, like the core of a nuclear reactor, with wildflowers. He stopped in the middle of this exotic place and unscrewed the thermos. He took a long drink of whiskied coffee. "I'm lost," he said.

"Good," said Amy. "Keep driving."

On the other side of the meadow, the mountains began. Gene found an old logging road. It was very steep and he had to keep the Toyota in its lowest gear to manage the climb. Their ears popped and the air became noticeably cooler. The silver-gray stumps of ancient clear-cuts studded the steep slopes like rooted tables. Patches of snow between the great stumps looked like dropped linen. The air was purer here and the sky was so blue it seemed like the inside of an enameled egg.

They entered an area of standing-dead trees. "Good pickings," Gene said, stopping the truck and setting the brake.

"Keep going," Amy said. "We didn't come all the way up here for firewood, damn it."

Gene sighed and restarted the engine. They drove for another hour, passing more groves of dead trees, slash piles, and old, abandoned logs that sawyers had left behind for unknown reasons. The sun was low and smoky in the sky. The children, cold and hungry, were whining and tapping on the rear window of the truck cab. "We're almost there!" Amy yelled through the glass.

Gene looked at his wife. There was something in her face he had never noticed before but would always see from this day on. If he had to name it, he would call it "grim determination," but even this description seemed to fall short. Amy was an attractive woman, but the set of the jaw and the cast of her eyes undercut her beauty. It was as if another Amy, the "real" Amy Underhill, had surfaced at last. Gene felt a sinking sensation in his abdomen, which he mis-construed as excitement.

When they were at an altitude where only stunted dwarf trees grew, they stopped and got out of the truck. There were a few beetle-killed trees, none of them more than twelve feet tall, on the upslope side of the truck. Gene went after these with the smaller of his saws. Amy took the children for a walk to gather berries. She herded them across screes of unstable shale, through thick, angry patches of scrub pine, across snowfields, and, finally, to a sheltered area where an abundance of huckleberry bushes grew. She gave the children a large plastic bag each. "Fill them with berries," she said, "while daddy cuts a load of wood. Then we'll go into town and eat at McDonald's. You'll have a real appetite by then."

She walked swiftly back to the truck, which was half loaded with firewood. "Shut off that saw and let's go!" she yelled at Gene, who was about to fell another dwarf tree.

Gene switched off his saw. "Hey, no sense in going back with half a load," he said, grinning sheepishly. She still had that look on her face, the look that made him believe no one ever knows the person they live with, and that nothing in the world is constant.

"Don't play for time. It won't work. We're going through with this, Gene."

"Whatever," Gene said, realizing that he could not match her resolve. He started the truck, hoping the children would not hear it, then hoping they would. "We are pretty darned evil," he said, mostly to himself.

"Uh-huh," Amy answered. "We're real novelties."

"But people just do not abandon their kids in the mountains!"

Amy didn't respond to this outburst. How could she respond to a silly remark that represented, so unconditionally, the generic pudding that served as her husband's brain?

I left them just as Gene was about to notice that Amy had changed again, and not just in her expression. She seemed *physically* different now. The bridge of her nose, for example, was beaky and shinier than before, her lips thinner, the angular jut of her jaw more acute, her tall forehead striated with astonishing areas of depleted pigments. He would tell himself (what choice did he have?) that these were only shades of difference that he might have noticed earlier had he been more attentive—people do change, after all—but this threadbare argument would be shredded before the honest rage of his nightmares.

I soared into the sky on my glossy black wings and sailed toward the children. They hadn't heard the truck start and were still picking berries. I watched them from a majestic altitude, enjoying the thermals, the heckling squadrons of starlings, and the unmatched beauty of the northern forests.

By the time their plastic bags were nearly filled with the dark red berries, the sun had slipped below the horizon. The cold mountain air crept out of the shadows, where it had survived the day, to reclaim the evening and coming night. "We'd better head back to the truck," Buddy said, looking up into the deepening sky, where the brightest stars were already twinkling.

But the long shadows the mountain put down obscured the trail. When they arrived at the steep scree of shale it was too dark to find the path that crossed it. And as Buddy stepped out onto the precarious slope of loose rock, he started a small landslide. The lonely echo of clattering rocks made Jill whimper. Buddy scrambled back to safety.

"What are we going to *do*?" Jill cried.

Now an ambassadorial bear with cubs, I ambled out of some huckleberry bushes behind the children, my long, red mouth dripping with my favorite fruit. My two cubs rollicked alongside.

"Oh no!" Jill cried. "It's a bear!"

"Don't move," Buddy said. "They can't see very well. Maybe she hasn't noticed us."

"Don't be afraid, children," I said, sweetly as my crude vocal cords would allow. I stopped directly in front of them and rolled on my back. My playful cubs pounced on me and bit my furry breasts. I slapped them away and growled, startled somewhat by the aggression of the little beasties, then gathered them up in my arms and we rolled together through thick spears of bear grass, chuffing and moaning with bear-family pleasure.

The boy hugged his little sister protectively. In the dying light their pale faces glowed supernaturally. Bears can see these auras; most humans cannot. "Follow me, children," I said. I turned from them and ambled away, downslope, into the thicket below.

It was almost dark by the time they arrived at my house. I vanished into my own shadow and watched them from several vantage points at once. What fine, holy animals they were!

"What is that?" the girl asked her brother.

"A house," he said. "A funny-looking little old house."

They came closer, close enough to reach out and touch the delicious walls. "I think it's made out of food," the boy said, licking his sticky fingers.

"Cake!" shrieked the girl. "It's a cake house!"

They pushed open the hard marzipan door and entered. I was seated at the table in more customary form. "Good evening, little ones," I said, my ancient voice scratchy and dry.

The girl screamed and the boy picked up a piece of firewood, which he held in both hands as a weapon.

"There's nothing to be afraid of, children," I said, smiling.

"It's a witch!" cried the girl. "A horrible old witch with dead gray teeth!"

"Let's go," the boy said, pulling his transfixed sister toward the door.

"You must stay at least for supper," I said.

Because they were very hungry by now, they approached the table but took seats at the opposite end. I smiled at their caution. "Too much caution can become a bad habit, my dears," I said, though they could not understand the significance of my words. I changed the subject. "Let's play a game, children."

"First we eat," said the boy. He was a hardheaded little rascal who appeared far brighter and more sure of himself than his slipshod, weak-willed father.

I set a good table of venison, broiled grayling, wild asparagus, goat's milk, sunflower bread with dandelion honey. They ate like little pigs. Their naïve unchecked appetite made my heart expand. Too soon they would be concerned with calorie counting, cholesterol content, and all the other drivel that makes the alimentary canal a quivering battleground of false causes.

When they finished this fine meal, they sighed in real contentment and gratitude. "You're welcome," I said, not in rebuke but in response to their little burps and the slack-jawed trance of happy satiation.

The girl became drowsy and fell asleep at the table. I carried her to a bedroom I had prepared in advance. When I rejoined the boy, he said, "Jill's had a hard couple of days, ma'am." His eyes held mine and did not blink. I liked him. He seemed to grow more mature by the minute. He would do well in the difficult world ahead.

"How about you?" I said. "Are you ready for a little game? You might win a nice prize."

"Sure," he said. His trust was edged with a steely-eyed wariness, but he was not one to play it safe, knowing instinctively that the only real way to lose was to not play at all.

"Then come with me. I'll show you something you won't forget."

I took him out to my barn. "Where are the animals?" he asked. I held up my stick and pointed upward. "Hey, there's no *roof* on this barn. How come?"

"To let the starlight in," I said. I touched his shoulder with my stick. He jumped straight up as if I'd given him an electric shock.

"What's that music?" he asked.

"Stars," I said. "They sing on long wires of light. Listen." What the boy heard was this:

> only the child
> can see the hand
> that made the wild
> mysterious land

I touched his other shoulder with my stick and he jumped again. When he came down, he landed on his hands and knees. "Enjoy yourself," I said. "I'll be back for you later."

The boy had jumped the line that separates human folly from the natural order, and he was at that moment running through the woods on all fours with a pack of wolves. He ran and ran, chasing the hart, feeling the joy of speed and strength, the comfort of the tribe and the unchecked lust of the hunt. When he grew tired, he returned to his slumber, then woke to the music of the stars, which he would forget only at his peril.

The next morning the girl demanded to know what I'd done with her brother.

"He's been playing a game," I said.

"You lie," she said, stern as her mother.

I gave her a witchy smile, sinister and cunning. "Help me clean this house, you snot," I said.

My profound ugliness intimidated her. She picked up a broom. Then, as was customary, I made what all the children see as my fatal mistake. I bent over next to the open door of my oven, pretending to scour a spot of grease from the floor, and waited for the blow. She delivered it on schedule. The broom whacked me across my bony old buttocks and I obliged her by falling headfirst into the oven. For effect, I let loose a blood-chilling scream of vile curses that antedate the development of speech organs in the so-called *Homo sapiens*. She slammed the iron door shut and wedged her broom handle against it so that it could not be opened. Then she turned the gas up high. I heard the pilot light ignite the ring of gas, and searing heat blew up into my face.

The boy entered the house then. He was still groggy from his hard sleep and was trying to adjust the vagrant grammar of his dreams to the tight parsings of authorized reality. When he understood what his sister had done, he became upset. "She didn't mean us any harm, Jill," he said.

"Yes, she did!" Jill cried out, wounded by Buddy's ingratitude. She had saved them, hadn't she, from the witch's evil schemes?

Buddy noticed the Polaroids I had taken of them while they slept. I'd tacked them up on the wall. He went to the pictures and stared at the angelic towheads, who resembled their parents only superficially. "See," he said, "she liked us well enough to take our pictures, Jill."

"What's that *smell*?" Jill asked, her eyes widening in delight.

The house was filling with a fragrance that was so sweet, so tempting, that their mouths began to water instantly. They forgot the Polaroids, forgot their argument, and could think of nothing else except the wonderful aroma and where it might be coming from. It was coming from the oven, of course, and as if to underscore this fact, the buzzing of the timer rattled the air.

The boy went to the oven and peeked in. Inside, perfectly baked, was an angel food cake. (*C'est moi.*) The boy took it out, using pot holders, and set it on the table.

"Maybe I was only dreaming about a witch," the children said in unison.

Only dreaming or, worse, *It was only a bad dream* are the formulas that have exiled me from the world for several hundred years. Children would have those scoffing catchphrases stenciled into their brains and the useful truth of their dreams would be dismissed time and again until the children grew into gray, dreamless entities of no consequence who would commit blunder after blunder on their murderously banal trip to the grave.

I suppose the story must end there, though the writer is pressing for one of his patented, neatly delivered, full-circle endings. For instance, he would like to see Buddy and Jill, older and honed to an edge by the harsh world, make their way home and confront their parents. Buddy would have a Ruger .357 Magnum in his belt and Jill's purse would be stocked with street drugs. (The writer has other murky ideas, generated by his need for what he thinks of as *neatness*. He calls these blind spots "satisfying endings." My motto is: Never trust an anal narcissist. The flattering mirror he cavorts in front of shows a geometrically precise world, tied up neat as a Christmas package.)

The writer would like to tell you something about me, as an object of (in this case) blame. But he hasn't understood yet the extent of my influence, the depth of my interest, or how he is my last refuge in a world that has excluded me. He is one of you, after all, no better and no worse. For example, he would like to know where I am *now*, when he needs me most. He doesn't realize that I'm always here, in his word processor, among the binary digits of the software, in the wiring and microchips, in the copper and silicon atoms, down among the leptons and quarks and gluons, and further, where time and space no longer exist, in the null of nulls, riding the crest of wave after wave of pulsing energy, a cosmic surfer, everywhere and nowhere, inside and outside, locus of a geometry of tucks and puckers. And I am in the stymied axons and dendrites of the writer's poor brain, break-dancing on the cerebral dunes as he rises from his desk and goes out to the kitchen for his twelfth cup of coffee, hoping for the final rush of syllables that chase and corner all the meanings of the story and truss them up with granny knots of inevitability. But there are large densities in the dross of his being, crazy opacities, flashes of perfect nonsense. He tries so hard, but he never says exactly what he means. (Though he means everything he says.) He is my puppet, but, alas, he is on very loose strings.

Just now, he's in his backyard sipping tequila from a flask, refusing to let the story go. He has climbed up to the top branches of his willow tree. It is a windy summer's night, and the stars are blowing through the whipping leaves like hissing, incandescent moths. "If I end it there," he complains to me, "no one will get the point!"

Let's leave him up the tree. He's not quite bright enough to trust you. Also, if we allowed him to design an ending and bandage it to the story, who's to say he wouldn't produce a monster? No. It's *your* story, reader, and you are always in the middle of it.

The gray Bavarian yodeling in the bathroom sent the New Year's party into a terminal slump. It was Dr. Selbiades's annual get-together for his patients. I'd been there less than an hour and had watched the party go from white-knuckle cheerfulness to unapologetic gloom.

Selbiades had been my shrink for almost a year. He was known as Doc Dow, after the chemical company. He believed in psychoactive drugs, not psychology. Psychology, he said, is rooted in semantics and semantics is rooted in the mind and the mind is a myth. There is the brain, the central nervous system, and there is the World. Sometimes they don't mesh. Chemistry is learning how to make them mesh. "We're in the Model T era of psychopharmacology," he once said. "The future is gleaming with Volvos, BMWs, and Ferraris."

I believed him. Why shouldn't I have? The yodeling Bavarian only last year was a cataleptic wallflower in the State Hospital. One dose of a new compound and he was goose-stepping to Wagner and asking for beefy women. I'd been brought from severe, broad-spectrum anxiety to chronic sulkiness in less than a year. I expected, any day now, a new ordering of the psychoactive rainbow to nudge me into a semipersistent state of kindhearted tolerance.

Pagans

Nirvana, according to Doc Dow, always happens on the molecular level, regardless of the method used to achieve it. Without drugs it takes Spartan restrictions of sensory inputs, dietary extremism, and a kind of self-hypnosis. Our Puritanical heritage, said the Doctor, makes us scoff at the notion that spiritual bliss can be gotten by swallowing capsules. But we are learning how to play the brain note by note, he said.

I was still a half-turn out of tune. It made me snappish and fussy. I affronted strangers for reasons I could not later explain. The yodeling Bavarian in the Selbiadeses' shower was a good example. He had wanted the tiled walls of the shower to call up the effect of sheer alpine slopes so that he could show us how it had been with him when he was a Nazi ski trooper during the War. I was in the bathroom at the time, taking my second Elavil of the evening. The Bavarian had left the bathroom door open so that everyone could hear him. When I went out, I closed the door behind me. His yodels softened to a chirping lament. The stiffly seated guests looked at me, some with anger in their eyes, some with cruel hilarity. All rode the black horse Despair.

"Some Nazi bastard like him killed my uncle," I said to the group. It was a lie, but I was shameless. That was another feature of my untuned brain. Cheap lies. I used them like salt and pepper. They gave an edge to the watery soup of my life.

I put on my parka and cap. "Leaving us so soon?" said Beth Selbiades, the Doctor's stunning wife. What a full-blown, fine-haired animal you are, I wanted to say, but one does not speak churlishly to the high priest's wife.

"Got to get home," I finally mumbled.

I went out into a whirlwind of snowflakes. A warm, southerly blizzard had moved in, blanketing our town with heavy wet snow, pretty to remember from the safety of July, but a misery to stroll through. I was dressed for it, except for my shoes, which were loafers.

I had walked out of my own New Year's party. Raquel had kissed Sloan Capoletti, our milkman, hours before midnight. I took umbrage. Having been out of work for some time, I was oversensitive to the carefree revels of the employed. Sloan had been giving us free cottage cheese (unsalable cheese that had survived its expiration date) because he felt sorry for our economic plight. Or so I thought. Then, as I watched the prolonged, open-mouth kiss, I understood that his dated cheese was meant to woo. After the hot kiss under the parasitic tree-killer, mistletoe, they went into the kitchen, where Sloan showed Raquel how to brew saloop, a hot drink made of sassafras, sugar, and milk. A blood purifier, Sloan said. I was suspicious. Why did Raquel keep sassafras in her spice and herb cupboard? To please the milkman? Excellent for the bowels, Sloan said. Why did the milkman want the bowels of my wife to be excellent? The party became a forest of symbols, all of them unfriendly to me, even dangerous—pagan symbols, witch symbols: mistletoe, sassafras, and scented candles, the over-decorated Christmas tree fat and gaudy as an old whore leaning drunkenly in the corner. And then, as if I'd been the victim of an openly wicked practical joke, I began to receive heartening winks from total strangers. I needed to walk.

I put on my parka and watch cap. Raquel cornered me in the hallway. "What do you think you're doing?" she said.

I gave her the look I felt she deserved. "He's in love with you," I said.

"I know," she said.

"You *know*?" I felt dizzy as my blood pressure wobbled and peaked.

"Of *course* I know!" she said, with unashamed spunk. "It's very harmless. He's a cute guy, Sloan is."

All I could do was stare at her as I zipped up the parka.

"Love is not harmless," I said, measuring out the words with some care.

She slapped her forehead and rolled her eyes. "Jesus, *listen* to what you are saying for once," she said. She turned away from me and walked back into the chaos of tooting horns, paper streamers, and the wet mouths of strangers. It was midnight in the eastern time zone, two hours away, but that was reason enough to toot your horn and stick your tongue down someone's throat.

I slammed the door behind me and started walking the seven blocks to Dr. Selbiades's house. The planet had French-kissed itself through several time zones as it mindlessly rolled down its doomed orbit. Though bells were ringing, horns were tooting, champagne corks were popping, I skulked away from it all, hating the manic pagans and their endless whoopee.

After I left the Selbiadeses' party, I walked aimlessly. I wandered into the North Side, a poorly lit district of tall Victorian houses. The area was famous for night crimes. Muggings, rapes, vandalism were the nocturnes played in these shadowy streets and alleys. I half expected a mugger to put a knife to my throat, and didn't care. Then a man waved to me from a front porch. He was a tall, heavy man in a metallic green suit. "That you, Roger?" he asked.

I shrugged. "Why not?" I answered.

"Then come on in, we've been waiting to start. Did you get lost or something?"

"Yes and no," I said.

I climbed the sagging boards of the porch stairs. When I reached the big man, he threw his arms around me. "Peg Munson is nervous as hell," he whispered into my ear, his warm spittle electrifying it. "I'm Jerry Peters," he said, pumping my hand. "You know," he added, seeing my blank look, "group coordinator."

He took my arm and steered me into the house. Inside, seated on sofas, love seats, and armchairs, were about a dozen people, men and women in their late thirties or early forties. "Here's the missing person," Jerry said, slapping me on the back. "Roger" —he fumbled with a piece of paper, a computer printout, squinted at it—"Roger *Flexnor*. Now we can get the show on the road."

It was easy to figure out that everyone here was a stranger to everyone else and that Roger Flexnor, whoever he was, was expected to round out the group: six males, six females. I guessed it was some kind of dating club for hopeless cases. I felt right at home.

People on one of the sofas scooted over, making room for me. I sat between a pale, bearded man and a small, plump woman. "I'm Peg Munson," the woman said.

I shook her hand. "Roger Flexnor," I said.

"Where's your data sheet?" she said.

I slapped my coat pockets, dug in my pants.

"Here's an extra," Peg Munson said, giving me a carefully folded computer printout. I saw her name, a paragraph giving a general (somewhat generous) physical description, and a personal statement ("Professional woman, Master's degree, likes walks in the rain, poetry that speaks directly to the soul, good conversation over gourmet dinners; expects to share her considerable resources, both physical and spiritual, with a man of corresponding substance").

I refolded the data sheet and slipped it into my pocket, wondering what Roger Flexnor had to offer such a woman.

"...tall, scientifically oriented man," Peg read, from the data sheet of Roger Flexnor, "desires *affaire d'amour* with mature Christian lady with unusually small features..." She giggled self-consciously; then, splaying her fingers in her lap, revealed to me a set of miniature hands without visible knuckles. This is what Roger Flexnor desired most in a woman. I glanced down at her feet and saw that they were also miniatures. Flexnor would be seriously awash in lust by now.

Jerry Peters, our host, said, "All right, one and all, let's get right down to it. We're not children, and it's a brand-new year. At least it will be in fifteen minutes. There's no need to stumble and bumble. I suggest we break with the past, whatever *that* might be, and give our Rocky Mountain Dating Service partners a big how-do-you-do Happy New Year kiss."

A woman, almost as big as Jerry Peters, stood up and kissed him with shocking energy. I leaned toward Peg Munson and she closed her eyes and offered me her Kewpie-doll lips.

"You're shy," she said, after the pecking kiss. "I am too. I guess the computer knows how to match personality types."

Peg Munson not only had little hands and feet, she also had tiny facial features. Lips, nose, and eyes were set close to one another to produce a smallish face. Her head was a distraction: it was nearly full-sized. "I've always wanted to know a Christian man who had a passion for nuclear science," she said, breathy with growing interest.

Then the real Roger Flexnor came in. "Sorry, everybody," he said, stamping snow off his shin-high mukluks. "I just could *not* get the chains on my car. I had to have the Exxon people do it." He was a tall, white-haired man in heavy glasses.

"Who are *you*?" Jerry Peters said.

"I'm Roger. Roger Flexnor, Ph.D. You're expecting me. I'm here for Peg Munson." He waved his printout as his glasses fogged over in the warm room.

I got up and walked through the awkward silence until I was back out on the street. The street seemed the place for me that New Year's Eve.

Jerry Peters called to me from the porch. "Hey, it's okay, citizen," he said. "Next time, though, try going through Central Data. We've got uplinks throughout the Northwest. Check out our ad in tomorrow's paper. There's someone out there who loves you. Believe it."

I didn't believe it. I waved to him and walked toward downtown, another two or three miles into the wind.

The city streets were bright with holiday decorations, but empty. I went into the first bar I came to, a place I'd never been in, called The Loose Caboose, a velveteen-and-Leatherette night spot with a scandalous reputation, but I was cold, and brave with self-pity.

The Loose Caboose was nearly empty. One drunk in a three-piece suit at the bar, two guys in designer sweats huddled in a booth. A big TV over the bar was showing us what New Year's Eve in New York was like. I ordered a bourbon and soda, and then another. An oily, old-time band singer in a tux began his version of "I'll Take Manhattan," Times Square celebrants roaring behind him.

My feet were aching with cold. The third bourbon made them feel like they were Roger Flexnor's feet.

"I know utter dejection when I see it," said one of the designer sweat-suit guys. He was at the bar, ordering drinks for himself and his friend, but looking at me.

"Good for you," I said.

"Say, listen," he said. "Delvin and I are going dancing later. You want to tag along? My name is Jeffrey, Jeffrey Hazeltine."

Delvin came up behind me. He put his arm around my shoulders. "Do I get the first dance or not?" he said to me, his voice sharp with a habitual pout.

"Not," I said.

Outside The Loose Caboose I realized that the walk back home was close to four miles and most of it was uphill. I jerked the strings of my parka hood tight and set out.

Three blocks into my trek, a car pulled alongside me. It was the pair from The Loose Caboose. "You need a ride?" Delvin asked.

"I need a ride *home*," I said.

"Hop in."

I did. I sat in the back while the two friends cuddled up front. I held no opinions about all this. Opinion holding had been one of the first causalities of my condition. Not that I didn't have opinions, I just didn't *hold* them. Everything was open to dispute, mutation, or outright cancellation.

I had an opinion about everything that had happened to me that evening, but also knew that I would not defend it tomorrow even if I could remember what it was. It seemed to me that all the people I had been with were puppets to a hidden agony, and could not find simple peace until the puppet master had lost interest in them. They had been yanked down their lives with seismic disregard. They didn't know where they were. They wanted their bearings and were willing to risk a lot to find them.

I revised this opinion a few times before giving it up. I wished the whole stumbling lot of us a lucky New Year. Then I remembered Sloan Capoletti. I leaned into the front seat. "Drive faster, Jeffrey," I said.

I lie on the nail-bed of my life still believing I am a good-hearted, sensitive man who would never beat his wife. You know my type: the afflicted, back-sliding liberal, self-aware to a fault—narcissistic, my shrink would say—but above all, not a man who would pound on a woman with his fists.

I stood over my wife telling myself these things. Her lip was bleeding. She was sobbing silently into her hands, her shoulders lifting and falling in heart-breaking shudders. I looked at my still-smoking fist. It was hot and tingling with the shock of what it had done. *Was* it my fist? It looked alien. It was too big, too cabled with blue veins. The middle knuckle was red, the flesh dented and raw where it had scraped a tooth. It was the fist of the Brute: the blunt club-end of a Stone Age arm. I opened it and looked at the trembling fingers that had once stroked and probed the woman on the floor in the name of love and tender lust.

Your Burden Is Lifted, Love Returns

I looked at myself through the one-way glass of my tricky brain: I saw a stranger in the bedroom, unshaven, drunk in his underwear, the blood draining from his face as the enormity of what he has done begins to sink in.

He is a great fool.

He has just put his life on a steep downgrade slope and his brakes are questionable. He feels sick to his stomach; he wants to cry.

Raquel is sitting on the floor in her panties and bra, holding her mouth. The bedroom seems to dilate and contract in sympathy with her sobs. A line has been crossed in this marriage. Would it be possible to pull it back to the other side? The mortified assailant thinks not.

"You *hit* me," she says, rising, the nonchalant globes of her breasts swinging, the wonderful curving flex of haunch and calf reminding the fool of what has been forfeited here.

"You *hit* me," she repeats, unable to believe it herself. "You bastard son of a *bitch*!"

"My God, Raquel, baby," he says, his heart a brick of remorse in his unquiet chest.

"*Do not use my name,*" she says: it is a careful instruction to the humiliated beast. The intimate syllables are no longer his to use. From this day forward, her name on his tongue will not be her name. It will ring oddly in his ear, and though he will say it over and over in tearful rages and in the half-sleep of early-morning dreams, he won't be able to get it right.

Even her face is the face of a stranger. This is some random woman, he thinks. A woman he might spy in Safeway fingering the eggplant. He would appreciate her fine Latina profile, how it hones itself with a shopper's glancing hesitations. Her eyes sharp with intelligence and dark with explosive desire. This is a woman he could love if he weren't already married to the women he loves. And she, of course, is happily married, too. She will not be picked up in the produce section of Safeway like a common aisle-walking tart. This last notion puts a wry twist on his lips and dilutes his remorse with bile.

While he is occupied with this reverie, she kicks him. Her strong foot rises up swiftly to his crotch, the instep impacting with a rumpling thump. In his Jockey shorts, standing flatfooted before her, he has offered a choice target of opportunity. He doubles over, sick, and manages to get into the bathroom before he loses his lamb chops, rice pilaf, and ratatouille. Not to mention the three or four tumblers of Old Taylor.

"You *bastard!*" she howls, following him into the bathroom. Her rage is on the upswing while his has peaked and dissipated. *Do not start fights if you cannot sustain your rage*, he muses. He is on his knees before the toilet, hugging the cool porcelain. Lemons of sick light float before his shut eyes.

"I think I'm hurt bad," he manages to say between convulsions.

"Not bad enough," he hears her whisper. He notices that her breath is choppy. He imagines that a dangerous wind has blown open the house, that she is teetering in it, holding on to a wall for support. He sees her hair standing out from her head, her eyes wild. Rags of rage snap in this insane wind. He sees the house lifted off its foundation, transferred by storm to a country without maps.

Then she touches his shoulder. He almost sobs aloud with gratitude. But it is not a forgiving hand. It is her foot again. (The foot he has kissed and tickled.) This time it shoves him into the toilet tank. His head gongs off the hard surface. A thread of blood weaves itself into his philosophic eyebrows.

By the time he has cleaned himself up and stopped the oozing blood from the hairline laceration, Raquel has dressed and packed her suitcase.

"Don't go," he says. "I think I have a concussion."

"Fine," she says briskly. "Perhaps in the future you will use your head more wisely."

"You won't find a motel this time of night," he informs her.

"I'll sleep in the car, then," she says, snapping the locks on her suitcase.

"Or maybe not," he says, alluding to the subject that had put the evening's events into suicidal fast-forward.

"I am not going to dignify that sick remark with an answer," she says.

Sick remarks, he thinks, *have become my specialty*. He tries to reconstruct the last three hours. It seems more like days than hours. He, the responsible house husband, is out of sorts. Raquel, the breadwinner, has come home late and dinner is cold on the table. He could have kept it warm in the oven, but the cold and coagulated dinner makes a better *statement*. He is being spiteful. Spite: the bitter pill that spoils love's slim chances. It hardens the soft core of stumblebums and statesmen alike. Spite: the great rotten god with baleful glance who systematically unravels the good world.

Through the smoked glass of memory, he watches his fist floating toward her. It seems, at first, that it only wants to deliver a semi-playful chuck under the chin. But he is grossly self-deceived. (Because of self-deception and spite he sees little hope for the human race.) The first has energy and hidden purpose. It is not as playful as he thought it was. Her lip cracked. A tooth stung his knuckle. She sat down.

Earlier he received her explanation with an indifference he almost believed. But it was spite again, masking itself with reason, mocking reason's coolness with sub-zero rage.

"Oh, *no*, honey," she said. "Look, it's past *eight*. I didn't realize... I'm really sorry, but—"

He turned his back on her then and mixed himself a drink. Bourbon, because he knew she detested the smell.

"Doug Thurston called a supervisory meeting because of the pothole crisis in the South End," she said. "I had to take the notes."

"Until eight?" he said mildly, speaking into his glass.

"Well, no, not until eight. We finished at six-thirty. But Doug—"

"Doug?"

"Mr. Thurston. He wanted to buy me... *us*, I mean... a drink. You know, for being good sports. The secretaries."

"Where did you go?"

"The Yucatán Room, at the Sheraton. Lowell Black was there, and Mary and Charlene. They want me to play racquetball with them. Mary Tyson had to drop out because of shinsplints. So their foursome is shot."

"I'm sorry...?" he said, setting his glass down carefully, his brow creased with the mock-sincere but game effort to understand her.

"But I told them I'm not the racquetball type."

"What type did you tell them you were?"

Raquel searched his face for the possible joke, but his face was neutral. His intentions were hidden, even from himself.

"You could have called me," he said, still without rancor.

"I know, I know, hon," she said indulgently. "I *should* have called. I just lost track, you know? And Doug—"

"*Doug*?"

"Mr. Thurston, the boss. Doug Thurston. He wanted to make it up to us." She gave him a small pecking kiss on the ear, notable for its motherliness and parceled heat. He clenched his jaw against it, and against the thing that was trying to surface in his mind.

He smelled, then, the tequila sunrises, the barroom smoke, the cologne of self-important bureaucrats. He felt rocked back by those essences. "God damn it," he said, convinced of the awful thing that had been skirting his thoughts the past few hours. For this was not the first time Raquel had come home late from her job at the Department of Streets. Once last week, twice the week before, and several times the previous month.

She looked at him, her head cocked inquisitively, like an alerted robin sensing the stalking cat. She heard the octave difference in his shaky voice as events began their sickening climb toward the blooded summit. "What's wrong, honey?" she said.

He finished his drink in a single corrosive gulp and set the glass down with a slam that startled both of them. "Wrong?" he said. "Nothing's wrong. What makes you think something's wrong?" Yet all this insistent innocence was betrayed by the tremors in his voice.

"I—"

He cut her off: "Let's eat this slop before it walks off the table."

He picked up the plates and put them into the microwave, hers first, then his. The food came out gummy but warm, and they sat down to their evening meal. Since he had been out of work, he'd become a passable if somewhat paranoid cook. If praise wasn't forthcoming after the first or second bite, he was thrown into a grievous sulk.

After dinner he went back to the Old Taylor. Bourbon pacified him, oddly. He became more civil as the evening progressed. She went on about racquetball, about how great Mary and Sally were (he was not clear who these women were—secretaries, apparently, but Raquel seemed to be flattered to find herself in their company), what a great boss Doug Thurston was, how he had promised to consider her for the next opening at the Administrative Assistant level, and so on. He began to feel, gradually, like a ball of string being unwound at the hand of an idiot child, even though the bourbon helped him maintain the illusion of solidity. While Raquel spoke, he touched himself surreptitiously a few times to see if he was still there. Yes, yes, his body seemed to say, we are still here, all of us: meat, bone, gristle, blood, marrow, the beating, secreting, and pumping organs, the wiring and plumbing, all present and accounted for. As it was in the beginning, so is it now, and so shall it be at the end of time. The false alpha and omega wisdom of bourbon, storming through his tender corpus, led these wacky musings. But there were always the tricyclic antidepressants to help him through the day-after black-hole blues.

"I'm sorry, I missed that last thing you said," he confessed, suppressing, now, a smile that he knew would be hellishly dashing if he let it break out.

"*Tomorrow*, I said. I'll be working late again, so you might as well cook only for one. Or maybe you can go to a restaurant. I'll give you an extra ten dollars."

"Oh, yes," he said. "That will be fine."

He managed to sit through three back-to-back sitcoms. He listened to Raquel's tinkling, careless laughter as Bob Newhart's stammering attempts to claim patriarchal authority elicited gales of laughter from the audience. He hated Bob Newhart suddenly, recognizing himself, and half the men he knew, in that beaten, paunchy little guy: twerps, nerds, schlepps, and all the unremarkable cuckolds—*cabrones*, Raquel would say if moved to Hispanic cruelty—portrayed so perfectly by the Everyman for our times, Bob Newhart. It occurred to him that if the sitcoms were uncensored, if commercial considerations were not a factor, and if the writers were given a free hand, then we would see ourselves as no dramatic literature has ever made any nation see itself. What the Newhart show needed was one more twist toward the black end of the spectrum. A little manic wobble to worry its too-tidy spin.

Raquel was laughing lightly at Newhart, who once again was left holding the bag. She laughed, too, at the troop of fools who complicated his life, while the women moved handily toward the things they wanted, unimpeded.

"God *damn* it," he said later, when they were undressing for bed, in answer to no remark but to an image in his mind of Newhart standing in a snowbank outside his lodge so that he could peek into a window to spy on his wife. Inside, by the fire, she was allowing an insurance adjuster to pat and paw her, hoping to get a higher estimate on a claim. It was vital to Bob that she succeed, though her sheer skill made him bite his knuckles.

"What?" Raquel said, unable or unwilling to acknowledge the gripe that had quietly soured the evening.

"You're sleeping with him, aren't you?" he said. "You're sleeping with Doug."

"*Doug*?"

"Doug Thurston, Your boss."

"*What?* Are you crazy? Did you take your medication today?"

This made him laugh. He approached her. "My medi*cation*? Is *that* what I need? Get the hubby zonked, then everyone's free to play? Is that the way it works?"

"You are being an incredible asshole, you know that, don't you?"

"Just answer the question, Raquel. Are you sleeping with Doug or not?"

Her eyes flashed in that Latin way he was crazy about. It opened glandular spigots everywhere. It made his hair flex. "Okay, sure. I'm sleeping with him. Is that what you want to hear? Does that thrill you a lot? I'm sleeping with him two, three times a day. In his office, in the janitor's closet, out in his Mercedes. The Mercedes is best, all that leather and the stereo system..."

Denial by exaggeration, as a technique, bored him. He laughed again. His laugh was dry and weak, as though his vocal cords were made of paper. He felt an itch in his right hand. The itch made the hand curl into a fist. He thought of giving her a little "chuck" under the chin. But his glandular spigots had been opened wide, amplifying the gesture: the chuck had steam.

I didn't sleep that night. Or the next. I took my medication but that didn't bring her back. I called Doug Thurston. Raquel hadn't been to work for two days. (He said.)

I called my shrink, but he had flown his Piper Cherokee to Alaska to video-tape caribou migration. Several times I found myself standing in the bathroom with large quantities of pills in my willful hand: cloud-gray bullets, tiny disks the tired pink of haze-dampened suns. On these occasions I became afraid of the unshaven stranger in the mirror.

I took refuge in chores. I cleaned the house to showplace perfection. I resumed half-finished projects—the windows needed caulking, the patio slab needed paint. While rolling a new layer of insulation across the attic, I found a newspaper dated March 15, 1949. The quaint headlines amused me for a while. The world of thirty-eight years ago seemed only *knee*-deep in quicksand. It was up to its armpits now, praying for a rope. My horoscope was short and sweet: "Your burden is lifted, love returns." I took it to heart. In the mantic arts, thirty-eight-year discrepancies are trifles only the literal-minded take seriously.

It was a pleasant day, sunny with promise. I took a six-pack of beer out to the front porch and waited for her.

Louis Quenon can make you feel better than you had any right to expect. You'll hear it said he's trouble in the long run. You'll hear it said he'll drink a week and disappear for two. They'll tell you he's a Feejee Indian from Africa. They'll call him a breed, oily customer, quack, boomer, con man, crook. Someone will get around to telling you he was born in a canebrake on the Guadalupe ten miles below Duck Pond, and a lot of other fairy tales. His wife, Lily, will tell you he's irresponsible and doesn't care what becomes of her in this life or the next. "You morons!" she yells at us. We'll be sitting there with him in Lucky's, drinking beer or sweet wine, listening. Lily will come in, a hard, narrow-hipped, bony woman of fifty. She'll start in swinging her big red purse, knocking glasses and pitchers to the floor. Louis looks at her as you might look at a waxwing mindlessly hurting itself against a plate-glass window. "Useless old drunks!" she yells. "Stupid retards!" We all scatter to the dark corners of the bar, except for Louis, and wait for the storm to blow over. Louis takes his time. He

Medicine Man

has the patience of a mountain, whatever else they might say. He lights up a cigarette. He arranges his lighter and tobacco pouch on the table neatly before him. He asks Leonard, the bartender, who's winning the ball game. He tilts his chair back. He looks up at the TV set as if at the blue sky. His smile has never had any meanness in it. He looks at Lily. Her anger, which was a solid brick wall coming in, is now like a flimsy membrane thinning out and getting weaker, yielding to a stretching force in the air. Louis will pat the table, rub his stomach, or stick a wood match in his ear for wax, and Lily's temper will come to heel, snap, and it's gone. Louis beams. He takes her by the wrist, easy, and she sits down, shaking her head at her own bad manners, but feeling a whole lot better. Louis makes a sign to Leonard, and everyone in the bar resumes his conversation and drinking. The incident is forgotten. Someone will usually dump a load of quarters in the jukebox, and everything is back to normal.

Now, this is what you *won't* hear: Louis Quenon was a real medic in the U.S. Army. He saw action in Sicily and North Africa. He got to know the local herb doctors and practitioners of antique medicine. They showed him things they usually never showed to outsiders. They warned him against surgery directed against the major organs, indecision, and a generally unrecognized plague they called, in a half-joking way, "glitter-blindness." He ran across a cell of modern Pythagoreans who claimed the universe was nothing more than an idea about tight bundles of woven lines. He who masters the art of line-bundling geometry, they said, will see the Weaver's Hand. When he returned to the States, Louis refused a scholarship to a big midwestern university that he had won in an open competition. In his letter turning down the offer, he said, "Dear Dean, This is to let you know that I've had second thoughts after reading through your catalog and that you are probably barking up the wrong tree over there in Madison."

His tribal name is Then-He-Sees-It, but he is only a fraction Assiniboin. His great-uncle, Willard Quenon, was a medicine man and they say that's where his talent comes from. But Louis says no to all of that, insisting that what he knows comes from a marabout he got acquainted with in Marrakech, and from the Sicilian herb specialists. What his Indian uncle Willard knew worked pretty well among the Tribe, but Louis said it wasn't very effective with white people. For the white man's diseases, you've got to go to the roots of the old white world and find the ancient remedies.

He cured me of a delicate constitution with a snail-water recipe that is still widely used in southern Europe by rural people. That's how I met Louis. We were at the bar, in Lucky's, accidentally sitting next to each other. He's a big, heavy man with a wide Indian face, but his hair is blond and he has a full beard that scratches against his chest. Our eyes met in the mirror behind the bottles. "How long have you had these fainting spells?" he asked me. Right off, my heart did its butterfly imitation and the barroom tilted.

"How did you know about that?" I said, short of breath.

"You write this down," he said.

I started to slide off my stool, but Louis touched my arm and that stopped me. I borrowed a pencil from Leonard and wrote down what Louis said on a paper napkin. Here's what put me back on my feet:

"A fourth bushel of good garden snails," he said. "Put them in a deep clay pot and lay some mint on top of them along with some balm and fennel to clean them. Let them stand all night like that with a colander over them so they can't creep out. In the morning wipe them one by one with a clean cloth and then bruise the snails, shells and all, into a fine mortar. Mix this mortar into six quarts of red cow's milk and set it on a medium fire, stirring all the while until it is thick as cream. Have a big pot ready. Lay a double handful of mint, half as much pennyroyal, ale hoof, and hyssop, then pour in the mixture. After two hours on a high flame stir it up, or else it will scum on top. When it cools off some, but before the pot gets comfortable to the touch, put it into as many Mason jars of any size as the mixture will fill. Put three ounces of white sugar candy in the bottom of each jar to kill the taste."

I had a hard time admitting to myself that I wanted to find those ingredients, and a lot harder time actually finding them. But I did, and right away, after the first quart or so, I began to take on color. In six months' time I'd gained thirty pounds. My lungs began to take in more air than they'd ever been able to, and my heart felt like a big fist opening and closing. I moved out of my small room above Lucky's and rented a little three-room house outside of town and put in a big garden where I could grow the hard-to-find herbs along with a good variety of greens. I felt like a healthy man of forty-five, and I'd been on a railroad pension for several years.

There's always a table or booth at Lucky's with a crowd of us believers trading stories. The younger customers, of course, think we're a bunch of senile old fools. They think Louis is a common type of gyppo artist, although he's never asked one of us for money, help, or goods. No one ever asks him why he offers to pass on a cure to ailing folks, because the question won't come up. You'll be sitting there, telling stories, adding a few frills here and an outright lie there, held in place by a common denominator of unswerving belief:

"You remember that black spot on my neck? Well, it got big and began to spread out like a stain. When it was as big as a dollar, I went to Louis. He gave me this yellow paste that smelled like antelope musk and in a week it went back to normal."

"I couldn't put any weight on my right leg. Louis said the big vein was shutting down. He gave me a blue unguent. Now I can dance all night."

"I was growing what I took to be a sixth finger."

"My left ear had a bell in it."

"I'd wake up every other night hollering for my brother, who drowned when he was only three."

"The wife thought the lead slipped out of my pencil fifteen years ago."

"My eyes were turning into bone."

"I'd sit down to grunt and nothing would come out but this nasty blue twine. I'd have to cut it off and hope for better luck tomorrow."

Here's another one. They took Moley Gleeson to the county hospital in a taxi. Moley had the room next to mine on the second floor above Lucky's. This was about a month before I moved out. I'd heard him blubber. I went into his room and found him sitting on the john, shaking with a chill and biting his hands. His eyes were quick and scared. There was a lake of slick brown blood on the floor and a terrible stink they'd never be able to scrub out. At the hospital they said it was cancer, a big one impossible to get at. They gave him sleeping pills and morphine and said it was only a matter of a few days now. A bunch of us would go up and visit with him. He'd forget who you were and once began to call himself Robert Dickinson. "I don't know this Moley Gleeson. In the hospital with cancer? That's too bad. That's a real shame." It was as if his mind were trading places with someone named Robert Dickinson and in that way freeing itself from the bad business of being Moley Gleeson. We figured it was the drugs that were doing this to him.

We went over to Louis's house and asked him if there was anything he could do for Moley. We didn't think there was, seeing as how the doctors themselves said that his cancer was out of reach, but Louis dipped into his big doeskin medicine bag, took out some fine orange, brown, and green powders, and went into the bathroom with them. When he came out, he said, "Let's go see Moley."

The nurse who brought us to Moley's room wasn't too happy to see us again. "Now, don't you boys tire out Mr. Gleeson. He's got about as much strength as a squashed cat." Louis closed the door behind us and tried to lock it, but there was no way to do that from the inside. There were four or five of us in the room with him. Louis went to the window and looked skeptically at the light coming in. He adjusted the blinds, dimming the air. Moley was lying there, half-asleep. His eyes, when they opened, were covered with that glazed look of fear and loneliness the dying usually have. Louis looked at us with a strange expression in his eyes, as if we were familiar and new to him at the same time. We didn't know what to make of it, and so we kept ourselves at a respectable distance, figuring it was his show anyway. He bent his big shaggy head down to Moley and whispered something in his ear. We couldn't make out what it was, but it took a long time, like a priest's last rites, so it was probably more than just "How ya doing, Moley?"

Louis pulled the sheet off Moley and then opened up his hospital gown. Moley looked like hell. There were bruises up and down his side and his arms were swollen up from the injections. His skin was soft and mushy-looking. He looked like a big wingless moth. He looked like he would come apart in your hands if you tugged at him. Louis rolled up his sleeves. He began to open and close his hands. His eyes were shut tight. Then he opened his hands wide. His hands began to stretch and taper out. They became long and narrow as snakes. They started to move toward Moley's underbelly and when they reached the pasty-white skin they didn't stop. His hands slid *into* Moley. Past the wrists. Up to the forearms. Moley's eyes were popped wide now, his mouth was ajar. I could see his tongue clicking around in there. Out of his mouth, from deep inside, I could hear a clacking, hammering sound, like wood on stone. The sweat was boiling out of Louis's forehead. He was searching around for something inside Moley, the way you'd feel the bottom of a swampy slough for something you'd dropped there. Then all at once the nurse comes busting into the room. She saw what was going on and began to holler for help. Louis was dragging something up. His forearms were dark red and the room smelled—a thin, sharp smell like arsenic smoke, comparable to what you'd expect just downwind of a smelter. What's coming out of Moley looks like an oblong head of lettuce. It's dark purple, nearly black, and wriggling like a speared eel. It was coming out of Moley's belly, just at the left of his navel and under the heart. If the thing had a head, then what I saw in it might have been eyes— dull and ugly, three of them in a row, looking around at the world of hospital rooms. The hammering sound that was coming out of Moley's throat had quit and Moley was grunting low and strong, with a kind of hard pleasure, like a woman giving easy birth.

A doctor came into the room. He hollered at Louis and then grabbed him by the beard. Another doctor came in and began to punch Louis in the back. But Louis hung on to the black lettuce eel, which, by the looks of it, was halfway out. The doctors were grinding their teeth and spitting curses at Louis and the nurse was running in and out of the room screaming for the cops. A young intern came in then with a steel chair in his hands. "Leave it to the Marines," he said. He took a baseball swing at Louis's head that landed with a gong. Louis staggered away from the blow but he didn't let loose of the thing in Moley's belly. The young intern swung the chair again and this time it dropped Louis to one knee. He lost his grip on the lettuce eel and it slipped back with a dark murmur into Moley to clack away at whatever was left of his innards. Moley sighed and went back to sleep, calling himself Robert Dickinson and telling us it was too bad about that poor bastard Moley Gleeson, whoever the hell he was. There was no mark or anything unusual at all on his belly. The blubbering nurse closed up Moley's gown and pulled his sheet up to his chin, and Moley, a kind of dying amusement in his old black eyes, caught her trembling hands to steady her.

The police came in then and carried Louis off to jail. Three days later, Moley died.

Any prosecutor in the state would have had a hard time convincing a jury to lock up Louis Quenon because he had entered the insides of a dying man with his bare hands in order to prowl around in there for dangerous lettuce eels, and so, after holding Louis for a while, they decided to let him go, fining him twenty dollars for disorderly conduct.

They say that while he was in the pokey, Louis cured the police chief's wife of her insomnia by having the chief cut the ears off a live wild rabbit and strap them, still warm, to her temples before turning in at night. They say it cured more than her insomnia, though, and she began to want more in bed than her husband, who was almost sixty years old, could deliver. This made the chief think poorly of Louis, and the word was put out that Louis had better keep his nose clean while in the city limits.

Louis got the blues after that episode. He'd come into Lucky's, but his smile was thin and far away and not meant for any of us who sat at his table. He didn't have any new stories to tell. We went ahead and asked him, "What's troubling you, Louis?" He'd take a deep lungful of air and let it sigh out. "You don't seem like yourself, Louis," He'd shake his head as if to unseat a fly and raise his beer to his lips. "Does it have to do with Moley?" we asked. "Or being in jail? Are you worried about the chief?" But he'd just look puzzled as if he didn't have the first idea of what we were talking about. Finally, after about a week of this, he said, "Step away." We did what he wanted because of our respect for him, and no one tried to figure out why he said it.

It was about this time that Louis took a sales job with a farm implement company. Louis was well liked by the business people and could get work whenever he wanted it. Most people in the selling business knew that Louis had the power to move merchandise. They'd put him on straight commissions and he'd earn enough in three or four months to last him and Lily the year. I saw him one hot July afternoon driving a big Farmall down the middle of the main drag leading a parade. He was wearing a wide-brim straw hat and sunglasses and I could tell by his color that he'd been drinking for a while. There was a troop of horsemen behind him, and behind them there was the high school marching band. A small crowd had gathered along the sidewalks to watch the parade, which was being held to celebrate the invention of the internal combustion engine. Behind the high school band there was a float that was supposed to illustrate the theme of the parade. It was a ten-foot-tall piston made out of silvered cardboard. Two girls in bathing suits were cranking the piston up and down. A three-year-old boy on top was dressed up like a spark plug. I saw Lily, narrower than ever, in the crowd of onlookers. She was walking slowly, so as to not get ahead of Louis's tractor. Her face was as colorless as skim milk. She was carrying her big red purse, but she wasn't holding it like a weapon. I could see by the look in her eyes that she was worried. I knew Lily didn't have any use for me or for any of us from Lucky's, but I caught up with her and touched her elbow anyway. "All of us over at Lucky's are pretty worried about Louis," I said.

"You have reason to be," she said without taking offense or getting that look of total disgust she reserved for Louis's friends.

"What's troubling him, Mrs. Quenon?" I asked.

She looked at me then and the old contempt came back into her eyes for a second. "Dreams," she said.

She told me that Louis was having dreams he couldn't figure out. They'd started up when he was in jail and they got worse after they let him out. The dreams didn't scare him any, but he was having trouble reading them. He wrote to a man in Morocco, but all his letters had been returned unopened. Every night for a week he'd called an old friend of his named Art One Pipe who lived in the far northeast corner of the state. One Pipe told Louis that he was well known for his patience and not to act like a teenage girl with acne when he needed his best quality most. One Pipe drove the three hundred miles to see him and to help him work things out. "All they did was drink bourbon and puke," Lily said.

The word began to go around that Louis was in a bad way. He'd quit his job after he'd made a couple of thousand dollars and had gone on a two-week tear, dropping most of it. Those of us who understood that Louis was the indispensable center of our circle as well as the spokes of the wheel that held it together, decided that something had to be done. I was elected to go to his house and make a plea, reminding him how important every one of us felt him to be. Lily let me in. She had an abandoned look on her face as if she didn't care what might happen next because the worst had already come about.

I found Louis in bed with a bottle of Canadian whiskey. He was naked and covered with a sheet. The room smelled fiercely of the rancid oil only a sick body can produce. He saw me and smiled a little. He tried to sit up. I helped him and fixed the pillows behind his head. He took the bottle of whiskey by the neck and poured some of it into his glass. He handed me the glass and took a drink himself directly out of the bottle. He had that same faraway look. I started to say something because I felt the time had come for me to say what I had come here to say, but he held up his hand to stop me. "Step away," he said.

I sat there for a full minute, not knowing what to do. Then I finished my drink and stood up. "Okay, Louis," I said. "But I'll come back a little later on, if that's all right with you."

Louis shook his head, frowning at my failure to understand him. "Me, I mean," he said. "*I'm* a step away. I think I always have been."

I guess I just had a blank look on my face. It seemed to exasperate him.

"The farther upstream you go," he said slowly, as if he didn't trust my ability to understand simple English, "the meaner becomes the terrain. I'm tangled up in some high brush country, and it's beginning to look like there's a real chance I won't be able to go any farther or even find my way back."

"Uh-huh," I said.

"Sometimes these dreams say, 'Yes.' Sometimes they say, 'No.' Sometimes they say, 'You are ninety percent stone, and should spend the rest of your time selling tractors and making Lily happy and quit tampering with what you are not going to be able to figure out,'" He grunted at the humor of such a possibility.

"Do they ever tell you to go down to the yards and lay your head on a rail?" I mumbled into my empty glass.

Louis looked at me, his eyes sharp and mean. He hadn't had his hair cut for some time and it hung down over his ears, damp and oily-looking. He scratched his beard and chest. Then he grinned. I could see that his gums were nearly white and his teeth looked bad, too. "Maybe so," he said. Then he threw off his sheet and swung out of bed. "Hell," he said. "Let's go down to that place on the corner and hear some music."

That place on the corner, the closest bar to Louis's house, was a mean little cowboy bar called the Bar-None. The Bar-None was a long, narrow hole-in-the-wall with no elbowroom, no light, and no way to keep out of trouble. I thought it was the poorest idea Louis could have come up with but decided to string along, hoping that maybe we wouldn't get that far. Louis had to walk slow, with me holding his arm, because he'd been lying in bed for nearly a week with nothing but whiskey for food and feeling bad about everything. But by the time we got to the Bar-None, the fresh air and exercise had perked him up. "Why don't we go on down to Lucky's?" I suggested. It was only another four blocks.

"No," he said. "Too far. Too many leeches."

I can only say that I was knocked flat. It was the first truly unkind words I'd ever heard from Louis Quenon. I looked at him and he didn't try to avoid my eyes, but there was still too much distance in his face for it to mean anything to me.

We went in. There was the usual crowd of rough trade you never see anywhere except in places like the Bar-None. We took two stools toward the dark end of the bar. The jukebox was turned up loud and thumping. The lights were flickering—bad wiring. A fight was getting under way someplace in back. Louis ordered the first round of drinks. The cowboy next to me knocked my arm off the bar with his elbow. He didn't say he was sorry. He looked at me and then at Louis and then went on with his conversation. He was talking in an enterprising way to a nearly unconscious hawklike woman. A bloody face pushed itself between me and Louis and whispered hoarsely for a bottle of gin to go. Someone was trying to waltz with an Indian woman who hated the idea. She had dropped something on the floor, but the hardleg she was with wouldn't let her stop long enough to pick it up. I decided to keep my eyes on the few square inches of bar in front of me until Louis figured he'd had enough of this place.

Someone came in by mistake. It was a woman and her husband. They had a dog on a leash. They stood in the doorway, squinting through the smoke haze and hammering roar. The woman said something to the man and they turned to leave. Something stopped them. Their dog, a gray poodle with a red ribbon on its neck, had gotten loose. Someone had scooped it up and set it on the bar. It skittered along, dodging glasses and hands, looking for a place to get down. The woman was trying to make her way toward it. "Banjo!" she yelled. "Banjo!" And pretty soon everyone in the place was yelling, "Banjo! Banjo!" and laughing crazy. Banjo was trembling, and even though you could tell he didn't want to antagonize anyone, his lips began to curl back over his teeth in spite of himself, and he growled. This made everybody at the bar laugh all the harder. A cowboy with a long mortician's face stuck a Polish sausage into Banjo's mouth. The bartender snapped the bar rag at him and said, "Off, mutt." The strain was too much for Banjo. He peed. The pee rolled down against the face of a garage mechanic who had passed out on the bar. The woman next to the passed-out garage mechanic woke him up by tickling his throat with her fingernail. "You're laying in a puddle of poodle piss," she said, straight-faced. Those at the bar who heard it passed it down. "He's laying in a puddle of poodle piss," they said. Pretty soon nearly everyone in the place was saying it. For a minute there you couldn't hear yourself think. The garage mechanic began to realize that he was the butt of a joke of some kind. He wiped his face on his sleeve and looked at the trembling dog. He took the Polish sausage out of its mouth. Banjo tried to bark but only managed a humiliating whine. The mechanic grabbed the dog's leash and jerked it up into the air. The woman who had been trying to retrieve her dog broke into tears. She made a kind of high-pitched yelping sound that cut through the general racket. The mechanic held the dog over the bar by its leash. He looked at it as you might look at a wriggling fish on a line, trying to decide if it's a keeper or not. The dog's hind legs were digging frantically at the air. Then the mechanic began to twirl the dog in big lazy circles, letting the leash out to its full length. Everybody near them had to duck as the dog went by. The woman who owned the dog was screaming, "No! No! Please!" Her husband was still in the doorway, his hand on his forehead. Someone had put a country tune on the jukebox about a man and his hound. "Me and my hound, we go round and around." The woman had made her way to the mechanic. She began to punch him in the face. She didn't know how to punch, though. It looked like she was knocking at a door shyly, hoping that no one was home. The mechanic laughed and twirled the dog all the harder. Then his face went vicious and he gave the leash one more hard swing and let it go. The dog helicoptered through the air and landed somewhere in the dark rear of the bar. The woman was still putting her balled-up little fists in the mechanic's face. He grabbed her by the coat and lifted her off the floor. Then he set her down on the bar. Someone handed her a glass of beer. Her husband was still in the doorway, his hand on his forehead.

Louis sat through it all as if it were a partway interesting movie he was watching on the TV set above the bar. He took his whiskey neat and sipped it. Someone said, "This dog here is suffering." An old cowboy with the face of a child had picked up Banjo. The dog was having a convulsion. Louis slipped off his stool and went over to the old cowboy. "Look here," said the cowboy. "He needs a vet, real quick."

Louis took the dog from the arms of the old cowboy. He brought it over to the bar and laid it down on its side. He felt along the dog's spine and the back of its neck. He ran his fingers along the rib cage. The dog was jerking and its hind legs were trying to get traction. Louis opened the dog's jaws and put his fingers into its throat. The woman, who was still sitting on the bar holding the glass of beer they gave her, yelled, "What is he doing! What are his qualifications!" Her husband was still in the doorway. He raised his hand as if to get someone's permission to speak. Louis pressed his ear against the dog. He straightened up then and looked at the woman down the bar.

"Your doggie is dead, ma'am," he said.

She heard him. "No!" she yelled. "Look, he's still moving his legs! Here, Banjo! Here, my darling!"

Louis pushed the dog aside to the man next to him and he in turn pushed it aside, and so on, until the dog finally got to the woman. She picked it up and held it close to her face. She began to speak to it in baby talk. Banjo began to wag his tail.

"No use," Louis said. "That dog is dead."

Banjo got to his feet and began to dance up and down, trying to lick the woman's tear-streaked face. A man and a woman were trading Sunday punches next to the men's room. The woman would take a punch, then grin and spit at the man. Then the man would take a punch from the woman and he would also grin and spit. It was some sort of contest. They were both heavyweights, two hundred pounds or more.

"No use," Louis said again. "No use in carrying on like that. The doggie is dead."

The garage mechanic helped the woman down from the bar and she and her poodle made their way back to the man in the doorway. The little dog was barking happily and jumping up and down against the woman's legs.

"It's dead," Louis said. "They shouldn't fool themselves like that. It only makes it harder."

Louis left town for a couple of months. No one knew where he went. When he came back, Art One Pipe was with him. One Pipe had brought most of his belongings. Louis put him up in a spare room. Lily, by that time, had had enough. One Pipe was the last straw, and she moved out, taking a room in the George A. Custer Hotel, uptown.

Louis had changed. He'd lost a lot of weight and he looked ten years older. I never realized how tall he was. When he was filled out, you didn't notice his height so much. But now he was skin on bone and had taken off his beard. His hair was cropped short. We'd see him, now and then, walking uptown, his clothes flapping on him like there wasn't anything inside them. His big round face looked sunken in and his shoulder blades poked up against his shirt like broken-off wings. He must have been close to seven feet tall, and it looked as though he had all he could do just to keep standing upright, like a narrow reed that had outgrown its ability to keep itself straight. He never came into Lucky's, and those of us who once counted on his being around gave him up for lost. No one came right out and said it, but it was in the air every time two or more of us would sit down together. Then the stories began to come in.

Louis had begun to stop people in the street to tell them what they didn't want to hear. He would block their way and point a finger in their faces, like a crazy prophet, drunk on his own visions. "Your baby will likely be torn up pretty bad in a baler," he told a woman, who fainted dead away on the spot. "The day after you have the family photograph taken, happiness will fly out of your window forever," he told a young pair of newlyweds. "In the little sealed-off rooms behind your eyes there is a coiled-up animal itching to drill holes in your ability to figure things out," he said to Nestor Claig, the high school principal and supposedly the smartest man in town. Sometimes he'd act as if he were listening to people's deepest thoughts. He'd cock an ear at them, squint, then put his big hand on their shoulders. "No, never do that twice," he whispered into the long hair of a beautiful young woman. "The corrected promise is all you can hope for," he said to a tired-looking man of fifty. And to a bank vice president, he said, "Her mind, you know, is shot through with tidy lies. Leave her before she drags you under."

Someone called the police and they threatened to lock him up again for disturbing the peace. The chief went to Lily with a plan to have Louis put away in the state mental hospital. But Lily didn't want any part of the chief's plan. "He keeps this up, Lily," said the chief, "and we won't need you to sign any papers. I'll get the court to put him away."

"Do what you want," Lily said. "Just don't ask me to do your job for you."

Then one day Lily showed up at Lucky's with a gentleman friend. He was over seventy and wore a fine silk suit. He carried a black cane and had a little white mustache. Lily had a proud look on her face. Her eyes dared anyone to say something. No one paid them any attention except when they moved their hands or opened their mouths to speak. Lily didn't care. She talked in a loud, relaxed voice about the big savings-and-loan company her gentleman friend used to work for as chief accountant. He didn't seem to mind her bragging him up. He'd sit with one hand in his lap and his other hand on a glass of sweet port, a real gentleman. He had a calm, distant gaze on his face that seemed to reach all the way back to Minneapolis, where he'd spent his best years. His name was Roland Towne. He lived in the room across from Lily's in the George A. Custer.

This went on for a while. Then Louis caught sight of them together, on the sidewalk, heading for Lucky's. He trailed them to the door but he didn't follow them inside. We could see him in the doorway, silhouetted against the light, like a staring pile of bones. Lily ignored him. Roland Towne ignored everything. Leonard would get a worried look on his face every time Lily and Roland came in trailed by Louis. "This is coming to a head," he whispered to me.

He was right. You could see that Louis was becoming agitated. He began to pace up and down in front of Lucky's, biting his fingernails and scratching his beard, which he'd begun to let grow again. He was still skinny, though, as if he'd given up the idea of eating proper food. One evening he came into Lucky's with Art One Pipe. Lily and Roland weren't there. "I'm going to tell you people something you probably don't want to hear," he said, to all of us. Art One Pipe shook his head. "Hell, Louis," he said. "It's better you just kept quiet."

Louis ignored him. "I was in the Badlands. Don't ask *me* how I got there. It was a dream. There had been a terrible drought. I hadn't sold a tractor in over a month. A custom cutting crew brought their combines in from Kansas, took one look at the dead, empty land, and got mean drunk for a week. And then, all at once, I was up north, in the Badlands, alone. What am I doing here? I said to myself. I met a woman who called herself Mrs. Tree. She was big and fat. She didn't know what I was doing there either. She lived in a mud-wall cabin. She said that she was responsible for the weather. She'd been sick. The wind had blown something bad into her ear. She couldn't remember things. Like the patterns of her stones. She had to line up some stones, big round ones that she had to shove with her shoulder. Every day she had to line them up in a different pattern just so the weather would stay normal. But the bad thing that had been blown into her ear made her forget the patterns."

Louis took a swallow of beer. One Pipe was staring into his whiskey glass. He had a slightly disgusted look on his face. Louis paid him no attention. "So I told her," Louis continued. "I said, 'I can fix up your memory with a little bit of this tea here.' I made her some and she drank it down. Her eyes lit up. 'That's real good,' she said. 'I almost remember everything now.' 'Almost?' I said. 'There is one more thing,' she said. She took off her dress and laid down in the dirt. 'You have got to be my husband for a little while.' There was a dangerous look in her black eyes, but at the moment she only seemed flirtatious and coy to me. So I piled on her and we were getting to it before long like a husband and wife."

"Take it easy, Louis," Leonard said. "There's mixed company here."

"Filthy lunatic," said an elderly prim woman in a flaming-red wig.

Louis ignored these protests. "But just as I reached the point of no return, I felt myself starting to shrink. At the same time, I got groggy and weak. Something was pulling me in, a powerful suction that had started to fold me in half, backward, at the hips. I mean to tell you that it came from *her*, that I was being sucked up into *her*, like the reverse of being born. Everything went black and warm and I could hear her heart thudding over me someplace like a rhythmic thunder. I moved upward, sort of swimming, sort of flying, in the pitch-black dark. Then there was something in front of me. A big, hard-shelled bug of some kind, like a sow bug, only it was half as big as me. It blocked my path. 'Kill it,' said Mrs. Tree. I was real surprised that I was able to hear her voice. It was like she was behind me someplace, talking through a culvert. I picked the sow bug up in my hands and killed it easy enough, but it took a while and it stank something terrible. Then I felt myself falling. Down down down I went until I hit something soft and warm. Pressure like I never felt before pressed me from all sides. I was being squeezed down smaller and smaller. I wanted to cry out, but there was no air to be had. Then the light hit me again like the blast of an atomic bomb. I was out in the open air flat on the mud floor of her hut, covered with blood and crying. She had given birth to me. I was her baby."

"Will someone please call the police?" said the prim woman in the red wig.

"When I was myself again," Louis said, unbothered by the interruption, "Mrs. Tree said, 'Thank you. You killed the thing that had gotten into my ear. I feel a lot better. I remember everything now.' We crossed over to where her stones were kept and she shoved them around with her shoulders until they formed a pattern of X's, circles, and stars. It was a lot of hard work and it took a long time. When she was done, she went into her mud hut and laid down to sleep. Pretty soon a big black cloud comes boiling out of Canada. 'Going to hail,' I said. Mrs. Tree pokes her head out of her hut and gives me a funny look. 'Be quiet, you,' she said. 'I got to sleep. The weather is back to normal now.' And sure enough, the white stuff starts jumping all around us, hail, big and lumpy. But something's wrong with it. It isn't exactly hail. After it hits the ground, it moves around and tries to sit up. I bend down to get a closer look. It's the figure of a man. Millions of them. They are all pasty white and naked as day one. They can't be alive, but they are. Half-alive anyway, and cold to the touch, cold as the hail I thought they were. You'd pick one of them up in your hand and he'd turn over and look at you with those sad icy-white eyes. There was no real energy in them. They seemed to be carved out of soft white soap. They didn't have any mouths to speak of, and they didn't have any assholes. You can't get the medicine into them and you can't get the poison out. They would just turn over and look at you with those miserable dead-cold icy-white eyes. They had little frosty mustaches and each one of them was holding on to a little glass of that sweet port. They made you want to puke. All they can do is think about how it used to be back in Minneapolis a hundred and ten years ago. I hollered into Mrs. Tree's hut that it would be better to have the drought, but it was too late, she was dead to the world of ordinary people."

He told this story as a daily routine. The details of Louis's dream would change, but it always ended with the little ice-cold men falling out of the cloud. I believed it was a real dream and that he'd just doctored it up a little so that it seemed to be especially about Roland Towne. Then one day, he told it while Lily and Roland were in the bar. Leonard looked like he expected trouble. The rest of us went on with business as usual. When Louis finished with the story, he stared directly at Roland. Roland nodded to him, amiable, and took a sip of his port. Lily was red as a turnip, having been insulted by the off-color dream and its outrageous ending. She had her big red purse with her, ready for action.

Louis had something with him. It was a moth-eaten blanket with wheels and thunderbirds stitched on it. He walked over to the table where Lily and Roland were sitting. He took something out of a pouch he was carrying and sprinkled it in the air over Roland's head. Then he unfolded the blanket and tossed it on top of Roland so that the old man was completely covered by it. Lily's jaw dropped. She gave Louis a thud on the back with her purse. Louis mumbled a little hocus-pocus in a foreign language. Roland didn't move. You could see his outline under the blanket. He was a cool old man. He let Louis ramble on. I saw the shape of his glass slide up the blanket as he raised it to his lips and then back down as he returned it to the table. He was drinking his sweet port as if nothing at all peculiar was happening. Louis took the blanket off with a big swooping yank. Roland's white hair was mussed a little but he looked serene as ever if not slightly bored. He nodded to Louis, still amiable, and took another sip of his wine, his mind nine hundred and fifty miles dead east. Some people are like that. Something inside of them is solid as rock even though their exteriors seem frail and delicate. I had to give old Roland credit. Louis gave him too much credit, though. He stumbled backward, swallowing hard, as if Roland had leveled a

Smith & Wesson .38 at his nose. I don't know for sure, but I think Louis had tried to make the old accountant disappear. It didn't work.

Louis got desperate after that. He got an old Model T ignition coil from the junkyard and began to give himself strong electrical shocks with Art One Pipe's reluctant help. These shocks were supposed to rejuvenate something that had gone dormant inside of him. When winter came, he stood for an hour in a blizzard without any clothes on, singing magical songs into the north wind. In the spring, he went on a diet of berries, bark, and roots. He slept in the skin of a grizzly killed eighty years ago by an Indian's arrow. The Indian had broken some kind of spiritual law by killing the grizzly and the skin was said to be inhabited by an angry spirit. Louis wanted to strike a deal with this dark spirit.

The dreams he had while sleeping in that skin led him to do things to himself that were painful and dangerous. He stuck long pins into his feet. He swallowed ordinary garden dirt, worms and all. He nearly blinded himself in the left eye with some kind of caustic. He dunked himself into the June rapids of the Sweetroot River and was swept downstream a mile before he could beach himself.

He learned new songs and sayings all the way from Alaska. He made a telephone call to North Africa and talked for an hour to a hostile bureaucrat who wouldn't give him the information he wanted. He rode freight trains to the West Coast and drank salt-water out of the Pacific Ocean where two great currents met in a war of waves, and when he came back he set fire to everything he owned except his medicine bag and his house.

He was thrown in jail again, let out, thrown back in again, forced to spend a couple of months in the state mental hospital, let out, and so on, in a battle between the authorities and Louis's ever-widening circle of desperate actions.

The town formed a committee to deal with the problem. He visited the committee meetings in white skins and paint on his face. He would sit in the back row, by himself, staring at the members of the committee without comment. One by one the committee members found strange-looking figures carved out of wood stuck into their front lawns. The chairman of the committee found a necklace of dead mice hung on his mailbox. But the committee members, all hardheaded businessmen, scoffed at Louis's mumbo-jumbo. Once Louis brought his moth-eaten blanket to the committee meeting, threw some of that green dust into the air, sang something in a falsetto voice, waved the blanket, but if it was meant to make the committee disappear into thin air, it didn't work. A couple of the members, though, came down with the flu shortly after that.

Art One Pipe had long since gotten fed up with Louis and had left town. Lily filed for a divorce. She got it quick and without any catches. She married Roland Towne a few days later and they went back to Minneapolis, forever.

Louis moved into an old mineshaft on a hill just south of town and was rarely seen anymore. People began to think of him as a harmless old hermit. They liked it that way. So long as he stayed up in his cave brooding, everybody was happy. Everybody got the idea that Louis had found his proper place in the world. "That crazy old hermit" is what you'd hear, always said with a kind of relief. And then all the old stories would take on a comic element. There had always been something awe-inspiring about Louis, but now people would chuckle and shake their heads remembering the funny side of his antics. Only a few of us remembered how it really was. Even some who had been given a cure for one thing or another would now tell you how most disease was really ninety percent in your head, anyway. "One cure is as good as the next if you believe in it, for the mind is the true healer." Or, put another way: "If you think you're sick, then by God you *are* sick, or soon will be." One old fool who Louis had raised up out of a hospital bed argued, "It wasn't my heart that was bad, it was my *attitude*." A husband who had promised to give Louis a two-year-old Cadillac if he could help his wife said, "Hell, she wore that cancer like a glove. When she decided to take it off because she wasn't getting any *mileage* off it anymore, off it *came*." Louis got the Cadillac, but it had piston slap and the transmission was balky.

After hearing this sort of talk one afternoon in Lucky's, I jumped up and yelled, "You're all ingrates and liars!" I danced a little old man's war dance, holding a chair out in front of me like a weapon or a dance partner. "Look at me!" I said. "I had one foot in the grave all the way up to the hip before Louis came along!"

But no one pays much attention to a white-haired seventy-year-old man doing a war dance with a chair. A few of them chuckled, and Leonard turned up the TV so that the baseball game would drown out my little commotion. An Indian woman named Nan Person came over to my table and sat down. She was about sixty years old, tall and angular. She had a fine long jaw but not many teeth in it. Her leathery hands were beautiful—slender and calm.

"They only feel betrayed," she said.

"What?" I was still a little hot. I stared at her and she didn't look away. "You don't make sense," I said.

"They are mad at him for going crazy," she said. "They feel like fools, having put their faith in a crazy man. Now they are proving to themselves that nothing ever happened to them."

That made me laugh. I touched Nan Person's hand. "One thing is sure," I said. "Nothing will ever happen to them again."

She laughed too, and I picked up her fine hand and kissed it.

But another thing did happen to them. It was a Sunday afternoon, maybe as much as a year later. A few of us were sitting around having some muscatel. Nan

Person, who had moved in with me, was holding my hand under the table. A love affair so late in life is an undreamed-of thing. But there it was, full-blown and real. A gift from nowhere for no good reason, but taken with gratitude and no questions asked. We never discussed it, Nan and me. It was there, in our eyes, a crazy thing that made us sweet and giddy.

Something was in the air that day. I saw Nan shiver slightly, with that nervousness you feel before an important event. It was quiet. The quiet was inside of you and outside of you. I didn't know I was holding my breath until I got dizzy. A few others were glancing at the doors every now and then. Leonard was sitting at the end of the bar where he kept the 12-gauge shotgun, pretending to read the newspaper. The TV set was on. A bullnecked preacher was hollering to beat hell into ten microphones. The sound was turned off, but the address of where you could send your money was being flashed across the bottom of the screen. Bullneck wasn't taking any chances.

I excused myself form the table to get a little air. The street was empty. It had rained hard earlier that day and everything was still wet and clean-looking. I was thinking how fine and permanent everything is in spite of all the individual comings and goings and the hoopla that goes with it, when a big hand touched me on the shoulder. It was Louis.

"Must have been the Apple of Peru," he said as if resuming a conversation we might have been having two or three years ago. I looked at him. He looked good. He was filled out and he had gotten himself a clean suit of ordinary clothes that almost fit. His hair was plastered down and his beard had been combed. My eyes must have been watery because he also seemed blurred around the edges, like an old photo that had seen too much sunlight. "Also known," he went on, "as the angel's trumpet, stinkweed, night-shade, and Jamestown weed. You may have heard the bastardized version, which is most popular in this neck of the woods. Jimson weed. That's what it must have been."

I figured he meant for me to ask him what he was talking about, so I did.

"I grew some," he said, "up on that hill, among a lot of other things. I sang a number of serious lamentations, and I needed helpers. But living up there in that mineshaft aggravated my piles, and my gonads had begun to produce severe and regular aches. Apple of Peru is a good helper for such troubles."

I wiped the blur out of my eyes. He came into focus for a second; then his edges got threadbare again. "Have you come back down?" I asked.

He didn't say anything. He stroked his beard and looked up and down the street as if it were the first time he'd been on it. He seemed to be vibrating like a tuning fork. I don't mean he was trembling as if he had the shakes after a killer binge. I just mean you couldn't concentrate on his *edges*. "Let's go have a drink," he said. "I'll tell you about it."

There was a general shamefaced welcoming commotion inside. Tables were shoved together and pitchers of beer were ordered. Leonard brought over a fresh bottle of Louis's favorite whiskey. Louis poured himself a generous shot. He stared at the glass for a minute. We waited. Then he pushed it slowly away. "I'd better not," he said, and everyone murmured something in an understanding way, since it was pretty clear that Louis had been dry for quite a while.

"Apple of Peru," he said. "That, and the fact that there's a big deposit of pitchblende in that hill. It wasn't hard to figure out what happened. At first, anyway. Then..."

You could hear everyone suck air as Louis picked up the shot glass and sipped at it. "What the hell," he said. "Spirits for the spirit, what's the harm?"

We didn't ask him what he was talking about. But Nan heard something in his tone of voice, a change, that made her dig her long, slender fingers into my leg. She leaned on me and her lanky body suddenly felt frail.

"Apple of Peru," Louis said again. "It has a characteristic way of getting down into your marrow. It probably had some pitchblende in it, too. I got real sick. But I got... *healthy*, too. Healthy in a way I'd never been."

He looked *too* tall all of a sudden. It was as if he were sitting on a pillow, giving him a few extra inches of height. A humming swarm of small white moths flew out of his left ear. I blinked and looked around to see if anyone else had seen them, but no one looked amazed. I took a long drink of wine.

"Leeches," Louis said, looking directly at me. He was smiling a little, as though we were sharing a private joke. A few people took offense at the remark and left the table, but they were the ones who had scoffed loudest at the memory of Louis's cures.

"Fever moved into me like a weather front," Louis said, resuming his story. "I went into a coma, I think. I was way back in that mineshaft, wrapped in a tarp. I think I was unconscious for two or three days. It's dark way back in a stope, darker than any night in the woods, and when I woke up... I would see a glow. It was coming from me, from my bones, from my blood, greenish-white, like I'd swallowed a quart of radium."

A round of throat clearing passed through Lucky's. No one was willing to swallow this part of his story. Some chair legs scraped the floor as the doubters got ready to depart.

"I was crazy for a while. I would run around the hillside, hollering and throwing myself down, flailing and kicking at imaginary beings. You could probably hear me all the way in town on a clear night. Once I tried to bite the moon, which had hooked itself onto my shoulder like a big cocklebur. It was trying to turn itself into a pair of wings. Owl wings. These were dreams and they were not dreams."

Louis got up and went to the front windows of the bar. He pulled down the shades. He then turned off the overhead lights. That made it pretty dark inside. At first you couldn't see anything except the blue glow of the TV set, where the bullneck preacher was now crying like a child, his thick, ham-pink face straining under a perfectly timed emotion, since the service was about over. He bit his lip and blinked back tears.

"I'm crouched down behind the bar, I think," Louis said. "Or maybe I'm behind the jukebox. I'll give your eyes another minute to get used to the dark, then I'll come out. Then you'll see what I'm talking about."

It was a long minute. The preacher had finished weeping and was now smiling up at the sky, where heavenly approval fell on him in the form of swiftly moving spotlights. Then someone slammed a glass down. I guess I was looking in the wrong place. I turned to the left and then to the right. Nan caught my face in her long hand and aimed it straight ahead.

The white moths I had seen swarming out of his ear had now formed themselves into the shape of a skeleton. The jaws of the skull opened. "Pitchblende," it said.

"Turn on the lights!" someone begged. A chair was knocked over. Someone bumped into someone else and cursed. Nan stood up, dragging me out of my chair. The glowing bones drifted toward us. But now their shape changed. They weren't bones piled on bones anymore. It was a circle of moths.

"I'm dreaming on my feet," Louis said, but his voice wasn't coming from anywhere near the moths.

Nan jerked me to one side as the moths came closer, but it was too late to avoid them. We were in them, passing through them. It was like passing through an electrical portal of some kind that took you from one place to another. I felt the hair on my head move.

Nan and I were running, hand in hand, over chairs and tables, over the bar, over brick walls and alleys and parked cars until we were nowhere near Lucky's or town but in a big, grassy, sunblown field, not scared but *eager*, not escaping but *finding*.

We were young. I saw how beautiful she had been, and I felt my own young strength as we loped across that meadow, kicking the heads off dandelions, the bees thick and busy, the cottonwoods at the meadow's end leaning pleasurefully against the perfumed breeze. "Keep going!" I yelled. "Don't stop!"

Leonard raised the shades and switched on the lights. I sipped my muscatel, Nan sipped hers. Louis raised his glass of whiskey and squinted at it. "Whew," he said softly.

"Louis," said some old man with rheumy eyes. "I got this numbness in my foot..."

"No more cures," Louis said. "The world has gone stale. Not the world of trees and rocks and animals, but the world that men have made. We hate it so bad we are itching to blow it up. I didn't go up on that mountain to figure out some new cures. It's useless to get rid of cancer in a man who can't tell the difference between the urge to grin and the urge to spit."

The baseball game came on and Leonard turned up the sound. Attention drifted gradually from Louis to the television set.

"Let's take a walk," Louis said to Nan and me. "There's more to tell."

Outside, Louis said in a dreamy way, "I was born with a caul, you know. My mother wouldn't have anything to do with me for a month. She figured it meant I could see and converse with ghosts. She was superstitious." He laughed. We laughed too, but we weren't too sure of what it was we found funny.

We walked up Main Street. The air was thin and cool for midsummer. Out of the corner of my eye I saw Nan shiver. I wondered if she had dreamed of a perfect meadow, felt her strong young legs pounding the grass as the pollen-heavy bees bounced off our bare arms.

"I'm not here," Louis said.

Nan grunted, as if her suspicions had been borne out.

"I'm in that shaft," Louis said. "I'm in that tarp. I could already be dead. Maybe dead for weeks."

Nan let some air hiss out between her teeth.

I felt light as a moonwalker. It seemed that I might float off if a good breeze came up. Some Sunday strollers were out. Louis nodded to them and they nodded back. Louis's nod seemed to say, Let's let bygones be bygones.

I was tingling all over. The atoms of my skin and the atoms of the air were mingling. The sidewalk felt like it was paved with marshmallow. Nan squeezed my arm until it hurt. She nodded at Louis, meaning for me to take a good look.

Although his edges were blurrier than ever, he looked good. I was proud, as I always had been, to be his friend. I was thinking, Isn't it nice that things never really end and what appears to be finished often fools you and more often than not comes back to start all over again with only minor changes for the sake of variety. Louis turned and smiled at me. It was a smile that could make you feel that you'd finally gotten the point after years and years of pretending there wasn't one.

We walked to the far end of Main Street, where the town ends. Then Nan and I, on our own now, turned and drifted slowly back.

From THE VOICE
OF AMERICA
(1991)

M ore people had been blown up or burned to death in 1945 than ever before in history thanks to aerial bombardment. I was eleven years old and in love with aerial bombardment. What could be more elegant than a squadron of B-29s unloading five-hundred-pound bombs or clusters of incendiaries on Tokyo, Nagoya, or Yokohama. My nightly prayer to Jesus included a plea that the war last at least until 1952 so that I could join it. I wanted to be a pilot or bombardier aboard a stratosphere-skimming Superfortress, our first true strategic bomber. So, when VJ Day came on August 14, all my dreams were vaporized in mushroom clouds of despair.

I was out on my ice-cream route in the Oakland suburb of Sobrante Park when victory was declared. My pushcart was full of 7-Eleven ice-milk bars, Fudgesicles, and orange sherbet push-ups but sales were slow. I rang the bells that were wired to the handle of the pushcart hard and loud, but the streets remained empty. Then, as if they had been given a signal, people rushed out of their houses. I gave credit to my energetic bell-ringing. I felt the power of my bells. But they didn't approach

Safe Forever

me. They gathered on their lawns and in their driveways, drinking liquor directly out of bottles. Some were singing and cheering. Men and women kissed each other wildly, and children, infected by the frenzy of the adults, ran in circles, screaming. It was a warm afternoon and there was no reason these people shouldn't have wanted ice cream. I rang my bells at them. I yelled, "Seven-eleven bars! Fudgesicles! Push-ups!" My ears rang from my own clamor.

Two men approached my cart and yanked open the heavy, insulated lid. They reached into the smoking-cold box and helped themselves to boxes of my stock. They started passing out handfuls of Fudgesicles, 7-Eleven bars, and push-ups to the cluster of children that had followed them. I held out my hand for payment, but they ignored me. They reached past my outstretched arm and helped themselves to more of my stock. "Wait!" I said. "You have to pay me!"

"The war's over, buster," one of them said. "The Japs said 'uncle.'"

I tried to grab back a carton of Fudgesicles, but he held it over his head. Women and children began to reach into my cart as if it were their right. "Don't!" I said. "You can't do that!"

"What are you, some kind of war profiteer?" one of the men said. "I got news for you, the war's *over*." He was about twenty-five years old and healthy-looking. Though I was panicky now, wondering how I was going to explain the loss of my stock to my boss and stepfather, Dan Sneed, a calmer part of my mind wondered why this man wasn't in uniform. Why weren't *all* these men in uniform? Dan Sneed was 4-F. What excused them?

I guess the question was visible in my eyes. It made him nasty. "Put a smile on your kisser," he said. "This is the happiest day of your life. Or maybe you're a Jap-lover."

He took my pushcart and wheeled it away from me at a fast trot. When he made a severe turn, he dumped it. The rest of my stock, along with several steaming blocks of dry ice, shot into the street. The children swarmed on it, screaming happily. Then someone came up behind me and untied the strings of my change apron. All my quarters, dimes, and nickels fell around my feet. I dropped to my hands and knees to retrieve them, but I had to compete with other children and a few adults.

I was paralyzed by defeat. I sat on the curb. After the money and ice cream were gone, the crowd moved away from me. I righted my cart and wheeled it back the way I came, my bells hanging silent.

An elderly woman who lived a few houses from ours tried to buy a 7-Eleven from me. I told her I was sold out. She put her dime back into her change purse. "You be *sure* to pray thanks for our atom bombers," she said as if scolding me for taking victory over Japan for granted.

"I will, ma'am," I lied. I felt no gratitude. God had not granted my prayer that the war go on for another seven years. Why should I be thankful for early victory?

"Many won't have to go now," the woman said. "Many will be safe forever."

She looked at the closed lid of my pushcart and sniffed. "Sold out already?" she said. "That seems unlikely."

I pushed my cart away from her.

"You remember to pray thanks," she said. "Your mother might have lost you to the war, save for our bomb."

"I know," I said gloomily.

The house was empty. Mother and Dan Sneed were still at work. I fixed myself a bacon and American cheese sandwich and listened to my radio programs. Terry and the Pirates were still fighting Japs somewhere in Burma. Jungle Jim was still tracking Nazi agents in a South American rain forest. Superman had located Hitler's secret weapon that would have guaranteed a German victory and was carrying it into outer space where it could be disarmed safely. It was all anticlimactic. The war was a dead issue.

I switched off the radio and carried my plate back into the kitchen. That's when I saw Mother's note, taped to the icebox. "Charlie, put the roast in the oven at 3:30. 300°. Boil ten spuds. Wash some lettuce. Shell peas. Set up the bar. Company tonight." It was almost 4:00. I'd been doing all the cooking since Mother had been hired as a welder at the Kaiser shipyards up in Richmond. Dan Sneed worked until dark, managing twelve pushcart boys as well as operating his own ice-cream truck in the Piedmont and Emeryville areas. He wore an all-white uniform. The jacket had a "Mr. 7-Eleven!" patch stitched over the left breast pocket. I put the bloody rolled rib roast into the oven and turned on the gas. After I rinsed the lettuce and shelled the peas, I carried the card table out into the living room and covered it with a white tablecloth. I took Dan Sneed's stock of liquor out of a kitchen cabinet and set the bottles in a neat row on the card table. I set a row of drink glasses in front of the bottles. Later, I would chip enough ice from the twenty-five-pound block in the icebox to fill the pewter bucket. I rechecked Mother's instructions to make sure I hadn't forgotten anything, then went back to the bar and poured myself enough sloe gin to darken my tongue. A thread of fire tickled my throat. "Banzai!" I yelled, holding my glass high. "Take that, Jap!" I yelled, making ack-ack sounds between my teeth.

I went out to the garage, light-headed, to visit my B-25. It was spread out on the workbench, half finished. It had been the hardest model I'd ever attempted to build. I knew I would not finish it now. A freewheeling sense of despair overcame me. The B-25 Mitchell was the first bomber to strike at the heart of Japan, back in 1942. But now it was ancient history, just as the war itself would soon be. Next to the B-29 and its atomic bomb, the Mitchell was as dated as the Wright brothers' "flyer."

The two Olson gasoline engines that would have powered my B-25 sat in their mounts, bolted to the workbench. I primed one of them with a little gas, connected the spark-plug wire to the big Eveready dry-cell battery, and spun the prop. The little engine sputtered, then caught, instantly filling the garage and neighborhood with a high-pitched roar. I opened the needle-valve throttle all the way, my mind happily saturated with noise. A haze of pale smoke hung in the garage in layers. I filled my lungs with it. Burning gasoline was one of my favorite aromas. I bent down to the exhaust port, mindful of the invisible propeller, and sucked fumes up my nose. A climbing tide of vertigo rocked me back.

The concrete floor of the garage felt like rubber. So did the driveway and sidewalk. I knelt down and ran my hands through the dry August lawn to see if the grass felt rubbery too, but it felt like the weak legs of docile insects. I pulled a gray tuft out of the dry ground and tossed it across the street. Then I went next door to see Darwin Duncan, not my best friend, but convenient.

"You want to go to Hayward?" I asked him.

Darwin was a small boy with an unhealthy yellow glow. His mother was a registered nurse. She kept a bookcase full of medical texts. Darwin and I would often study the *Human Anatomy for Nurses* text when no one was home.

"What for?" Darwin asked suspiciously. He was wearing heavily padded earphones. There was a soldering iron in his hand.

"What do you mean, what for? To go swimming, why else go to Hayward?"

Darwin and I went to the Hayward Plunge at least once a week during the summer. It was a big indoor pool. I'd learned how to swim there, and how to dive. My favorite dive was illegal, but the lifeguard didn't stop you unless you were bothering people with it. You'd spring along the edge of the pool, then dive with a kind of spinning, corkscrew twist. The motion caused your body to auger its way to the bottom. It was frightening because you didn't have control. Hydraulic pressure seized you, applying an uncancelable torque that you had to ride out. You had to see the corkscrew dive to its end. Then, when you hit bottom, you had to figure out which way was up, even though it was obvious. You were disoriented.

But Darwin didn't want to go swimming. He was working on his radios. He was a radio nut. His room looked like a repair shop . Every flat surface, even his bed, was littered with the scavenged parts of old radios. His current project was a nine-tube, four-band superheterodyne. He was a genius, but his parents worried about him. They wanted him to be normal, like me. "Why don't you play baseball, like Charlie?" they'd ask him in my presence. "Charlie, why don't you teach Darwin how to throw a football?" But they were wrong about Darwin. He was probably a better athlete than me. I knew he could beat me in a footrace, at least. He just preferred to work out technical problems in the privacy of his cluttered bedroom.

His room was hazy with solder smoke. I liked the smell of solder smoke, too. Not as much as the smell of exhaust fumes, but the nose-pinching, acrid taste of hot solder had its appeal. It was like sour incense. I cleared a spot on Darwin's bed and sat down to watch him work. He slid a thin screwdriver into a tangle of multicolored wires to make an adjustment of some kind. "I'm aligning the intermediate frequency amplifiers," he said. Darwin was a year older than me and had skipped the fifth grade.

Human Anatomy for Nurses was shoved under his night table. I picked it up and thumbed it open to the section on Human Reproduction. The illustration of a woman lying on her back with her legs up and thighs held wide always made my heart lurch. This reaction was instantaneous and reliable. Then my mouth would go dry, and if I swallowed, my throat would click. All her parts, interior and exterior, were flagged with Latin labels. In my bed at night, after my routine prayers, I would whisper the forbidden Latin names as if I were preparing myself for some dark, subterranean priesthood. The pages of this section of the book were greasy with use. I thumbed ahead to the cutaway view of a tumescent penis fully encased by a vagina. My throat clicked loud enough to be heard, but Darwin didn't look up from his delicate adjustments. I'd seen this drawing a thousand times, but the red machinery that allowed human beings to repeat themselves endlessly down the centuries made my palms sweat.

Darwin handed me the earphones. "This is London, England," he said casually. "Loud and clear, with some selective fading."

I put the earphones on. Behind a roar that sounded like a waterfall, I heard two comedians exchange quips about Adolf Hitler as if he were still alive and subject to the sting of ridicule. They were hanging on to the war, too.

When I went home, Mother had dinner on the table. "Where have you been, Charlie?" she asked.

"Darwin's," I said.

"Dan's not too thrilled with you."

I went into the front room. Dan Sneed and a lanky WAVE were drinking highballs. I started to tell him that the loss of my stock wasn't my fault, but he spoke first. "You didn't chip any ice, Charlie. How am I supposed to make drinks for our guest if there isn't any ice?"

"I'm sorry, Dan," I said. "I forgot."

"You forgot," he said. He leaned down to get a good look at me. "Your blackheads are coming back again," he said. He was a tall, narrow-shouldered man with thin brown hair combed straight back. "Use the washcloth on your face, Charlie."

"Don't be too hard on him, Dan," said the WAVE. "He's got beautiful manners. He's got the manners of an officer and gentleman." She touched my cheek with her open hand. Her hand was damp and chilly. She had a long, melancholy face, but her eyes were bright and fun-loving. I decided to tell Dan later about what had happened on my route. Nothing could be done about it now anyway.

I went to sleep that night trying to picture the secret Latin parts of the WAVE, but I had trouble getting past her crisp blue uniform, which I admired extravagantly. The next morning, I found that uniform strewn down the length of the hallway, as if she had undressed on the run. Mother and Dan's bedroom door was not completely shut. I pushed it open an inch. The lanky WAVE was in bed with them. She saw me. She sat up and stretched, the sheet falling away from her breasts. I ducked, as if from a wild pitch. "Wait up, Charlie," she said. She made a halfhearted effort to pull the sheet up. *Ampulla, areola, adipose tissue, epithelium*, I thought. "How about starting the coffee, kiddo?"

"Yes, ma'am," I whispered. Mother and Dan Sneed were still asleep on either side of the tall WAVE.

I made the coffee, then started some bacon frying. I broke six eggs into a bowl and whipped them until they were foamy. Then I collected the full ashtrays and drink glasses from the living room and brought them into the kitchen. I dumped the ashtrays into the garbage, then put the glasses in soapy water to soak. I laid six slices of bread on a cookie sheet and put them under the broiler. When she came out, all made up and in her uniform, breakfast was ready.

"You run a right ship, Charlie," she said. "But I don't know if I can deal with all this." She lit a cigarette and blew smoke out one side of her mouth, away from the food. "We drank a bit last night." She sipped her coffee, but did not touch the food.

While she smoked cigarettes and drank coffee, I ate. Her breasts were large and slung low. I made myself see them through the fabric of her uniform, the dark pink *areolae*, the abrupt nipples.

She shoved her plate across the table. "Here," she said. "You're a growing boy. You've got room for this." When she yawned, the low breasts rose, straining the buttons of her tunic.

I walked her to the bus stop on East 14th Street. She worked at the Alameda Naval Air Station. She said she was two hours late. "Not that it matters," she added. "Nobody but the fanatics are going to report on time today. Ask your folks."

We waited together for the bus. She sat like a man, her legs stretched out in front of her, crossed at the ankles, her arms resting on the back of the bench. A cigarette dangled from her full lips. "I'm from Iowa, Charlie," she said. She stared into the distance as if she could see cornfields. "Christ. Iowa. If they think I'm coming back to Dubuque after working in the Bay Area for two years, they've got another think coming. This is paradise, for my money."

The bus came. We stood up together. She straightened her uniform and crushed her cigarette out on the pavement. She shook my hand. "You're a solid citizen, Chas," she said. She pulled me close and hugged me, her chest pillowing my face.

On my way home I bought a twenty-five-pound block of ice from Mr. Salas, who ran the ice dispenser. Mr. Salas didn't speak English, but he was in a joyful mood. He cupped his hands in front of him, then threw them upward. "Boom!" he said, shaping the air between us into a mushroom cloud. I smiled because he expected me to, and he patted and tousled my hair.

It was the job I hated most—carrying a block of ice home. Mr. Salas had tied twine around it so that I could carry it, but the twine cut into my fingers and I had to set the block down on the sidewalk every so often, and its awkward weight made the muscles in my arms burn. Now that the war was over, we would be able to get a refrigerator. The atom bomb had made that possible. The first time I saw a photo of that mushroom cloud, I thought of Aladdin's lamp and the genie that rose out of it as smoke. Because of that cloud of magical smoke, we would have all the things that were impossible to have during the war. I realized I should be thankful, and I prayed my thanks that night, just as the old woman had suggested, but my heart wasn't in it. Mid-prayer I lost the drift and wandered into dreams of combat: P-47 Thunderbolts strafing German supply trucks, airborne troops engaged in door-to-door combat in French villages, destroyers dumping depth charges on Jap subs. When all my combat scenarios had been exhausted, I watched the lanky WAVE sit up in bed and stretch, her long breasts reaching upward. I fell asleep with the incomplete prayer on my lips and dreamed of refrigerators. I opened one of three that sat in our kitchen and took out a heavy roast. Blood from the roast splashed my feet. I didn't have any clothes on. The WAVE said, "You're an officer and a gentleman, kiddo." She sat at the kitchen table sipping coffee. I asked her what time it was. "It doesn't make any difference," she said. "Yes it does," I said. "No it doesn't," she said. "Not anymore, Chas." The natural melancholy of her face seemed a thing apart, something that could live on, long after she was gone. I ducked away from it.

I felt like I had been asleep for days, but when I woke up, it was only half past midnight. I got dressed and went out to the backyard. There was a short fence between our yard and the Duncans'. I hopped the fence and rapped on Darwin's bedroom window. He opened it and I climbed in. I knew he'd be working on his radio, and he was. His room was hazy with accumulated smoke. His eyes were red. "I'm adding a two-stage RF amplifier," he said. "It'll triple the sensitivity."

I nodded. I couldn't think of anything more boring than working on radios. "Can I get the book?" I asked. He was bent over the upside-down chassis, soldering iron probing the tangle of wires, threads of white smoke curling past his ears. He shrugged.

I tiptoed down the hall. Darwin's parents were asleep in their bedroom. They were both snoring—almost in harmony. I didn't need to turn on the living-room lights. I knew exactly what shelf the book was on and where it was on that shelf. I drew it out of its place slowly with my already damp fingers. It's familiar weight and texture excited me.

I cleared a spot on Darwin's bed, and the book fell open to the well-visited pages on Human Reproduction. Even though I had seen those illustrations a hundred times, the sexual architecture of human beings retained its power over me. The scrupulously detailed perineum, the seat of mystery, the dark valley between the columnar cliffs of the thighs, always made me catch my breath. In the same way, years later, the Grand Canyon would make me dizzy with the belief that surprise and whim ruled the visible world.

The clicking of my throat exasperated Darwin. He unplugged his soldering iron and sat on the bed next to me. "Why don't you look at something else for a change?" he said.

"What for?" I asked.

He took the book and thumbed through it. "The side view of the skull looks like Africa," he said, holding up a red, white, and blue illustration. "The mandible goes from the Congo River to Cape Town. The parietal bones are the Sahara desert." He turned pages. "The heart looks like Africa, too," he said. "The bulge of the left atrium looks like Egypt."

Darwin could be as boring as his radios. I grabbed the book away from him. It fell open to the posterior view of the external genitalia of the female. We studied the layers of complexity in silence.

"It looks like a church," I said.

Darwin often boasted about being an atheist, but his parents were religious. He hit me on the shoulder. I dropped the book and it walloped the floor. We held our breaths, but the harmonious snoring from his parents' bedroom didn't pause. "You want to see Vicki Zebard?" I said.

He shrugged. "Sure," he said indifferently, as if I'd asked him if he wanted to go to Hayward.

The Zebards lived on the last street of the development. The field behind their house was staked for a hundred new homes. With commando stealth, we crept up to the dark house. "Maybe it's too late," I said, my cowardice beginning to assert itself.

"It doesn't matter what time it is, stupid," Darwin said.

I knew that, of course. All we had to do was tap on her window. It made no difference that it was nearly 2:00 A.M. I groped in the dirt for a small stone. I heard my blood billow past my ears. I was breathing hard but not hard enough to keep up with my accelerating heart. I felt dizzy. Darwin took the stone from me. He lobbed it against Vicki's window. The light came on after the third stone almost cracked the pane. The blind rose slowly, and there was Vicki Zebard. She peered out at us. She held a hand up to her eyes, as if to shade them from the dark. Then she yawned, or pretended to yawn. She sat down on her bed and lit a cigarette, legs crossed, nightgown hiked up to her thighs. She seemed oblivious of us, lost in her own thoughts. We hopped around in the dirt below her window without making a sound. "Do it, do it," Darwin hissed. She enjoyed torturing us. Finally she stood up. She raised her nightgown over her head, very slowly, in one-inch increments. Vicki had just turned thirteen. She was a heavy girl no one really liked. She walked to school alone, and she was always alone on the playground, unless someone wanted to torment her a little. She picked up her cigarette and paced back and forth in front of the window, her large, flaccid breasts opulent in the dull light from her bed lamp. To enhance the idea that she was unconscious of us, she talked to herself. She poked a finger into her cheek thoughtfully, as if stumped about something. She'd cock her head to the left and then to the right. Her public hair was dark and powerful, fully adult, rising almost to her navel. Darwin was still hopping silently, but I was partially paralyzed. When she pulled down her shade, Darwin jumped on me. We rolled around in the dirt for a while, in a kind of celebration. Then we had a footrace home, Darwin beating me by a full block.

The darkened neighborhood seemed strange to me. Did I actually live here? Did anyone actually live here? Bats flitted around the streetlights, eating millers. How strange the world was, how beautiful. I didn't feel so bad about the war being over. But I wondered, what's going to happen next, and could I bear to wait for it?

"Pudenda!" Darwin yelled.

"Mammaries!" I responded.

"Infrapubic ramus!" Darwin screamed.

"Sphincter ani externus!" I yodeled.

Like medieval monks gone berserk, we screamed the Latin names of the lower anatomy until lights began to come on in the dark little houses.

The next day was the hottest day of the year. I sold out early and came home, my change apron bulging with silver. I went to my room and stacked and counted my gross earnings, then subtracted my profit. I rolled the nickels, dimes, and quarters into paper wrappers. Dan Sneed was in Emeryville and wouldn't be back for several hours to restock my pushcart. I had an afternoon to kill. my mother was still working at Kaiser, but now that the war was over, there was no need for Liberty ships. She expected her layoff notice any day now. Then she'd be a normal housewife again, she said. The world was going to be normal again. I didn't remember what normal was since I was only five or six when the war began to change everything.

The elation I felt the night before didn't have staying power. I made a pitcher of Kool-Aid and filled it with chopped ice. I carried the pitcher and a glass out to the garage. I picked up the skeletal wings and the half-finished fuselage of the B-25 and crushed them into a soft wad of balsa wood and tissue paper. Then I started one of the Olsons and breathed exhaust fumes until my depression was gradually replaced by a brain-spinning giddiness.

Darwin came over, attracted by the screaming Olson. "Let's go swimming!" he yelled.

I took one last lung-sweetening breath of burned gas and pulled the sparkplug wire loose. "Okay," I said.

"Not the Plunge, though," Darwin said. "The bay."

The Hayward Plunge in hot weather was like a greenhouse. It sapped your energy. After swimming across the pool a few times you felt dead. You felt like you were sweating even under water. And afterward you felt waterlogged.

We walked to San Leandro Bay. It was a place forbidden to swimmers because raw sewage from south Oakland and San Leandro was pumped directly into the water. Parents tried to keep their kids away from all swimming areas in that big polio year of 1945, believing that the virus was carried and spread by water. San Leandro Bay was especially feared. But the fear of parents was an abstract thing, an irrelevancy, like the rusted BB-pocked signs that warned against trespass or dumping, or commanded, "No Swimming."

The beach was lumpy with seaweed and garbage. Broken bottles gleamed in the oily sand. Small waves lapped at a mossy mattress someone had tried to launch. None of this seemed ugly or inappropriate to us. It was San Leandro Bay.

There was no one else around, so we stripped. Darwin sprinted into the half-hearted waves screaming. I followed him. The water was warm and thick, like soup. It stank, but it was not like the eye-burning chlorine stink of the Plunge. I loved swimming here, in salt water, because you could not sink. The heavy water made you buoyant and you felt you would stay afloat even if you dozed off.

Darwin was floating on his back, his small erection periscoping the brown water. "Penile distension," he yelled.

"Corpus spongiosum!" I screamed, sending up a periscope of my own.

We swam for hours, then walked home sunburned, salt-crusted, and weak. I sat on a curb next to an idling delivery van and breathed its exhaust. Darwin sat next to me. He wasn't a habitual sniffer of exhaust fumes like me, but he didn't mind them. School would begin in three weeks. Darwin had already graduated from Stonehurst elementary school and was attending junior high, and he hated it. He looked like a fifth-grader. The big eighth- and ninth-graders picked on him mercilessly. I hated the idea of going back to Stonehurst, even though I'd be a sixth-grader, loaded with seniority. I had squandered summer. And now that the war was over, school was bound to be more boring than ever.

The last Saturday before school started, Darwin and I went to Emeryville, where the Oakland baseball stadium was, to watch the Oaks play the hated San Francisco Seals. We bought tickets for the right-field bleachers, the cheapest seats in the park. We wanted to be out there in right, where the left-handed sluggers would hit their homers. I brought two gloves—one for Darwin—anticipating free baseballs.

It was a dull game for seven innings. The Oaks hadn't hit a ball out of the infield. My personal hero, Les Scarsella, the aging slugger who had hit .300 for the Boston Braves back in 1940, had struck out once and had popped out to shortstop. He was closing in on another forty-home-run season, so my hopes were high. Gene Bearden, ace of the Oakland pitching staff, had held the Seals to four hits and one run, a line-drive homer by their powerful first baseman, Ferris Fain. Then, in the bottom of the seventh, Scarsella slapped at a three-and-oh pitch and drove it over the center-field scoreboard, with Wally Westlake on second. Darwin and I went crazy, pounding each other with our gloves and screaming out the Latin names for the sexual apparatus. In the top of the ninth, though, Ferris Fain, with Hugh Luby on first, caught a hanging curveball and drove it deep to right. It was a line drive all the way, still climbing as it passed over our heads and out of the park. We'd been calling him names at the top of our lungs—mons pubis! ductus deferens! labium majorum!—and, as if he'd heard and understood and wanted sweet revenge, he straightened out Bearden's sloppy curveball and laced it into the streets of Emeryville.

The weak end of the lineup came up in the bottom of the ninth and the game ended on three dribbling ground balls, all to Hugh Luby, the Seals' great second baseman.

We rode the bus home depressed. We both felt a little queasy from all the hot dogs we'd eaten. Darwin looked more sallow than usual. A glaze of sweat made his face shine. He complained of a sore neck. "I'm going to puke," he said.

"Wait till you get home," I said.

He stepped between two parked cars and vomited. Hearing someone vomit always made me want to vomit, too, and so I kept walking until I couldn't hear him. When he caught up to me, he said, "I don't feel so hot."

"It was all those hot dogs," I said.

"No, I think it's the flu."

We walked the rest of the way without talking. When I opened the front door of our house, I heard arguing. There was a man I didn't know sitting at the kitchen table. He was short and nearly bald, but he had thick, muscular wrists and forearms. His forearms were tattooed with American flags. He was sipping from a bottle of beer. Mother and this man had been drinking for a while. "I'm going to celebrate!" Mother said, smiling viciously at Dan.

"Celebrate *what?*" Dan said. "Unemployment?"

"Look here," said the man at the table. "I don't think I want to get into this."

"Shut up, Weldon," Mother said. "You're an invited guest. I'm going to make you supper. I invited Weldon for supper. He was laid off today, too. I don't see why he can't have supper. We're going to enjoy ourselves."

"Looks like you've already been enjoying yourself," Dan said. Dan, still in his whites, had just returned form his Piedmont route.

Mother threw a dishrag at him. It hit the window, then draped itself over the curtain rod. Dan lit a cigarette and blew smoke thoughtfully at the seated man. Then he saw me in the doorway. "I need to look at your books, Charlie," he said. "You're running short. What are you doing, giving away ice cream?"

I hadn't told him about my VJ Day disaster yet. I shrugged and went to my room. He followed me. "I think you owe me thirty dollars, Charlie," he said. I had a mason jar full of dollar bills and another one full of change on a shelf in my closet. I took the bills down and counted out the money I owed him. He took the bills and stuffed them into his wallet. But that wasn't the end of it. He looked at me for a while, studying my face. "Stay put," he said. He went out. When he came back he had his Vacutex. "I told you a thousand times to use a washcloth on your face. You can't be meeting the public with blackheads all over your face. Blackheads and ice cream don't mix." He'd ordered the Vacutex from an ad he saw in *Popular Science*. It was a syringe that sucked blackheads into it. I hated the thing. It was painful and it didn't work.

Dan pushed me into my chair. He cupped the back of my head in his left hand and applied the Vacutex to my face. The tip of the Vacutex was hollow. He pressed it on a blackhead, then drew back on the syringe. Supposedly the blackhead was lifted out of my face and sucked into the body of the syringe. It didn't work, but Dan Sneed believed in it anyway. He believed that if he pushed it harder into my face, the blackhead would eventually loosen its grip When he gave up, my blackheads were haloed with bright red circles.

I washed my face in cold water, then went out to the kitchen to see if Mother was really going to make supper. She was sitting on Weldon's lap. Dan Sneed was leaning against the sink counter, looking forlorn. "We're going to San Francisco," Mother said. "We're going to the Top of the Mark to celebrate. Vaughn Monroe is playing there." She gave Weldon a sloppy kiss. Weldon turned bright red and tried to show Dan Sneed a "no harm done" smile, but Dan was staring at the wallpaper.

I went back to my room and took a few dollars out of my money jar. There was an Abbott and Costello movie playing at the Del Mar Theater in San Leandro. I went next door to see if Darwin was feeling good enough to go with me, but his mother said he was running a temperature. She looked at me suspiciously, as if I had something to do with Darwin's illness. "Did you boys go swimming in the bay?" she asked. She was a huge woman, tall and thick.

"No, ma'am," I said. "Just the Hayward Plunge."

She squinted at me. "Do you have the measles?"

I touched my still-smarting face. "No, ma'am. My stepfather squeezed some blackheads."

"You shouldn't squeeze them. All you need to do, wash twice a day with soap and water."

I went to the movie alone. I loved the Del Mar Theater. It had a huge photograph of Harold Peary on the billboard. Harold Peary was a Portuguese actor who played the Great Gildersleeve on the radio. He was from San Leandro and the entire town was proud of his success.

Darwin had polio. I visited him once in the Oakland Children's Hospital. He was in a long white room that had a dozen iron lungs in it. The breathing sound of the twelve iron lungs was eerie. The lungs were silver canisters about seven feet long. The paralyzed children were lying on their backs inside the canisters. Only their heads were outside the lungs. I sat next to Darwin and looked at his face in the mirror that was placed at an angle directly above him. The mirror allowed you to sit down and talk face-to-face to the person in the lung. The trouble was, the person in the iron lung could only talk when the machine had allowed his paralyzed lungs to draw enough air, but the machine was slow. I asked Darwin how he was feeling, and the machine would click and sigh and then Darwin answered, "Not too good." I wanted to cheer him up, but it didn't seem possible.

"How's your transversus perinei profundus?" I said.

A nurse making an adjustment on the iron lung next to Darwin's turned to look at me.

Darwin's machine clicked and sighed. His face in the mirror was expressionless. "How's your clitoris?" Darwin asked. The nurse raised an eyebrow and shook her head at us. Darwin closed his eyes and when I spoke to him again he didn't answer. He'd fallen asleep.

Shortly after school started, Dan Sneed left home for a job in Fort Worth, Texas. I wasn't sure if Mother and I were supposed to join him later or not. Mother found a job in an Oakland department store demonstrating yo-yos, which had become a postwar fad. It didn't pay nearly as much as her welding job, but it was all she could get. The job market, now that the defense plants were idle, was depressed. A man moved in with us. His name was Mel Sprinkle. He'd worked at the Kaiser shipyard, too, and had yet to find another job that suited him. He made me nervous. He hung around the house most of the day, reading the newspaper and making phone calls. "There's not much work for a man like me," he'd say. I took that to mean either that he was overqualified for most of the jobs he saw advertised or that his skills were rare and generally unappreciated. He was muscular and athletic-looking and he ate everything I cooked, but he didn't seem to have much energy. He wore one of Dan Sneed's old bathrobes around the house while he drank coffee and studied the want ads.

Now that Dan Sneed was gone, I was out of work, too. I hated hanging around the house with Mel Sprinkle, and so I spent afternoons and weekends out in the garage or wandering through the neighborhood, watching work crews frame new houses in the bare fields next to Sobrante Park.

On the Sunday before Thanksgiving, I went to an air show at the Oakland airport. The Army Air Corps's first jet fighter, the Bell P-59 Air Comet, was the star of the show. It flew circles around the heavy, slow-moving fighter planes of World War Two. It was a point on the horizon, coming at you, making no sound. Then it was right in your face, fifty feet over the field, a silent flash of silver followed by its own slow thunder. One by one, the outclassed piston-powered fighters landed, clearing the sky for the future. They taxied to their hangars in an embarrassing flourish of waddling turns as they exercised their obsolete maneuverability. Quaint propwash made skirts billow and hats fly while the Air Comet stood on the fire-belching nozzles of its twin jet turbines and climbed vertically into complete invisibility. The crowd, faces painfully upturned to the zenith, made no sound.

The week Darwin came home from the hospital—on crutches with steel braces holding his useless legs rigid—I broke my arm in two places. I jumped a curb on my way home from school and lost control of my bike. I came down hard in the middle of a busy lane of traffic. A woman screeched her brakes to avoid running over me, then pulled her car over to the curb. She saw my bent arm and told me to get into the car. She picked up my bike and put it into the backseat. It was a bad break, a compound fracture. A shaggy tip of bone peeked through the ripped skin. I gave the woman directions to my house, while marveling at the fragile architecture of human anatomy.

"You're a calm one, aren't you?" she said. "Are you in pain?"

I looked at my wrecked arm. It fell away from itself midway between wrist and elbow, making a perfect Z. *Ulna, radius*, I thought. "No, ma'am," I said. I was insulated from pain by shock. I felt light-headed, as if I'd been breathing gas fumes in the garage. I let my face rest against the cool glass of the window. She drove slowly, in second gear, trying to avoid bumps that might jar my arm. She talked to me as she drove, her soothing voice rich with motherly concern, as I imagined myself in the Plexiglas nose of a B-29, on the one-way mission that would carry me into the rest of my life.

Fred Ocean wrote to his wife, Sara, twice a week—amusing, energetic letters meant as much to cheer himself up as to entertain her. He made the stark Arizona landscape bloom with Disneyesque exaggerations: "It's so desolate out here the red ants look up at me beseechingly when I walk to the post office. They want me to kill them." He described with good-natured cruelty the geriatric midwesterners who came here to Casa del Sol to retire among the scorpions, lizards, and black widows. He assembled the details of the daily skirmishes between their sixteen-year-old daughter, Renata, and his mother. So far it's a bitchy little war of hit-and-run raids and long-range sniping," he wrote. "But it's going to escalate into a full-scale nuclear exchange if we don't get out of here pretty soon." He didn't tell her that his panic attacks had returned full-blown since he and Renata had arrived in Casa del Sol, or that because of them, he'd started drinking again. Nor did he mention the woman in Tucson, Germaine Folger, who had become his de factor drinking partner.

The high spirits he mustered for his letters home did not extend to his daily life. He was exhausted from

Desert Places

being on edge most of the time, anticipating the inevitable snide remark from his mother, Mimi Ocean, and the wild mood swings of his daughter. He felt like a tightrope walker, his mother and daughter sitting on opposite ends of his balancing pole. Renata hated the desert retirement community and begged at least once a day to return to Seattle. "I need *green*," she said. "Nothing's green here. I've got to see a green tree, green grass, green water. I feel like I'm stuck in a million square miles of kitty litter." But he had promised Sara to keep Renata here for at least a month. What had been a close mother-daughter relationship had become a contest of wills, beginning about the time Renata started high school. Renata hated high school and wanted to quit. Both Sara and Fred believed that a month of exile would give Renata the perspective she needed to take stock of her life and to reconsider.

So far the strategy was a failure. The hoped-for tranquilizing effect of the remote desert community did not materialize. The opposite happened. Renata had become more hostile, more headstrong in her poorly thought-out plan for total independence. She wanted to go to work as a gofer for a rock band, eventually breaking into the management side of concert tours—all this on the basis of having talked to one of the Eurythmics for three minutes in a Portland hotel lobby. They had tried to force her back into school, but neither Fred nor Sara— aware of what went on in big-city high schools these days—had the necessary belief in the quality of the education Renata was receiving to give their efforts moral authority. In any case, they would have had to tie her hand and foot and deliver her to the school grounds, but even then she'd eventually walk away, refuse to do the work, or find some other way to defeat them.

Fred's mother hadn't seen Renata for three years. In that time, Renata had grown to adult size. She was five feet ten inches tall, with a strong, wide-shoul-dered build. Her only interest in high school had been the swim team, but that hadn't been sufficient to hold her. Her punk costume and hairstyle—a collection of colored spikes that made her look like an old representation of Miss Liberty—put Mimi Ocean off immediately. "Good Christ, what in the hell did you let her do *that* for?" she asked Fred at the airport in Tucson, well within Renata's hearing. "She looks like she's on leave from some halfway house for mental cases." His mother, who had just had cataract surgery, inspected Renata at close range through special eyeglasses that looked like goggles.

"Luckily," Fred wrote, "Rennie finds the wild life around here interesting. For example, there's a swallow's nest in the entryway to my mother's house. It's tucked up in a corner and has three or four baby swallows in it. Rennie checks on them every morning, fattening them up with toast crumbs. There's a big aggressive roadrunner that passes through the backyard every afternoon. He pokes around for a while before moving on. Rennie calls him Big Bopper."

It struck him that his letters to Sara were a kind of espionage, treasonous to both his mother and his daughter. For that reason, he had to write them late at night in the privacy of his bedroom, or at the local cemetery where his father was buried. Needing an afternoon escape, he'd drive his mother's white Cadillac convertible out to the local "boot hill," the grassless, hardpan graveyard that had once served the adjacent nineteenth-century mining community of Doloroso. Doloroso had been partially restored into a certified "ghost town," the owners of which had their cash registers primed for the permanent tourists of Casa del Sol. "I like this cemetery," Fred wrote. "It's filled with the bones of miners, gunfighters, and Civil War deserters—a worthy cast for a big-budget western. I think of Dad and the other retirees who are buried here as sort of underground tourists, mingling with the local color." He wrote his letter seated on a bench-high stone next to the flat concrete slab that marked his father's grave. His father's slab looked—appropriately, Fred thought—like a section of prestressed concrete used in bridge construction. It was more of a barrier against burrowing animals than a memorial.

Renata hated the cemetery and would not accompany him there, even though it meant that she'd be in the house alone with her grandmother. She liked Doloroso, though, because it had a café, and this was where Renata took most of her meals. She couldn't bear her grandmother's cooking. "Mother is essentially blind," Fred wrote. "All kinds of debris winds up in the food—hair-pins, buttons, even animals. Last night—I swear to God—something crawled out of the paella. It was cricket-size. Rennie and I watched it drag itself across the table trailing a saffron slick. It moved badly, as though it had left a couple of legs back in the casserole pan. Rennie retched, excused herself, plunked down in front of the TV with a can of cashews and a Pepsi."

The stone Fred sat on marked the grave of one Henry Phelps, a man killed in something called "The Arrowhead Mine Disaster of 1912," according to the inscription on the brass plate attached to the front of the stone. He imagined that Phelps and his father would have had common interests—Ivan Ocean had started out as an iron-ore miner in northern Michigan back in the 1920s. The notion that the two men were somehow compatible satisfied a relic curiosity in Fred. Perhaps they were sharing a mild and unharried eternity, trading memories in the closeted earth. Why not? If the Mormons could give their honored dead entire *planets* to rule, why not this simple and unembroidered afterlife for the honorable bones of Henry Phelps and Ivan Ocean?

When Fred wrote his letters in the cemetery, he felt as if he were addressing both his wife and his father. He whispered each word out loud before committing it to paper, even though he knew his father wouldn't appreciate his humor, or, more accurately, the whimsical melancholy in which it was couched. He remembered how his father would sit behind his no-nonsense steel desk, his barrel-like torso erect, glancing at his watch impatiently, only half listening, picking out a phrase now and then to single out as evidence of his son's faulty and perilous grasp of reality. "Life makes no apologies, son," he once said. "And self-pity is the *worst* reaction to hard knocks."

The mottoes of rust-belt capitalism had always been easy to make fun of, but Fred had come to understand that, hokey as they were, these mottoes aptly represented his father's honest strength, his untethered spirit. Ivan Ocean had risen out of the iron-ore mines of northern Michigan to become the owner-manager of Decatur Metal Fasteners, Inc. "Rennie is Dad all over again," Fred wrote, "just as stubborn, just as impatient, hating all forms of dependence, waiting for her chance to cut the ties. No wonder she wants out of high school. Yesterday she called it a 'day-care center with team sports.' Dad quit school when he was fifteen—did you know that? Ran off to Escanaba, lied about his age, got a job in a Negaunee mine, worked his way through Michigan Tech, bought his ticket for the capitalist gravy train. He doesn't know it—" Fred scratched that out and rewrote, "He didn't know it but he was never able to accept discipline, either. He was a wild mustang with frontal lobes. They say character traits leapfrog the generations. Think of the Fords. Henry was the mustang, his son Edsel a sweet old plug—nice guy, but he went swayback under the saddle—but Henry the Second, the grandson, was the mustang reborn. So it is with Rennie, me, and Dad. (Hey, am I leaving you out of this formula, darling? But you've always said that Rennie is one-hundred percent Ocean.) Mother can't see the similarities, but I can, and they are real, even to the physiognomy—the big, peasant build, the tough jaw, the unblinking eyes that both you and I have trouble meeting head-on. I'm the Edsel of the clan, honey, the rageless caretaker, the nice guy with a music box tinkling where there ought to be a snarling dynamo. I'm just the conduit for the genetic fire."

Whoa, he told himself, dropping his writing pad and pocketing his pen. He didn't like the drift of this letter. He didn't like the metaphors, the deft but unconscious switch from witty reportage to dark confession. (He could almost hear his father coax, "Don't stop now, Freddy, you're on the right track. You're headed for a solid dose of reality. Go for it, boy.") "Reality is overrated, Dad," he said out loud. A sudden gust of wind, a dust devil, sucked a plastic rose from the grave of another retiree, carrying it high in a violent spiral. He watched the dust devil vandalize the old graveyard, scattering the unwilted artificial bouquets. It rocked the Cadillac as it crossed the road that paralleled the cemetery and moved toward Doloroso, where it seemed to lose interest, allowing its hoard of fake roses and bits of twigs and litter to settle back to earth.

That night he dreamed of dust devils grown to tornado size. They were coming for him. He drove the Cadillac into the desert, trying to escape, but the engine gradually lost power and finally quit. He put the top up, rolled up the windows, turned on the air conditioner, the tape deck, the radio, but nothing worked for long and the wind chuckled insanely against the pitching car. He woke up sweating, sick to his stomach. He reached for the Rolaids on the night table, then realized that the nausea was from adrenaline and that he wasn't sick but frightened, the fear coming to him disguised as an idea that could be worked out or ignored. He rolled over, pulling the covers up, hoping to slow down his accelerating mind in the bogs of sleep, but the adrenaline kept coming and he began to shake. He got up, moved down the dark hall toward the living room, switched on the lights. His mother kept a stock of gin and tequila in a cabinet against the wall. He took down the gin from the top shelf, poured himself a quiet glassful, drank half of it down. He went out then onto the patio, under a night sky that seemed blistered by a million stars. He sat in a deck chair and took small gulps of gin. "Jesus, Jesus," he said, rocking back and forth.

When he went back into the house, it was nearly dawn. His mother was already up, making coffee. He tried to slip back into his bedroom unnoticed but she saw him and called him into the kitchen. "You're drinking," she said.

"Medicinally," he said, not wanting a lecture or an argument or even permission, but she was a drinker herself, well into her cups early every evening, and did not press it.

"When are you leaving, Freddie?" she said.

"Eleven days," he said—too quickly—and he realized that he'd been marking time.

Without her goggles his mother's eyes seemed unnaturally dark and liquid—nocturnal eyes capable of absorbing more of him than ordinary sight would permit. "Eleven days won't change anything," she said. "Eleven hundred days won't be enough.

"Oh, Mother, come on," he said. "Rennie's not that—"

"Rennie's not the problem, Freddie. *You* are. You're afraid of your own daughter."

"Brilliant," he said, turning away from the black, unfocused eyes.

"Say what you want, it's true. You're afraid of her, afraid she won't love you. But you're fooling yourself, Freddie. Rennie's a whole lot tougher than you are. She's a steam roller and she knows it. As long as you treat her with kid gloves, she's going to walk right over you."

"Fine," he said. "I'll take the belt to her."

His mother sighed. "No you won't. You couldn't. And even if you could, it's far too late. Let her do what she wants. She will anyway." The coffee finished perking, and she poured out two cups. After taking a small, hissing sip, she said, "Freddie, I'd like the two of you to leave. I'd like you to go back to Seattle as soon as you can."

He almost took advantage of this remark. It was an old habit. He put on a wounded look, the phrase he wanted was on his lips, but he saw a tear start out of an old ruined eye and he held back.

"You miss Dad a lot," he said.

"I do," she said. "I really do."

When he went back to his room, Renata was sitting on his bed. "I want to burn down this house," she said.

"You can't," he said. "It's made out of clay. Adobe."

"Then I'll turn the hose on it and dissolve it. Ashes to ashes, mud to mud."

She was actually smiling. She smiled so seldom these days it almost broke his heart. "Brat," he said, slapping her lightly on the thigh.

"I want to go home, Daddy," she said, her voice small, like a remnant of childhood.

"So do I, baby," he said.

He sat next to her on the bed. Renata put her arm around his shoulder. "Daddy," she said. "You're out of your envelope, you know that, don't you?"

"What?" It was hard to keep up with teenage jargon. He wasn't even sure it was jargon, since Rennie tended to invent her own.

"You're over the edge, out of your element," she translated. "You're red-lining, Pop."

"Look, Rennie—"

"I heard you talking to Grandpa yesterday. You were in the bathroom, shaving. I think you're weirding out. Daddy, I want to go home for your sake, too."

"I am surrounded by Wise Women," he wrote later that morning in the cemetery. "I guess I'm either lucky or cursed." He started to cross that sentence out but dropped the pen. Sara had been after him lately to "rethink his situation."

He was in a dead-end job, but it was secure and he liked it. He'd been a technical editor for Boeing for twelve years and he'd reached the ceiling as far as pro-
motions and big salary jumps were concerned. He didn't mind—he liked the job
well enough to excuse himself from the lures of ambition. He had no desire to
climb the corporate ladder. He was paid decently, he got an annual cost-of-liv-
ing raise, he was well liked, and he had managed to make himself as indispensable to his unit as the man he worked for, maybe more so. He had what all reasonable men wanted: job security—and this long leave of absence bothered him.
Sara thought the time off would make his boss realize just how important he was
to his unit, but Fred was uneasy. His work would pile up or be done poorly by
someone else. But more than that, he missed the job itself. He actually relished
cleaning up the strangled prose of engineers, who, left to their own narrative
devices, could make the operation of a pencil sharpener seem as arcane and as
potentially dangerous as the operation of a breeder reactor. His was a small job
in the great world of jobs, but it was what he wanted. He was content. At forty-
two, life had become pleasantly fixed and unchanging for Fred Ocean.

"You're an old man already," he heard his father say. He could see how his
father must have appeared to the other retirees of Casa del Sol: the big, sturdy,
peasant features, battered but unhurtable. Ivan Ocean: even the name was
strong, suggesting both the Russian masses and the sea. Ocean was a retooling of
a difficult Russian name, Ozhogin, which was a bit too slushy for the parochial
phonetics of American rust-belt English. Ivan Ozhogin, son of Vladimir. Born in
the U.S.A., in postfrontier North Dakota, moved out of his home after knocking
his father and older brother down a flight of stairs, rode the rods to Escanaba,
buried himself in the red rock of iron country, emerged as a man with a slashing,
take-no-prisoners vision of America. He was a happy man, but not a content one.
Never content. The content do not contend. The happy people of this earth are
the fighters, the conquerors, the risk-takers. Fred, lovingly, put a Mexican wedding shirt on his father, white slacks to match, huaraches on his big wide feet. He
saw him tanned Apache brown, saw his white teeth flashing as he shouted, "You
think you've got it made. Let me tell you, you don't deserve what you have. You
don't deserve Rennie or a wife like Sara who only wants you to do your best.
You're going to lose all of it. You'd let the world go to hell and not blink an eye
as long as you were content. Men like you, my boy, can't hold on to anything
except by luck." Even in death his father was full of instructions and warnings.
The trouble with such advice was that it only made sense to those who gave it.
Crazy mustangs did not travel with dollar-a-ride ponies. Advice from his father,
he always believed, was like clothes handed down: you could wear them only if
they fit. His father's instructions fit him like a shroud. "Back off, Dad," he said
gently. He watched his father, as if on a freight elevator, sink down into the hard
ground to resume his reminiscing chats with Henry Phelps, a man more to his liking. Fred picked up his pen and pocketed it.

He drove into Tucson, ostensibly to make reservations for weekend tickets to Seattle. But he didn't drive out to the airport. Instead, he stopped at the Conch, where Germaine Folger would be waiting for him.

"Well, gracious," she said. "Look at you, tiger."

He glanced at himself in the smoky mirror behind the bar. He'd driven in at high speed with the top of the Caddy down. His hair was wild and his eyes were spooky—wide and wind-whipped red. His heart was tripping along at highway speed, and he was very thirsty.

"What's been chasing you, honey?" Germaine said. "A ghost?"

Judging from her cozy slur, Fred knew that she'd been here for a couple of hours already. Germaine was older than he was by at least ten years. She was a tall woman with a doughy but still pretty face. She had a small mouth. Her lips were thin and pouty, like the lips of a child. He liked her looks. He liked the wet brown eyes that seemed to have been evolved specifically for barroom light. And he liked the way an old torch song would send her gaze into the middle distance as if she were revisiting scenes from a bittersweet past. He'd never seen her in sunlight, and he could not imagine her squinting her way across a sun-bright parking lot. She was a barfly. He smiled at the old-fashioned word. She was half ruined but not destitute. She dressed well, her credit was good enough to allow her to run a tab, and the stones in her rings looked genuine. Her husband sold real estate in Scottsdale. He'd made a fine art of keeping his distance from her.

"It's been a hard week, Germaine," he said.

"Could be a trend, baby," she said, patting his hand.

Fred ordered a bourbon and soda. The jukebox in the Conch specialized in ballads from the 1940s. Dick Haymes was singing "All or Nothing at All," saturating the dim air with a dangerous nostalgia. Everyone in the Conch looked on the verge of making a serious, life-upsetting error.

"Maybe you ought to start thinking about heading back to Seattle," Germaine said. "This country can be tough on you webfeet."

"That's for sure," he said. "In fact, that's why I'm in town. To make reservations."

"But you came here first.

"I didn't say I was in a hurry," he said, clinking her glass with his.

She smiled—bravely, he thought, because her eyes seemed resigned to a future measured in hours. She still had the power of her former beauty, and though the reason he was attracted to her was not that simple, he didn't try to find a deeper motive. He'd wanted her strictly as a drinking partner. That was safe; anything beyond that could be avoided.

"Hell, webfoot," she said, recklessly. "Maybe we should say good-bye in style."

He sipped his drink, as if thinking it over.

"I've got to get to the airport," he said.

"The *air*port isn't going anywhere," she said. "Besides, there's a travel agency around the corner from me." She put her hand on his, a proprietary gesture that took away his right of withdrawal. "Listen, Freddie," she said. "We're friends, aren't we? My apartment's a minute away. I think I know what you like."

Fred believed her. He believed that she possibly knew what he liked better than he did himself. She was a student of the small variations that made one man different from another. It accounted for her wrecked life.

"My dad says what I like isn't good for me," he said.

"Then it's time your dad minded his own business, I'd say."

They went outside, where the sunlight instantly betrayed her face. Her eyes tightened to leaky slits, and her chalky skin, blasted by the desert sun, became mottled and rough. In the darkness of the bar she had seemed melancholy and wise, but out here in the harsh light she only looked mournful and perplexed, as if the pain of old abuses was still alive.

He walked her to the parking lot. "I'll follow you," he said, and he did—for five blocks, where they were separated by a traffic light. He saw her pull over on the other side of the intersection to wait for him, but when the light turned green he made a hard right and headed for the airport.

"Well, say it, Pop," he said as he eased the Cadillac onto the freeway.

"There's nothing to say, Freddie. I would have done the same thing. You have to weigh the consequences of your actions, since only you can be responsible for them."

He gave his father a diction and vocabulary in death that he hadn't had in life. It was easier to talk to him that way. The blunt homilies and warnings needed a good technical editor if they were to be taken seriously.

"Did you ever play around, Pop? Did you ever find a woman who knew what you liked?"

It was the sort of personal question ghosts can't answer. Fred found one of Renata's tapes in the glove compartment and plugged it into the deck. The flogging beat, the tortured guitars, and the brainless lyrics eliminated the possibility of further conversation.

At the cemetery the next morning, Fred added a paragraph to the letter he'd been working on the last few days. "You'll probably get this after we're home," he wrote. "But these communiqués from desert places are habit-forming. I'll probably continue writing to you twice a week for the rest of my life. Proximity is our most deceptive enemy, I think. Distance is more than simple geography. Ask Rennie. I'm closer to Dad now than I've ever been, and he's somewhere across the universe. He thinks I'm incorrigible. It's true. But so is he. So is Rennie. We all are. Just like the tarantulas. We've got them, you know, big across as tortillas. Early this morning I escorted one off the premises. He'd done an incorrigibly tarantula thing. You know that nest of cute swallow chicks Rennie's been monitoring? Well, Nature's got no use for cute. The tarantula got them. I found him, after noticing the empty nest, sitting fat as a cat among a litter of darling little feathers. I eased him out of the entryway with a broom. He was so bloated on infant swallow meat he could barely waddle out of there. Then I dutifully swept up all the feathers. I pinned a cute note to the nest: 'Bye-bye, Rennie. We've flown away to become rock-star swallows. Thanks for everything. Wish us luck.' Dad would say, 'No one was ever hurt by a light dose of reality.' My answer to that would make him slap his forehead in disgust. Reality, Dad, is public enemy number one, truth be known."

When Fred got back to the house, it was still early. Rennie was asleep and his mother was sipping warm gin in the bathtub—her arthritis was acting up again—and his father was whispering sharp warnings in his ear. As a concession to all of them, he took the note off the empty swallow's nest and threw it away.

Hart is dead. Cancer got him. He died well. What I mean is, he died pretty much as he lived, without fear or dread, and he died without the sort of high-torque pain or mind-gumming drugs that would have blunted his ability to find interest in the process of dying. We still talk about him in the present tense. "Hart has presence of mind," we say, and "Hart can't tolerate French movies," and "Hart likes his beer freezer-cold." His gray stare, somewhat quizzical due to the tumors thriving near the occipital region of his brain, asks you to be honest: Never say what you don't mean. If in doubt, remember, silence is incorruptible. You can spend half a day with Hart and maybe trade three opinions. But he likes his jokes. He likes the sharp observation that punctures the gassy balloons of hypocrisy, pomp, and self-importance. As a photographer and poet, that's what he's about. And so he can get you in trouble. He's a little guy with a proud chest.

Paraiso: An Elegy

His camera bag, always slung on his shoulder, makes him list ten degrees to port. It makes him walk with a limp.

It began with an omen. We were in Juárez, Christmas 1988, fending off a gang of seasonal pickpockets who had moved into the border town from somewhere in the interior. They circled us like a half-dozen bantamweight boxers, nodding and shrugging, feinting in and dancing back, bumping us, confusing us with large, friendly smiles. Hart pulled out his little Zeiss and started to spend film while our wives, Rocky and Joyce, dealt with the footloose thieves. These wives are tough, friendly women from the bedrock towns of Butte and Anaconda, Montana, respectively. When a quick brown hand slipped into the throat of Rocky's purse, she slapped it away, brisk as a frontier schoolmarm, and my tall, strong-jawed Joyce yanked her purse clear with enough force to start a chain saw. The thieves tap-danced away from the white-knuckled determination of these good-looking *güeras*, with no hard feelings, no need to get righteous. The phrase *No me chinguen, pendejos* was ready on my lips, and I whispered it in rehearsal since I am fluent with set phrases only. And Joyce, who *is* fluent, hissed, "Don't you *ever* say that in this town unless you want to take your gringo whizzer back across the bridge in segments."

Joyce works in a Juárez industrial park, teaching idiomatic, rust-belt American to executives of the *maquiladora* industry who need to travel north. Her company assembles computer components for GM, and pays its workers an average of five dollars a day, which is a full dollar above the Mexican minimum wage. Joyce gets eighteen dollars an hour because she insists on being paid what the job's worth, having come from Anaconda, a town so unionized you can't pour tar on your leaky shed without getting hard stares from the organized roofers. It troubles her that the Tarahumara Indian beggar women on Avenida

Diez y Seis de Septiembre can make twice as much on a good day as a worker in a *maquiladora*. That's why she didn't get hysterical over the pickpockets. Their mostly seasonal earnings are on a puny scale compared to what the foreign-owned *maquiladoras* siphon into their profit margins. If anyone was close to hysteria, it was me (the gringo instinct to protect and prevail knocking at my heart), not the iron-willed women from Montana. My fists were balled up, and my mind was knotted, too, with such off-the-subject irrelevancies as my honor, my male pride. *¡Lárguense a la chingada!* I felt like saying, but I also knew that if I did, things would get serious in a hurry because these thieves from Chihuahua or wherever have a more commanding sense of honor than I do. We gringos might have a more commanding sense of *fair play*, but honor is too abstract to touch off instantaneous grass fires in our blood. It applies to flag and parents and, at one time, to a young man's conduct in the vicinity of decent girls, but it has never functioned as a duty, uncompromising as the survival instinct, to oneself.

And if I did get lucky and scatter them with a few wild punches, then what? The streets were dense with locals who do not think the world of these pale, camera-toting, wisecracking, uninhibited laughers from a thousand miles north of the Río Bravo. And when a nearby *tránsito*—a black-and-tan-uniformed traffic cop, the local version of the *guardia civil*—strolled by to see what was what, speaking the same street Spanish as the purse-snatchers, whose story did I think would be heard? Who did I think would go to jail? This was before Hart's diagnosis, when we were all planning a succession of trips starting with the thrill-a-minute train ride from Ciudad Chihuahua to Creel and on to the Barranca de Cobre, and later in the year, to Puebla and Vera Cruz. "*Que le vaya bien*," Joyce called to the retreating pickpockets. And a smiling thief replied, his Spanish courtly and dignified, "And may it also go equally well for you, lady," Rocky, a former parachute journalist who now teaches Bullshit Detection 101, rolled her black Irish eyes and muttered, "Jesus. Joyce must be campaigning for sainthood. The Bleeding Virgin of the Cutpurse. They wanted to take your MasterCard, honey, not test your Spanish."

We stopped in the Kentucky Club on Avenida Juárez for a round of self-congratulatory margaritas, then crossed back into Texas, purses and wallets intact. We felt generally upbeat. But in the river, on the north bank, we saw a decapitated mule. We hung over the rail, staring at the mud-colored carcass bloating in the silty river, as if this had been the planned high point and ultimate purpose of our tour. Hart said, "Omen, troops." We looked at him. This was one of those moments in life when things get too slippery to catch in a net of words. We looked at each other. An innocence rising up from childhood struck us dumb as Hart attached a long lens to his Zeiss and photographed the headless mule.

2

Joyce and I are on this trip with Hart and Rocky, looking for something in the desert. A kind of comradely spitefulness has made us rowdy and solemnly amused by turns. I guess it is Death we are spiting, though no one comes out and says so. We like each other because we know we are misfits who have found our niche in the friendly halls of universities.

We are western by chance, and remain so by choice. We love cars and rock and roll more than we love fine art and baroque music. We wear this preference on our pearl-buttoned sleeves. We've been antsy from birth: The verb "to go" was the first one we learned to conjugate. We've got Cowboy Junkies in the tape deck and a six-pack of Lone Star balanced on the console between the seats. Drinking and driving is a western birthright. This is Texas, where it's legal to have opened containers in a moving car. This law (known affectionately as the Bubba Law) may be repealed soon, but we're not in a mood to worry about it: the lab report on the biopsies is in and now we all know the worst. Hart has six months, if he's lucky—six months, that is, if the tumors crowding his vertebrae don't break in and vandalize the spinal cord tomorrow or the next day.

Hart has the perfect vehicle for this type of travel. A 1972 Chevy Blazer with the big 350 long-block V-8 throbbing under the hood. The Blazer is a two-ton intimidator. Hart is not into intimidation, but the slender Celicas, Maximas, and Integras that pull into our slipstream don't know that. They tend to keep their distance from the big, rust-brown, generously dented Chevy. Hart and I sit up front, Rocky and Joyce sit in back—a western arrangement not meant to signify the relative status of the sexes. A traveler from New Haven, say, might look into the Blazer and see Hart and me up front in straw hats with beer cans on the dash, and the women eating coffee chews in back, perhaps catch a strain of the Cowboy Junkies' visionary wailing, and think *highway buckaroos and the little women, tsk, tsk*. This is unfair to the Yankees, of course. You might find the same arrangement in a dented Blazer in New Haven. Only in New Haven, I suspect, the highway-buckaroo remark might be justified. Two couples riding this way back there *would* be making a statement, whether they wanted to or not. Turning ourselves into an illustrated idea is the last thing in the world the four of us would do.

We're heading, in our roundabout way, for Tucson, normally a five-hour trek from El Paso, where we live. The sandstorms have raised cubic miles of desert, turning it into coastal fog. Our running lights are on and we've slowed to forty and the wind is making the big Blazer rock and roll. Hart is feeling the strain, having just undergone his first series of radiation treatments, which he found entertaining. ("Star Wars, troops. They levitate you into the center of a big dome where smart machines that know your body better than you do sniff out and then zap the intruders.") I have offered to drive, but no one drives the

Blazer except Hart. He loves this truck as a settler might have loved his big-bore buffalo gun, his horse, or his quarter section of homestead bottomland. And so it's decided: We'll turn off at exit 331, get on U.S. 666, and head for my widowed mother's adobe hacienda in Paraiso, Arizona, where Death has left his stain and dull gloom not long ago.

It is late afternoon when we pull into her driveway, and Mom—Sada—is already in her cups. She's been working all morning on *Storm over the Dragoons*, a six-by-three-foot oil painting, and now is drinking ruby port to unwind. Painting has helped fill in the gaps left by the removal of Lenny Burbek, her husband for the last twenty-six years. Cancer got him, too.

Sada pours wine for us at her kitchen table. The house smells of oil paint, even though her studio is out in the attached garage. "Hart, you look fer shit," she says. Sada, at eight-two, has dispensed with all the social delicacies.

"Fer shit is an improvement over yesterday," Hart says, holding the cup of ruby port but not drinking. The road beers have already given him grief. Alcohol, mixed with the tumor-poisoning chemicals circulating in his system, makes him sick. He's got a tumor in his liver, too, and his liver won't forgive and forget. Hart puts the wine down and takes a picture of Sada. She is a mask of fierce wrinkles and looks more like an old Navajo or Apache squaw than the immigrant Scandinavian that she is. Hart has this theory: The land eventually has its way with us. Live in this desert long enough and sun, wind, sand, and thirsty air will eventually give a native shape to your clay, just as thirty years in Oslo will fade, elasticize, and plump up the austere skin of an Apache. The land works us like a craftsman works maple or oak. Ultimately, the tools and strategies of the craftsman overcome the proud immutability of any hardwood. The land owns us, not vice versa, the current triumph of the capitalist zeitgeist notwithstanding. This is Hart's pet idea. The land owns us and we had better treat it with the proper deference. You can see it in his prints. It is often the text and always the subtext of his poems. "We all need a pet idea," Hart says, "even if it's a stupid one. Even a stupid idea, pursued long enough with enough dedication, so that all its dead ends are discovered, will lead you to the same place as a nifty one." We don't ask Hart what or where that place is. We act like we know, and maybe we almost do. "Besides," Hart says, "*ideas* are ultimately wrong anyway."

Sada fixes her favorite dish that night, linguini with clam sauce, along with big prawns from Puerto Peñasco, down on the Sea of Cortez. Tyrell Lofton, Sada's boyfriend, eats with us. Tyrell is a West Virginia mountain man bent on turning his piece of Paraiso into mountaineer country. He's planted black walnut trees, tulip trees, and a variety of conifers, and has a fecund greenhouse that produces several tons of winter tomatoes. He dreams of building a small still—a genetic mandate. And his house, made of scrap wood, has been half built for twenty years. He's a lean, hard-knuckled seventy-five-year-old widower who also has the weathered Apache look. As we eat, I can tell Hart is planning photography sessions with Tyrell and Sada, for no one we know proves his pet idea better than these two.

After dinner, Sada begins to fidget around. She wants to go dancing. "Have you kids been to the Duck Inn?" she asks coyly. The Duck Inn is a little geezer saloon that caters to the population of Paraiso. "They've got a terrific little band there. The ex-sheriff of Tombstone owns the place. He's also the bandleader."

Sada was a dancer in the Ziegfeld Follies and there is no quit in her. Her bottle-blond hair is startling above her brown, massively grooved, big-cheeked, purse-leather face. "I think we'll pass, Mom," I say.

She scoffs. "Don't be an old fart, sonny, you're not even fifty yet. Come on, we'll have a few laughs."

Tyrell, who always has a twinkle in his faded blue eyes, says, "Goodness me, I don't think they ever had *four* professors in the Duck Inn all at once." Tyrell is quick to spot the potential fun in a given situation, but his remarks are never mean or sour. According to Tyrell, it's okay to take the light view of humanity, since only trees have honest-to-God dignity. It's his pet idea.

"Hart doesn't feel up to it," I say.

"The hell I don't," Hart says, his face drawn, his jaw tight enough to reflect light.

And so we all walk to the bar, surrounded by black night and the thousand unblinking stars of this high desert. Hart amazes me, plodding along, one painful step after another, Rocky hanging on his arm. What amazes me is his placid indifference to the Big Change coming his way, his refusal to let it become the major dramatic event of the season. And then I think of his pet idea, and how the desert might shape a body for pain, too. The Apaches took pain in stride, even sought it out as a measuring stick of their individual worth. The deserts of the Near East have produced prophetic pain-seekers for thousands of years. Jesus, destined for pain, did not pile up annuities or build Alpine retreats to hide himself from it. Blood and sand are the primary colors of the desert. The agonies of crucifixion are storming in Hart's bones and guts, but he won't let us in on this internal secret. I am reminded of Sada's third and last husband, Lenny (another de facto Apache), settling into his easy chair gingerly, as if some wickedness had turned his burly, ex-ironworker's frame into crystal stemware. Lenny and his pal from down the street, also dying of cancer, would sit in their bathrobes and watch the Playboy channel for hours at a time, sampling each other's painkillers. There they were—two old men, all the vigor of their lives sucked into the unappeasable black hole of cancer—denying the sex-hating Intruder by watching the rosy, pile-driving rumps of fornicating youths hour after hour, snacking on chips and *queso*, washing down opiates and tranks with beer, giving a thin cheer now and then to the gymnastic skills of the actors. Lenny died in bed pushing himself up to a sitting position while insisting that he felt much, *much* better.

Paraiso is not exactly a retirement village, though most of the residents are retired. There are a few younger people who commute the ninety miles to Tucson to work. They live here because real estate costs half as much and because the air is about as clean as late-twentieth-century American air can get. A few of these people are in the Duck Inn, dancing and carrying on. Sada knows them all and shouts their names. She backs her straight shots of vodka with draft beer and she has a what-the-hell look in her eyes. Soon she is up on her feet, dancing alone among the younger folk, holding her peasant skirts up over her old hardscrabble knees and yelling, "Yippee, son of a bitch, yippee!" while her carpet slippers flap. Then Tyrell leaps up, his wide pale eyes almost glassy, and does a solo mountaineer buckdance which no one challenges. Rocky is laughing her choppy, nicotine-stained laugh, and Hart, though he's got a white-knuckled grip on his untouched mug of beer, is smiling. Joyce nudges me under the table, whispering, "Hope you feel strong. You and Tyrell are going to have to carry Sada home." And the fiddlers chop down feverishly into their fiddles as if everything now depended on this crazed music.

Later that night, as the coyotes howl and the screech owls make their eerie electronic screams, Joyce and I hear Rocky crying softly through the wall that separates our bedrooms, and under the crying, Hart's laboring snores. Unable to sleep, I get up and prowl the house. It is 3:00 A.M., the hour of the wolf, dead center of night when all of us are naked in our small separate selves. At this hour all the technological wonders and powers of America seem like a feeble dream: the optimistic cities of glass and steel, the superhighways, the elaborate networks of instant communication, and the medical colossus that, for all its precise weapons and collective strategic genius, cannot discourage the barbarous imperialism of a wretched horde of mindless tumors.

The garage light is on. Sada is up, too, working on her big landscape. She doesn't hear me come in, and I watch her drag a broad, paint-fat brush across the base of the Dragoons, the range of mountains where Cochise and his band of righteous Chiricahua warriors held off the U.S. Army for ten years. The mountains are blue-black under the angry flex of muscular storm clouds. All the rage of Sada's eighty-two years is in this canvas, which, the longer I look at it, seems more like a thunderous shout than a painting. "Some painting, Ma," I say.

She whirls around, her leaky Apache eyes burning with a warrior's need to run a spear into the dark gut of the beast.

"It's all I can do now," she says.

3

As we head south toward Douglas and Agua Prieta, I am thinking of the strange girl who lives across the street from Sada. She is sixteen and suffering the pain of boredom and the deeper pain of her own oddness, which will isolate her more than geography ever could. Joyce and Rocky found her lying in the middle of the street, her hair chopped close to her scalp, as if by a hunting knife. Thunderclouds sat on the Dragoons. Joyce thought at first that the girl had been run over, but she was only waiting. I am waiting for something to happen to me, is what she said. Joyce and Rocky left her there, spread-eagled in the road, as the tall clouds moved closer and God's original voice began to rumble with its old no-nonsense authority. Red-tailed hawks lofty as archangels swept down out of the dark sky, choosing among opportunities. Joyce and Rocky decided: Maybe the odd girl was right and was playing her aces now, while she still had them. Maybe we are all waiting for something to happen to us—death or life— but for the girl lying in the street the issue was unclouded by career, marriage, property, and all the other trump cards that must be deferred to before we can clear the slate and move on.

Hart's Blazer pitches and yaws over a rough highway that will take us into the mountains. We have turned onto a narrow, shoulderless road that cuts west into the southern foothills of the Dragoons as we head now for Bisbee instead of Douglas and Agua Prieta. "I've always wanted to see the Lavender Pit," Hart says.

Traveling by whim is touring at its best.

The old houses of Bisbee cling to the sides of the mountains, prayerfully as exhausted climbers. And the streets, angled like derailed trains, work their way up to the highest ledge of dwellings. We walk these steep streets, finding level ground in a doorway now and then to catch our breath. Hart's been taking painkillers and tends to stagger against the unexpectedly oblique tugs of gravity that have made the older buildings lean into each other like amiable drunks. He stops now and then to photograph the odd geometry of a ruined hotel, the grit-pocked face of an old miner, the bands of Japanese tourists who photograph everything in their path as if making a visual record of what will one day be all theirs. The four of us often agree that World War Two is still being fought, that the atomic bombings of Japan merely forced a change in weaponry. After Hiroshima and Nagasaki, the tide turned, and now Japanese samurai in three-piece suits, portfolios in hand, are succeeding where Tojo's fanatic armies failed. Choice Hawaiian beachfront and Rockefeller Center are theirs, the great ever-green forests of Oregon are theirs, and lately, giant cattle ranches in Montana. "I could settle down here," Rocky says. "In one of those shacks on the side of the mountain. This place is like Butte, without Butte's winters."

Rocky prides herself on being realistic. She knows we all understand that she is imagining her life without Hart. The terms are hard, but they always have been. We are alone, we have nothing to sustain us but a few pet ideas fueled by a dram of courage. The rest is a pipe dream. Not that pipe dreams are not nec-essary, we've just got to know the differences. This is Rocky's pet idea, and it's one that she's earned. Ten years ago she survived the removal, from her brain, of a benign plum-sized tumor that made her trade her career in parachute journalism for an academic one.

We are required to be brave. Another pet idea. Also Rocky's.

The Lavender Pit is really two pits, big enough to drop a pair of medium-size cities into. On the way out of Bisbee, after getting half-drunk in the Copper Queen Hotel (Hart managing this with a carefully sipped double shot of mescal), we stop with the tourists to gape at this man-made Grand Canyon. Rocky, who has seen her town, Butte, more or less consumed by such a pit, says, "Sucks, don't it?" to a tourist lady from Arkansas. The tourist lady smiles stiffly and turns her camera on her husband and daughter, who backstep dutifully toward the Cyclone fence that guards the lip of the pit and the thousand-foot drop beyond. The red gouge in the earth looks like a fresh wound, the god-size tumor removed, the lake of blood vacuumed out. A lifeless pond at the bottom of the pit glows like iridescent pus. Oh yes, the planet here is dead. It is deader than the moon, because it was once alive.

"I'm losing my buzz, campers," Rocky says. "Let's clear the fuck out." The lady with the camera gives Rocky a murderous look, protecting the innocence of her child. Rocky grins good-naturedly. "Too late for Miss Manners, hon," she says cryptically, swinging her arm out to indicate the pit, the precarious town, the silent witness of the elderly mountains.

4

We skip Tucson and head back, but the Blazer heats up outside of Deming, New Mexico. We were headed for Palomas, the little Mexican town where General Pershing launched his failed attempt to bring a taste of gringo justice to Pancho Villa, but are now stalled in a gas station where two head-scratching mechanics decide the problem is in the fan clutch and that it will take about an hour and a hundred dollars to fix it. It's hot, over a hundred degrees, and we sit inside the crankcase smell of the garage drinking lukewarm Cokes and watching a TV that seems to have only one color: puce. One of the advertising industry's truly horrifying commercials comes on: "Your marriage will never end. Your children will never grow old. Your pets will never die." It's an ad for a video camcorder, showing a family watching their dead past captured and preserved forever. Whatever unhappiness lies ahead, it cannot touch these moments of joy. Mom kissing Dad in the kitchen; Junior chasing a ball; Rover begging for table scraps—immortal, immutable. Old age, sickness, alienation, divorce: all our little hells defeated by videotape. Paradise secure in a cassette, the grim episodes edited out.

We step back into the heat and stroll up the desert road. To the east, the gray humps of the Florida Mountains wobble in the corrugated air. A man, ragged and barefoot, approaches us. He's so far beyond the liberal dream of salvage and social recycling that he almost seems happy. His weak hair and crosshatched sunburned skin make him look sixty but, his clear blue eyes put him closer to thirty. He is hashed with small cuts, as if he's been climbing through barbed-wire fences all morning. Hart greets him with the head-on nod of equals. Hart and the ragged man are down to common denominators, and they recognize this in each other. The man asks for a cigarette and Hart gives him one, then lights it for him. As the rest of us stroll on, Hart reaches into his camera bag. When Hart has his camera ready, the man begins to shift his weight from left foot to right and back again. The asphalt road is burning hot and I assume the man is moving oddly because his bare feet are giving him trouble, but then he raises his stick-figure arms as if they were big sunny wings and begins to turn in half-circles, first one way, then the other, his cigarette held delicately in his fingertips. He lifts his face up to the sky to let God see him better, and chants a broken-throated nonsense. It's an Indian dance, or his idea of one. "He didn't want any money," Hart says when he rejoins us. "He said all he needs now is smokes. He gave me permission to take his picture, but only while he was doing his atonement dance."

We continue our stroll; the man, who doesn't need an audience, continues his dance. The sun has baked curiosity out of our thoughts. Curiosity is a luxury of the temperate zone. When a shoeless man in a parched land tells you he's doing an atonement dance, you more or less have to accept him at his word. Besides, there's enough to atone for to keep half of humanity dancing shoeless in the desert for a century while the other half lights cigarettes for them.

A few months later I will think of this moment while looking at Hart's photographs matted and framed on our apartment walls, and it will seem as if all of us are moving to the drumbeat of some privately realized dance—the ducking pickpockets with large incongruous smiles under their stony eyes; Sada and Tyrell holding hands shyly but glaring like unyielding Apaches from their mountain stronghold, determined to make their stand; Rocky tugging defiantly on her cigarette as she fixes something at infinity with wide-open eyes that won't blink; even the headless mule floating near the concrete bank of the Rio Grande like an offering to the indifferent northern gods. And Joyce and me, caught looking at each other with slightly shocked expressions, as if on that very day, before the small white church in Palomas, we grasped for the first time that love is possible only because it must end.

—for Zena Beth McGlashan

The Dakemans were untidy degenerates, including their children and pets, according to Mom. "Some people make their pets and children as trashy as they are," she said, her voice hushed discreetly. "It's a well-known fact of life." She used me—in my crisp blue Air Force uniform complete with Expert Marksman medal and Good Conduct ribbon—and our dog, Pershing, as counterexamples. Pershing was a joyless yellow Labrador. We kept him tied to the mulberry tree in our front yard. He never barked or strained at his rope when cars, or people on foot, passed by. He was too intelligent, too dignified, to be ruled by the ordinary chaotic dog emotions. Several of the undisciplined Dakeman dogs would often come over to visit Pershing, and Pershing would allow himself to be sniffed, nipped, teased, and sometimes mounted, without protest, until Mom rapped the window hard enough to make the uninhibited Dakeman mongrels realize her anger. The motley gang of dogs would then chase each other back across the street

An Airman's Goodbye

to their house, which looked like it had been plucked up out of some 1930s dust-bowl state by a tornado and deposited twenty years later in our clean and tidy, middle-class, scrupulously manicured east San Diego neighborhood.

I had just gotten back home after twelve weeks of basic training at Parks Air Force Base outside of Oakland. I had caught the flu in the damp northern California climate and had lost twenty pounds. I went into the Air Force skinny—six feet tall and one hundred and sixty pounds—and now, at one hundred and forty pounds, I looked like I'd just been liberated from a Nazi concentration camp. Still dizzy and weak, I spent my evenings watching TV and listening to Mom whisper complaints, as if she wasn't in her own house and needed to be secretive. She complained about the Dakemans, about the rising price of meat, and, with tight-lipped bitterness, about Dad's boss, who kept him on the road six to eight months a year. I didn't mind listening to her. It was better than listening to a drill instructor scream a long list of your shortcomings into your face. And besides, the tedium I had to put up with was more than compensated for by her abundant, nonstop cooking.

"You need good, clean food, Miles," she said. "I'm sure they fed you nothing but filth at the training base." I ate the equivalent of six meals a day, hoping to put some bulk on my bones. My hair hadn't grown in yet, and when I looked at myself in the full-length mirror, it seemed I was all nose and ears. The thought of looking up my old high school friends depressed me. They used to call me Nose-with-Legs—in just that way, like the title of a painting, as if I were a walking Picasso—and that's exactly what I looked like at one hundred and forty pounds.

Mom's specialty was meat loaf. I could eat six or seven slices of meat loaf at one sitting, along with a huge baked Idaho potato buried in sour cream, two or three steamed vegetables blanketed by a lava of yellow sauce, a quart of milk, and a hot wedge of apple or cherry pie for dessert. I was determined to get back the weight I'd lost before I had to report to Keesler Air Force Base in Biloxi for airborne radar training, and I would eat until a comfortable pain tightened my belly. Mom, a short, fat woman and a big eater herself, was delighted with my performance at the table. She liked her men beefy as lumberjacks. All her brothers had been lumberjacks in the forests of Oregon and northern California—big-bellied, thick-wristed, hearty men with fine personal habits and positive outlooks on life—and Dad was a two-hundred-and-eighty-pound medical-supplies salesman who loved Mom's food so much he'd make small whimpering sounds as he ate. She connected my vulnerability to disease to my scrawniness, and now I was scrawnier than ever. She also saw evidence of a negative outlook in me, but this too, she believed, was a consequence of poor nutrition, the flu, and the influence of the riffraff who, she believed, joined the military only to improve their pathetic circumstances.

In the mornings, after my huge breakfast had time to settle, I'd go down into the basement and lift weights for an hour or so, tape-measure my arms, chest, and legs for signs of new bulk, then come upstairs to shower. I'd watch TV until early afternoon with a plate of meat-loaf or roast-beef sandwiches, then, in the evening, while Mom was getting supper ready, I'd sit out on the front porch and talk to Pershing. Pershing liked to be talked to. He would sit attentively on his haunches and study me with his big liquid eyes as I told him stories about life at Parks Air Force Base.

I was telling Pershing how two DIs had beat up a half-retarded kid for not changing his underwear often enough when a muffled bang from across the street startled us both. This was normal; you expected noises of all sorts from the Dakeman house. A thud, a bang, or a scream, and a door would pop open and dogs or children would come flying out barking, crying, or laughing, or issuing blood threats. Mr. Dakeman was usually out of work, but when he did work, he made good money. I think he was a welder or boilermaker, and he would leave the family for weeks at a time to work in such exotic places as Tulsa, Oklahoma, or Galveston, Texas. Sometimes he was home for half the year or more, and toward the end of one of these forced domestications, he would become short-tempered, often relieving his frustration or boredom with bouts of mind-numbing drinking.

This was one of those stretches of time when Mr. Dakeman was between jobs. The soft explosion I'd heard had to do with Nola Dakeman, his teenaged daughter. Nola came flying out of the house, slamming the door behind her and cursing tearfully. At seventeen, she was a tall, long-armed girl with crisp black hair cut Cleopatra-style, and absolutely no sign of breasts. After she calmed down, she started walking up the street backwards, her hands shoved into her pockets, muttering to herself and scowling at the house she'd left. She was barefoot, and wearing cut-off Levis and a yellow football jersey with the number 99 on it in big blue letters. It belonged to her brother, Eldon, an awkward giant of subnormal intelligence who'd played tackle on the varsity football team in his freshman year solely because of his size. He dropped out of school a few months short of graduation to join the Navy. Eldon Dakeman was the object of a lot of jokes among my friends, none of which were repeated to his face.

When Nola saw me watching her, she turned quickly and started walking normally, and then, as if seized by a better idea, she spun around and waved. I swung my arm in a casual arc. Pershing raised his sad eyebrows expectantly. Nola smiled. "Hey, *Miles*, you're back home," she said.

"Affirmative," I said, military-style.

She crossed the street. She was wearing makeup, a lot of it. The face she had painted on herself was pretty. I never thought of her as pretty—she was just a lanky Dakeman kid across the street—but three months away from home gave me a fresh perspective.

"So, are you a big jet pilot or something?" she asked, putting one long narrow foot on the first step of our porch, stretching her other leg behind her. Her calves rounded out nicely as they flexed; her haunches curved sleek as albino seals out of her skintight cutoffs.

"Negative," I said. "I just finished basic training. I'm going to Mississippi in a few weeks to study at the radar school."

"Eldon's not in the Navy anymore," she said.

"How come?" I asked. All the lights were on in the Dakeman house, even though it was still light outside. I could hear Mr. Dakeman yelling at someone, probably his wife, a slender, gray woman who always seemed distracted, as if she were trying to remember something important and couldn't go on with the next thing she had to do until she recalled it. I saw Mr. Dakeman drag her across the yard once by her wrist, pulling her into the house so hard that she swung from side to side like a kite being yanked out of a windy sky by force.

"He got kicked out," Nola said. "He did something weird, I think."

That didn't surprise me. Once during a scrimmage, Eldon pulled down his pants far enough so that his gigantic, ghostly-white butt was visible to the backfield. Mooning his own backfield was his idea of sophisticated humor. I was the third-string quarterback getting a chance to work with the starting backfield. We were in a T-formation set, and I was too busy staring over the center at a pair of growling linebackers to notice Eldon at his left-tackle spot. When I turned to hand the ball off to Joey Butterfield, the fullback, Joey wasn't there. I got creamed and fumbled the ball. Joey was on his back, laughing hysterically. I was facedown and writhing in the grass, taking late hits even though the wind was knocked out of me and Coach Stuckey was blowing his whistle so hard it hurt my ears even under the insulating pile of bodies. Coach Stuckey made the entire football team take ten laps after scrimmaging for two more hours because of our attitude problem. We wanted to kill Eldon, but at six feet six inches and two hundred an twenty-nine pounds, he was easy to forgive. It was hard to believe all this had happened just the previous fall. High school seemed like a century ago.

"What did he do?" I asked.

"I don't know. He won't say. I think he *wanted* to get kicked out, though. He hated it." She sat down on the first step of the porch, the back of her head level with my knee.

"Too bad," I said, trying to imagine hulking Eldon in a tight-fitting sailor's uniform.

Nola nudged Pershing's flank with her naked toes. "Hi, Pershing," she said. "Hi, you silly old zombie." She put her hand out, and Pershing leaned toward it an inch, his eyes melancholy in the waning light. Then Mom cleared her throat. She'd been at the screen door for a while, listening. ""Miles," she said in that soft, confiding voice. "I have your pork chops ready, dear." I left Nola on the porch talking to Pershing and went inside to eat.

Mom gave me free use of her car, a bright yellow 1950 Hudson Hornet. I loved its low-cut lines and power. When you got into it, you stepped down, as if into a private basement apartment. The upholstery was a dark beige plush and the dashboard held big, generous instruments and a chrome-plated push-button radio. Mom vacuumed it out once a week, as if it were part of her house. The car was clean and it still had a showroom smell to it, even though it was over five years old. Sometimes I'd have her pack a lunch—four sandwiches, pie, thermos full of milk—and I'd drive out to the beach. The surf at LaJolla Shores was perfect for body-surfing, and I'd spend an entire morning swimming out to where the big waves were breaking and then riding them in. I worked up a terrific appetite doing this, and by noon I was ready to eat my four-sandwich lunch. Then I'd drive around town for a while, looking at the sights, taking the long way home—through Balboa Park, past the zoo and Navy hospital, and then out onto the highway that ran through Mission Valley, where I'd open the big Hudson up and watch the red speed indicator dance on 90.

About two weeks before I was scheduled to take the train to Biloxi, Nola Dakeman asked if she could come to the beach with me. In spite of myself, I glanced quickly at the kitchen window of our house, knowing that Mom would be squinting out at us and wondering what Nola Dakeman wanted from her clean-cut airman. I told Nola she was welcome to come, but would she meet me on El Cajon Boulevard—four blocks away—in fifteen minutes. She shrugged—probably guessing what was behind my strategy—and said, "Sure."

In the car, she said, "What's the matter, don't you want your ma to know you're taking me to the beach?"

I glanced over at her, a nervous twitch of a smile trying to sabotage the cool, regulation military expression on my face. She sat close to me, and I realized that she smelled. It was a strong, domestic smell, a mixture of sweat and kitchen odors—the Dakemans were known to fry everything in deep fat: a haze of grease fogged their kitchen day and night—but under this was a rich, tropical smell that was as exotic to me as the air of an equatorial seaport.

By late afternoon I was in love with Nola Dakeman. I didn't realize it until a few days later, but thinking back on our day at the beach I saw that was when it started. After we swam and body-surfed for a few hours, we came back to the blanket to have some lunch. But I couldn't eat more than one sandwich, and even several hours later the undigested sandwich felt like a twelve-pound shot in my stomach as I saw again, in my imagination, her water-beaded face, the long strands of her wet black hair pasted to her neck and shoulders, and her electrifying eyes that seemed able to transfer some of their blue voltage into mine.

I lost my appetite. I began to meet Nola out in the street after dark, and the anticipation of these meetings was so intense that I had a hard time swallowing my supper. Mom thought I was having a relapse of whatever it was I'd caught in basic training. She wanted to call a doctor, but I begged her not to. "I'll be all right, Mom," I said. "All I need is to rest my stomach a little. I think I've been eating too much. Maybe I have a little indigestion."

She regarded me with a wounded look. Cold tears glazed her eyes. "My food does not cause indigestion," she said gravely.

I'd go outside when it was dark and give Pershing some leftovers, and then Nola would come out and stroll across the street. We'd talk casually until Mom left her vigil at the kitchen window to watch one of her favorite TV shows. When she was gone, Nola and I would slip around to the side of the house and kiss each other to exhaustion, each grinding kiss lasting minutes.

I loved her smell and would dream about it at night, and the dreams eventually became erotically specific. Mom began to regard me with a kind of shy disgust when she changed my bedding. I'd never been in love before. I'd gone steady twice in high school, but that was part of an expected routine. Nola and I met every evening at the same time and would wind up necking heavily either in our side yard, between the house and the garage, or in her backyard.

The Dakeman backyard looked like a graveyard for the Industrial Revolution. The shrubless, grassless yard was strewn with the massive hulks of old arc-welding generators, compressors frozen with rust, and gutted prewar cars waiting patiently to be repaired or further cannibalized. Unidentifiable fragments of machines grew out of the sterile soil like exotic rust-colored wildflowers.

We made love for the first time in the rotting, mushroom-sprouting backseat of a prewar Buick that sat wheelless in a far corner of the Dakeman yard. It was a passionate, flailing, short-lived attempt, charged with the sort of desperation people who leap from the windows of burning buildings have, but it was the real thing: sex. "I love you! Oh dammit, I think I love you!" I said, joyous and amazed. I hugged her hard and rocked her from side to side against the mildewed mohair as disturbed moths banged into my face and neck.

She drew back, putting some distance between us. "It'll be way better next time," she said. It was a thin-lipped declaration of superior knowledge. It was my first time, but it was not Nola's. "It won't be such a great big deal for you next time, Miles."

We took a walk through the neighborhood. The nearly full moon transformed lawns and sidewalks into pewter, and the sparse fronds of the date palms that lined the streets seemed like the motionless wings of astonished angels. As we passed the dark windows of my house, I sensed Mom's unhappy, vigilant eyes watching us. I put my arm around Nola's bony shoulders. "You're really kind of okay," Nola said, as if she had heard strong arguments to the contrary. "You remind me of some movie actor."

"I do?" I was thrilled, because just that morning, while studying myself in the bathroom mirror, I'd thought that I had something of Rory Calhoun's looks—a blade-thin but muscular body; sharp, crafty face with a handsome, hawklike nose tilting out of it.

"Who?" I asked. "What actor?"

"Jack Webb," she said.

I tried to hide my disappointment. I laughed. "Dum-da-da-*dum*," I sang, thinking that the stupid *Dragnet* theme would haunt me for the rest of my life.

"You remind *me* of a movie star, too," I said.

This seemed to startle her. "Really?" she said eagerly. "Who? Tell me."

I almost said, because I was still smarting from the Jack Webb comparison, *Lassie*! But then my devotion to her overcame my anger and I quickly blurted out, "Debra Paget." And it was true, she did look like Debra Paget, the beautiful actress who played Indian princesses almost exclusively, except that Debra Paget had a magnificent body with powerful, coppery breasts that looked like they could punch holes into sheet metal. Nola had no breasts at all.

"Oh, you're *crazy*," she said, obviously pleased.

We returned to the prewar Buick after a while and did it again. When we finished, Nola said, "See? That was a thousand percent better than the first time, Miles, wasn't it?" She patted the back of my head. I'd seen her pat Pershing, whom she regarded as an emotional cripple, in this same encouraging way.

"Affirmative," I said.

I began to think that I could not bear to go to Biloxi, Mississippi, and leave Nola Dakeman behind. Life without Nola seemed like no life at all; it seemed like death. Nothing that would happen from now on could excite or motivate me if Nola was not at my side sharing every detail of the experience. I'd be no better than a zombie, sleepwalking through the world. Mom knew something was wrong, and she probably knew what it was, but she couldn't bring herself to discuss it. At best she would whisper abstract complaints, to no particular sympathizer, about the endless housecleaning, laundering, and cooking she had to do for little or no thanks.

In my lovesickness, I had become a slob. My hair was growing back unevenly in scruffy patches, but I wouldn't go to a barber shop. I didn't shave for days at a time. In the mirror, to my disgust—despite my general lack of grooming and military neatness—I began to look more and more like Jack Webb. I twisted what forelocks I had into curls, greasing them and making them hang on my forehead, hoping for a dashing, Rory Calhoun effect, but I only looked like a Picasso caricature of Sergeant Joe Friday. I even started smoking, because I had never seen Jack Webb with a cigarette in his mouth.

"I won't have you leaving filthy cigarettes around my house," Mom said, a new coldness in her voice.

"Roger, wilco," I said, stubbing out my Chesterfield in the kitchen sink.

"My car is full of beach sand," she said.

"Sorry about that," I said.

"Don't sorry-about-that *me*, young man. I want you to clean it out or not use it again. Do you understand me?"

I rolled my eyes toward the ceiling in the now-universal James Dean manner. "Affirmative," I said.

And later, adopting a more conciliatory tone, she said, "Miles, I know you're seeing that... that *skinny* girl. I really don't understand it, not that it's any of my business, but why can't you look up your old high school friends? Why are you avoiding them?"

My old high school friends had their own lives. They had jobs now, or were in the military. We were all light-years removed from the kind of shoulder-punching, smart-mouth, street-loitering way of life we never once saw as limited, shallow, or futureless. I thought of them now, at Mom's insistence, and could not clearly remember their faces.

We were sitting at the kitchen table. Mom slid a wedge of peach pie in front of me. She pressed a scoop of vanilla ice cream into it, and then another. The fatty pink flesh hanging from her arms jiggled with the effort.

"No thanks," I said, pushing it away.

It's hard for pale blue eyes to look tragic, but when they do, it takes your breath away. Tears in unreal abundance flooded down her face. She turned and stumbled out of the kitchen making warbling, wet moans. I was too shocked, for a moment, to move.

Inexplicably, my reaction to Mom's outburst was *rage*. I dumped the pie and ice cream into the sink and stormed out of the house, slamming the door so hard that something inside fell off a wall. I crossed the street to the Dakeman house and knocked on the door. I'd never gone up to the Dakeman front door once in all the years we'd lived across from each other. After at least two minutes, Mr.

Dakeman himself answered. He squinted at me through an alcoholic mist. "She's out," he said. Then he grinned a little. "Come on in and wait, Captain."

We went into the living room, where Mr. Dakeman had been watching the wrestling matches on TV and drinking Seagram's 7. An angry crackle of frying meat came from the kitchen. I could almost feel beads of drifting fat settle on my face. On the TV screen, Lord Blears was stomping the throat of Antonino Rocca, the great acrobatic wrestler from Argentina.

"You want a drink, Captain?" Mr. Dakeman said.

I started to say no, but hesitated a beat too long and Mr. Dakeman filled a spare shot glass to the brim. "Down the hatch," he said, filling his own glass and lifting it to his lips with the grace and efficiency of a journeyman drinker. I raised my glass more cautiously and then leaned forward so that my puckered lips would catch the rim before any whiskey sloshed over it. Mr. Dakeman was a round-bellied, narrow-shouldered man with big, dark-knuckled hands. He smelled of sour, days-old sweat, booze, and fried meat. He had little, intelligent eyes that glinted with a mean-spirited self-satisfaction. Though he seemed to be absorbed in the wrestling match, I knew he was watching me out of the corner of his eye as I sipped from my shot glass. I swallowed all the whiskey then and set the empty glass down. My face got hot. He refilled my glass. I lit a cigarette. Antonino Rocca had recovered from getting his throat stomped and now had Lord Blears trapped in a grapevine twist. Lord Blears, monocle in place and bellowing in pain, tried to hop to the ropes. "Phony limey bastard," Mr. Dakeman said.

"Break his back, Rocca," I said, feeling the whiskey.

"Rocca could do it," Mr. Dakeman said soberly.

We spoke of wrestling and drank as the whiskey-loosened minutes got away from us and the room darkened. At one point, Mrs. Dakeman came in with steaks fried to the density of leather and covered with scorched onions. She set the plates down on the coffee table, one for Mr. Dakeman, one for me. Mr. Dakeman accepted his dinner without acknowledgment. I started to say something, but thought better of disturbing Mrs. Dakeman's perfect distraction.

"Salt," Mr. Dakeman said, his eyes fixed on the TV set, and his wife returned with a shaker of salt, again without apparent expectation of a mutter or nod of thanks from her husband. Rocca had beaten Lord Blears, two falls out of three, and now Gorgeous George was taking on Wild Red Berry in the main event.

"Red Berry's tough," Mr. Dakeman said, a wad of steak in his cheek, "but he's too small. That hairy fruitcake's got forty, fifty pounds on him."

The front door opened and Eldon Dakeman came in. He stood in the half-light of the living room, steel lunch pail dangling at the end of his long arm. He was as big as ever but there was a curvature to his back I didn't remember. He had developed an older man's stoop. Nola had told me that Eldon was now working for Ducommon Steel down in National City, making good money unloading finished steel products from railroad cars.

"Hey, Eldon," I said.

He peered into the dim room, gradually recognizing his father and me sitting on the couch. "Hey, Mike," he said.

"Miles," I said, but Eldon ignored the correction. He had finished socializing. He went into the kitchen and came out gripping a steak in his hand. Then he went off to his room, his footfalls shaking the house. I tried to imagine what Eldon looked like in a sailor uniform. The effort made me smile. He must have seemed dangerously improbable to his superior officers. They must have come to believe that the entire hierarchy of naval command would have been compromised if Eldon was allowed to wear, and distort, the uniform.

"Miles," Mr. Dakeman said, in a musing tone of voice. "Who the Jesus gave you a handle like that, Captain?"

Gorgeous George took something out of his trunks while the referee wasn't looking. He had Wild Red Berry's arms twisted into the ropes. He rubbed the stuff from his trunks into Wild Red's eyes.

"That's cayenne pepper!" Mr. Dakeman said. "That pansy can't win without pulling a stunt like that."

"I don't know who gave it to me," I said.

"What?" Mr. Dakeman said, leaning toward the TV set. Wild Red Berry had just drop-kicked Gorgeous George into a corner post and was now working him over with flying mares. I refilled my shot glass.

"It was probably my mother," I said. "She likes dignified names like Miles and Terence. Jonathan, Carlton, Emory. Do you know what my dad's name is? It's Leland." I was sitting on the floor by then, my legs stretched out under the coffee table. I forgot myself and spit angrily into the dog-stained carpet, thinking of my name and how I hated it. The lumpish body of a big, sleeping mongrel pressed against my thigh. A smelly child in diapers stood next to me and touched my ear with a Popsicle. I saw Mrs. Dakeman come and go a number of times, carrying dishes or whispering the names of children. I saw that my glass was full again, so I emptied it as Wild Red Berry defeated Gorgeous George with a punishing Boston crab, a submission hold, the inescapable hold all wrestlers feared.

A sound from the street pierced through the cheering crowd and Mr. Dakeman's rumbling snores. It sent a spasm through my drunken heart. It was the sound of Nola's wild, rebellious laughter. I started to get up, then decided to stay put. I thought I should be seen sitting on the floor with a shot glass in my hand watching TV with her father, as if I were one of the family. But she didn't some in. When she laughed again, I got up and went to the door and opened it a crack.

She was leaning against a '52 Ford Victoria. It was a beautiful car—lowered, leaded, chopped, channeled, with a custom paint job, a metallic maroon so deep and liquid it looked like you could slip your arm into it straight to the elbow. The driver of the car had his head tilted out the window. A cigarette hung from his lower lip. He was a Drifter. The club's name, carved into a cast-aluminum plaque, dangled from the rear bumper of the Ford on chromium chains. He had long sideburns and his hair was sculpted into a well-greased duck's ass. He gunned the engine now and then, filling the semidark neighborhood with a window-vibrating roar. When he let it idle, I could hear the radical camshaft make the engine stutter. It was a street dragster, meant for high RPMs. It idled nervously, the timing unsure of itself. Nola, her hands shoved into the front pockets of her cutoff Levi's, leaned down to the indifferent Drifter and waited for him to remove his cigarette. He took his time, but when he finally flipped the butt into the street, she kissed him. Her head and shoulders gradually entered the narrow window. Then the upper half of her body was inside the car, lost in a well of shadow. It looked as if she were sinking into a maroon lake. Her long foot rose, slowly, and the sandal it was wearing slipped off. The toes of the foot curled tightly. Then they splayed.

I switched the porch light on and off several times, as any father might have done. Of course, Mr. Dakeman would not have stood at the door observing his daughter protectively. The dignity and responsibility of fatherhood were not high on his list of personal standards. I glanced over at him. He was awake again, staring wearily at Dick Lane, the ringside announcer, who was giving his redundant analysis of the matches we had seen and what we could expect in the future. I snapped the porch light on and off with the outrage of someone who had rights—a father, an older brother. A lover. And, of course, I immediately felt like an idiot, like a coward. The truth was, the Drifters were a legendary car club, known for their fearless run-ins with the cops, their lead-pipe-and-chain-swinging brawls with other car clubs, and for their amazing *cars*, each of which was a legitimate work of art. I was in awe of the Drifters and their cars, and couldn't have gone out in the street to claim Nola: Without a car of equal beauty and sophistication, I could not have competed.

I sat down on the couch and poured myself another shot of whiskey. I let my glass rest on my teeth and I felt, along with the burning trickle of booze, the throbs from the radical Ford as it eased away from the house.

My heart speeded up, anticipating Nola, but as minutes passed I realized that she had gone off with the Drifter again. My irate-father-at-the-light-switch act probably meant something altogether different to her than it would have meant to a girl from a decent family. She probably thought it was her mother, or a sister or brother, warning her away from the house because her father was on a blood-letting rampage.

I left Mr. Dakeman sunk into the corner of his sofa, his sagging face pale in the TV's gray flickering light. When I crossed our lawn, Pershing grazed my knee with his big sad head. I knelt beside him and hugged him until he trembled with anxiety. He wasn't accustomed to physical demonstrations of emotional need. Then I took his rope and unhooked it from his collar. "You're free, Pershing," I said. "Go piss on a tire." But Pershing just stood next to the mulberry tree and quivered.

I was very sick the next day. Physically more than emotionally, but as my strength came back, this order was reversed. I packed, halfheartedly, the things I needed to take to Keesler Air Force Base. Civilian clothes were not permitted in basic, but in technical school we would be allowed to spend weekend passes out of uniform. Not that I looked forward to weekends. I didn't look forward to anything. I had made the mistake of waiting for the Drifter to bring her back. I'd waited out on the porch, talking to Pershing, who stayed under his protecting tree, tethered to his own timidity. I waited an hour. Then the customized Ford turned the corner and rumbled down the street. The Drifter eased up to the curb in front of the Dakeman house and turned off his lights. Then he turned off his engine. I watched the dark, unmoving car. A silence, like the hush of conspirators, sealed our neighborhood from the rest of the universe. But Pershing's keen ears twitched and he glanced quickly at the Ford, then guiltily back at me.

I imagine he heard the secret friction of flesh, the fluid roar of hearts. He looked at me in alarm, his sorrowful eyes understanding, but not quite condoning, my apparent complaisance. "I don't own her, you idiot," I said.

I tried to eat breakfast and failed. After picking at a four-egg cheese omelet for a few minutes, I had to run to the bathroom. Mom seemed sympathetic, but her sympathy came from a distance. She'd lost faith in me. I was not going to be a robust eater with a positive outlook like Dad or my lumberjack uncles. I skipped lunch, went for a long walk instead. When I got home, I saw Nola sitting on her front porch. She was wearing her cutoffs, her round white thighs held wide in brave unconscious welcome.

"Hey, Miles," she said.

I didn't trust my voice, so I just waved. I was wearing my uniform. The crisp, silvery-blue sheen of it had a good effect on me. It took away some of my bitterness. The uniform reminded me that I belonged to something much larger and far more dependable than this narrow street with its tense little lawns and hedges and the Dakemans' dust-bowl eyesore. I was an airman third class, soon to be a trained specialist, destined to fly in the RC-121-C Super Connies, the radar picket planes that defended the coastlines of our nation from sneak attack. I felt sorry for Eldon, who had lost his chance with the Navy. But it was the kind of pity that gives you a warm feeling of comfortable self-regard.

"You look sharp, Miles," she said.

I stopped. I pulled my cigarettes out and lit up. "Thanks, Nola," I said. Then, touching the bill of my cap, I added, "For *every*thing." It was a scene from a movie, an airman's good-bye to the things that would grow small and quaint as he rose higher and higher into the blue yonder. It was the right thing to say. It was exactly what Rory Calhoun would have said.

A salt tide broke through Hornbeck's antiperspirant and the high reek of the hot afternoon was on him. He parked his truck in the driveway and went into the house. Roberta met him inside the door. "Your son mutilated his new teddy bear with a steak knife," she said.

He followed her into the kitchen. The table was set. Hornbeck was hungry and dazed with fatigue. He had skipped lunch because he'd had to help Cosmo Minor take a pair of vintage Corvettes from Mexicans in Boyle Heights, and things had gone from tense to freaky when the Zambrano brothers locked themselves into the cars and the tow trucks and cops had to be called in.

Hornbeck took off his jacket and sat at the table. The hot kitchen smelled of old grease and Lysol, and now, of him. A covered aluminum pot rattled on the stove, steam jetting from the lid.

"Beam me up, Scotty." He sighed.

Aliens

Roberta, a thin woman with a long, angular face etched with disappointment, opened a beer and put it on the table within his reach. "Get Lance washed up before your shower, will you?" she said, adjusting the heat under the pot. "Say something to him about teddy. He thought teddy had one of those horrible creatures living in its chest, like in that movie you brought home last week."

Hornbeck carried his beer out to the backyard, where Lance and another preschooler were playing trucks. Both boys were cranky and overheated. The few rules of order they had created for their game were crumbling. Lance was using his truck as a hammer against the other boy's truck. The other boy was trying to withdraw his truck from the onslaught, but Lance followed it with relentless blows. The other boy was on the verge of tears.

"Hey, soldier," Hornbeck said. "Time to wash up for din-din."

Lance ignored his father and swung his truck with increasing savagery, rising up on his little haunches for added leverage.

"Whoa, big guy!" Hornbeck said, chuckling a bit at the boy's determination. "Time out, my man! Mommy's got our dinner almost ready." He set his beer down on the lawn and stepped into the circle of combat. He caught Lance's truck on the upswing. Lance, enraged, pulled his truck back, but Hornbeck picked up the boy and carried him toward the house. Lance kicked and punched. His round cheeks shined explosively red. He twisted away from his father's mild rebukes, arching his back and holding his breath between screams. Hornbeck, a tall, slope-shouldered, bearish man, held the boy at arm's length and gave him a light shake. "That's *enough*, son," he said, and Lance hiccuped once and was quiet. "All right, that's fine. You're safe now in a Federation Starship tractor beam. The war with the Klingons is over, okay?"

Hornbeck put his son down. As soon as his feet touched the ground, Lance ran over to the other boy, who was still on his knees making truck noises, and swung his truck into the side of the boy's head. The crack of hard plastic on flesh made Hornbeck wince. The boy ran screaming from the yard, leaving his truck behind. Lance sat down and resumed hammering the other boy's truck, all hindrances finally removed.

Hornbeck sipped his beer and waited for his son to exhaust himself. Then he called and the boy came running happily to his dad. "Okay, war's over, soldier," he said. "The Federation wins. But look, you can't be giving major headshots to your little buddies, okay?" He scooped the boy into his arms. "Let's beam up to the *Enterprise* for our pseudo-soup and miracle-meat." Hornbeck made the high-pitched hum of the transporter beam and Lance giggled with delight.

"Lance has the attitude of a Klingon warrior," Hornbeck said to Roberta later that evening. They were in bed, reading the paper.

Roberta put her section of the paper down. "The attitude of a Klingon warrior," she repeated. "And just what *is* that? Tell me, I'd honestly like to be educated about this."

Hornbeck leaned his head back into his pillows and looked at the ceiling. "Beam me up, Scotty." He sighed.

"No, I mean it. I'd like to know, really. Let me in on how you see us. I'm really curious."

"You're a Vulcan beauty," Hornbeck said, turning toward her. "I'm insane over Vulcan women. Vulcan women drag the one-eyed nasty from Neptune out of me."

He reached for her, but Roberta pushed him away and got out of bed. She lit a cigarette. "I don't think I can deal with this," she said.

"Captain Kirk won't like to hear that, Roberta," Hornbeck said. "Maybe you'd better report to Bones for attitude rehab."

Though it was often not possible, Hornbeck preferred to work alone. This, and his addiction to science fiction movies, had earned him the nickname Han Solo. Most of the repo men at the Bolton Agency liked to work in pairs. Especially when they had to go into the neighborhoods. Having gone into Boyle Heights for the vintage Corvettes with Cosmo Minor had made a difficult situation nearly impossible. Cosmo, a stocky, impatient black man, and Hornbeck, a six-foot-six-inch hulk, had created a confrontational atmosphere that eliminated any chance for calm negotiations. And while two men were needed to get the cars back to the bank that had financed them, the presence of both Cosmo and Hornbeck at the front door of the Zambrano residence lit an us-against-them fuse that couldn't be snuffed. There was the exchange of insults, the inevitable shoving match, the gathering of hostile neighbors.

Hornbeck felt far more effective in one-on-one situations. People, when he had to confront them, didn't feel threatened by him despite his size. He had a sincere, friendly manner, and a shy, boyish smile that encouraged trust. If he had to take a car or a stereo, the delinquent owner was usually willing to listen to Hornbeck's reasonable arguments. And he, in turn, was willing to hear their hard-luck stories. Often the delinquent owner would invite Hornbeck into his or her house for a beer or coffee. On more than one occasion, Hornbeck was so moved by their hard-luck stories that he volunteered to make the back payments on the merchandise himself, provided the payments were small. He saved the TV set of a stroke-paralyzed widower once by paying eighteen dollars on the man's contract with the appliance store. He became deeply sympathetic to deserted women with children to support.

Bonnie DeLuca had missed four payments on her washer and dryer. She'd met him at her door in a bathrobe. "Don't tell me," she had said. "Pay the hundred-sixty now or its bye-bye Maytag, right?" She began to cry. She opened the door wide and he went in.

"I'm really sorry, ma'am," he said, pushing his hand through his hair, unable to hide his discomfort. He found the utility room and looked at the washer-dryer set. He checked the width of the machines with his tape measure, then checked the width of the utility-room door. When he went back into the living room, Bonnie DeLuca was sitting on the couch staring into her cup of coffee. A small child pestered her knees.

"I wish I could just do what I'm thinking," she said into the cup, "but, God help me, I'm not that type of woman."

Hornbeck pretended he didn't hear this and went out to his pickup and skidded the hand truck off the bed. He rolled it around to the back of the house and pulled it into the utility room. Bonnie DeLuca was there, her robe partially opened. "Goddammit," she said. "I *need* my machines."

"I feel rotten about this, ma'am," Hornbeck said. He knelt to detach the hoses from the washer.

"Feel rottener," Bonnie said, kneeling beside him. She was small and vulnerable next to the sweating bulk of his long torso.

He was surprised at how easy it was to let this happen. It was a first for him. Six years of faithfulness ended, easy as hanging up the phone.

Bonnie had said, "What do you think of me? I mean, what do you *really* think of me?" They were in her bed. The weak springs of the bed had made distracting hee-haw sounds, like the braying of a donkey. In another room the child had imitated those sounds in a dreamy singsong, and was now whining for its mother.

"What do I think of you," he said, scratching his chin. "I think you're a warm-blooded earth woman. Unlike your Vulcan counterpart."

After they made love again, Hornbeck said, "And what do you think of *me*?"

"To be honest, I think you're real nice but kind of geeky," Bonnie DeLuca said.

That had been three months ago. Since then, Bonnie had not made any payments on her washer-dryer combination. The payments had been made by Hornbeck. "What are all these savings withdrawals?" Roberta asked him one morning at breakfast.

"What withdrawals?" Hornbeck said, studying the newspaper.

She tossed the bankbook onto the table. "Forty dollars, May ninth. Fifty dollars, June tenth."

"Oh that. It's a surprise, honey."

"We can't afford any surprises. I need a replacement crown on my molar, Lance needs school clothes."

"No problem," Hornbeck said.

"There's something else. I want to put Lance into Rage Reduction before he starts kindergarten."

Hornbeck's newspaper sagged gradually to the table. "I'm sorry? You want to put Lance into rage *what*?"

"Reduction. I'm very serious about this. His violence has got to be understood and dealt with."

"All healthy five-year-olds have some violence, honey. It's very normal. We begin in the jungle. They tame us, little by little. Look at me." He twisted a pair of paper napkins into cylinders and stuffed one into each nostril. He stuck out his tongue and rolled his eyes. He stood up in a half-crouch so that his knuckles dragged on the floor. He made urgent primitive noises in his throat. "Me, ten years ago," he said.

"Cut it out. I'm trying to be serious. He's destroyed most of his toys. He thinks hideous creatures live inside them. He hurts his playmates."

"Good Klingon warriors, from a very early age—"

"Stop it! You turn everything you can't face into a comic book!"

Hornbeck smiled, He thought he had an answer to this. Her mistake seemed clear to him. What, for instance, could he not face? He started to speak, then stopped. He ran his hands through his hair and shook his head, somewhat dismayed at his inability to state the obvious. "I'm a good person," he finally said.

"So is Jerry Lewis," Roberta said.

Sometimes he didn't mind taking things away from people. The Invernesses had bought a two-year-old Cadillac for nothing down and payments of over four hundred dollars a month. They were a couple in their sixties, living on pensions in Van Nuys. They weren't poor, they had a savings account, but it was convenient for them to skip payments from time to time. They had missed three in a row now, and the credit union that had granted the loan engaged the services of the Bolton Agency.

"I've always wanted a Caddy," Mr. Inverness said.

"Everyone wants a Caddy," Hornbeck said.

"Do you *have* to take it?" Mrs. Inverness said. They were in the Invernesses' living room. Mrs. Inverness had made tea, but Hornbeck wasn't drinking his.

"You've missed three payments, ma'am. The fourth is due next Friday. If you can come up with seventeen hundred and eighty-four dollars, then, no, I don't have to take it. That figure includes the late-payment penalties."

"It's our only transportation," Mr. Inverness said bitterly.

Hornbeck looked at his watch. "I'll need the keys," he said.

Mr. Inverness patted his pockets. "Don't have them," he said. "You have them, Polly?"

Mrs. Inverness shook her head. They both stared at Hornbeck. Behind their bifocals, their pale eyes were big with tentative challenge.

Hornbeck looked around the medium-to-high-rent apartment. Quality furnishings. Behind the leaded-glass cabinet doors of an antique sideboard, stacks of Wedgwood dinnerware gleamed. Mr. Inverness was wearing expensive burgundy wing-tips and Mrs. Inverness's dress did not come from a K-mart rack. They were plump, florid people who were not worried about their next meal.

"I can make my regular payment," Mr. Inverness said, "but not a cent more. We are not wealthy."

"That's not acceptable," Hornbeck said.

"Listen to me, you. I'm sixty-seven years old, I've put two snot-nose ingrates through college. I've worked hard all my life. I've had a little setback, but I *deserve* the car."

"Do I look like Father Christmas?" Hornbeck said.

"Don't take that tone with me, young man," Mr. Inverness said, rising.

"Now, Kenneth," his wife said. "Remember what Doctor said about temper and blood pressure." She turned bitterly toward Hornbeck. "You're *killing* him," she hissed. "Can't you see that?"

Mr. Inverness leaned toward Hornbeck, his jaw stiff with menace.

"Just give me the keys, Mr. Inverness," Hornbeck said, glancing at his watch again. "I've got other appointments this afternoon."

"More innocent people to crucify," Mr. Inverness sneered.

Hornbeck held his hand out for the keys. Mr. Inverness sprayed saliva into it.

"You've just made my job a whole bunch easier, Mr. Inverness," Hornbeck said.

Hornbeck went into the kitchen and looked on top of the refrigerator and then scanned the countertops. The table was empty. He entered the bedroom and went through the clutter on the dressers and night tables. Then he emptied the night-table drawers onto the neatly made bed. A collection of antique dolls were arranged on a shelf under the window. The tiny red lips of the dolls were puckered and their seductive, oversize eyes regarded Hornbeck coyly. While

Hornbeck was looking at the dolls, Inverness came in and grabbed his arms from behind, but Hornbeck threw him off easily.

"I'm calling the police!" Mrs. Inverness said.

"Do that, ma'am," Hornbeck said. "Tell them that you and your husband are trying to steal a car from people who trusted you to pay for it."

Hornbeck found the keys in the closet, hanging on a hook that had been screwed into the doorframe. Mr. Inverness lurched at Hornbeck, trying to grab the keys, but Hornbeck stiff-armed him in the breastbone, knocking him away. Mr. Inverness sat down, his shocked mouth wide open, unable to draw in air.

Hornbeck skipped lightly down the stairwell and into the parking garage, whistling. He found the Cadillac, a pearl-gray Coupe de Ville. He gave the thumbs-up to Cosmo Minor, who was reading the newspaper behind the wheel of the Agency's flatbed truck. Cosmo looked at his watch, then scowled at Hornbeck. Hornbeck grinned and waved Cosmo off. They wouldn't be needing the flatbed after all. Then he climbed into the Caddy and drove it away, hard plumes of blue smoke geysering from the tires.

He drove the car to Bonnie DeLuca's house and took her for a ride. They stopped at a bar for drinks, then drove off to a secluded area in the Santa Monica Mountains.

"Upper Crustville," Bonnie said.

"Don't count on it," Hornbeck said. "I hauled a boat out of here a few months ago with my own truck. Damn near burned up the transmission."

Hornbeck kissed Bonnie roughly and shoved his hands under her dress.

"Hey, Bonzo," she said. "Aren't we a little out in the open here?" She turned her face away from him to look at the wide houses and expensive landscaping.

"The windows are smoked. Besides, I feel kind of pumped up. I took this baby from bloodsucking life-forms hatched in the outer limits, Bonnie. Earthlings one, Evil Empire zero."

"You're a geeky kind of guy, you know that, Hornbeck?"

"But I've got a good heart," he said, pressing her down into the tangerine velour.

The house was dark and no one was home. Something was wrong, but it was past eight and Hornbeck was too hungry and tired to deal with it. It had been a long day, and he reeked. He'd taken back three cars, a living-room settee, an expensive stereo system, and, of all things, a satellite dish. The man who had the dish was crazy. He hadn't been using it to receive television broadcasts, but as a device to contact aliens. He had rigged a short-wave transceiver to the dish and was transmitting his voice into space. "I am on the brink of a monumental discovery!" the man had said. When Hornbeck started unbolting the dish from its mounts, the man became frantic. He ran around his backyard making odd gestures and babbling in a language he had made up. Hornbeck felt uneasy as he unbolted the dish. He had to kneel down and duck under the supporting struts to do the job, and the man could have clobbered him from behind with a rock or garden tool. Hornbeck knew the man was capable of doing something like that. One look at the man's face and it was clear he was crazy enough to do the next thing that occurred to him. When Hornbeck got the dish into the back of his truck, the man began howling in despair. "My research is ruined! I hope you and the slime that sent you realize that!"

"Sorry, Professor," Hornbeck had said. "E-Z Pay Appliances can't afford to support research projects."

"I was about to solve their codes, you Neanderthal!" the man had yelled as Hornbeck started his truck. "I could have moved humanity forward by a thousand years!"

"A thousand won't be enough, buddy. But I'll tell Mr. Sulu when I see him. He's good at cracking codes."

Hornbeck groped his way into the kitchen and turned on the light. There was a note taped to the refrigerator: "It's pointless to think anything's going to improve. We don't make sense to each other any longer. Dr. Korda pretty much summed it up: "The boy's father encourages a direct-line approach between desire and object. This is an extremely unproductive trend, and will most certainly cause the boy untold difficulty once he enters public school.' I guess Untold Difficulty is the name of the game, but I want to try one more time to beat the system. I hope you understand. You'll be hearing from Stensrud, Stensrud, and Levitz. (Legal firm.) Roberta."

Hornbeck read the note again, then opened the refrigerator. He took out the makings for a pressed ham and cheese sandwich, and two bottles of beer. He took his sandwich and beer out to the living room and then noticed for the first time that most of the furniture was gone. He went through the rest of the house. It had been stripped also. He went into the bedroom and felt the top shelf of the closet. The tapes of his *Star Trek* episodes were still there. He took a large bite of his sandwich and washed it down with beer. "Looks like she's gone back to Vulcan, Mr. Spock," he said.

"You want to go up to West Covina with me tomorrow, Hornbeck?" Cosmo Minor said.

"I guess so," Hornbeck said. "I mean no. Unless you really need me."

They were in Minor's small apartment watching one of Hornbeck's *Star Trek* tapes and drinking Canadian Club highballs. Cosmo Minor's wife, Trude, was making supper.

"This yo-yo's wanting to make payments on three computers," Cosmo said, "but he's too busy playing tug-o'-war with his dick to come up with it."

"Dumb shit."

"Hey, ain't they all."

Hornbeck felt agitated. "You're sure it's okay with Trude if I stick around for dinner?" he said.

Cosmo leaned back in his chair and called over his shoulder to Trude. "Hey, peaches. It's okay with you if Hornbeck stays for supper, ain't it?"

A sound came from the kitchen that could have been a confirmation.

"See? What'd I say, Hornbeck?"

Captain Kirk had walked through a time portal and found himself in Renaissance England. The portal sealed itself instantly, leaving Kirk stranded outside a pub in a dark street. He spoke into his communicator, but, he airwaves of the sixteenth century were dead. "Now what?" a bemused Kirk murmured to himself as a scornful swordsman belittled his futuristic clothes.

"Sometimes I feel like that," Hornbeck said, gesturing toward the TV set with his tumbler.

"Like what?"

"Like Kirk there. Like I was dropped into the middle of nowhere. I mean, in the middle of somewhere strange. I feel like I just materialized in L.A. thirty-nine—Jesus, *thirty-nine!* —years ago."

"Thirty-nine ain't old, man," Cosmo said, fixing himself another drink.

"I don't mean that. I mean, like I never had a basic say-so in all this shit. I mean, here I *am*. You know? But it's not my fault."

"Hey, man. Do I look like the fucking Prince of Wales?"

"What?"

"The fucking Prince of Wales don't need to figure out where he is or why they do him like they do. He just *is*. That's all he needs to know about it. The rest of us are accidentals."

Hornbeck took a pull directly from the bottle. "No one's going to tell me I don't belong, Cosmo. No one's going to tell me I'm a fucking accidental scab on the fucking accidental ass of society."

"Ay-fucking-men, pardner," Cosmo said. "But how come it's *you* feeling like that? No one's saying shit to you. You look like Merlin Olsen. You look like you fucking own the company, ace. You look like you got the world buttfucked and the world asking you to stay *on*."

Hornbeck allowed himself a small sob, but once that passed his lips, the dam behind it shook loose.

"Holy cow, Hornbeck," Cosmo said. "You want some coffee?"

An emotion he could not master stretched Hornbeck's face into acute angles. He rolled to the floor and brought his knees up to his chest. His chest hurt, as if it held a taloned creature. Stunned with shame, and afraid Trude might come in and see him like this, he hid his face in his arms and continued to sob quietly.

"Looky there, Hornbeck," Cosmo said gently. "Captain Kirk kicking serious ass in jolly old England."

Bonnie DeLuca's husband came home. Hornbeck found this out when he called her and Norman DeLuca answered the phone. "Who is this?" Hornbeck had said.

"Who the fuck wants to know?" DeLuca had replied, his diction elaborate with menace. Hornbeck hung up.

He drove by the DeLuca house once and spotted her in the backyard cutting back a rose bush. She was wearing shorts and a halter. The pink curves of her body made him ache. A wretched moan broke from his throat. Hornbeck parked the truck and walked up the driveway to the back fence. He opened the gate and entered the yard.

When she saw him, she dropped her clippers. "You can't come around here anymore," she whispered savagely.

"I thought I'd say hello."

"Say good-bye instead. My husband's home. He's in the house right now, taking his bath."

"This is a business trip," Hornbeck said.

"What are you talking about?

"I've decided to take the Maytags."

"You *what*? You can't take them. I'm up to date on the payments!"

Hornbeck got the hand truck and pulled it into the utility room through the back door. He unhooked the hoses from the washer and unplugged the dryer.

"You're crazy, you know that?" Bonnie said, watching him in disbelief.

Hornbeck wheeled the appliances out and loaded them into the back of his pickup. He tied down the hand truck, but not the appliances. Norman DeLuca came out wearing a red bathrobe embroidered with fire-breathing Chinese dragons. The robe had billowing, half-length sleeves. Beads of water glistened on the dense black hair of DeLuca's forearms. "I'm calling the cops, asshole," he said. Hornbeck got into the truck and started it. He looked back at Bonnie. She was standing at the edge of her lawn, her grimly folded arms pressing her breasts flat.

Hornbeck exchanged thrusting middle fingers with Norman DeLuca, then put the truck into first gear and eased out the clutch. He drove up the street a few hundred feet, stopped, then accelerated hard, in reverse. When he was in front of the DeLuca house again, he stomped on the brake pedal, sending both washer and dryer shuddering off the truck and into the street. The machines hit with grievous thuds and large pieces broke loose.

Later that day he was scheduled to go to Pomona to pick up a massaging recliner. An elderly woman had bought it three months ago but had yet to make her first payment. He imagined that she was on Social Security, a widow ignored by her middle-aged children, crippled with arthritis, and fed up with life. But not so fed up that she didn't want to retain a few creature comforts. He imagined himself having coffee in her kitchen, her shaky, knob-knuckled hands struggling with the pot. He imagined himself looking cautiously into her fogged eyes, half convinced he'd be able, now, to see the immortal parasite that thrived behind them. And it wouldn't matter. He'd make the back payments on her recliner anyway.

Because of a snag in my thinking I lost interest in both vector analysis and differential equations and had to drop out of college and hitchhike home twelve credits short of graduation. Home was a half a continent away and I didn't have a car or bus money and was afraid to ask my folks for help. They had paid my way through three and a half years of engineering school at Platteville, Wisconsin, and I couldn't have said to Dad, for instance, that I wanted to come home because the laws of thermodynamics bored the life out of me. He wouldn't have understood my reasoning.

I didn't have any reasoning. Something down at the underpinnings of reason had given way, and there was no explanation for it. I couldn't even explain it to myself. All I knew was that every time I opened a textbook something numbing, like pain, would stab the back of my head. Or my eyelids would feel thick, as if stuffed with sand. Or I would read the same page over ten, fifteen times and not one word would register.

Horizontal Snow

I kissed my girlfriend goodbye, packed my suitcase, and headed for the highway west. "What's *wrong* with you?" she'd asked, and I had no answer. I'd hurt her, I was aware of that, but my own feelings were in cold storage. I observed her pain in the way a surgeon observes the pain of his patient: with compassion but without involvement or remorse. I was strong and healthy, my appetite was good, I slept well, but nothing interested me. I felt like an animated corpse, moving through a world I had left behind. Greeting myself in the bathroom mirror each morning I would say, Hello, Zombie.

The first ride I hitched was with a family. They dropped me off on the far edge of Minnesota, in the middle of nowhere. It was a lonely stretch of road, and though the weather had been springlike for several weeks, the wind from Canada still had a threat of winter in it. My second ride came minutes before hypothermia set in.

A pickup truck with a homemade camper stuck on the back rolled to a gradual stop ahead of me. The camper was made of scrap wood and had a peaked roof, like a house, covered with tar paper. It looked like an outbuilding of a farm, modified for travel. The man driving said he was going all the way to Bonner's Ferry, Idaho, four hundred miles short of my destination. I hesitated before getting in because the man was so ugly he took my breath away. He may have been the ugliest man in the world. At least I had never seen anyone up to that time as ugly as he was, and I have not seen anyone uglier since. His face was flat as a skillet, even concave. His hammered-down nose was five fingers wide, and his short forehead had prominent supraorbital ridges thick as cables. He looked like something you'd see in an anthropology textbook, as if forty thousand years of evolution had skipped over him. This was 1958, and so much has happened since then that much of what follows seems more like a dream than personal history.

His name was Lot Stoner and he claimed to be a preacher. He drove slowly, under fifty, with both hands on the wheel. He had huge, amply scarred, thick-fingered hands that had seen decades of punishing work. We rode along without speaking for several hours, though now and then he would glance over at me and at the suitcase wedged between my legs. "I specialize in the defeated," he finally said. When I didn't respond to this, he went on to explain that he was a preacher of the gospel. He didn't have a church or a degree from a recognized seminary, but was a self-taught man of God. "You just lost a big tussle, didn't you?" he said. He had yellowing, wide-spaced eyes. They were slightly wall-eyed so that when he looked at you directly, it seemed as if he was seeing two of you—one slightly to the right, one slightly to the left. I guessed his age at about sixty, but his hair was bright red and youthful.

Again he waited for my response. I didn't have one. I shrugged and turned my gaze out the side window, where snow-patched fields drifted by.

"I saw defeat in your posture," he said, "while you were standing out there in the elements with your thumb out. I said to myself, 'Lot, there is a young buck who has been in the toilet. There is a boy who hit bottom but did not bounce.' Am I wrong?"

I didn't see myself as that bad off, but he was at least partly right. Articulated, the snag in my thinking went something like this: "This struggle is not worth the reward." It loomed in my mind like a huge door that had just shut, locking itself. I couldn't formulate it in words at the time, but I sensed that it had the clear-cut, irrefutable perfection of Einstein's discovery of the absolute equivalency of matter and energy. I had been an honors student headed for a job in the aerospace industry to help build rockets so that we could catch up to the Russians. Sputnik had been put into orbit the previous fall, and things did not look good for the U.S.A.

"Your hand looked like the hand of a mendicant, upraised for alms," Lot said. "I said to myself, 'Lot, there is a boy who has lost his way.' I am hardly ever off the target about such things."

Lot talked about himself for a while. He said he felt more like a traveling teacher than a pulpit-bound Bible thumper. He said he was too footloose to have his own church, and also that he was too broad-minded and generous with his biblical interpretations to follow the narrow and self-interested theologies of the fat-cat denominations. He gave examples of his broad-mindedness. "This may astound you, son," he said, "but I can see evidence of divinity in a cow pie, and again in the maggots that devour it." He reached under his seat and pulled out a microphone that had some wires dangling loosely from it. "Ain't that right, Willie?" he shouted into the mike.

A woman's voice crackled over a loudspeaker that was wedged between the seat and the back of the cab. "Ain't *what* right?" she said. She sounded sleepy and annoyed at being disturbed. I figured, correctly, that she was lying in a bunk back in the wood-slat and tar-paper camper.

"About me seeing the Almighty Himself in commonplace cow shit," Lot said into his microphone.

"Yeah," said the voice through an unrestrained yawn.

"I can see the Lord in all of it," he said. "In every piece of flotsam and jetsam, in every gnat and mosquito—there He is, doing business like He has every day for twenty billion years. History means nothing to Him. Yours, mine, or that of the damn fool nations."

Lot told me that he'd spent a good part of his life in prison. "I killed a man," he said. "I took his head into my hands and squeezed it until the pressure on his brain became intolerable. There were ruptures under the bone and then the bone itself gave way. He was stone dead before I released him, and the blood from his ears ran in abundance through my fingers. They said later they had to pry my fingers off of him with cold chisels and pliers. I had momentarily lost the sense of myself." He took his right hand off the wheel and showed it to me. The hard, walnut-size knuckles looked like the joints of a machine, the thick wrist timbered with straight shafts of bone.

He picked up his microphone. "Am I sorry? Tell him, Willie, if I am sorry."

"He ain't," Willie said.

"And I'll tell you why," Lot said. "The man deserved what he got. He was worthless. Worthless scum. I know I just told you I can see divinity in flotsam and jetsam. But this man was below that. He was filled to capacity with nothing. He was nothingness incarnate. He was a hole in God's blue air."

"He's getting up steam," Willie's crackling voice warned from the loudspeaker.

We were in the flat, rich farm country of central North Dakota, the landscape of boredom itself. A few years later, after having got past my motivational problems, I would be installing Minuteman missiles into this same wheatland for the U.S. Air Force.

"The man I killed was a two-legged lamprey," Lot said. "He attached himself to the helpless underbelly of good-hearted people and sucked their lifeblood from them until they were pale effigies of their former selves. He would fill his nothingness with their somethingness. He was a con artist who had taken my daddy's last dime for an electrical arthritis cure, coupled with painful injections of a useless saline solution. Can you blame me?"

"No," I said.

"And I accept no blame. But while I was up at the state farm, I had myself a long time to ponder it. My meditations led me to the light, the holy light, pure and simple. And I am going to reveal this holy light to you, son, free of charge.

Spreading the truth is my goal in life. I doff my cap to no sect, denomination, figurehead, or dogma. I do not take my notions from someone else's larder of so-called religious verities."

We passed a small lake and drove through a town where, four years later, I would betray my young wife by going to bed with a farmer's widow named Zola Faye Metkovich. My young wife would leave me, I would leave Zola Faye, but I would stay on at Minot Air Force Base, helping to redesign ICBM parts and support equipment that had failed their stress and endurance tests. I would make a lot of money, drive a big car—an air-conditioned Chrysler Imperial—and have a string of five girlfriends who lived far away from each other in the small isolated towns of North Dakota where people, though born in the United States of America, still spoke with foreign accents, German and Russian. It would be the most exciting time of my life, but of course I did not know it, and could not have imagined it, as I bounced along toward Idaho with Lot Stoner and the unseen woman he called Willie.

Now and then, Lot would take a dried-out sandwich from a paper sack on the floorboards or lift a thermos to his lips. He offered these to me, but I refused. Food from his hand was automatically unappetizing, as if contaminated by his ugliness. He hummed to himself for a while, ate a little more, gazed out at the slow-moving scenery from time to time. It took me a while to realize that he'd quit talking, and that I had been waiting for him to reveal this holy-light business to me, not that I believed in such things or had ever given them much thought. I began to think that he'd just forgotten about it, or had something more pressing on his mind. And then it occurred to me that I was being conned, or that he was self-deluded, maybe even brain-damaged. I leaned my head against the window and pretended to doze off. And then I did doze off.

A crackling electrical scream woke me up. It was Willie, yelling for someone to come back to her.

Lot slowed the truck and pulled off onto the shoulder of the highway. "Go climb into the back and take a look, will you, son?" he said wearily. He crossed his arms on the wheel and rested his knobbed forehead on them. "I'll catch a couple of winks while you're back there."

I got out of the truck into a northern gale. The false spring was over. A new storm from the Arctic was blowing in. In these latitudes you can smell snow in the air. It's not so much a smell as it is a pinching in of your nose, a tightening of the membranes inside. You turn your face into the wind, lift your nose to it, sniff in. "Snow," you say to yourself. "Blizzard."

When I climbed into the camper, I saw a narrow-faced woman with Indian cheekbones curled up under a heavy blanket. She had thin, stringy hair, and her haunted eyes looked like those of a trapped wolverine.

"Come here, dammit," she said.

She was lying on a bunk that ran the length of the camper. There was an electric light glowing in the ceiling. The only other light came through the back door, which I left open. She was trying to push herself up on her elbows.

"What's the matter?" I said.

"Lift me up," she said through gritted teeth.

She was young. Maybe twenty, but probably closer to seventeen. I slid a hand behind her back and muscled her forward. "Quit it," she said. "I just needed to get up a little so's I can get set. It's coming."

She scooted forward a little, then lay back down. Her knees were up and her belly was very big. She pulled the blanket aside and her naked belly rose up, tight and shiny.

"You're having a baby," I said.

"You don't say," she said. She spread her knees and screamed, loud and terrible, more rage in it than pain. I stepped back and my head hit the roof. Her microphone was on the floor, next to her bunk. I picked it up.

"She's having a baby, Lot," I said.

"Joy to the world," replied his weary voice from a tiny loudspeaker that had been stuck to the ceiling with electrician's tape.

I put the mike down. Willie was growling between clenched teeth, her head rolling side to side on her pillow. "Is there anything I can do?" I asked.

She waved her arm. It flapped like a broken wing. "Get me that pint-size green bottle out of the icebox," she said. "And don't be an asshole and faint."

We looked at each other for a few seconds. If anything, my heart was beating slower. "Don't worry," I said.

The icebox was a homemade affair with a heavy lid fitted into its top. Among cans of soda and beer and packages of food were a half-dozen pint bottles of gin. I took one of these out and uncapped it. She took a long pull from it, and then I did the same. It was cold in my mouth and warm going down.

"Glory, glory," said Lot, his grainy voice dropping like sand from the ceiling.

"Maybe you ought to be back here with your wife," I said into the microphone.

"We all can't fit back there, son," he said. "There's not that much to do, anyway. You just do what the girl tells you. She ain't new at this."

Wind from Canada mauled the truck. It howled in the wooden slats of the camper. I looked out the door and saw the blizzard, the horizontal snow.

"Give me your hand," Willie said. She squeezed hard enough to make the separate bones touch. The skin of her stomach was pulled so tight I could see my shadowy reflection in it. "Take a look, will you?" she said. "I want to know if he's coming out ass end first. I had two others that did, both stillborns."

She let go of my hand and I moved down to the foot of the bunk and peered between her uupraised knees. There, at the dark joining of her thighs, was a little face. It looked like a dried apple. Crimped as it was in those bearded jaws, it looked Chinese and ancient. Its eyes were shut tight, the mouth a stubborn line. The unbreathing nose was flat and wide. The idea occurred to me that this wasn't an infant at all but a tiny old man who had serious second thoughts about the wisdom of leaving the comfortable and nourishing dark for the starved light of North Dakota. The notion made me smile. "Welcome home, chump," I whispered.

"Well?" Willie said. "Is it coming out frontwards of backwards?"

"Frontwards," I said. "Frontwards," I repeated into the mike. "And I think it's got red hair."

"I'm kissing the Good Book," said Lot.

Once the head cleared the birth canal, the rest was easy. Willie leaned forward and took the baby up in her arms, nipped the cord with her teeth, tied it off with a length of nylon fishing line, and wrapped him in the blanket. A small cry—more like the ratchety chirping of a newly hatched bird than that of a baby—came from the blanket. I wiped the sweat off Willie's face with my handkerchief, and she took another swig of gin.

"You're a nice fella," Willie said, smiling up at me.

I thought about that. "I don't think so," I said.

I went back up to the cab. "Fatherhood," Lot said, "is a great responsibility." He gave me a sidelong look of high significance, his off-center eyes splitting me into twins. Then he started the truck and we moved down the white highway.

"You probably ought to get them to a hospital," I said. "Or at least to a doctor."

"We'll stop in Minot," he said. "We'll get some warm food and a place to rest. Doctors aren't important to our thinking. Are they to yours?"

I looked at him, but he was squinting out into the painfully bright air of the storm. "Yes, I think so," I said.

"Someday you'll wake up out of your little nightmare and click your heels, son," he said, shifting down to second as snowdrifts began to collect in the road. He picked up his microphone and said, "What are we going to name him, Willie?"

"Jesus Dakota Stoner," Willie said without hesitating a beat.

"Merry Christmas," Lot hooted into the mike.

"We'll call him J.D. for short," Willie said.

Lot drove even slower as night came on and the blizzard got worse. We stopped in Rugby, an hour or so short of Minot, at an all-night café called Mud and Sinkers. Lot pulled a tobacco can out from under the seat. It was packed with dollar bills. He counted out five, smoothed them out on this thigh. "We'll get us some coffee and doughnuts and sit out this storm. When it gets light, we'll hit the road again."

We found a booth near the warm kitchen and a waitress brought us coffee and three glazed doughnuts. Willie had Jesus Dakota tucked in a blanket. The dried blood and mucus of his recent birth still mottled his skin, which otherwise would have been a bright saffron-pink, but Willie didn't seem too concerned. She opened her wool shirt and drew out a long thin breast and gave it to the baby. The baby hadn't been crying, but he pulled at his mother with urgent power.

"It'll be good to get home," I said, for conversation's sake, but I said it mostly to myself.

"J.D.'s home already" Lot chuckled. "Home is a warm teat, wherever you happen to be."

"Seattle," I said. "That's home for me."

Lot sipped his coffee, squinted at me through the steam. "Better to be in exile sustained by a dream of home than to endure the disappointments of home itself. Home itself is an idea that never measures up. I speak from experience."

"You're too deep for me, Lot," I said.

"Don't mock him," Willie said. She said it simply, without taking her eyes off her baby.

"You'll find one day that what I said is true," Lot said.

And what good will it do me? I wanted to say, but held back. I was tired and a little fed up with his homespun homilies. I wanted to be back in West Seattle, in my parent's big house overlooking the Sound. I wanted to be in my upstairs room, at my desk, watching the ferryboats at night brilliantly spangled with lights. I wanted to listen to the lonesome call of their foghorns while snuggling deeper and deeper into my old bed.

There were some names etched by knifeblade into the table before me. Rena + Yank. Pete + Vicki. Remember Me, Annette. I concentrated on those names and sipped my coffee, willing the night to pass quickly. I would come back to Mud and Sinkers four years later as a Boeing field engineer, after completing my degree at the University of Washington, the snag in my thinking long gone and forgotten. Carline Minsky from the town of Balfour would be with me, and those carved names would still be here, among half a dozen more. Carline was pregnant and wanted to get married, but I told her I already was married—even though my wife had left several months earlier. Carline broke down, but what could I do? I said I'd pay for the abortion. She took the money, but our little romantic episode ended then and there. Maybe she got the abortion and maybe she didn't. I never found out, nor wanted to.

We'd gotten carried away down in a silo, next to a recently installed Minuteman missile. We were on a service platform, adjacent to the missile's third-stage motor, near the warhead access ramp, and Carline said, "Let's do it, right here." She wasn't supposed to be in this Top Secret area, but there was no one else around within miles who might object. "This motor is fueled by a ton of nitroglycerin, stabilized by cotton filaments," I told her. "It's very dangerous." This was a partial truth, but it made her moan with fear and excitement. We did it standing up, her bending over the rail and leaning out close enough to the Minuteman to kiss the megaton hydrogen warhead. "I'm so hot," she said, and I was too. *Too* hot, it turned out, because we neglected the usual precautions, and she got pregnant, somewhere under North Dakota.

"I saw something else in your posture," Lot said, startling me. He was slumped over on his side in the booth, and I thought he'd been asleep. "I saw something besides defeat, or maybe it wasn't defeat I saw at all. Maybe it was this other thing all along."

I held a picture of blue water and white boats in my mind, so as not to get caught up again in his stagey pronouncements.

"Don't you care to know what I saw?" he said.

Willie stirred. Jesus Dakota turned his face left and right before finding the breast she half-consciously offered him.

"Not especially," I said.

"I'm going to tell you anyway. I saw a dangerous hunger. I saw an unfeedable hunger."

His primitive head, his bright red hair, the fatigue that lined his face—the complete aspect of an outcast and loser. I smiled and shook my head, affecting dismay.

"You were going to tell me something about a holy light. You must have forgotten," I said.

The need for sleep pulled him lower in the booth. He closed his eyes. "I already did. You weren't paying attention, son."

After a while, they were all sound asleep, that odd and aimless family with no future and a harrowing past. Even when a trucker came stomping into the café, kicking snow off his boots, flapping his arms against his chest, and cursing the storm at the top of his lungs, Lot, Willie, and Jesus Dakota didn't wake up. It was 3:00 A.M. , and the trucker ordered hot cakes and coffee. He talked constantly at the waitress, and from this I learned that he was on his way to the West Coast. I saw my chance and sat next to him at the counter. He was a tall, thin, nervous man, but he was friendly. He was a talker who was starved for conversation, and so when I asked if I could ride along with him to the Coast, he said, "Just don't ask me to stop every fifty miles so you can piss. I've got to make Tacoma by tomorrow afternoon."

I went back to the booth. Willie had scooted over so that my coat was partly under her. I didn't want to wake her up, so I just left it there. It was just an unlined windbreaker anyway. I took one last look at them. I hoped they'd make it to Bonners Ferry, but given what they were, it didn't seem to matter much where they wound up. They'd be back on the road again before long, the road being the only place where they would feel welcome.

In the truck, a huge Diamond T hauling double trailers, the driver said, "Who was that ugly fuck and the bony squaw you were with?"

"Just a ride," I said, tossing my suitcase behind the seat.

The trucker poured himself a cup of coffee from a thermos, shook two white pills from a small envelope. He placed the pills carefully on his tongue, then swallowed them with coffee.

"Got to jump-start my fucking *brain*," he said, winking.

Then we roared out into the blinding storm.

D ave Colbert is sick of hearing about the geology of the northern Rockies, but the man driving the car, Marv Trane, is a relentless know-it-all who never passes up a chance to display his knowledge or to correct Colbert's less encyclopedic grasp of the earth's crust. The wives of the two men are chatting in the back seat of Trane's Isuzu Trooper. It was Colbert's wife, Rhea, who suggested the joint week-long trek to Montana. Trane's wife, Freddi—a small, high-strung woman whose eyelids flutter hysterically when she speaks—had been bitten on the arms by her husband and had found a sympathetic confidante in Rhea. They had met in Relationship Dynamics, a class taught in a local community college's adult education division. The two men had not met each other until yesterday morning, and Colbert—who has already had his fill of Marv Trane—is gloomy with the realization that there is no way to avoid the six days of misery that lie ahead.

Wilderness

Colbert is afraid of Trane, convinced that the man is dangerous. Now and then Colbert catches Trane glancing at him with narrowed eyes and sly grin, as if sizing him up. Trane has done this often enough to keep Colbert on edge. When they shook hands yesterday, Trane's grip had nearly made Colbert wince. Then, when Trane smiled, he exposed his teeth to the back fillings, a trait that Colbert has always associated with ambition, aggression, and the need to intimidate. People in the public eye, the great successes of our time, seem to have this mirthless smile, which Colbert has dubbed the Attila Grin.

Trane, however, is not in the public eye. He is an unemployed systems analyst, recently laid off by Lockheed. Rhea has argued that the bites on Freddie's arms were most likely inflicted in the heat of passion, and not intended to cause pain or damage. Nonetheless, Freddi was alarmed enough to seek out Rhea for support.

"He really loves her," Rhea told Colbert, "but he sometimes loses control, especially when he goes off his medication." Trane bit his wife in a Wal-Mart parking lot, during a lightning storm. He wanted to make love, right there in the Isuzu, as the sky convulsed.

"He *forced* her?" Colbert said. "He *attacked* his own wife in a parking lot?"

Rhea frowned, then said, "No. Not really. There was consent, but it *was* a bit surprising, and... in retrospect, frightening. Freddi was afraid of what might have happened if she had refused him." Trane, Rhea said, was very upset at losing his job. Being laid off had "unmanned" him somehow. He wanted sex to be random and violent or he didn't want it at all. His consequent mood swings were hard for Freddi to cope with. A psychiatrist had prescribed an antidepressant, then, after further diagnosis and consultation, lithium, but Trane hated the side effects of such drugs and would not take them regularly. Rhea thought a trip into the mountains would be therapeutic. "It will do *us* good, too," she said.

"Up there, above that scree!" Trane shouts suddenly, jolting Colbert out of his troubled reverie. "You can see some outcroppings of Precambrian basement rock!" He rolls down his window and leans out of it, pointing up the sheer slope to the left side of the highway. His face in the wind is Attila: challenging flash of teeth, the warrior's terrain-assessing squint, the taut jut of jaw. The Isuzu drifts over the center line into the oncoming lane of traffic. There is no traffic, luckily, and Colbert, though tempted to grab the wheel, lets the car drift, half hoping it will find its way to the far shoulder of the highway, maybe even roll over into the ditch that borders it. This is the morning of the second day of the trip and Colbert is desperate enough to sacrifice his own safety, and the safety of his wife, if it results in the abrupt end of this "therapeutic" trek.

But just as the car is about to stagger onto the soft shoulder of the opposite lane, the shoulder widens into a scenic turnout and Trane wheels the big Isuzu smartly to a sliding stop next to a rushing cataract, as if this was what he meant to do all along. Trane has his door open before the car stops rolling, setting the parking brake as an afterthought. Colbert leans his head back into the headrest and closes his eyes. *Jesus*, he thinks. *I took five days of emergency sick leave for this?* He turns around to give Rhea a scathing look, but both women are peering out the windows at the cataract that is roaring down a sheer rock wall. "My God, my God," Rhea says, her voice constricted with reverence, a tone that instantly infuriates Colbert.

Colbert is a high school social studies teacher who is in the throes of burnout. He has been in the grip of a fatigue so profound that he has lost his train of thought on several occasions recently while lecturing to his honors class. Each time this has happened, he has excused himself from the room. In the hallway, nearly in tears, he would try to collect his wits. He'd smoke to calm himself, and when he'd return to the classroom he would read aloud from the textbook until the bell rang, giving him reprieve. His honors class—good kids from good middle-class homes—listened to their Walkmans while he read, or they gossiped in small groups. Some of the bolder boys and girls would pair off and make out in the back of the room. Colbert didn't care. He read mechanically from the text, not listening to himself either, fighting the urge to put his head down on his arms and go to sleep.

Rhea, always alert to behavioral aberrations, sent him first to counselors and then to doctors. The diagnoses invariably described him as a candidate for "burnout" even though his physical indicators were quite good—a bit overweight, subpar muscle tone, cholesterol level a few points out of the normal range, blood pressure up a bit, but generally speaking, he was in tolerable good health.

One counselor suggested a career change. But, at forty-two, Colbert is terrified of this option. It isn't an option at all, as far as he's concerned. It's a one-way ticket to chronic unemployment and poverty, and to an even greater lethargy of spirit. He can endure things as they are now for another ten years, when he will be eligible for an early retirement.

Colbert sighs heavily, startling himself. He realizes he has been staring at Trane's wide back, unconsciously curious, and is now abruptly recognizing Trane's posture: legs apart and loose at the knees, elbows out, head bent forward slightly in concentration. In full view of the women, Trane has unzipped his pants and is urinating next to the picturesque waterfall, the hot urine steaming in the cool mountain air. That Trane is relieving himself in front of everyone doesn't surprise Colbert at all, it only adds to his general peevishness. Rhea and Freddi, however, are looking in the opposite direction, squinting at a ridge of snow-capped peaks to the south.

"I *love* this country," Rhea says. "I don't know why we just don't *move* here. My God, imagine waking up every morning to that view!"

"I'm sick of Sunnyvale," Freddi agrees. "I mean, you can't even *see* the coastal mountains anymore because of the smog."

"I could get work making birch-bark canoes," Colbert says. "Rhea could weave baskets from the native grasses and sell them to tourists. We could chew peyote and commune with the mountain spirits."

"David's first response to beauty is cynicism," Rhea says to Freddi. "Depend on it."

"I'm not a cynic," Colbert protests mildly.

"You've got to earn your stripes to be a true cynic," Trane calls over his shoulder as he yanks up his zipper. Colbert is shocked that Trane has heard them. It seems impossible. *The man must have the ears of a bat*, he thinks. Trane leans into the Isuzu. "You've got to understand the system completely before you have the right to doubt it," he says, his teeth exposed in a white challenge that makes Colbert look away.

"Who understands any system completely?" Colbert mumbles.

"I don't mean to pull rank, Davey, but I'm a senior systems analyst, remember? It's my job to understand systems."

An unemployed senior systems analyst who bites his wife and pisses in public, Colbert thinks, and, as if Trane's keen hearing can even pick up thoughts, his smile collapses into a thin sneer and he slaps the side of the Isuzu hard, making the women, and Colbert, jump.

Colbert opens his door and gets out to stretch his legs. He walks to the rear of the car, then beyond it to the edge of the turnout. He hears a diesel truck laboring up the grade, the caw of crows, the rush of wind in the stately Ponderosas. Northern Idaho is more beautiful than he expected and he is momentarily confident that the trip might not be so bad after all. Trane is a bully and a jerk, he knows, but easy to ignore once you stop reacting to his insufferable running commentary and aggressive glances. Colbert fills his lungs with the nippy autumnal air and heads back to the car. For the first time he notices the big red-and-white bumper sticker, glued diagonally—with swashbuckling carelessness—to the back of the Isuzu: "Crisis Doesn't Make Character—It Exhibits It," and Colbert's moment of optimism fades as quickly as it came.

By midday, they are almost in Montana, nearing Lolo Pass. "I've got a surprise for you," Trane says, taking the Trooper off the highway and shifting it into four-wheel drive. Colbert, who has been dozing, is instantly alert. He feels his innards rise, weightless, as the car drops down a steep dirt road that winds through a stand of beautiful old cedars. "There's a natural hot springs down here not very many people know about," Trane says.

"You've been here before?" Colbert asks, alarmed. It occurs to him suddenly that this trip was Trane's idea to begin with and that Rhea was finessed into thinking it was hers. Rhea, for all her night-school classes in pop psychology, could be astonishingly naive. She tended to think that most people were as straightforward and honest as she was, that they meant what they said, and that liars and cheats were their own worst enemies—to be pitied, or rescued by therapy, rather than feared or avoided. She often argued that good therapy could transform the world. She believed that people were basically decent and that civilized behavior was instinctive, not an extrinsic ideal (as Colbert has often jibed) that has teased humanity for ten thousand years like a mirage in the desert.

Trane hesitates, then says, "Oh, sure. I've been here. Years ago, when I was a kid. My dad used to take me to Montana to hunt."

"How wonderful to have a *committed* father," Rhea says. "I mean, I don't approve of hunting per se, but I think a father taking his son on outings and so forth is so... *beneficial*, in terms of the son's future stability. I only wish David had had a father like that. A father like that gives his son *permission*, ultimately, to become a man."

"What kind of father *did* you have, Davey?" Trane asks. "Did he give you permission to become a man?"

Colbert ignores Trane's glance, though he can see, out of the corner of his eye, the glare of teeth. "He was a son of a bitch," Colbert says.

Trane releases a single angry bark of laughter and downshifts abruptly, making the Isuzu fishtail. "So was mine," he says. "He gave me permission to get the fuck out of his house."

"Aren't you driving a little too fast for this road, darling?" Freddi says.

"No, actually I'm not, darling," Trane says, mocking his wife's tone. He presses the accelerator to the floor and upshifts, making the car lurch into a nearly broadside skid.

"Please slow down," Rhea says. Her voice is reasonable, but Colbert knows she is terrified. He turns around so that she can see his I-told-you-so smile. Her face is rigid, her eyes are wide.

"Marv knows what he's doing," Colbert says to Rhea. "He's obviously an experienced off-road driver, no need to fret."

Rhea leans her head back and closes her eyes. "Don't take that tone with me, David," she says. "I'm not a child."

"There it is," Trane announces, bringing the Isuzu to a hard stop. They are in a clearing: a bowl with steep granite sides, the high, sky-touching rim of which is screened with thick stands of larch and fir. At the bottom of the bowl is a steaming pool of water about the size of a baseball diamond. The pool is studded with large gray boulders. "Hot springs," Trane says. "This is part of the Lolo batholith."

"Remarkable!" Rhea says, her voice resuming the irritating pitch of reverence Colbert has not heard before today.

"Molten granite magma rose into the earth's crust here about fifty million years ago," Trane says, lecturing again. "What you see all around you is young granite. Now, fractures in the granite and in the Precambrian sediment rock permit rainwater, or the runoff from snowmelt, to circulate deeply enough to get heated by the still-hot batholith before it percolates back up to the surface at the springs."

"Nature's own hot tub," Colbert says.

"Right," Trane says, winking archly. It's a conspiratorial wink that annoys Colbert. "*Better* than a hot tub, in fact," Trane goes on. "The Indians claimed these waters had healing powers And not just for your usual aches and pains, but for your spirit. Water like this will put your body and soul back into alignment."

Colbert can almost sense the thrill that Rhea is experiencing. It is the sort of thing she needs to believe in, having given up on all the conventional forms of belief.

"Is it safe?" she says. "I mean, can we go in without getting scalded?"

Trane leans into the backseat and puts his hand on Rhea's knee. "A little scalding is just what the medicine man ordered," he says, winking again. He shuts off the engine, and the silence moves in on them like a forbidding presence. For a while no one speaks; they even breathe cautiously. Finally, Trane opens his door, and the slight wheeze of dry hinges releases a worm of sound into the body of silence.

Rhea is first to speak. "My God but this is beautiful. Are we allowed to camp here?"

"Who's going to tell us we can't?" Trane says.

The cool, piney air, Colbert notices, has a slight sulfurous stink to it. The disk of blue sky above them seems unhappily far away, an optical illusion generated by the steep granite walls and the tall conifers that grow at the high rim. Trane opens the back doors of the Isuzu and pulls out the camping gear. "I'll set up the tents," he says. "Why don't you ladies try the healing waters? Then we'll have a good lunch."

Colbert starts to undo the ties on one of the bundles, but Trane takes him by the elbow and pulls him aside. "Let me deal with this stuff, Davey," he says. "I've done this a thousand times. You could be a big help by digging the slit trench, off a ways in the trees."

"Slit trench?" Colbert asks, confused. Colbert is not a camper, has always felt uncomfortable in the woods. He prefers picnic grounds with tables and fire rings. He likes to know that convenience stores and telephones are not far away.

"You know—an outdoor crapper," Trane says. "Dig it about a foot wide and about three feet long. Maybe a foot and a half deep." He hands Colbert a short narrow-bladed shovel, then returns to the job of laying out the tents and other equipment.

Even a brief walk into the woods makes Colbert nervous. And these are real woods, the wilderness, not a neighborhood park. The ground is carpeted with pine needles, the scented air is thick and unmoving. Colbert feels that he is being observed by animals he cannot see. Behind a large, privacy-giving, lichen-covered boulder, he starts to dig. The ground is hard and his progress is slow. He has to remove stones of varying sizes from time to time, and the slit trench that gradually takes shape does not have the square dimensions Trane described. It's more of an oblong hole, the size of a steamer trunk. It has taken Colbert an hour to dig it, and his arms and back are burning with fatigue. When he returns to the campsite, the tents are erected side by side with a fire ring made of stones set between them.

"David! David!" Rhea says. "Where have you been? Get *in* here, it's wonderful!" Her voice has a haunting quality, as if it is coming from all directions at once, a voice in a dream.

All three of them are in the water. Colbert sees their heads floating together at the far side of the pool, partly screened by mist. He stares at them for a while, as if he doesn't recognize what he's looking at. "Rhea?" he says.

"Take your clothes off and get in here, honey!" Rhea calls again. Her voice is textured and amplified by the heated water and surrounding granite. He is momentarily transfixed by this vision of the floating heads and by the odd resonance of Rhea's voice.

"Come on, Davey," Trane says, "we'll baptize you. Old Wakantanka lives here." Trane's voice, enlarged and timbered with authority, is doubly obnoxious to Colbert. He turns his back on them.

"Marv says Wakantanka is the Indian name for the Great Spirit, honey," Rhea calls after him.

"Does he," Colbert says under his breath as he pulls back the flap of a tent.

His and Rhea's suitcase is inside, and he rummages through it until he finds his swim trunks. He strips, then pulls on the trunks, a boxer-style pair he bought twenty years ago, imprinted with white sailboats against faded blue. The trunks no longer fit. His pale belly falls over the waistband. Colbert leaves the tent and his skin is immediately assaulted by the cool, humid air, as are his bare feet by the pine-needle loam. When he steps into the misting pool, he chokes back the urge to cry out in pain. The water is *hot*, well over one hundred degrees, but the apparent comfort of the others makes him wade bravely forward against the instinctive urge to recoil. The notion that he is wading not into water but into pure *pain* gives Colbert a moment of giddy panic. He grits his teeth and moves toward the smiling heads resting at the base of a granite boulder the size of a small house.

"David," Rhea says, "those trunks are ridiculous."

"The trunks are fine," Colbert says. "It's the body in them that's gotten ridiculous."

"Don't knock yourself, Davey," Trane says, pulling himself strongly out of the water and onto a shelf in the stone. Colbert tries to hide his dismay at seeing that Trane is naked. He looks quickly at the women, still up to their necks in the opaque water. Their faces, red and finely beaded with sweat, betray no sense of shock or uneasiness.

"Get all the way in, David," Rhea says. "It's more therapeutic that way. It feels fantastic."

Freddi climbs up next to her husband, and Colbert sees that she is also naked. She is even more fragile-looking without clothes. Her small, chalky breasts, webbed with networks of fine blue veins, seem as breakable as china in the early-afternoon sunlight. The Tranes, on the gray rock, look like a posed tableau—Marv, the muscular Roman god; Freddi, the water nymph.

"This place is magical!" Rhea says, apparently unaffected by the casual nudity of the Tranes. She submerges herself suddenly, then springs up pink and laughing, and Colbert—as he has begun to suspect—sees that Rhea is naked, too.

"You'll smooth the kinks out of your system here, Davey," Trane says lazily. He's lying back now, taking the sun, his genitals lolling on his thigh, while Freddi, on her haunches beside him, looks dreamily content, as if water, sun, and the passivity of her husband have conspired to put her into a happy, self-satisfied rapture.

Rhea's large breasts, buoyant and flushed pink in the hot, silty water, embarrass Colbert. Colbert is a private and shy man who has always shunned openness in public. Rhea, early in their marriage, would sometimes hug him impulsively, no matter where they were. She'd kiss his cheek or ear, comb loose strands of his hair with her fingers, but Colbert put a stop to it. "I'm sorry, honey," he'd said, on more than one occasion, "but I can't be intimate in public. It's like exposing my private life to an audience of strangers." Rhea said she understood, but often forgot herself, drawing sharp rebukes from Colbert. After their marriage crystallized into routine, the subject never came up again. But now, what the years solidified has become, in one afternoon, loose and undefined, and Colbert feels sick with humiliation; he feels betrayed.

"Take those outrageous trunks off, honey," Rhea laughs, climbing out of the water and stretching out on a rock slab of her own, without any apparent self-consciousness. Colbert regards his large-breasted, wide-hipped wife gleaming in the sun and is suddenly moved to the brink of tears at the mindless generosity of her ample body. The body is so helpless, he thinks—a poor pack animal bent under the crushing weight of a confused, unteachable ghost. This thought depresses Colbert further, and he turns his back on the three glistening bathers. "The trunks stay on," Colbert says, wading away. His heart is pounding hard enough to hear. He is sure the others can hear it, too. He crawls into his tent and puts his clothes back on. Then he goes out and gathers dry sticks for the fire ring, taking Trane's hatchet with him.

Trane, using a high-tech two-burner propane stove, fixes a late-afternoon lunch of wild rice with mushrooms and chicken breasts in wine sauce. He takes a container of prepared asparagus vinaigrette out of an ice chest, and there is a good Sonoma white zinfandel to drink. They sit on folding chairs at a card table draped with a linen tablecloth, and they eat off real china.

"God, I expected to eat Beefaroni off paper plates," Rhea says, delighted. "Whose idea was this?"

"*Mea cullpa*," Trane says. "But I'm glad Davey collected all those twigs anyway. Later on we can make us a little fire and have a sing-along. I brought my twelve-string. How about it, Dave? You remember Dylan? I do passable Dylan."

"David's being a poop," Rhea says. "He's a world-class sulker."

"I'm telling you, Davey," Trane says, "you should have adopted the right attitude out there in the water. A *wicasa wakan*—holy man to you—would have warned you about taking these waters with a bug up your ass. There's probably not a lot of time to get yourself in tune."

"What do you mean by that, Marv?" Rhea asks.

She sounds like a schoolgirl, Colbert thinks.

"I think I'm boring Davey," Trane says.

"Well, you're not boring me," Rhea says.

"I just meant," Trane continues, "that according to precepts found not only in Mahayana Buddhism but in nearly all of the nondualistic religions, including Native American animism—"

"Excuse me," Colbert says, standing up abruptly. "I have to go to the slit trench."

Trane releases a burst of hard laughter that puts Colbert on alert. "That's *funny!*" Trane says. "Davey said something funny." He cups his large hand on Freddi's shoulder and rocks her. "Don't you want to say something funny, too? Show these people that you can say something funny, too, Freddi."

"I can't think," Freddi says, smiling self-consciously.

"Try," Trane says. "Try to think. Who knows, you might get to liking it."
Colbert is awakened out of a dream in which his bare feet are being snuffled by large rodentlike animals. Rising voices have pulled him out of his disturbed sleep, and he lies on his back staring into the close black air of the small tent.

"I don't know why they have to fight," Rhea says.

"I wouldn't call it fighting," Colbert says, yawning.

Trane is talking with the speed and intensity of a manic auctioneer. His rant is punctuated every half minute or so by a whimpering response from Freddi.

"These tents should be farther apart," Colbert says, recalling, wistfully, their widely separated motel rooms of the night before.

"Listen to that," Rhea says, sitting up.

The sound is unmistakable, but Colbert just shrugs.

"He's *striking* her," Rhea says. Freddi is crying softly, begging him to stop. Trane's angry chant has become a barely articulate growl.

"We don't know that," Colbert reasons. "I think it's just a performance for our benefit."

"We'd better do something about this, David," Rhea says.

Colbert lies back down and pulls the sleeping bag over his head. "I didn't bring a revolver," he says.

"I'm *serious.*"

"I know it's hard, but try not to be," Colbert says, rolling over into his sleeping position. The cold, unyielding ground under the tent floor makes his shoulder ache instantly.

Abruptly, the commotion in the Tranes' tent shops. There is a canyon of silence into which Colbert has begun to fall, the dream of rodents nuzzling his feet returning, but before the fall is complete he is pulled back into consciousness by a string of urgent moans.

"They're making love," Rhea, who is still sitting up, says.

"No, it's just sex," Colbert mumbles. "Tarzan's reward."

Rhea sighs. "Everything is a great big joke to you."

Colbert doesn't respond to this. The remark strikes him as not only off the mark but, in light of what he has been going through the past few months, *unfair.*

Then Rhea's searching hand is in his sleeping bag. "Come on," she says. "Let's."

"Rhea, for Christ's sakes."

"It's been a long time, David," she says sternly.

"It's been a week," he says.

"I'm not taking no for answer," she says. Her hoarse voice in the disembodying dark becomes a curiosity, as if it is the voice of a threatening stranger. Colbert imagines startled animals bolting through the forest at the sound of Freddie's eerie vocalizations, as Rhea unzips his bag and presses herself down on top of him, vibrant with a fierce, uncompromising energy.

But Colbert pushes her away. He pulls on his shirt and pants and leaves the tent. He walks to the edge of the hot springs and squats down. A crescent moon suspended in the narrow disk of sky is reflected perfectly in the black water. Colbert takes his shirt and pants off and wades toward the moon, trying not to disturb it. He wades to the far side of the pool and leans back against a wall of granite. He is surprised that he feels comfortable and relaxed, and soon his thoughts drift south, away from the wilderness of Idaho.

He remembers attacking the smug ignorance of his bored honors class shortly before he began to lose interest in them. "Your feelings and ideas, limited and confused as they are, have been *handed down* to you," he told them. "You don't know it, but you're wearing old, mismatched clothes. You think you're wearing originals, you're proud of the ridiculous costume you're wearing. But it's old, *old*, and stinks of the thousand dead bodies who wore it before you!" ("*Gross*, Mr. Colbert," offered Betty Vukovich, a cheerleader, sticking her finger into her mouth as if to induce nausea.) He began to tremble. He had to blink away a shock of burning tears. But the kids just stared at him with drooping interest, like sheep momentarily distracted from their browsing by the irrelevant natterings of a possessed shepherd.

A splash breaks his reverie. Something has entered the water, and Colbert feels his neck hairs bristle. He starts wading stealthily back toward the tents, but he is sure that whatever it was that made the splash is aware of him. A catalogue of wild animals races through his mind, from otters to mountain lions to grizzly bears, and when he reaches the opposite shore, he is breathless with terror. He looks back at the water expecting to see a dark presence leaving a heavy wake, but sees only the rippled moon.

"Hidden in every shaman is a hunter," Trane pontificates. He's been in the water for over an hour and his skin is dangerously pink as he lies on the rock slab, recovering.

"That's it," Colbert says. "I've had it up to here. We're going home. Drive us to Spokane and we'll take the next flight to San Jose."

"Whoa, bud," Trane says, easing himself off his rock with the grace of a sea lion.

Colbert wades away from the group, suddenly fearful. He hears, behind him the water parting furiously before Trane's churning thighs.

"You're acting like a spoiled child, David," Rhea says. Her voice is languid, almost disinterested, and this makes Colbert doubly fearful. Something has changed, but he can't decide what it is that has made today different from yesterday. He is aware of his poor physical condition more than ever, how his pale, shapeless legs cannot move with strength and speed through the dense, sulfuric waters.

"Wait up, Davey," Trane says, his voice cajoling now, seductive.

Then Trane's hand is on Colbert's shoulder, stopping his retreat. Colbert turns to face Trane and realizes, for the first time, the true difference in their sizes. His eyes are level with Trane's chin; to meet Trane's gray gaze, he has to look up. Trane's eyes are benevolent and manically intense at the same time, and Colbert tries to turn away, but Trane has tightened his grip, making escape impossible.

"What do you think you're running away from, Davey?" Trane says. "Remember: Wherever you go, *there you are.*"

"Take your hand off me, you fucking creep," Colbert says, his voice trembling.

But Trane throws his arm around Colbert in a brotherly embrace that makes the stiff bones in his shoulder crackle. Then, with Colbert in tow, Trane starts wading back toward the stones where the naked women lie easy in the sun.

"Let me go, you crazy son of a bitch!" Colbert says, close to tears.

"I've told you, Davey," Trane says, unmoved by Colbert's rage, "you've got to show the right attitude in these waters. This isn't your backyard pool, this is a holy place."

"You goddamn phony," Colbert sobs. "Everything you say..."

But suddenly Colbert finds himself underwater, held there, unable to wrench himself away from the arm that has him in a headlock, keeping him submerged. The water makes his nose and eyes feel on fire, but the arm will not release him. It occurs to him that Trane intends to drown him, and he begins to fight for his life, but he has no leverage and poor footing, even if he could match Trane's strength.

Then, just as suddenly as he was submerged, he is hauled up out of the water, gasping. He tries to work free of the headlock, but Trane tightens his grip. Colbert's face is crushed into Trane's rib cage. He tries to look to the women for help but is unable to lift his eyes to them.

"Baptism, you realize," Trane says blandly, "did not originate with the early Christians. It's a rite as old as mankind itself. Man, very early in his history, realized that he was vulnerable to all sorts of false systems springing from values rooted in the survival instinct—you believe what you *need* to believe—and false *systems* invariably deny the heart's desire to transcend the mundane. Man wants to feel exalted. And so, baptism was seen as the symbolic washing away of the things that clog one's ability to experience straightforward truth."

"Then it's meaningless to baptize infants," Colbert hears Rhea say. He is astonished that she has maintained her bright and banal sophomoric tone.

"A man like your husband here is unable to experience his own life. He's locked into a totally flawed system. You're right, Rhea. Infants should baptize us."

"Please," Colbert says, his voice muffled. He is becoming vertiginous in the vise of Trane's arm. "Let me go."

"We should *all* be baptized," Rhea says gaily, pushing off her rock and entering the water. "We all need a new start."

"Out with the old, in with the new," Freddie giggles, joining her.

"This, of course, is my point," Trane says, muscling Colbert under the hot water again. This time Trane takes him deeper, and Colbert loses his footing altogether. He feels helplessly buoyant as his boxer-style trunks break the surface and balloon, and though he is terrified, he thinks of how foolish the trunks must look, billowing pneumatically, exaggerating his clownish rump, the faded blue sailboats stretched tight. When he feels he has held his breath as long as possible, he begins to claw at Trane for mercy. And when this fails, he puts his hands flat on the silty bottom and tries to push himself up.

Something moves under this left hand. It is a jagged wedge of granite, roughly the size of a brick. He digs it out of the soft silt and shifts it to his right hand and when Trane finally pulls him into the air, Colbert swings the stone upward with as much force and accuracy as his awkward position will allow and it hits the side of Trane's head, close to the temple. He believes that if he allows Trane to dunk him again, his breath will give out and he will drown, and so as Trane bellows in pain and surprise, his hands now shielding his bleeding head, Colbert drives the heavy stone into Trane's face as hard as he can and this time he hears the wet collapse of cartilage and bone. Trane staggers backward, thrashing the water, trying to stay on his feet. Colbert follows him until Trane slumps down in shallow water. Dimly aware of the screams of the women somewhere behind him, he raises the stone with both hands and hammers it into the top of Trane's skull, an though Trane's eyes are red and blind, he is able to say, "Oh now wait, Dave. Please, Dave, wait," as the water around both men turns flagrantly red.

Colbert, sobbing for breath, wades back to the tents. The bones of his right hand are cramped with pain, as if his hand has suddenly aged and every joint has been frozen with severe arthritis. He looks at his hand and sees that it is still gripping the blood-smeared stone. He tries to will his fingers open but the fingers, white as sun-bleached bone, refuse to comply. He holds his arm out from his side, puzzled, waiting for the rock to drop. He is shaking wildly. His knees unlock, nearly causing him to fall. It is as if all the strength of his body has been concentrated in the hand that holds the stone. He tries to throw it into the trees, but only throws himself off balance, and he falls to all fours, still gripping the wedge of granite.

It is not until he sees Trane's hatchet, leaning against the ice chest, that his hand relaxes. He leaves the stone behind and crawls toward the hatchet. He feels as if he is swimming, his movements slowed but also sustained by water. The hatchet feels good in his hand—it is light and well balanced, and it has kept its edge. It is much superior to a stone. The teacher he once was recalls the dozens of millennia between stone and steel, how the efficient steel blade of progress joyously cut down the astonished enemy.

Colbert feels refreshed and clear-headed as he wades back out to the annoying gabble of voices. He feels as if he's just awakened from ten thousand years of nightmare.

Pop hit Mom. I heard it, then I heard Mom. She yelled. She started to cry. I unplugged my earphones from my shortwave radio and came out of my room, blinking in the bright light of the kitchen. Mom was sitting at the table, and Pop—Wade Eggers—was leaning over her. I went up to him and hammered him. I nailed him. He went down in slow motion, like a swamped boat. I still had my earphones on. I started to kick him, but Mom said, "Don't, honey," real loud, in that voice of hers that makes you think Jesus is in the next room, watching. So I quit. I had no great hate for him. I had no feeling for any of them. By "them" I mean the men she picked out for herself. I was just sick and tired of it. "It" meaning her life and what she dragged along behind it, me included. If I'd had some dynamite

The Voice of America

just then, I probably would have lit it. In my mind I have burned that house in National City down to the foundation a thousand times, everyone asleep inside. I dreamed of waking up as someone else, in a different place, where things were decent. "Good-bye, forever," I said. I meant it this time.

Mom was drunker than Pop. She got up and went into the living room. I followed her. Blood hung on her lip like a dark red grape. A drop fell onto her carpet. She always said she loved that carpet. It was a fake oriental made in Mexico. "I'm gone," I said. I kicked the television. It was a big cherrywood Packard Bell with a twelve-inch screen. A clay penguin on top fell off and broke, but Sid Caesar on the screen didn't flicker.

"I don't want you to leave," she said. "Where can you go, honey?"

I picked up the Packard Bell and let it drop. I looked around for something else to pick up and drop. The china cupboard.

"Stop it!" she yelled. She held one hand up to her face. "Stop it!" Her fingers trembled, like she had taken all she could. But I had seen all this before many times. There was no end to what she could take. That's how it seemed. It was an act. Everything is an act.

I went back into the kitchen. Pop had pulled a bread knife out of a drawer. *That* made me blow up. I hit him as hard as I had ever hit anyone. This time he flopped when he went down. His eyes rolled up, showing the whites. His mossy tongue hung out. I put my hands around my mouth and called down to him, like he was in a hole. "Pop, I'll hurt you this time, I mean it," I said.

To show I was serious, I kicked his gut. I walked on him. He started arching his back and waving his arms so as to call me off. I picked him up by his shirt and slammed him a few times on the wall. His head bounced. During all this I still had my earphones on. "Stop it, baby!" Mom yelled. "You'll kill him!"

In my earphones her yelling sounded like so much whimpering music. Let her whimper to Jesus, I thought, as I drummed the wall with Pop. I thought about all the times—when I was younger—how I cried in my bed while she and whatever man she had at the time fought and yelled, sometimes with strangers they had brought into our house. I would put on my war-surplus earphones with the big rubber pads and plug them into my war-surplus BC-348 shortwave receiver and try to pick up the Voice of America. But I could hear them right through the Voice of America.

I thought, as I slammed Pop, about the many times I had sat alone in a car outside some bar in Marquette, Michigan; Fort Worth, Texas; Bakersfield, California; or Tijuana, Mexico. I thought about the motel and hotel rooms I had slept in as a child waiting for someone to come for me while a world of strangers cursed and cried in the hallways and small rooms above and below and to all sides. These things are not so terrible—I have heard of worse—but they add up after a while and you learn to hate them. We had no real home and the stink of liquor and the noise of their lives was something I always ached to get away from. But leaving isn't easy. There are things you have to think about. Mom married Wade when I was thirteen. He was her fourth husband, if I have counted correctly. None of them was any good. Wade was the worst. I had seen him pick up a knife before, though he never had guts enough to use it.

I went back into my room. The yellowish glow of the dials on the BC-348 looked like two sour smiles. I plugged my earphones back in and searched around for the Voice of America. I loved to listen to the Voice of America. You could listen to all your favorite radio programs as they were broadcast across the oceans to Communist countries so that the people who lived in them could hear how it was to live in the Land of the Free. *Jack Benny, Duffy's Tavern, Truth or Consequences, Counterspies, The Great Gildersleeve*, and so on. I had copper wire strung out to the eucalyptus tree in the backyard for good reception. I found the Voice of America in the thirty-one-meter band, but they just had Walter Winchell on or somebody like that with the latest bad news.

"I don't want you to go, baby," Mom said. She had come into my room. She stood behind me and my radio equipment. She lifted one earphone away from my head so I could hear her. Then she put her hands on me. I shook her off. She was so stupid with booze she didn't know how to act. She hardly ever knew how to act. Some people just aren't ready for the world from the time they are born. She is one of them. This had to be the tenth time she'd begged me not to leave.

"I'm going anyway," I said. I was seventeen, almost eighteen, and big. I had talked to a Marine recruiting sergeant. Korea was still going on. They needed men. I lifted weights at my friend Dick Drummond's house. I could military-press two hundred and dead-lift three. I was ready. To leave her behind.

She put her hand on my biceps, which I hardened. "I'd be here alone with him if you went away, honey," she said, squeezing around on my arm as if looking for soft spots.

I took off the earphones and turned around. "That's your problem," I said. "Leave him if you don't want to take that crap," I said.

"You know I've stayed with him for your sake, baby," she said. "Baby, you *know* that's the only reason I've stuck it out. I wanted you to have a home."

This was too stupid for words. But I had heard it before and was tired of telling her how stupid it was. It was worse than stupid. It was a lie. This was a lie that she believed herself. How people could lie to themselves, and *believe* it, was the miracle of human life as far as I was concerned. I'd seen her do it, I'd seen Wade Eggers do it. I have seen others do it since. If you need to believe something bad enough, you *do*. She sat down on my bed and started crying again. "You could be like Jesus," she said. "Any boy could, if he wants to let it out, if he isn't too scared." This was booze talking. Her Jesus talk made me want to hit her. I got up and left the room.

Pop was puking into the kitchen sink. The kitchen was heavy with the stink of bourbon-puke. She could really pick the winners. I went into their bedroom and took the keys to the Pontiac off the dresser. Then I went out to the car and unlocked it. Pop, at the kitchen window, saw what I was up to. He rapped the glass with a knife. He came stumbling out of the house.

"Don't you dare touch my car," he said.

"Go to hell, you goddamn Communist," I said, ramming the gear lever into first and spraying gravel.

I don't know why I called him Communist. He considered himself self-educated and had a superior attitude. He read books, and when he came to a good part, he'd read it out loud, no matter who was there or whether or not they cared about the good parts. Pop drove a sandwich and coffee truck and parked it outside the gates of defense plants at lunchtime and at shift changes. That's how he made his living. It gave him a lot of time to read books. Walter Winchell said the Communists were in high places, getting ready to take over the country. They wanted to change how we thought. They had sneaky ways to do this, so you had to keep your guard up. Watch out for those teachers and professors who say things that downgrade our nation. I didn't worry about it. I figured my teachers were too stupid to be Communists. But Pop wasn't stupid. He'd put on his F. W. Woolworth reading glasses and say things like "Jesus Christ was not the son of God. He was just a good magician. He fooled the gullible with sleight-of-hand tricks and with hypnotic spells. Just add him to your list of egomaniac Jews." Mom hated this type of talk, since she was religious, or at least she believed in God and Jesus, and that it was bad luck to bad-mouth them. Pop deviled her for fun.

I drove over to Dick Drummond's house. It was still early enough for him to be up, though his folks were in bed. I honked the horn in his driveway, two longs and two shorts, so he'd know it was me. He came down in about a minute.

"What's happening, Shit-hook," he said. Dick was a wiseass. He got in the car and the first thing he did was switch on the radio. He searched around until he found the L.A. station that played nothing but R and B, which you could not find on a local station. Local DJs thought Johnny Ray was as cool as it got. They thought Les Paul and Mary Ford were hip.

I burned rubber coming out of his driveway and caught a yard of second-gear rubber in the street. Dick whistled, but he was being a wiseass. Dick had this chopped deuce coupe with a full-race '51 Merc engine in it and he could lay a mile of high-gear rubber shifting up from second doing sixty. So a 1949 Pontiac with a low-compression six didn't exactly impress him, even though I was pretty good at nailing second with a speed shift.

"Check the mirror, Dad," he said. "I think you left the transmission in the road." Coming from Dick Drummond, this was a compliment. Dick was tall and lean. He could bench-press a ton, but he couldn't clean-and-jerk worth spit. No legs.

I headed out to the beaches. Dick had the radio turned up full-blast. Lloyd Price was singing "Mail Man, Mail Man." We were on a dark street in Pacific Beach. Dick said, "Stop here a second, Dad." I pulled the car over to the curb. Dick got out and walked over to a storefront. He raised his foot, then looked over at me with a comical expression on his face. Dick could be a bad actor. I knew he could do it if he was in the mood. He was wearing his engineer boots. I shrugged. He straightened his leg into the window and it bowed in, then exploded. Dick danced back from the falling glass. Then he reached into the window and picked up a suitcase. He carried it to the car and threw it into the backseat. I popped the clutch, laid yards of rubber, speed-shifted into second, caught another yard of rubber. I hit third with another speed shift, but there wasn't any top-end power left and the Pontiac just wobbled a little and flattened out.

Up in La Jolla where all the bankers and doctors live, Dick had me drive alongside parked cars, real slow, while he reached out of his window with a jack handle and knocked off side mirrors and punched holes into windows. I saw a kid's bike lying out on a sidewalk. I hopped the curb and mashed it. Dick laughed.

Back down in Mission Beach we picked up a couple of girls. They were gang girls who'd been dumped. Their hands were tattooed. Dick had Julia and I had Inez. We drove up to Torrey Pines and found a dark spot looking over the moonlit ocean. On the radio: Earl Bostick playing "Flamingo." It was real romantic, and Dick had Julia's pants off in half a minute, but I had too much on my mind for it. Inez said, "What's wrong, mon? You feeling out of it? *No quieres* nookie, mon?" She was good-looking enough, but my mood was wrong. I just didn't feel like it. She was in my lap. Her breath burned my eyes. I turned the radio dial, looking for more L.A. R and B stations. I found Ray Charles. "Lonely Avenue." This made it worse.

We drove the girls back to Mission Beach, then headed home. We didn't talk. We listened to music.

"You okay, Dad?" Dick said when I let him off. "That was prime muff, man. You missed some choice gash."

I shrugged. I backed out of his driveway and headed home. Two blocks down the street I caught high-gear rubber by floorboarding the fat Pontiac for a full three or four seconds before I popped the clutch. There was a gravel patch on the street. I slid. The rear fender hit a parked car. This made me laugh. I drove home laughing, tears on my face, singing like Lloyd Price.

It was late, almost morning. I let myself in through the back way and went to my room. I felt ripped, like I'd been into the wine. I turned on the BC-348 and looked for the Voice of America. It was lost in static, on every band. Then I found an American-sounding announcer saying how the Chinese were kicking the Americans out of Korea and how cities in the U.S.A. were full of crime and how the whites hated the Negroes. It was Radio Moscow. I shot Radio Moscow the finger through the glowing dials. Then I went to bed.

"Jesus planned this out," Mom was saying. She was sitting on my bed. The sun was up. She'd been talking, thinking that I was awake even though my eyes were closed.

"What?" I said.

"He's gone, honey," she said. "Pop. He left an hour ago. He's not coming back." She dabbed a tear out of the corner of her eye. "He was destined to stay four years three months, and now he's gone. I believe Jesus had this in mind for me."

My hand was sore. I looked at it. It had swollen up and the knuckles were raw and blue. I wondered what he had in store for me. I didn't believe there was anything in store for anyone. People just let themselves believe any bullshit that makes things easier for them. I said it before: This amazes me.

"Oh God, you gave him a terrific wallop, honey," she said.

"He's gone?" I said.

"I've never seen a terrific wallop like that."

"You mean' he's not coming home tonight?"

She sneered, and for a second, though everyone always said she was a very pretty woman, she looked ugly. Then she smiled and was pretty again. "Not tonight, not any night. He's gone." She picked up my hand and kissed it. Her lips lingered on each battered knuckle as if to heal it. "I'll make you a nice breakfast, baby," she said.

Breakfast sounded good. It had been a long night. I was hungry.

I am haunted by lightning. When the sky is streaked with jagged blue flame, when the blue-white tongues fork the earth, when the deep-throated anvils or hammerheads drift their weightless tons over my house murmuring my name in the oldest language men know, it is time for me to put insulating miles between myself and the weather or dash quickly to the rubberized shed in the backyard.

Conductivity runs in my family, reliably leapfrogging the generations. My father was not affected by voltage from the sky. My grandfather, however, was lifted out of his Adirondack lawn chair by a furious bolt arcing, literally, out of

Insulation

the blue: no storm, no cloud, no freak manifestation of ionized dust—just naked *a capella* lightning. The empty windless sky gave him false security as he sat reading the papers in the lovely light of an August afternoon. Grandmother was watching him fondly from the kitchen window as she stirred batter for peach cobbler, her specialty. Then the blue shaft, thick as God's middle finger, lifted him out of a satisfied doze as she watched, not in horror, but as one might relive the strangeness of one's dreams.

Shock and horror came later when she found herself in the yard standing at the edge of a burned area in the lawn, Grandfather still smoking at the ears and nose, his head a violent shade of vermilion, his hands clutching with the strength of a strangler his evening *Tribune*. Grandfather had flown up and over the back of the lawn chair, tossed like a toy, the vermilion glow fading to something darker, a grim tattoo coarse and ugly, zigzagging from scalp to the conductive center just above the navel—our genetic fault line.

I am not superstitious. Just the opposite. I have degrees in mathematics and physics from a better-than-average university; I have made my living for twenty-two years by analyzing failure rates for the aerospace industry. I along with three colleagues designed the multipurpose Unplanned Event Record, which is now used universally.

But there was a close call last summer, and it changed everything, made me attractive in ways you would not imagine. Now I am preoccupied with insulation. I have had all the tall trees that once surrounded my house cut down. No TV antenna festoons the roof. I wear thick-soled rubber boots, even to church. (The steeple of our church was demolished by lightning a year ago. A char of skeletal beams points skyward, aspiring hope mutilated in a single, heaven-sent stroke.)

This is the truth we live by: A thousand repetitions of an event give you every right to expect the one thousand and first. This is what lies behind the reassuring phrase "Laboratory-Tested." You rely on it. Your warranties would not be worth the paper they are written on if not for such testing. This is why, despite your romantic longings for a less technically suffocating world, you do not believe in ghosts, mental telepathy, synchronicity, healing crystals, New Age music, or the zodiac. Go to two astrologers on the same day and you are likely to have a head-on collision with yourself on the expressway to confusion.

We have a fine new world. It works repeatedly, not in random fits and starts. We have what the ancients only dreamed of: reliability. Chicken guts, crystal balls, tea leaves, tarot cards, *I Ching* sticks, drug- or starvation-induced hallucinations do not produce the reliable and specific data required by jumbo-jet pilots, brain surgeons, market analysts, or, for that matter, wheat farmers. Bypass hard knowledge at your own risk. The "right-brain" enthusiasts, the gurus of intuition, are simply lazy. They want the shortcut that bypasses the difficult road between cause and effect. But no one gets off this road. Superstition remains superstition and it can only lead to the dark side of the mind, where illumination is scant and quirky, and those who travel there soon find themselves lost in the eclipse of reason.

I am haunted by lightning, but I believe in reason. I won't produce convincing evidence here. I am not trying to convince anyone. I am only trying to save my life, my sanity, though it is too late to save Eugenia.

Eugenia had come to fear me. If I reached across the breakfast table to touch her hand, she pulled back, goose bumps spreading up her arms. I would see her counting, though she tried to conceal it. I saw the slight up-and-down ratcheting of her eyes as they numbered the vertical peonies in each panel of wallpaper to distract herself from her fear. A good-bye kiss at the doorstep had become an ordeal for her. Our lips no longer met. We kissed the neutral air. In the bedroom—but I am not one to discuss the bedroom. Suffice it to say that when the forecast was bad, our nights were spent in the stomach-souring dread of distant thunder.

Eugenia had evolved rituals for such times that made the traditional Latin mass seem accessible and abrupt. She made the bed seven times, spraying, again and again, the underside of the blankets and sheets with an antistatic aerosol. She stood on a chair and unscrewed the light bulbs, thinking, foolishly, that by disconnecting them from their source she would safeguard the bedroom. For this same reason, she unplugged the radios, clocks, and television set. She kept crystals under her pillows. Sometimes they found their way into the bedclothes, where they scratched us. But she would not hear my complaints. A sudden breeze with the smell of rain or ozone in it sent her running. She claimed she could see the fine hair along my upper arms rise up as if from sinister sleep when ordinary unmenacing clouds drifted overhead.

She knew—to give her credit—that she was made up of positive and negative charges. We all are. The universe is. There is nothing else. This is the bottom line, perhaps the only line. The play of human events—a phantasmagoria imposed on an electromagnetic field. You knew this, of course. There is nothing more to say about it.

When the electron-hungry clouds—anvils, hammerheads—began to track me down with the same inexorable logic that describes the fall of an apple, Eugenia believed the danger was a consequence of moral fault. She made the sign of the cross before receiving me.

"I am entitled to some affection!" I have cried out on occasion.

"I am giving it to you," she'd remark. "This is it." But she'd wear electrician's gloves with rubber gauntlets that reached her elbows. Gum-soled shoes covered her feet. She coated herself from ankles to earlobes with a nonconductive oil used in the manufacture of electrolytic capacitors that smells vaguely of burning dogwood. I still keep a steel drum of this oil in the garage. The insulation, naturally, also involved the place of intimate connection. The bolt of passion, needless to say, was often neutralized by such rigorous precaution. I won't say more.

I have been to famous clinics. They find my blood, bones, and tissues normal in every way. They find no pockets of ionization, no secret micro lightning rods wired into my femurs or tibiae. My hair has been studied for excesses of copper, zinc, and iron—elements that might seduce electrons out of the sleeping ground. I have been wired to ultrasensitive meters while spinning dynamos were passed over my body, but the indicators did not leap.

The doctors advised psychiatry. They ignored the evidence I offered. One hundred years of empirical proof: grandfather in the lawn chair, *his* grandfather struck down in a pasture, the several attempts on me. My cousin Priscilla was electrocuted by her telephone during a storm. My eldest brother, Paul, his pacemaker dazzled by a faulty microwave oven, causing his heart to wreck itself with fibrillations; my young brother, Warden, dead on the putting green. And of course there's me: the scalp-tightening sensations whenever a storm gathers, and then the close call of last summer. Evidence. But evidence without theory is noise. I have no theory.

Desperate for a theory, I wrote to Dr. Helper. Helper is a psychologist who writes an advice column in our local paper. I signed my letter "Haunted." "Dear Haunted," he replied. "The abnormal fear of lightning is a well-documented phobia. Like the other common phobias—fear of the marketplace, fear of heights, fear of confinement—it can now be safely attributed to brain-chemistry deficits. Rest assured, you can be cured through appropriate medication. As for your 'evidence'—your 'close call'—please, in the future, do not go fishing in aluminum boats."

I didn't know the boat was aluminum. It was painted dark green and had a woody look to it. The seats were wood, the gunwales were wood, and the oars were wood. I saw wood, I believed wood. It was Ted Lardner's boat. I had checked the weather forecasts and there were no thunderstorms within two hundred miles. I cannot spend my weekends reading technical journals in my rubber shed. I need recreation.

I should have realized the boat was not wood by its action in the water, but Ted had distracted me with the tradition of sky burials in Tibet. The bones of the dead are crushed and mixed with yak butter so that the scavenging birds will eat the remains and carry them, along with the spirit of the deceased, into the sky. Ted teaches comparative culture at the community college and is endlessly fascinating, but even so, I should have been more conscious of the boat.

I caught a fish, then Ted caught a fish. I caught another fish, a trash fish, and then Ted caught a water snake. I saw a terrapin leaving a wake. There were mergansers, fish hawks, and an occasional heron. It was lovely, we had a fine time, and Ted, who makes his own guitars, talked melodiously of how lightning-struck wood is soft and easily worked. It bends cooperatively with applied heat and produces, in the finished product, an incomparable tone. He had his guitar with him, and when we began to believe the fishing would not improve, he strummed and sang. It was idyllic. Even so, I should have been more conscious of the boat.

"My guitar speaks," Ted said. "This is a concert guitar, the back and sides made of struck rosewood, the top of struck cedar."

But there were other voices speaking, and I heard them too late. "Looks like rain," Ted said.

"What?" I gasped. I swiveled about, rocking the boat.

"Boom, boom," Ted said, and strummed, and then I heard it too: thunder filtered through trees and hills.

I dropped my pole, heard the gong of metal on metal, and it was then I realized the boat was made of aluminum, not wood. "Jesus, Ted!" I cried out. I picked up the oars, clambered into the rowing seat, and headed the craft back to the dock, which looked to be at least two miles away. Even as I bent to my labor, wind wrinkled the lake.

The first angry white billow appeared at the crest of a hill, and as if announcing its arrival, a basso-profundo roar caromed through the small green valley that held the lake and a few small farms. Unaware of my fear, Ted strummed folk tunes from the 1960s while drawing peacefully on his pipe.

The last remaining god is weather, someone once said. Clouds are bundles of electrical charges. The earth yearns with free electrons for the upward leap. Overhead the great white muscle of stratocumulus gathered itself toward the lethal flex. The weightless tons drifted silently over us, staining the water dark green. I rowed hard. At last Ted noticed my terror. "Not to worry, old son," he said blandly. "Lightning can't strike twice in the same place, or haven't you heard?" He held his lightning-struck guitar high and grinned. "We're safe," he said. "Guaranteed."

"There was fire in your mouth," Ted said later. "The water glowed so that you could see huge mackinaw trout eighty feet down. They looked like swimming angels."

All I remember is the taste of sweet onions, the flavor of lightning. You must survive in order to remember it, however. My brother Warden was killed on a golf course. Jean, his wife, was coming up behind, working her way out of a sand trap. It knocked him sideways, off the green, his putter a black wand in his dead fist. Jean said, "I bent down to give him CPR and smelled onions, but he'd only had fruit for lunch."

For some reason, I had my net in my hand as I rowed. The aluminum frame, I am told, turned into a hoop of fire. The oarlocks were welded to their seats. The oars splintered. The fish we caught were instantly cooked. Brass rivets melted and the boat opened. Ted swam, towing me behind. Though I cannot swim, I was extraordinarily calm. I give credit to the strike, which had momentarily reorganized my mental processes. I felt holy in the lake, on my back, Ted's hand gripping my collar, the sky blue and clear again above me as we made our slow way to shore. I believed I was dead and that Charon was towing me across the River Styx.

This mood stayed with me for a long time. I remember it so vividly that sometimes I believe it isn't a memory but an ongoing condition. "Your jacket filled up with light," Ted said. "You were a one-man monster movie." Ted is one of the lucky insulated ones. He can touch exposed house wiring and not feel the thrilling vibration of alternating current. "It was liquid light," he said. "I thought I saw your bones. They were red and alive under your shirt. I saw your heart."

My fillings had melted, burning my mouth. I developed a permanent cramp in the rictus muscles, forcing an engaging smile on my face I was powerless to remove. Behind my back, and sometimes to my face, I was called Smiling Jack. At work, my lead engineer, Phil Stratton, a good man, tried to put a stop to it, but the name stuck nonetheless. Nicknames, however, were the least of my worries. Without warning, I had become attractive.

In K-mart, car batteries inched toward me until they teetered on their shelves. Computerized cash registers at my approach gave out tiny electronic screams, losing track of their sums. The ignition of my car would suffer from confused timing, often leaving me stranded. My Timex flowed backwards. Eugenia's hairpins, like a caravan of army ants, followed me out of the bathroom.

There is an explanation for everything. This is no idle assertion. It is the philosophy that made the modern world possible. Next to Newton in my den is a portrait of Einstein. The thoughtless believe the latter superseded the former. No. The latter, using the same methods, holding the same belief in *reason*, and guided by the same faith in the certainty of explanation, *extended* the former. If you lose your belief in explanation, you have lost your mind. Your mind is a representation of a five-century-old trend. What is preparing to replace it offstage, in the wings, grinning in the shadows? I tremble to think. So should you.

One day I will find an explanation for Eugenia's tragic death. I could not attend her funeral because of my relentless smile. Her relatives might have understood, but in my grief I found it monstrous, a senseless affront. We are electrical. But shall I declare a conspiracy of electrons Should I fix blame on the microcosmic field of positive and negative charges Should I say my vulgar smile in the face of my loss was arranged by an evil jocularity of atoms?

She was insulated. Boots, gloves, electrolytic oil, emotional distance. Yet the bolt found her. There was no storm. I admit to anger. A man is entitled to some affection. Yet prolonged contact frightened her. She ran, stumbling in her boots, through the house, from imagined danger. I could not help myself: I thundered. I roared. A man is entitled to some affection. I did not feel attractive, though a mob of paper clips, straight pins, tacks, scraps of foil, swarming in the air like gnats when the bright afternoon is cooled by storm clouds, followed me as I roared in pursuit.

I found her in the laundry room, wedged between the dryer and washer. I felt calm, reasonable, prepared to discuss the issue in a rational way, but I knew I was also roaring at her. She looked up at me as if at a bad sky. "Eugenia," I said, but the syllables came out as claps of thunder.

Something kicked her. It reached me as a spent corona, a blue glow that washed over me like a wave, and, like a wave, receded. It came from the 220-volt outlet, domestic lightning, wanting *me*, I believe, but passing through Eugenia en route. I tried to dial 911, but the phones were hot. Storm clouds arrived on the scene, warning me to keep silent, keep insulated, whispering my fate in small cyclones that bent my neighbor's trees and carried spirals of dust into the darkening air.

I have faith that a scientific explanation for these events will soon occur to me.

BORROWED HEARTS
(NEW STORIES)

Leon woke up smelling the past. The past smelled rank, a funky odor: sex, sweat, and broth, a foul soupy cafeteria smell, or worse. He needed to remember it, the time and place where the smell originated, but could not. It was important, crucial, but it was impossible. He felt like crying, and then he did cry. He choked back the sobs, but could not hold back the tears. He was wracked with pointless nostalgia and then by free-floating remorse. It made no sense.

He rolled toward Maisy, his wife, thinking she might be the source of the smell. She was sleeping on her back, snoring lightly with her mouth open. He leaned close to her face and inhaled her breath. He slid the blanket down and sniffed her body, beginning with her armpits and moving to her neck and breasts. He sniffed her navel and pubic tuft. He sniffed her

Borrowed Hearts

knees, and finally her feet. But he smelled nothing, not even her sweat. She woke up, muttering, "What are you *do*ing, Leon? Stop that. Where are my blankets?"

"Sorry," he said.

"You have to see a doctor," she said. "I mean it."

"It's not medical," he said. "It can't be just a medical thing."

"It *is* medical. It *is* a medical thing."

Maisy got out of bed and found her robe. She grappled with it, looking for the armholes. Leon still desired her, though her belly in recent years had gotten large. It fell like a roll of silver-white dough over the long horizontal scar from a decades-old hysterectomy. The fine geometry of her face was becoming obscured by thickened flesh. Her hair was thin and mostly gray and her eyes had lost the startling blue urgency they'd had when he first met her thirty years ago. Even though she was sixty-six, time's relentless anvil had not been completely punishing. She still evoked the image of the woman he'd married—the dancer with the long-legged twirl, her lean back descending in a subtle arch to the abrupt hillocks of her firm rump, the wide, generous breasts, the smooth neck, and the classic planes and hollows of her lovely face.

The smell that woke him up was fading. It had not come from his wife, he knew that now. Alone in bed, he smelled himself, his pits, his wrists and hands. He was still limber enough to pull his pale white feet up to his nose, but he had no odors at all. The odors—*fumes,* really—that he had smelled hadn't come from anything in his present surroundings. They had come to him from the past, like a memory, a memory without images. The odor lacked a name and convayed the feeling that if he could only pin it down—soup, sweat, candle wax, glue, sulfurous tar, the gamy residue of sex—then something momentous would be revealed to him, something linked to a past event of pivotal importance. But it remained abstract, and by the time he got out of bed and brushed his teeth, it was reduced to a memory of a memory, insubstantial as a pointless dream. None of it made sense.

He joined his wife in the kitchen. She'd already finished making coffee and was reading the paper at the table. He poured himself a cup and sat down. He inhaled the steam rising from his cup but could not smell the good coffee aroma. He went to the pantry and found the can of coffee and removed the plastic lid. He inhaled deeply, his nose almost touching the rich, dark grounds, but he smelled nothing.

"It's completely gone, isn't it? Your sense of smell," Maisy said, studying him now.

He sat down, sipped his coffee. "I could smell it even after I was awake," he said. "It lasted about a minute, then it went. Same smell, every morning. I can't pin it down, but it's so real."

"Something's not right."

"It can't amount to much, Maisy."

"You walk around the house trying to smell things. The other day I saw you light a match and inhale the sulfur. Only someone who couldn't smell would do a thing like that."

"Maybe it's just an allergy, a temporary thing," he said, making a show of inhaling coffee steam with unrestrained pleasure. "The mulberry trees are budding out now. You know how bad that pollen can be."

Maisy sighed. "I don't like being waked up like that, Leon. I don't want you smelling me every morning. It gives me the willies. Something's wrong with you."

"Nothing's wrong with me," Leon said. "I feel fine. A lot of people lose their ability to smell things. I'm sixty-five. I can't see as well as I could twenty years ago, either."

"But you smell phantoms. I want a doctor to look at you just in case. I'm thinking a neurologist."

"It isn't a medical problem," he said. "How could it be a medical problem?"

"Milder symptoms than that are medical. I'm going to call the clinic." Maisy had been an army nurse, and had served in Korea and then again, after an interlude as a surgical nurse in Tucson, in Vietnam.

Leon chuckled, shaking his head, but it was an act. He felt like crying again. It was frightening, this sudden deprivation of one of his senses. He remembered being inducted into the army, a hundred naked boys bending over and spreading their cheeks for the examining doctors, the overpowering anal stink misting his eyes and making him gag. Oh! if he could only smell those scared young sphincters again!

The loss was frightening, but it was more frightening that he would receive powerful smells in his dreams, smells that were so insistent that he woke up with them still present, his heart pounding and his mind reaching back for something in the distant past that cried out for recognition. It was like a blind man waking up from strongly textured visual dreams in which an unidentifiable scene from his past presented itself and continued to present itself in the minutes after he was fully awake, mimicking restored sight.

Maisy opened the morning paper. "I think you're having seizures of some kind," she said, scanning headlines.

Leon put on his sweats and walked down to the workout room, angry at Maisy's casual diagnosis, a diagnosis that implied a serious medical condition. He looked forward to working out his anger on the weight machine. One of the reasons they had moved to this new retirement community—Sierra del Monte—was the splendid exercise facilities. A personal trainer was available, but Leon preferred to work out using his own routine. The trainer held group sessions in the afternoon. Leon worked out in the morning.

Dick Drake was standing in front of the universal gym when Leon arrived. Dick was a big man with long, scraggly white hair that still showed shocks of red in random patches. He stood like a stone image contemplating, it seemed, the lat machine. Leon knew him well enough to give him a nickname. He called Drake "Rasputin." Drake, in turn, called Leon "Captain." Leon assumed this was because of his silver crewcut and for the pressed khaki slacks he wore exclusively.

Drake, in his early seventies, had a recent heart transplant and was exercising now under his doctor's orders. He was broad-shouldered, slim-hipped, and tall, a onetime college basketball player. He enjoyed his special status as a transplant patient. He told the details of his operation to anyone who would listen—how the heart-lung machine's connection to his aorta had failed and how his blood left red slicks on the operating-room floor. Drake was full of life and bravado and endless talk. He had neither self-pity nor conceit, which, Leon thought, ennobled him. Leon liked Dick Drake; Maisy did not.

"I'm defibrillating," he said to Leon's greeting. "I've got to stand still."

Leon sat down at the leg press and started exercising. There was too much weight on the rack, but he didn't stop to change it. After half a dozen presses, he quit. Drake was still standing in front of the lat machine as his defibrillator hammered spikes of voltage into his misfiring heart.

"Son of a bitch," Drake said, touching the bulge in his side where the defibrillator had been implanted.

"You okay?" Leon said.

"Sometimes I feel like I'm on a high wire stretched over Niagara Falls."

Drake's forehead was yellow as wax. His grand nose hooked out of his face like a damaged keel. He grinned, his pale eyes alive and merry under shaggy gray eyebrows. "What do you say we trash this for today and go out for a plate of bacon and eggs?" he said. He raised his arms and flexed the biceps. The lumpy muscles bucked erratically under the sagging skin. "I'm in good enough shape to miss a day. What do you say, Captain?"

Maisy wouldn't go with them. She didn't want to hear Drake describe his operation again. Leon showered, put on his gabardine slacks and a Hawaiian shirt, then walked to the Lanai room, one of three cafeterias in the Sierra del Monte complex. Drake was already there, seated at a table. He hadn't changed out of his sweats. Leon pulled out a chair and sat down.

"You didn't have to dress up for me, Captain," Drake said.

"I didn't," Leon said.

A pretty waitress came by, a girl just out of high school. Leon ordered corned beef hash and poached eggs. Drake asked for the fruit plate.

"Damn," Drake said, leaning sideways to watch as the girl moved briskly between the tables. "Doesn't that make you want to start the nonsense all over again, Captain?"

"She's a baby, Rasputin," Leon said.

"I was a baby once, too," Drake said gravely. His collapsed lips drooped into a sad inverse smile.

"What's wrong?" Leon said.

"I feel so goddamned useless. How come Dick Drake gets a brand-new heart when he can't do anything with it anyway? I'm just waiting to die, like the rest of us. Seems like a waste."

Drake never talked like this. "Something's bothering you," Leon said.

"I think the Nigerian wants his heart back, Captain."

Leon knew that Drake's heart had come from a Nigerian cab driver, killed in a head-on collision in Washington, D.C. The Nigerian was twenty-eight years old at the time of his death. His heart was flown to El Paso from D.C. in four hours. Except for the heart-lung machine problem, it had been a perfect transplant.

"Fibrillating again?" Leon said.

Drake shrugged. "Off and on. Nigerians are big on ghosts. Maybe the cabby feels he can't break away from the earthly bonds until his heart is buried, too."

"Mumbo jumbo, Rasputin," Leon said, though he did not think Drake's superstitious fear was unreasonable. He was tempted to let apparitions, visitations, or vibrations in the ether account for the phantom odors he woke up to every morning.

Drake raised his napkin to his face. He coughed and something came up. He folded the napkin and put it on his plate. "I'm okay," he said. "Sometimes when I retch I can put pressure on the vagus nerve. That makes it quit."

The young waitress came by and leaned over their table. "Is everything okay, guys?" she asked.

Her thick auburn hair, electrified by the dry desert air, fell inches from Leon's face. He closed his eyes and breathed in, nostrils flared, but he could not smell her fragrance.

"I was as good as dead," Drake said to the waitress. "Now look at me." He opened his shirt and showed her his smooth wide scar. He raised his arms and made the gnarly biceps leap. The shadow of melancholy and doubt that had obscured his optimistic nature had passed. "I'm going to live forever, honey," he said.

Leon got up and went into the men's room. He stood in front of a urinal. Before he unzipped, he tried to smell the powerfully astringent deodorant bar that lay next to the drain. He knelt in front of the urinal and breathed in the fumes. His eyes watered, but he smelled nothing.

A man in a wheelchair rolled into the men's room. "Are you okay, buddy?" he said.

Leon stood up, embarrassed. "Fine," he said. "I'm fine."

Age had not made Maisy lose interest in sex. Leon was capable, but had little staying power. "Sorry," he said, breathing hard. He rolled away from her. "I'm short on wind these days."

"Don't worry," Maisy said. "I'm not going to start trolling the playgrounds for teenage distance runners."

They both laughed. It had been a good marriage. They had no children and were content with that. Maisy had been thirty-six when they got married, Leon thirty-five. Ten years before that, Maisy had been married briefly to an army officer.

They took a shower together. Leon put his face directly under the spray. He smelled roses in the steam. The showerhead ovevwhelmed him in fragrance. He stepped back, startled. "Is that your shampoo, Maisy?"

"What are you talking about?" she said. "I'm not shampooing yet."

It was roses and more than roses. He could almost remember the place—a riverbank, maybe a lake, a fine house in the country. And there was a gathering of some kind, people he knew but could not name. There were voices among the roses, by the river or lake, and the familiar house, a handsome place tucked in green hills, was full of music and roses, thousands of roses. *He's here,* he heard someone say. Someone else said, *Sure enough.*

He fell to a squat on the tiles, shaking. Maisy turned off the water and left the shower. When she came back, she toweled him dry. "I've called for an ambulance," she said.

"I'm okay," Leon said, standing up. "I almost remembered it that time, Maisy." Tears rolled down his face and his voice shook.

"There's nothing to remember," she said. "You had a seizure, a bigger one this time."

"Maybe heaven," he said. "Maybe heaven smells like flowers, and the houses are full of roses and music, and the people are sweet."

"Take it easy, hon," Maisy said. "They'll be here in a minute."

It was an aneurysm. A bulging vein, dangerously fragile, had pressed hard against a branch of the olfactory nerve. The pressure the aneurysm had exerted on the brain had also stimulated the seizures. The seizures—the nostalgia-rich odors of nowhere—stopped after the operation. And after a while his sense of smell came back. Leon was able to smell ordinary everyday things again, but his dreams were odorless. Stripped of fragrance, they no longer had the power to draw him into haunting and familiar landscapes where people he recognized but did not know welcomed him. He missed this, which was foolish, and made no sense.

He wore a cap to hide his shaved head. A long red arc traveled from his right temple, across the top of his skull, ending just over his left eye. He wanted to show Dick Drake his scar, wanted to bore him with the details of his surgery—Rasputin had it coming, after all—but discovered that Drake had been taken back to the hospital where he'd received his heart transplant.

Leon visited him. Drake's Nigerian heart was failing rapidly and he was waiting for a new donor.

"Jesus, I hope this time they give me the heart of a goddamn Swede. Swedes don't believe in ghosts, do they, Captain?"

Leon went along with it. "You want a *Swiss* heart, Rasputin. The goddamn Swiss only believe in money."

They were out in an open-air plaza between buildings. Fast-moving springtime clouds moved them in and out of shade. Dick Drake sat bundled in a wheelchair. He looked thin and wasted, but his spirits were high.

"The Nigerian's calling it in," he said. He looked up, as if he could see the Nigerian cabby gesturing among the clouds. "He can't travel without his heart."

Leon stopped at a flower shop on his way home. He bought a dozen roses for Maisy, a mix of reds and yellows and pinks. The roses filled the car with perfume. It was a happy smell, the fragrance of optimism and hope, a fragrance that would be welcome in anyone's idea of heaven.

He knew he did not need to, but he wanted to win her heart again. He wanted to win her heart every day for whatever time they had left together. It made no sense, but it didn't have to. Nothing had to.

He came into the Lost Cause Bar and Grille out of the noontime desert heat and began to suck down Bloody Marias as if they were snakebite antidote. Ever since his wife left him, it had become a lunch-hour ritual. But today the generous hits of Herradura Reposado—a very good tequila— pulled him into a situation he ordinarily would have backed away from. He antagonized a woman who carried a .22-caliber mini revolver in her kangaroo pack. He should have been sensitive to the situation, but he persisted in stumbling blindly through life on the thorny path of his nagging sorrows.

The woman didn't seem unapproachable. Hadn't she been sitting alone for the better part of an hour at the bar? Didn't that give him license? Anyway, his remark had been mild by any standard. "You have priceless Virgin Mary skin," he said. "Unblemished as the Jesus-haunted communion wafer itself. I raise my glass to original *skin*." He chuckled attractively, monitoring his performance in the bar mirror. "I hope my little pun is acceptable to you, Miss."

"Keep your little pun in your shorts," she said unpleasantly, not bothering to turn her head. Her voice was flat, without nuance. A bored voice, a dead-end voice. The voice, he realized when it was much too late, of a woman on a mission. "Drinking your lunch again, I see," she added.

He regarded her. Did he *know* this woman? Was she a regular at the Lost Cause? She was dressed in light work out clothes: nifty half-zip sweatshirt, the chopped-off sleeves revealing weight-

A Romantic Interlude

trained biceps; teal-blue nylon running shorts; canvas kangaroo pack snugged against her flat lower abdomen; expensive cross-training shoes—a lunch-hour jogger or power-walker. A dark hourglass of sweat sopped the area between her compact breasts; her hair was tied back in ordinary twine. She was pretty, but this wasn't immediately apparent. Melancholy overruled her natural beauty, made it irrelevant. She reminded him of his ex-wife: big-boned, solid, good neck, tennis-firm legs and arms, and—he glanced down at the brass rail—-long, narrow, highly arched feet. He pictured her in a low-cut cocktail dress, her face made up and her hair sexily crimped, and he felt an old sentimental attraction.

"Just what do you think you're staring at?" the woman said.

"At a memory of loveliness," he said.

He meant it. The salt of nostalgia stung his eyes. Sentimentality lurked in his blood like a defective gene. The divorce papers had arrived earlier that day and the bottom dropped out of his world. He was sick with the vertigo of weight-less fall.

The woman sipped her club soda. "You insincere prick," she said quietly, facing him now. It was an impersonal observation. The world was plagued with insincere pricks, and this was just one more confirmation.

He regarded her, his mood souring. He shrugged. Then he made a critical mistake. "Okay, then: Doleful dildo banger; lonely rider of the electric zucchini," he said. "Midnight baton twirler," he added.

It seemed reasonable: if this woman took compliments as insults, she was likely to take an outright insult as a compliment. He winked at some of the regulars down the bar, sharing his amusing inverse logic. He searched his memory and came up with a choice fragment of an Irish curse: "May the devil take the whey-faced slut by the hair, and beat bad manners out of her skin for a year." This couplet from a James Stephens poem presented at auditorium volume in a makeshift brogue drew more phlegmy cackles from the afternoon corps of drinkers.

The woman crooked a beckoning finger at him. She smiled. Believing that he'd been correct, that she had been favorably stimulated by his crude remarks, he leaned toward her. She brought her lips close to his ear, reached between his legs. She found his balls and squeezed them with a need that made his spirits rise. He waited—hope soaring—for her electric tongue.

"You are going to die for that filthy remark," she said, squeezing harder. "And you're going to die *shitting* yourself, like the dirty little sewer rat you are."

His bowels acknowledged the threat: eruptive liquid gaspings. He tried to lurch away from her, but her gym-trained hand on his balls became a vise. Embarrassed by pain, then fear, he said, "Look—she wants me, guys!" The regulars made uncivil noises, signifying approval. He rolled his eyes and bit the tip of his tongue puckishly.

He didn't see the slap coming. It was not a hesitant slap, flicked ladylike from the wrist. She held him in place with her left hand and walloped him with her right, the blow achieving maximum velocity at the radius of her long arm. It caught him flush against the ear. He'd been leaning backward to offer yet another raffish observation to the regulars and was swept off his stool by the force of the blow. She gave his balls one last iron-fingered squeeze and let him go. He hit the floor on the point of his tailbone and yelped, his head roaring with colossal chimes. This amused the regulars greatly. He picked himself up to a grainy chorus of barks and hoots. He dusted his jacket and slacks with nonchalance, but then the stab of pain in his lower back made him grab the bar and cry out.

"I meant what I said, bozo," the woman said, with a calmness that he finally realized was pathological. She stood before him—ready for war, her knees bent—anticipating his first move. Bands of visible muscle writhed in her legs. Her biceps were veined, the muscles round and hard as baseballs.

"You don't remember me, do you?" she said.

"You're confusing me with someone else," he managed.

"Am I? Maybe so. But I don't think I am."

"I'm not the guy," he said.

She shrugged. "What's the difference? You'll do."

"Look," he said. "Whatever it is you think I've done, I want you to know that I'm...

"Sorry?"

"Yes. Sorry. Really."

"You insincere prick."

It was an argument he wasn't going to win, that was clear. She had singled him out as an adequate substitute for the guy who had fucked her over, and there was nothing he could do about *that*. He bowed elaborately in a small effort to save face, then left the Lost Cause by the back door, fighting nausea.

The woman wasn't willing to accept his retreat. She followed him out into the weedy field behind the bar and down the steep banks of the arroyo that tunneled under a railroad trestle—his shortcut back to his office. Thinking that he had taken enough humiliation at the hands of this woman, he decided to wait for her and give her the confrontation she wanted. He'd never hit a woman before, but equal opportunity was a two-way street, he reasoned. He was near the bottom of the arroyo where the greasewood bushes and ocotillo were tall and thick. The woman made her way down the embankment—not tentatively but quick and sure-footed, and this athleticism made him think twice about the wisdom of confronting her. When she was within a hundred feet, he saw the missionary adrenaline in her eyes. He back-pedaled, turned, and ran. Even so, she gained on him. But just as he broke into a full sprint, he stepped into a rabbit burrow and went down, his ankle exploding with pain.

The woman stood over him, digging into her kangaroo pack as if looking for some private, feminine thing. The tiny, snub-nosed revolver she drew out of it fit her hand as comfortably as a tube of lipstick. "I won't take it anymore," she said. "Not from any of them, and certainly not from *you.*"

He cringed and rolled away from the righteous steel finger of the tiny pistol. It was pointed at his head. He offered it alternative targets on the meatier backside of his anatomy. He covered his head with his arms and hands. A small-caliber bullet in the brain was a terrifying thing: he might vegetate in an irreversible coma absorbed in hellish dreams for twenty years before he died. And given the subjective nature of the mind, twenty years might easily translate into eternity. The horrors of hell, he believed, were very real and always close at hand. A fallen-away Catholic—though no Catholic, as the Jesuits often observed, ever falls completely away—he made the sign of the cross on his forehead with his thumb, giving himself emergency absolution.

When the shot came, as he knew it would, he felt nothing for several seconds. Then a burning shaft of pain, as if a white-hot poker had been laid across his bare shoulder, made him scream. The scream was involuntary. It embarrassed him. It was high-pitched, unmanly, without timber—an infantile shriek, a frightened primate's formless vocalization. He rolled over, the flats of his hands held up as if they could catch bullets. "Ho now!" he said. "Don't! Jesus!" The words were his but the voice was not. Somewhere behind these bursts of sound, a calmer part of him hoped no one besides this woman was listening. "Don't kill me!" he begged, his hands up and moving. He'd experienced some bad depressions after his wife left, and had toyed with the idea of ending it all, but now he saw that life was sweet and necessary. He wanted to live. Life—weird and frightening and tiring and repetitive as it was—was *good*.

The drone of cicadas answered his plea. He braced himself and sat up. The woman was sitting in the weeds, holding the gun carelessly in her lap. "I've decided against it," she said.

"Thank Christ," he whispered to himself, like an amazed car dealer who had just sold a lemon. He decided to press his luck. "I promise I won't report this. I was out of line. I admit it. It was my fault. I see that now. But really, I think I should go to a hospital."

She raised the gun. She looked at the small revolver as if holding wordless dialogue with it. "I hate guns, really," she said. "I supported the Brady bill."

"Oh, yes! I did *too!*" he quickly agreed, happy to have found common ground.

She looked at him, almost shyly, as if she had seen something in him that should not be seen. "I can't take you to a hospital," she said. "They have to report gunshot wounds. It's the law."

He kept his eye on the gun. "Okay, fine. Look, let's let bygones be bygones," he said. "It's not a bad wound. It's just a scratch. I can take care of it myself." He felt faint. A film of greasy sweat glistened on his face. His arms were tingling.

"No, you need attention," she said. "I'll take you to my apartment."

He sagged. He could hear his blood's strong arterial roar.

"Will you agree to that?" she asked.

"Oh, please," he said as if waving off a second helping of a rich dessert. "Don't trouble yourself. I'm fine. Really."

The gun wobbled in her hand, the barrel cutting zees in the air. "I can't go to jail. I just can't—I have two children at home. Rolfe refuses to send child support."

"Rolfe?" He saw a reassuring character trait emerge: The Mother. The Madonna. The Homemaker. The Giver, not the Taker, of life.

"Rolfe is my ex," she said. "The bastard who gave me this." She pulled up her sweatshirt, then her jogging bra. She pointed with the gun barrel to striated scars above her left nipple. Someone—Rolfe—had tried to brand her. "He did it with his salad fork. Pretty, isn't it?"

An impersonal mask hardened her expression again. The awful migration of conscious personality left vacuums in her eyes. A faraway train, the afternoon Amtrak, gave a lengthy blast of its horn. Two longs, a short, followed by a long.

Did railroad men *want* to visit loneliness and despair upon the land with their great melancholy horns? *No no, oh no,* it grieved—and he felt abandoned in a dark and lonely place without hope or luck or the last-minute clarity of grace.

The gun drifted down again. It occurred to him that he could easily reach out and snatch it away from her, but he was wounded and felt light-headed, while she was athletic and supercharged with craziness. If he made a move, she might empty the revolver into him. He knew that, if he survived this, he would emerge with a severely downgraded opinion of himself.

The woman's arm stiffened suddenly as she leveled the gun directly at his crotch. He felt the blood drain from his head. He saw the darkness behind the daylight—a consequence of the heightened vision of the doomed. "I suppose you think you can do me, now that you've seen my breasts," she said.

He caught himself thinking this over. "*Do* you?" he said, three seconds too late. "I never thought that! I wouldn't have. I mean, Jesus what do you take me for? I *respect* you, I sincerely *respect* you!"

Her breasts were lovely: sturdily conical and tipped with pink rosebuds. The unfortunate thought—that the salad-fork tattoo only made them more interesting—he was sure was readable in his face. And now he had broken a drenching sweat. He could smell his bitter vapors.

"Shut *up*," she said, taking aim. "I think I know when I'm being manipulated. I've gone to *graduate* school in manipulation."

She approached him. Her eyes were bright and unblinking. She nudged his crotch with the gun barrel. He felt his genitals make the anatomical equivalent of a heart-stopping scream. They tightened and shriveled into microscopic pods—no doubt an evolutionary duck-and-cover cringe meant to let the hopeful tribes of mankind survive crisis and continue.

"Gee, looky there," she said, suddenly cheerful again. "You've wet yourself!" She raised the gun and held it against his temple as she watched the rapidly expanding stain.

He looked down at his crotch, also surprised. The body had its own agendas. "Looks like I've made your day," he said, disgusted with himself but suddenly very calm.

The afternoon Amtrak clattered frantically across the trestle. Passengers in the Sightseer Lounge waved at them. They believed they were witnessing a picturesque southwestern tryst—secret lunchtime lovers meeting at the bottom of a charming arroyo.

The roar and clatter of the train bullied everything else from his mind. He sat still, the barrel of the woman's small pistol pressing a tiny O into the thin skin of his temple.

Abruptly, she put her gun away and stood up. "I have a first-aid kit in my car," she said. She did some stretching exercises for her hamstrings and calves. He watched melons of lively gluteal muscle lift and tighten her shorts. A vein in her calf stood out with pre-varicose intensity. She had slim ankles, a patch of hot-pink razor burns rising up the inside of each.

The arroyo hummed with a million cicadas, and it seemed to him that he could hear each one individually. A breeze moved in the ocotillo, the tall flowering stalks swaying voluptuously. She turned to face him and he saw, with a surge of gratitude, that her madness had subsided. She was relaxed, and a bit concerned, though not precisely contrite. She was not going to kill him, he knew this now, and he wanted to kiss her hand.

"I'm not sorry, you know," she said. "They might put me away again for a while, to stabilize my medication, but I did not instigate. Or do you feel I am mistaken?"

"No, no," he said hastily. "I instigated. It was me. I'm the one who should be sorry."

"Should be? Then, you're *not*?"

He bit his tongue. A bird with bright-red chevrons under its wings flew between them. He believed he and the bird had exchanged a microsecond glance. He felt he could have counted its feathers. The pain of the wound—a hot, steady throb—did not distract him. If anything, it sharpened his senses. He felt doubly alive. His ability to smell things, which had been wrecked by thirty years of Pall Malls, came back, bringing him the heady strangeness of a thousand subtle emanations. He felt overwhelmed with gifts. Life was not merely good, it was explosively good; it was singular, it was everything, it had no counterpart. Passionate tears of gratitude dripped from his chin. He was glad to be alive; not glad, ecstatic. This was pure gift: the afternoon, the woman, the wound—all of it. He'd been on the roller coaster of death and redemption, a five-minute ride that had taken an eternity. An educational trip, superior and more instructive than any sky-diver's adrenaline rush. And he knew he would come out of it a better person. *That which does not kill you makes you stronger.* This Nietzschean sentiment always seemed bogus to him, especially since it had the cachet these days of a bumper sticker. But now he believed it.

She saw his tears and was affected by them. Her own tears came then, and he saw each one of them as they found pathways in the ridges beside her nose. He saw them, and *smelled* them, their human salt, their bittersweet strength. He smelled the dirt he sat on, the creosote bush that shaded him, the dry husks of dead insects scattered around him. He smelled his own blood, caking on his shoulder. He smelled his urine. And he smelled her—her perfumed sweat and her minted breath. He smelled the fragrance, stimulated by exercise and the desert heat, radiating from the dignified mound of her sex. He was sorry he had spoken crudely of that lovely mound, the *mons venus,* as the medical texts called it, sorry he made it the object of an ancient and worn-out contempt.

"I was wrong to speak as I did," he said with a formality he believed the situation required.

"And I was wrong to shoot you," she replied, also recognizing a need of formality. They had both been something less than fully human; now, in this moment, they were something more. He felt exhilarated. He believed she did, too.

She stepped toward him, placed a heatless kiss—the ethereal buss of an angel—on the top of his head. He caught her hand in his and pressed it to his lips. It was like the final reconciliation of extremes; a moment prefiguring the end of a worn-out world.

He felt suddenly bold, even inspired. "Lunch tomorrow? he offered.

She studied his face, searching for insincerity. "Why not?" she said. "Same place, a few minutes before noon—before the lunch-hour crowd."

She smiled then for the first time and it was dazzling with the unguarded brightness of restored sanity. She was lovely in a way that humbled him. He watched, not daring to breathe, as she cinched her kangaroo pack tight, the outline of the revolver visible under the Gore-Tex. Then she turned abruptly and charged up the steep embankment.

He felt light and porous. He felt defenseless and glad. He stood, shaky at first, then climbed out of the arroyo and into the new world that lay ahead.

C onsider, if you will, the ancient Egyptians," Stan Duval said, just as we were sitting down to dinner. "They had the correct attitude, in my humble estimation."

I usually acted as though I hadn't heard him. He made me nervous; I couldn't get used to him being around. My mother had married him in Yuma, Arizona, a year ago. I couldn't figure out why. He was twenty years older than she was and he always wore his green pin-striped suit at the dinner table even if he'd been walking around the house in stained underwear a half hour earlier.

Stan always characterized his estimations and assessments as humble. "In my humble way, I believe I am one of the most valued employees at Ryan." He'd said this more than once, as if he suspected we had our doubts. He was in charge of an equipment shed at Ryan Aircraft. His job was to check out machine tools, and then check them back in again. Inventory Control Engineer. That's what he called himself.

Experience

Mom had fixed fried chicken, lima beans, and scalloped potatoes, Stan's favorite meal.

He made a point of bringing up obscure subjects at the dinner table in order to educate us. Mom had quit school after the eighth grade, and I was going to be a freshman at Lowmont High School, a school Stan had no respect for.

"What do you mean, dear?" Mom said. She didn't care about Egypt, but she knew Stan liked to be drawn out after he'd made a thought-provoking statement. It was a routine of theirs.

Mom's eyes were glazed. She was still young-looking and almost pretty, even though she'd gotten thick around the hips and had developed a sizable double chin.

Stan leveled his fork at her. "Firstly, their social organization—*sine dubio,*" he said. "Secondly, their thoroughly worked-out religious bureaucracy. Thirdly, their corps of civil-engineering professionals, *par excellence*. Those chaps knew who they were and had no doubt about their self-worth."

He forked some potatoes into his mouth and chewed them thoughtfully, jaws rotating side to side, camel-style, his heavy-lidded, Levantine eyes studying the ceiling. His phony British accent got on my nerves. Stan had grown up in Boise, Idaho and had lived in California most of his life. He'd never been to England, or anywhere else, as far as I knew.

"They had slaves," I said.

"Ah, slaves," he said. The word seemed to stir up favorable memories for him. The long syllable slid down his tongue like gravy. "As an institution, slavery was not the social horror the present-day liberal thinker makes it out to be," he said, smiling abruptly.

The accent was bad enough, but it was this smile that unnerved me most about him. Out of that gray, half-collapsed face came a sudden specter of long, black-edged teeth that animated his entire being with a parody of life-loving vigor. It was a smile meant to charm and convince. But it was as if a corpse in its coffin had leered flirtatiously at the passing line of mourners.

"Take some more chicken, Tony," Mom said to me. "There's more than enough for your lunch tomorrow."

"I'm not hungry," I said. In fact, my stomach was jumpy. Dillard Burdett was coming over in a few minutes. We were going to have Cokes in my basement room. My stomach was jumpy because Dillard's sixteen-year-old cousin, Wanda Schnell, from Escondido, was coming with him. Dillard had told me incredible stories about Wanda. Once, when he was visiting his aunt and uncle in Escondido, he and Wanda went out into a grove of avocado trees where she took off her underpants for him.

"I—saw—it—*all*," Dillard had said. He spoke gravely, with arresting eloquence. "I—shit—you—not—Tone," he said.

"Did you show her yours?" I had asked. This question was out of line, but my curiosity got the better of me. Dillard, like me and most of our friends, preferred the mutual presumption of experience. Innocence and fear, our true condition, could not be admitted. This was the unstated given that made our friendship possible. We never challenged each other's boasts in the area of sexual experience, though we understood that none of us had any. Of course the boasts had to be reasonable—flights of fantasy were shouted down instantly.

"What do *you* think, turd?" he'd said, annoyed with me. We dropped the subject, lit cigarettes.

"The slaves of Egypt were well taken care of," Stan continued. Stan was a speedy eater. He took large bites and worked his sideways-grinding jaws fast. He usually finished minutes ahead of me, and I was often reprimanded for inhaling my food and bolting from the table. But I couldn't finish tonight. I was too jumpy.

Stan lit a Chesterfield and blew a cloud of smoke into the hanging lamp above the table. "Slaves were highly prized possessions. And most certainly they were not excessively abused. You do not abuse your valuable possessions. It would make no sense to do so," he said. "Are there any vestiges of doubt in your mind, Antonio?"

I hated my name. The way Stan dragged it out made me hate it more. He gave it the correct foreign pronunciation. It made me feel like an immigrant. My real father *was* an immigrant, a barber from Palermo who now cut the hair of movie stars in Beverly Hills. "Georgio Castellani—Modern Hair Styling." He wore his hair long, like the TV wrestler, Baron Leone. Sometimes he tied the back into a ponytail. When I visited him, which was three or four times a year, he would give me a haircut that made me feel like a scented and oiled Sicilian hit man. I'd seen him just a week ago, and my hair was still squared-off and crisp. I could still smell pine trees and lemons.

"I guess not," I said, wanting to leave the table. I didn't like to argue with Stan. He was an educated man, having graduated from Cal Poly at San Luis Obispo. He spouted Latin at us as if it were our second language.

"*Quae nocent docent,*" he said. "'That which hurts, teaches.' You need to be a realist in this turbulent world of ours. Slavery was cradle-to-grave welfare, all needs and wants attended to." He flashed his dark smile engagingly. "Now, Antonio, I've often mentioned how adamantly I am against the socialistic welfare system inspired by our late president, Franklin Delano Roosevelt. However, in ancient Egypt the social structure required a ready-and-willing work force of considerable proportions. And remember, the Egyptians did not have the gasoline-powered machinery to do their work for them such as is available to the so-called modern world." He leaned back in his chair and puffed his cigarette. He held it in the European style—cradled between thumb and forefinger, palm up. He blew a cloud of smoke toward the ceiling and squinted into it as if he could see pyramids and pharaohs assembling in the haze.

I saw Egypt in my mind, three thousand years ago. I saw myself as Mark Twain's Connecticut Yankee making modern devices for the astonished pharaoh, such as the two-way radio, television, the internal combustion engine, and the airplane. Diesel-powered vehicles trucked stones the size of bungalows through the desert as the astonished pharaoh applauded. Pharaoh's daughter thought I was some kind of god. She came to me bearing gifts. "I'm not a god, Laura," I told her. "I'm just a regular guy with some American know-how."

I liked the name Laura.

My rumbling stomach interrupted my daydream. I needed to get ready for Wanda Schnell. I couldn't believe Dillard was bringing her over. I'd seen a snapshot of Wanda wearing a bathing suit. Though she was only fourteen years old in the photo, she already had the full breasts and flared hips of a grown woman. Her face was blurry, but she seemed to be smirking at the photographer, her slitted eyes dark with knowledge. She was now sixteen, two years older than me.

"What about freedom?" I said.

"Freedom?" Stan passed his hand over the table, like a magician casting or removing a spell. "Bloody hocus-pocus, Antonio. Freedom is an earned condition of the mind. It has nothing to do with the ideals and schemes of a society. Socrates in his cell, staring at his cup of hemlock, was freer than you or I shall ever be. Freedom, Antonio, cannot be conferred upon the *profanum vulgus*— that is to say, the common riff raff—by fiat alone."

Mom snatched up her wineglass and drank it down in audible gulps. "What about their creepy ole zombies?" she asked, laughing with a kind of merry desperation. Stan was her fourth, and worst—I thought—husband.

He flinched as if someone had flicked ice water in his face. Blatant ignorance always took him by surprise. He regarded her with his big, moon-yellow eyes. "I believe you mean *mummies,* dear. The so-called *zombie* is a vulgar Hollywood exploitation of a West Indies folk myth."

I pushed away from the table. "Well, I've got to cut out," I said. "Dillard's coming by."

"Clean your plate first, Antonio," Stan said. "Food such as this is the exception, not the rule. In Ethiopia or Zanzibar, the peasants are often forced to eat insects for want of grain and meat."

"Did you really like it, Stanley?" Mom said. She looked hopeful, and a little nervous all of a sudden.

Stan looked confused. "The chicken? Of course I liked it, dear," he said. "You *know* it's my favorite meal. Why do you ask?"

"Because, well, it's not really chicken."

Stan looked at his plate, frowned, then looked at Mom. "I'm afraid I don't..."

"It's bunny rabbit, honey, not chicken. Safeway had a wonderful sale, and..."

Stan jumped up from the table, his face turning a lighter shade of gray. He brought his napkin to his mouth and made a dash for the bathroom. He didn't have time to close the door. We heard him vomit.

"Guess he doesn't like rabbit," I said.

"He had three helpings," Mom said. "Of course he liked it."

Stan moaned horribly between upchucks.

"Lepus cuniculus," I said. "A burrowing rodent. He liked it as long as it was chicken. When it was *lepus cuniculus,* he hated it. He's vomiting an *idea."*

Mom tapped a cigarette out of a pack of Lucky's and lit up. "I suppose you think that makes sense, smarty-pants," she said.

I heard Dillard's shrill whistling out in the street. Then he yelled my name in big baritone shouts. His voice had changed in the last year. He sounded like a fully grown-up man, and he vocalized the change whenever the opportunity presented itself.

"See you later, Mom," I said.

"Does he have to bellow like that?" Mom said.

"He's showing off," I said.

I gave her a kiss and then smelled the booze. Even under the rabbit, potatoes, lima beans, and cigarette it was strong. Vat 69. She'd been drinking it most of the afternoon. When you considered who she'd married, it was easy to figure out why. What did she ever see in him? I felt sorry for her, wished she could have the man of her dreams, whoever that might be. I pictured someone like Gary Cooper, a tall, quiet man of unshakable integrity who never in a million years would lecture us about the ancient Egyptians or socialistic welfare. Gary Cooper, the brave yet modest man of *High Noon,* who didn't like to fight but could if forced to. Not a man full of fancy ideas, but a man who was silently wise.

A man who ate slowly and chewed his food with good square jaws that went up and down, and who did not puke at the thought of eating rabbit.

I flooded and combed my hair at the kitchen sink, then went out to meet Dillard. His cousin, Wanda, lagged a few yards behind him. She seemed to be examining the neighborhood—the houses, the shrubs, the cars parked in the street. "Hey, neat-o," she said. "Whose Stude?" She didn't direct her question to either me or Dillard, content that someone would feel obliged to answer her.

"My stepdad's," I said.

"Neat car," she said, still not addressing anyone in particular. She touched the long, sleek fender, then began to stroke it.

It *was* a neat car, a brand-new 1948 Studebaker Champion, pearl gray and fast-looking. I oftened wondered how Stan had managed to pay for it, since he was always complaining about how much it cost to support even a small family like ours.

"You wanna see his stuff?" Dillard said. He meant my radio gear, which was down in the daylight basement where I had my room.

Wanda shrugged indifferently and sauntered towards us. I got my first clear look at her as she moved into the glow of our porch light. She was wearing flip-flop clogs and a loose-fitting cotton dress. Her face was round and puffy, and she had short fleshy arms that she kept folded against her breasts. Her eyes were small and deep-set. I couldn't see them even when she faced me. She looked like a mature woman who'd already had her quota of disappointments.

I led the way down the driveway to the basement. The house was built on a slope, and my room, along with the garage, was under the daylight end. I switched on the lights.

"What's all this *junk*?" Wanda said.

"That's his radio stuff," Dillard said. "Tone's a ham, a radio head. He got his license last year. Hey, isn't that right, Tone?"

"Right," I said. It always embarrassed me a little when strangers came into this room. My radio gear was a very personal thing. When strangers looked at it, I felt naked.

The gear did look like junk, to the untrained eye. My homemade work table was crowded with steel chassis studded with vacuum tubes, power transformers ,and coils. Tangles of green, red, and yellow wires were strung between them. Large-faced ammeters and voltmeters gleamed from hammered aluminum panels. A wall was covered with QSL cards from other hams around the world.

"Show her how it works, Tone," Dillard said.

Dillard and Wanda sat on my bed, a war-surplus cot covered with surplus wool blankets. I kept a big Westclox alarm clock under it. When I wanted to raise stations in New Zealand or Australia, I'd set the clock for three or four in the morning, the hours when darkness covered most of the Pacific Ocean. That was the best time for long-distance communication.

I switched on my receiver, a Hallicrafter S-40A, and tuned it to one of the busy ham bands. A garble of voices mixed with Morse code whined from the speaker.

"Yuck!" Wanda said.

I turned down the volume and spun the dial to one of the commercial short-wave bands. A suave British voice was giving news items in brief sentences, pausing after each one to let the foreign listeners catch up. "Cairo's response to the Crown was ambiguous at best," the suave voice said.

"Pretty cool, huh?" Dillard said.

"Parliament will take up the question of policy concerning future relations with our former protectorate," the slow-speaking Englishman said.

Wanda was looking around the room. It wasn't much of a room—the walls were concrete blocks, except for the far back one, which was just dirt. I'd been digging in that dirt to increase the size of the basement—Stan wanted more storage room—but I hadn't made much progress. Stan paid me fifteen cents for every wheelbarrow of dirt I hauled out.

My work table was against a wall. High up on that wall was a short window at ground level. Antenna wires passed through this window and into the back-yard. I'd nailed some two-by-fours together, braced them with one-by-four splints, set them in three-foot-deep holes sixty-four feet apart, and cemented them in. A folded di-pole antenna hung between these masts, suspended on pulleys. Guy wires anchored to wood stakes webbed the back-yard, which made careless strolling hazardous. Neither Mom nor Stan spent much time outside, so it didn't matter.

"What's all this stuff for?" Wanda said. She'd shoved Dillard off the cot so she could have it for herself, and was now lying on her side, her head propped on her hand. Her puffy face and stringy hair made her seem exotic. The great arc of her hip rose and fell slightly as she dangled her foot over the side of the cot and kicked rhythmically. Her flip-flop hung precariously from her toe.

Dillard sat on the concrete floor, spinning a king-size marble he'd found. His legs had outgrown his torso. They took up most of the space between the cot and my work table. His size-twelve shoes scuffed against my chair. He was only about five foot seven, but he had the legs and feet of a six-footer. "Hey, talk to somebody, Tone," he said. "Show her how you do that."

I put on my earphones and turned on my homemade transmitter. When the tubes got hot, I tuned it. The electrical smell of hot insulation filled the room. It was a smell I liked. I liked the smell of hot solder, too. I glanced quickly at Wanda to see if she had noticed the change. Her nose was crinkled a bit, so I guessed she had.

I tapped out a series of CQs with my telegraph key. I got an answer right away. I pulled the earphone jack out of the S-40A so that the code would come over the loudspeaker. It was a strong station in Bakersfield, someone I'd contacted before. I didn't like this guy because he used a Vibroplex semi automatic speed key and sent his messages too fast. He had a lousy "fist." His dashes were too short—you could easily take them for dots—and his spacing between word groups was erratic. He also bragged too much about his rig. A thousand watts generated by a pair of big Eimac tetrodes in the final amplifier. Anybody could do that if they had the money.

"There it is," I said as code thumped through the basement. "Bakersfield, California. Over two hundred miles north." I was a little vain about my ability to send and receive Morse code over long distances.

"Bakersfield, huh?" Wanda said. "You actually *want* to talk to somebody you don't even know in Bakersfield?"

I tapped out the usual greeting with my old-fashioned brass key, a relic of the 1920s spark-gap days, a present from my uncle Lamar. Then I turned to Wanda. Her small dark eyes seemed oriental to me. Her flip-flop had dropped off, and her little painted toes splayed and unsplayed in time to some rhythm she was hearing in her head. "I've raised stations in Japan," I said, trying to recover lost ground.

This seemed to interest her. "How can you do *that?*" she said. "You don't even speak Japanese."

"It's just the same as Bakersfield," I said. "It's just farther away. You have to wait until the atmospheric conditions are right. Radio waves bounce off the ionosphere, hundreds of miles up. It's like banking a pool ball. And language is no problem. We just use international Q signals."

"Oh, I'm sure," she said, rolling her eyes.

"Tone's a whiz, no lie," Dillard said. "He can tell you how the stuff works, can't you, Tone?" He flipped the marble all the way into the dirt hole at the back of the basement. He went to look for it. "Tell her how it works!" he yelled from the dark excavation.

"It's actually pretty simple," I said. I signed off with Mister Vibroplex from Bakersfield and unplugged the crystal from my transmitter. "This is a quartz crystal. It vibrates at about seven million times per second once you excite it with a small amount of electricity. Then this seven-megacycle oscillation is amplified by this Pierce oscillator—" I tapped on a glowing vacuum tube. "And the signal is fed into a final amplifier—" I tapped on the bigger of the two tubes in my transmitter. "This boosts the power of that seven-megacycle oscillation to about twenty-five watts. Next, I tune the final amp with this knob here, which is connected to a variable capacitor under the chassis. This plug-in coil is designed to match the crystal's frequency—" I tapped on the forty-meter coil at the back of the chassis. "And then the tuned signal goes into the half-wave folded di-pole antenna out in the backyard, where it is radiated into space. You understand any of this, Wanda?"

She was lying on her back now, hands behind her head and chewing gum methodically. "Any of what?" she said. She stared into the joists of the kitchen floor, which was directly above us. It was an indolent, small-eyed gaze.

"How I can talk to Japan," I said.

"How do you know if it's really Japan?" she said. She blew a bubble, popped it. "How do you know if it's even coming from Bakersfield? Maybe it's just some joker down the street yanking your chain." She raised up a little and looked at me. "Hey, Tony. Does that radio of yours play music?"

The sound of my name coming from her lips made me feel strange. My stomach lurched. I switched the Hallicrafter to the broadcast band and tuned in a local station. Dick Haymes was singing "Together."

"That's more like it," she said. She flopped her arms out to her sides and her bare legs dangled off the cot. She swung her feet lazily to the music. The thin cotton material of her dress gathered in the valley between her round thighs. The contours of her lower body were amazingly visible. Dillard crawled up to me on his hands and knees, pushing the big marble ahead of him. He tugged my arm hard. I bent down so that he could whisper in my ear. "I think she wants to show it to you, Tone," he said.

"You said we were going to get Cokes, Dill," Wanda said.

Dillard's words made my mouth go dry as paper. "I'll get them," I whispered.

When I came back down, Wanda was sitting in my chair, fooling with the dials of the S-40A. She had my earphones on. I looked at Dillard. He was sitting on my cot. He shrugged, then winked. I passed out the Cokes. Wanda pulled the earphones off and got up. "All I can hear is noise," she said.

We sat there, sipping our Cokes. Dillard burped every few seconds. He was swallowing air to do it. Wanda didn't seem to mind.

Dillard punched my arm. "*Ask* her, numb nuts," he said.

My face got instantly hot.

"Ask me what?" Wanda said.

"*You* ask," I said, shoving Dillard away.

The chair she was sitting on swiveled and she began to push herself in slow circles. "I'm dizzy," she said, letting her head loll about helplessly, as if her neck had been snapped.

"Tone here wants to see it, Wanda," Dillard said.

I could have killed Dillard on the spot. I couldn't swallow my last mouthful of Coke. It backed up into my nose.

Wanda got up and stretched, her woman's breasts rising inside the cotton dress. The she turned her back on us and strolled to the dark end of the basement where I'd been excavating. Dillard and I sat on the cot.

"Go on," he said.

"*You* go on," I said.

"I've already seen it," he said.

"Sure, two years ago."

"It was last year, chicken." He made a clucking chicken noise.

My heart was beating fast and a burp was trapped halfway between my stomach and my throat.

"We'll stroll the lane... to*gether*," Wanda sang at the dark end of the basement. Her voice contradicted her mature body. It was small and high, the voice of a little girl.

Dillard set his Coke down and pulled me off the couch. He gave me a hard shove towards Wanda, which gave me the momentum I needed, physical and mental.

"Sing love's refrain... to*gether,*" she sang.

Then I was standing next to her on the dark dirt floor, our shadows looming large and formless against the unevenly excavated area.

"What do you want, Tony?" she asked.

"You know," I mumbled. "What Dillard said."

"What did he say? I forget."

My pickax was stuck in the wall of compacted dirt. I grabbed it and took a few energetic swings. I hadn't worked down here in a week. I'd run into some rocks, and the going was slow. Fifteen cents a load wasn't half enough. For all his money, Stan was a cheapskate.

I hit a rock, and big red sparks flew down towards our feet. I put the pick down. "He said that you were going to show it to us," I blurted out.

"Dillard's a geek," she said. She folded her arms against her breasts. She bent and unbent a knee impatiently. "In fact, both of you are geeks. I bet you two are the geekiest freshmen at Lowmont." The knee rocked faster and faster, building up speed.

I started to leave, but she grabbed my arm and spun me towards her. She kissed me. Her hard lips were cold from the Coke and tasted of Double Bubble. She pushed me away but held me in place with her eyes. Even wide open they were small. But I couldn't turn away from them.

She drew up her skirt as if squaring a tablecloth. I saw it all—the trembling pink thighs, the anonymous dark where they met.

The skirt dropped. "You've got a real neat haircut, Tony," she said. "Does your old man let you drive the Stude yet?"

"No, I won't be sixteen for almost two years."

"Gee, *that's* hard to believe," she said.

This made me feel good for a few seconds. Then not so good.

I went back to the cot. Dillard had an idiot grin spread across his face. "Shut up," I said.

He grabbed me and wrestled me down to the floor. We rolled around, each trying to get an advantage. I could usually best him at wrestling, but now that his legs were long and his feet were size twelves, it was hard to handle him. We held each other in stalemated headlocks, unable to move.

Wanda put her bare foot on my shoulder and rocked our knotted, head-locked bodies back and forth. "Hey, geek," she said. "Time out. You got a toilet around here someplace?"

"Upstairs," I said. "Let go, Dillard."

He didn't. I got his arm behind his back and pulled his hand up to the nape of his neck. He made a squawking noise. Then let go.

I led the way out of the basement. The path to the front of the house was steep and unlit. Wanda grabbed my hand. It was surprisingly small in mine. It was also damp. She held on tight, as if she needed my guiding strength. I was embarrassed, but also flattered.

Mom and Stan were watching television and didn't pay any attention to us. We had an Admiral with a three-and-a-half-inch screen, and they were sitting up close to it, trying to watch *The Toast of the Town*. I stood behind them while Wanda went to the bathroom. Mom was sipping her Scotch and Stan had a glass of Bromo-Seltzer. Every so often he let loose a complaining belch.

Wanda finished peeing. We went back outside. Dillard was sitting on the curb, throwing pebbles into a storm drain. "You're a nice guy, Tony," Wanda said. "There's not many nice guys left."

She had a bruised look in the pale streetlight. She was only sixteen, but she seemed to know what was in store for her. There wouldn't be very many nice guys in her life.

"Stay fine, Tony," she said.

I cleared my throat once, then twice, but couldn't think of anything to say. My jaws felt wired shut.

There was something just out of reach in this stopped moment between us. She knew what it was but could not articulate it. And if she could have, I could not have grasped it. It was this: She knew her fate. I did not know mine.

A lfredo came home from work to find that his wife, Sabrina, had taped his son's mouth shut. It was duct tape, in double layers, from ear to ear. Gregory didn't seem to mind. He sat on the living room floor playing with his Tonka trucks under the shedding Christmas tree, humming through the tape.

"What happened?" Alfredo said.

"What do you mean?" Sabrina was at the stove, stirring a pot. It was stew, a good smell. He inhaled, his eyes closed. Garlic, basil, bay. Sabrina was a dedicated cook.

"Greggy, the tape on his mouth," he said.

"He was going on and on," she said, stirring. "You know how wound up he gets. I couldn't shut him up."

"I don't think duct tape is a good idea," he said. He looked at Gregory, who was now ramming a dump truck into an ambulance and humming furiously. Christmas had come and gone, and the toys were already boring the boy.

"You don't have to be home all day with him," his wife said.

"True," he said. "Even so, honey..."

"We don't have to talk about it right now," she said. "I've got your dinner ready."

He went to the bathroom to wash up. His face in the mirror was pale and rough with black stubble. He was not a handsome man. He had thick features—a wide, crooked nose, flat lips, and bulging, hyperthyroid eyes that always seemed alarmed. His strongly ridged forehead sloped back into a receding hairline. He was a gentle, uncombative man, but he looked like a washed-up boxer. His hair was turning gray and he thought he looked ten years older than he was. It didn't make sense, this biological injustice, but he could accept it.

Fault Lines

He had a good, well-planned life, and everything was on course. His stock portfolios were thriving, he was not outrageously in debt, and his job was interesting but undemanding. He sat at a computer screen all day long in a state-of-the-art ergonomic swivel chair, working with simple probability outcomes, writing memos, revising instructional manuals. He was a reliability engineer, working on a new project, a VLR (Very Long Range) cruise missile, nicknamed Gravy Boat by company insiders. His assignments were basic—writing instructional manuals that explained, in layman's terms, simple reliability concepts. The manuals were intended for nontechnical management types. It was easy work, even pleasurable, and he was paid well for it. It was not the kind of job that aged a man prematurely. He was even in line for a managerial post. In the year 2000, just around the corner now, he'd be wearing the orange and white ID badge of third-echelon management, the first step on the ladder to "mahogany row," the penthouse offices on the top floor of the Project Development Center.

After dinner Alfredo and Sabrina watched television. Gregory was in his room, talking to himself. He had a loud, raspy voice, and he used it with unself-conscious gusto.

"Hear that?" Sabrina said.

Alfredo looked away from the TV, listened to the boy's babble. "He sounds like an auctioneer. It's kind of cute."

"Try it all day long. He follows me around, clacking like a crow. It isn't cute."

"But duct tape..."

"Think about it," she said, her voice level. "You want me to go insane?"

He raised his hands off his lap, let them drop. He turned his attention back to the TV program. He liked the girls of *Bay Watch*. Liked to see them running, their moist, buoyant breasts rising and falling with each slow-motion stride. The stories were necessarily mindless. And that was fine. You didn't want to be distracted from the kinetic wonders of physical perfection by unpredictable trips into serious drama. Alfredo believed the world was purely and exclusively physical. All speculations on the never-observed nonphysical inevitably led to confusion and grief. No one could argue with that.

Alfredo had put on too much weight in the four years since Gregory had been born, and his blood pressure was up. One-sixty over ninety-five. The doctor had prescribed the drug Inderal to control it, which Alfredo took religiously. He was not religious about the doctor's other suggestions. He continued to smoke, he took no exercise, he ate too much. This evening he'd stuffed himself with beef stew and Parkerhouse rolls and pecan pie left over from Christmas. His pants were open in front and he was full of bloat.

His father died at fifty-six of clogged arteries. Alfredo vowed to not let that happen to him. For his New Year's resolutions he'd promise himself to cut down on smoking, eat more fruits and vegetables, and join a fitness club. He was only forty-three, but his body looked sixty. The *Bay Watch* girls, he knew with some regret, would not give him a second glance.

In bed that night his wife was not interested either. This did not surprise him. But it had been a week or more, and though he was not all that interested in it himself, he believed abstinence could become a de facto condition. "Use it or lose it," his doctor had told him more than once. Blood tests had shown that his testosterone was down a few dozen points. This was to be expected, at his age. Even so, the horomone level was still solidly in the normal range.

"I think we should," he said.

"*Should?*" Sabrina looked at him, her expression puzzled. She was five years younger than Alfredo and she was still attractive. She had not lost her figure. Her neck was long and smooth and her black hair spilled out on the pillow. She had broad cheekbones and small sharp eyes. When he first met her, he thought she was part Asiatic or maybe Indian, but her father was English and her mother was German.

Alfredo had been attracted by her long neck and thick black hair. She reminded him of a Modigliani figure. Modigliani was also in love with women who had long smooth necks.

"It's been almost two weeks, Sabrina," he said. He tried to kiss her neck, but she arched away from him.

"Maybe tomorrow," she said. "I can't predict my moods."

At work the next day, Rollie Pastorino gave him a ten-dollar chip he'd taken from a Las Vegas casino. "Here's a start on your new life," he said.

"Do I look that bad?"

"Worse."

Rollie was a small, dapper man. A Desert Storm vet who wouldn't talk about the war. "It was like coming after being in for only half a minute. Too embarrassing to talk about," he said. "Watch the replays on TV, you'll find out more from them than you would from me. I was just a thirty-second tourist. Didn't even get sand on my dick. The Arab women were given orders to stay the hell away from the infidel GIs. Infidels. Shit, those camel jockeys don't know the half of it."

Rollie flirted outrageously with all the secretaries, even the homely ones. He had a gigolo's style, but his boyish good looks made him seem harmless. Women were attracted to that combination. "I'm working my way through quality control," he said. "I've bagged half the unattached women in the Project Development Center and a couple of the married honeys down in the blueprint crib."

"You're full of crap, Rollie" Alfredo laughed, half-believing him.

After work they went to the Rogue Bull for Happy Hour. Rollie downed two double Beefeaters before Alfredo had finished his first.

"Fucking broads," Rollie said very loudly. "They don't want your dick for its functional value. They see that woody as opportunity knocking. They spread their legs and you can hear the gates of the mall grind open. You can get lost in there, buddy. A twat is a bottomless pit full of rug rats, mortgage payments, and Saturday nights at the bingo parlor. A man who doesn't look out for himself can get pulled around by his choad like Fido on a leash."

A man at the next table who was sitting with two women who could have been twin sisters said, "Hold it down, moron. There are ladies present."

"What are you, their pimp?" Rollie said. "Fuck you and fuck them."

Alfredo held up an apologetic hand. "I'll take care of him," he said to the man.

"Fuck you too," Rollie said to Alfredo.

The man stood up abruptly, knocking his chair over. The two women sitting with him grabbed at his sleeves. He tore himself away from them.

"I'm going to kick your ass, you mouthy little greaseball," he said.

Rollie Pastorino was half a foot shorter and seventy pounds lighter than the insulted man, but he hit the man first, a right to the belly and a left to the face. Rollie punched with his arms held close to his body for maximum torque. The man sat down, his mouth open, trying to draw air into his lungs. Blood spigoted from his nose. Rollie kicked him and the man toppled over. One of the women grabbed at Rollie, screaming. Rollie shrugged her off and kicked the man's head, heel first, until Alfredo stopped him.

"You tried to kill him," Alfredo said out in the parking lot. His voice was trembling and he felt queasy.

Rollie shrugged. "I don't see it that way," he said. "I just taught the stupid hump some basic manners."

Alfredo stopped at another bar on his way home. It was a quiet place in his neighborhood. He needed a drink to calm himself down. Rollie had surprised him. He'd gone for drinks with Rollie before but had never suspected this murderous streak.

Alfredo sat at the bar and ordered a shot of Bushmill's and a draft beer. A man in a Santa Claus costume sat next to him. The man was wheezing as if he'd been walking uphill.

"I guess you're wondering why I'm still suited up," the man said. He had a small silver bell with him. He picked it up off the bar and gave it a shake.

The last thing Alfredo wanted to do was antagonize anyone. He was still trying to sort out what had happened back at the Rogue Bull. Maybe, he thought, bars ought not to have inflammatory names. The bar he was in now was called, simply Ye Olde Pub.

"It's because I got locked out of my own place last week," the man explained. "The bitch wouldn't even let me get my clothes."

"Sorry to hear that," Alfredo said, trying to sound sympathetic. He saw that the man's costume was grease-stained, as if he'd been sleeping under parked cars.

"Here's the thing," the man said. "I'm a worthless piece of shit. We're all agreed on that, right? But on the other hand, who isn't?"

Alfredo felt his neck hair bristle. "Me," he said, looking into his glass of beer. "I'm not a worthless piece of shit. Not at all."

"Oh, Jesus," the man in the Santa costume said. "Another happy Christian." He picked up his bell and gave it a hard shake. He raised his drink, a whiskey and soda. His puckered lips reached needfully for the rim of the glass.

"You're worthless when you think you're worthless," Alfredo said, immediately regretting it. He hated aphorisms, especially uplifting ones. They were never true, or if they were, their opposites were equally valid. All abstraction was open to contradiction. The world may have been a dream, wave patterns focused by gravity, but humans were structured to see the dream as rock-solid real. In any case, the world, whatever it was, couldn't be known through abstraction. He thought, *bar, Bushmill's, bartender, deadbeat, me.* At this moment, that's all there was. You had to deal with things within reach.

"Thank you, Norman Vincent Peale," the defunct Santa said.

Outside it began to rain. Alfredo heard car tires hiss in the wet street. "You're welcome," he said, pushing away from the bar.

When he got home, he heard muffled crying. Sabrina was in the kitchen, eating a steak. "You're an hour and a half late," she said, looking at her wristwatch.

"Sorry, but you won't believe what happened. Where's Greggy?"

"In his toy closet. I gave him a time-out. What won't I believe?"

He went into Gregory's bedroom and opened the toy closet door. The boy was lying in the dark among heaps of stuffed animals, whimpering. Alfredo picked him up and carried him into the kitchen. "What did he do this time?" he asked.

"Ask what he didn't do," Sabrina said, cutting into her meat.

"He's only four, Sabrina."

She stabbed her knife into the steak and left it standing there. "You know what I hate?" she said. "I hate it when you talk down to me, like I was some kind of morally deficient nut-case. Maybe you should've been a priest."

"I'm beginning to feel like a priest," he said.

Sabrina responded to this by cutting into her steak again. Alfredo carried Gregory into the living room and set him down in front of the TV set. He plugged a Disney tape into the VCR, then went back into the kitchen. He put on a hot-pad glove and took his steak out of the oven. "This looks first rate," he said, sitting down opposite his wife.

"It's probably shoe leather by now," she said, sliding the bottle of steak sauce towards him.

Alfredo invited Rollie Pastorino over for New Year's Day dinner. "Rollie's a character," Alfredo told Sabrina. "He's likable as hell, but has this whacko streak. He's a real Jekyll and Hyde type."

"Sounds like loads of fun," Sabrina said, rolling her eyes.

When Rollie appeared at their door, he was soaking wet. "Had a flat on the freeway," he said. "Soon as I got out to change the tire, the fucking sky opened. I need a drink."

Sabrina regarded the little man. "That isn't real polyester, is it?" she said. "Why don't you take a hot shower while I dry your clothes?"

Rollie kissed Sabrina's hand. "See," he said to Alfredo, "this is why I'm not married. You got the last good woman on the planet, you greedy bastard."

They all laughed. Sabrina gave Rollie a warm glass of mulled wine and showed him to the bathroom. "Leave your clothes in the hallway," she said.

While Sabrina dried Rollie's clothes, Alfredo made a pitcher of martinis.

"This is going to be a long evening," Sabrina said.

"I don't follow you," Alfredo said.

"Your friend is a jerk," she said.

"I thought you two hit it off, honey."

"He put his hand on my ass when I showed him the bathroom."

After dinner, the men watched a bowl game while Sabrina stayed in the kitchen, cleaning up. "This Sabrina of yours," Rollie said, "she's the real article. I know the type."

"How so?" Alfredo said.

"Puts on this quiet, pouty, fuck-you act. Ice on top, but there's this huge festering lava bed underneath the permafrost."

"I don't think so," Alfredo said.

"Maybe you haven't tapped into it yet. Maybe you haven't figured out where the fault lines are. You want some expert advice?"

Alfredo raised his hand, stopping Rollie. "I think we'd better change the subject," he said.

"It's mental more than physical," Rollie said.

"Enough," Alfredo said.

Rollie slumped down into his chair theatrically. "I've offended you," he said. "I've made you uncomfortable with me. We're friends, but now you want to kick my ass. You want to bust me up."

Alfredo laughed. "I'm a peaceful man, Rollie," he said.

"That's the world's number-one oxymoron, Alfredo," Rollie said. "Makes me feel lonely to hear you say it."

Sabrina came out of the kitchen. "You two want mince meat pie, or are you just going to keep on drinking?" she said. Framed in the doorway, backlit by the bright kitchen lights, she looked alarmingly beautiful. Loose strands of her dark hair caught the light and became incandescent. Both men stared at her for a moment. Rollie said, "Awesome." He made a breathy, whistling sound.

Sabrina shifted her weight to one foot and put her hand on her hip. The sudden aggressive curvature of her body made Alfredo wish that Rollie was not there.

"I'll take the mince meat," Rollie said.

"I'm in the mood," Sabrina said after Rollie left. She led the way into the bedroom. Alfredo's heart beat like an untested teenager's. He went into their bathroom and took two Inderals, then undressed. Sabrina was already in bed, her small eyes slitted. Her black hair was spread out on the pillow like the wings of a raven.

Alfredo, his heart still hammering, spent some time looking for Sabrina's fault lines, but only aroused her impatience. "I know exactly what you're doing," she said. "I don't need that. I just want you, not your imagination."

Alfredo sighed. She had no fault lines. On the other hand, he didn't either. Rollie was dead wrong. I *am* a peaceful man, he thought, and Sabrina is exactly what she appears to be.

Alfredo made love to his beautiful wife in his usual straightforward way.

He couldn't sleep. He got up wanting a cigarette. The house was quiet except for a muffled singsong chattering. It was Gregory. The boy was talking in his sleep. Alfredo went into his son's room. Gregory's face was angelic in the faint glow of his night-light. Alfredo shook a cigarette out of its pack and held it in his lips but did not light it. He knelt down next to his son's bed.

The boy would have Alfredo's coarse features. He could see the process of genetic sculpture beginning to express itself. Which probably meant the boy would also share Alfredo's temperament—docile, calm, reliable, satisfied with minor achievements and moderate pleasures.

Alfredo knew that Gregory would be unaffected by the incidental abuses and unjust punishments of childhood, and that, in manhood, he would not be driven by abstract furies. His thirsts would be real thirsts, and his quests to slake them would be direct and practical. The boy was a simple expression of blood, bone, and flesh, forged in starlight and gravity.

He kissed his son's forehead, then went out into the backyard. The rain clouds had passed, the moonless winter night was strung with stars. He lit his cigarette and said a small prayer. Not of thanks but of acknowledgment. The universe did not require his gratitude. It was unholy and grand and without fault. Alfredo blew a lungful of smoke into his corner of it.

E veryone arrived in boots, but it was too hot in the house to keep them on. Before long the air was skunky with the intimate aroma of winter feet, feet that had been sealed in leather and thick wool socks all day long.

Most of our guests were half drunk and in an uncritical frame of mind when they arrived. Those who weren't wearing boots shed their shoes in the spirit of fellowship.

My girlfriend, Rocio Cantú, hated giving parties in this *el norte* country. She claimed she didn't know what white people liked to eat and drink. Even so, this party was her idea. "We *go* to parties, but we never *give* parties," she said, explaining why this one was necessary.

This was a sore point between us. Her reluctance to entertain embarrassed me. We were poor. I'd been out of work for almost a year, having quit my job teaching English as a second language in El Paso.

Rocio was born on a farm in Coahuila but grew up just out- **Feet** side Mexico City. When her family moved to Juárez, she came north. She took my class at the community college, and I fell in love with her. I talked her into moving north with me. "It's better up north," I said. "No hassles, plenty of work, good pay." It was a lie, but I'd been in El Paso for five years and needed a change of scenery. I thought the north Rockies would be good for us.

Throwing parties was an expense our budget couldn't tolerate. I knew this, Rocio knew this. Another thing: whenever we talked about entertaining our friends as potential guests in our house, Rocio suddenly perceived them differently. They were no longer just our friends, but finicky strangers—*guests*. What do you give to a guest? Guests are mysteries, they are full of unknown expectations. They come to you wanting happiness and cheer and good times, and how do you provide that?

We are not reasonable people. A few jugs of cheap wine, a pot of something hot—chili, fajitas, gumbo, stew. This takes no monumental effort. Even so, Rocio went catatonic. Such pockets of madness in the woman you live with are not negotiable. They are permanent topographical features of the psyche, and you either learn to live with them or they'll rip the bottom out of your love boat. Other things—the good things—even things out. My own unnegotiable psychic topography no doubt caused her some trouble.

Most of our friends were also unemployed. Even so, they are reckless with their food stamps and brought over generous pots of hors d'oeuvres. They even brought booze, an eclectic show of partially filled bottles—vermouth, single-grain whiskey, gin, blended rotgut sold only in one-quart bottles, and tequila.

A friend of mine who had just gotten married gave me his old stereo that afternoon, the very afternoon my temperamental old Emerson decided to stop working. His new wife had a brand-new Marantz, so he gave me his old Sanyo.

It had only one working speaker, but that was fine by me. Benny Goodman, Coleman Hawkins, Johnny Hodges, Lester Young, Duke Ellington don't require stereo, they come straight at you.

"Good crowd," said Duane Mercator, my counselor from the Unemployment Office. "I see some of them from time to time down at the Job Service. My kind of people."

"Gold bricks to a man," I said, offering him a tray of pumpernickel squares layered with brie and prosciutto.

Duane looked a bit out of place in his blue suit, paisley tie, and milky, blue-veined feet. Even so he maintained a kind of gloomy dignity that tended to make people keep their distance. He had a lean. hawkish face, the face of a dangerous Sicilian, I always thought. Sometimes he seemed more like a Catholic prelate, a man of importance in Holy See politics. Actually, he's an impressively accomplished amateur magician. His hobby.

"Got any good leads, Duane?" I said.

"Everybody's a teacher, Tony," he said. "This town is loaded with out-of-work professors. The Ph.D. mills are turning them out like Big Macs. McDoctorates are cluttering up the landscape. These people think they're lucky to get hired as adjunct faculty at minimum pay and zilch benefits. And the system is happy to use them. In fact, it feeds on them. These people are vampire meat, Tony."

His eyelids fluttered like willow leaves in a wind when he talked shop. Under the dancing eyelids, his pale gray eyes would travel upward and crescents of the moony, blue-tinged whites would show themselves.

The heavy, wet wind of a late-winter storm thumped and groaned against our little house. Taj Mahal rasped his blues through the single speaker. Morton Arthur, a big man with a ZZ Top beard, gave me a conspiratorial hug. "In your study, man," he said, laying a finger against one side of his ruined nose. I knew what he meant. Morton was connected, and liked to share his coke. He had money to burn, unlike most of the guests. He was our local celebrity. Any day now one of his science fiction novels was going to hit the charts. He wrote a kind of juiced-up 1930s space opera with Cyberpunk features: nubile earth women doing crack on crater-pocked *The Pusher Planetoids;* slave traders providing American teenagers as slave labor to work the bug farms of the spider people from *The Planet of the Arachnids;* hermaphroditic cowboys herding desexed human clones though underground *Labyrinths of Venus.*

"Feel free," I told him, but in truth I was uncomfortable with his habit. I glanced around the room to see if Rocio was watching. She did not approve of drugs. She always wore the red "I Am Drug Free" ribbon during drug-awareness week in El Paso.

Mort had been busted in L.A. while working on a screenplay for a mid-budget but never-distributed SF shoot-em-up called *Time Slot.* He'd spent a month

in jail, and then six more months doing public service. His public service con-
sisted of lecturing local high school audiences about the dangers of drugs. Mort
loved his drugs, and asking him to denounce them was like asking Jerry Falwell
to promote child pornography.

> "Champagne don't make me crazy,
> Cocaine don't make me lazy,
> Ain't nobody's business but my own,"

Morton sang, along with Taj Mahal.

Rocio came over to us, suspicious. "No *drogs,*" she said.

"*Deportes sí, drogas no,*" Morton said, laughing. It was a bumper sticker we'd
brought up from the border. It was on our refrigerator. It tickled Morton. Sports
yes, drugs no. "What sports do you play, Rocio?" he said.

In truth, he liked Rocio and Rocio liked him. Their play at hostility was a
kind of running joke. But Rocio drew the line at hard drugs. "I mean it,
Morton," she said. "*No pinchi drogas en* my damn *casa.*"

"Rocio, Rocio, Rocio," Morton intoned, giving her name its rightful Spanish
inflections. He passed his middle finger under his nose and inhaled noisily. "I
have given up the filthy habit, Rocio. I sniff only *taco pescado* now. It's cheaper
and gets you almost as high."

Rocio's eyes got big for a second, then she laughed. "I don't believe you,
Morton," she said, cuffing him lightly on the jaw. "You have a filthy mind."

This little house we rent used to be a barn. Legend has it that a horse thief was
hanged from its rafters. It's a legend that happens to be true. I call it a legend
only because hanged horse thieves in this part of the country are legendary. I
found out this piece of history from Peter Selvig, a one-hundred-year-old ex-
railroad conductor who lives across the street. He said that he witnessed the
hanging. He no longer remembered the name of the thief. He remembers only
that the man was tall and skinny and that there was a lot of drunken joking
among the grown-ups about whether or not he wouldn't slip the noose when
they dropped him. Someone suggested tying a sack of feed to his feet so there'd
be enough weight to cinch the noose and snap his neck properly. Peter wasn't
supposed to be present—it was strictly a party for adults. But he and his older
brother climbed, unnoticed, up a ladder in the far end of the barn and hid
behind a stack of hay in the loft. It was New Year's Eve, 1899, and the thief was
to be hanged at the stroke of midnight, ushering in the bright new thief-free century. Peter remembers the condemned man's face clearly as the sheriff's deputy
put the noose around his long, thin neck. The expression in the thief's eyes,
Peter said, was something to behold. It was calm and peaceful and, in a strange
way, *generous.* It suggested something extrahuman to little Peter, though he

could not have articulated this at the time. The look on that man's face was something Peter could not get out of his mind. It remains vivid, almost a hundred years later. Peter, who was on the edge of his own precipice, has something of this same unafraid look. His foggy old eyes are peaceful and generous. "That old boy's boots came off," he said. "They tied the mealsack to his boots, and when they dropped him the sudden stop yanked off his boots. He had little feet, like a girl's feet. Feet to break your heart." I liked Peter a lot and we spent many afternoons in his backyard whittling on pieces of maple. These afternoons were so enjoyable that I was almost glad to be out of work. *Deportes sí, trabajo no.*

After about six hours the party broke up into subparties. There was a group in the bedroom making militia jokes, a north Rockies pastime. Three wives sat on the sectional discussing the merits of discount warehouses. Mort Arthur had collected half a dozen people and had taken them into the double-size closet I call my study. I went with these. There were about six of us. "I lied to Rocio," Mort said to me.

He dismantled a picture frame to get at the glass. Then he chopped some generous lines. Someone provided fat Dairy Queen straws that had been clipped short, and we passed the glass around the small room like a communion palette. I was worried Rocio would come in. She had started going to church again after a ten-year layoff and had hung her grandma's old crucifix above our bed—a dark, twisted savior carved out of stubborn mesquite by an eccentric but faithful artisan. Under the black eyes of that Indian Jesus, Rocio was becoming less and less willing to participate in the mild exercises of foreplay. There was no telling what new extreme she might be pushed to if she barged in on Mort's cocaine ceremony.

I went back to the living room. Rocio had gotten uncharacteristically tipsy. Someone had brought a bottle of Irish Cream, and she indulged herself. She likes candy, and Irish Cream is the candy of hard drink. Manitas de Platas, the gypsy guitarist, was on the Sanyo, and Rocio, who claimed three-quarters Spanish blood, was demonstrating the flamenco. For castanets she was using spoons. Her skirts were flying, exposing her long silky thighs and smoky undies. A thin line of sweat gleamed on her temple. Perfume and pheromones mixed and radiated like woodstove heat from her spinning body. *Who is this woman I've tied my life to?* I asked myself, knowing the question was stupid as well as central.

I went into the kitchen where Duane Mercator was doing a magic trick at the insistence of a small crowd. "Everybody sit down and close your eyes," Duane said.

I sat on the floor, back against the wall. A woman I didn't know sat next to me. She offered me a hit from her joint, which I refused. "I don't mix my chemicals," I said. She shrugged and passed it the other way. "I'm going to count slowly to ten," Duane said, his voice beautifully modulated. We could have been in Las Vegas, watching an expensive act. His voice was the voice of a professional master of ceremonies. It made you feel that you were in competent hands. You left his cubicle in the employment office feeling that important jobs were being lined up for you.

When he finished counting, the woman sitting next to me slumped down. The *mota* dropped from her fingers. I picked it up and passed it to my left. I let my head thunk against the wainscoting of the wall behind me, giving in to a sudden postcocaine fatigue.

Duane said, "I want you to think of a white wall. It's fifty feet high and a hundred feet wide and it is pure, unblemished white."

The woman next to me slowly raised her head off the linoleum. "I see it," she said.

"Think of this wall," Duane said, "as a place of complete peace. It is untouched by petty aggravations. Nothing can mar it. Nothing has ever marred it. It was clean at the beginning of time, it is clean now, and it will be clean at the end of time. It is the wall that surrounds Eden."

"Wow," said the woman. "Man, I'm going snow-blind."

I didn't see any wall. Maybe a pale spot, wide as a quarter. But I had to push it to believe it.

"Try not to be so cynical," Duane said to me. I guess he read the expression on my face.

I made an honest effort. The little pale spot widened. This interested me.

"Now," said Mercator. "Open your eyes."

I opened my eyes. The pale spot was still there. Not fifty feet tall, but definitely there. Mercator opened the oven door. He took a bottle of milk out of the fridge and put it into the oven. He turned the oven on and set the dial to "Bake."

"I'm going to start counting again," he said. "When I reach twenty, I'll open the oven. He reached twenty, then opened the door again. The bottle of milk was gone. In its place was a package. Duane took the package out and removed the heavy brown wrapping paper that covered it. He tore the paper off the package and opened the box. A kitten raised its head and mewed. Duane closed the oven door. He counted to twenty again. Then he opened the oven again. Inside was the bottle of milk. He got a saucer out of the cupboard and poured some milk into it. I could see, from the way it steamed, that it was warm milk. The kitten ran to the saucer and began lapping it up, her tail erect and quivering with pleasure. We applauded.

I got up and went back into the front room. For some reason, Duane's magic trick had bothered me. The white haze he'd called up was still with me. It flared around the living room like a halo. Rocio had finished dancing and was now sitting on the sofa sipping Irish Cream.

I went down to the basement to lie down and watch television, hoping the party would break up pretty soon. I watched part of a T and A movie on the

Playboy channel. Then I switched to one of the Christian channels, where a pair of evangelists, a man and a woman, told their audience how at one time they did not have a measurable ounce of faith. "Hey!" the woman cried out with the élan of a cheerleader. "Look how far we've *come!*"

I slept for a while. When I woke, the party was over, our guests were gone. I found Rocio sitting on the floor of the shower stall. She sat with her knees pulled up, her arms crossed on her knees, her head on her arms, while tepid water lashed her brown back, the knuckles of her spine shining like wet stones.

I turned off the water. "Come on, let's go to bed, honey," I said.

She sobbed. One big, ragged sob. This is where she goes when she is sad, the shower. I lifted her up and held her against my chest. Her breasts turn outward in their fullness. I read that somewhere once—a generously erotic phrase—and it applies to Rocio. When she got her feet under her, I wrapped her in a towel.

I locked up the house and went to the bedroom. Rocio had collapsed on the bed in a careless sprawl—her thighs loose in a parody of invitation. But I knew, from experience, that it would have been a mistake to misread the moment. I left her there, her eyes half open, her mind halfway back to the slopes of Chapultepec.

I cleaned up the house, put the coke-dusty glass back into the picture frame, washed the dishes. When I went back to the bedroom. Rocio was kneeling at the head of the bed, kissing the gnarled mesquite feet of her grandmother's Jesus. She was still weeping, silently, and I knew that we would soon be going back to the border.

I knelt beside the bed, stroked her calves and her feet. They were perfect feet—long, narrow, highly arched. I touched the sweetly knuckled toes, traced the delicate webbing of veins under the transparent skin, the bleak and startling rise of the ankles.

As she kissed the tragic feet of her grandmother's Jesus, I kissed the fragile spray of bones that reached down from the instep and ended at the toes: for they too were fossils of starlight that had not forgotten their radiant freedom.

The summer I turned seventeen, freedom and boredom were two sides of the same equation. Total freedom equaled total boredom. I felt it physically. It squeezed me, it made me sweat. In dreams it hung in the air like a hot, paralyzing fog. It weighed on me, pressed me down. I was trapped under the weight of absolute liberty.

Both my parents were working a lot of overtime at Convair making B-36's—the intercontinental atomic bomber that would send the Communist world back to the Stone Age—and I was left to my own devices. But I had no devices and was caught like a fly in the web of my own sloth.

Out of desperation, after my mother and her latest husband, Ward Moseley, had left for the swing shift, I searched their bedroom looking for rubbers and other evidence of their sex life. I went through my mother's lingerie drawer, her jewelry boxes, and felt the top shelf of their bedroom closet. In Ward Moseley's underwear drawer I hit the jackpot. There among the sandalwood-scented boxer shorts was a nickel-plated .38-caliber snub-nosed revolver. I didn't know he owned a gun. Next to it was a box of shells.

Hormone X

I took the gun out and hefted it a while, watching myself in the dresser mirror. I was wearing Levi's, engineer boots, and a white T-shirt. My black hair was greased back into a slick duck's ass. I broke the gun open and spun the cylinder. Then I filled the holes in the cylinder with six bullets. I aimed the gun at my reflection.

"You've fucked me over for the last time, scumbag," I said. The image in the mirror pointed the gun at my chest. My heart vibrated with disbelief, then started to pound: I had put actual pressure on the trigger, enough to raise the hammer a fraction of an inch. I unloaded the gun, returned the bullets to their box and continued my search.

I found some pamphlet-size comic books. They were just like the Sunday comics but with perverted twists: Blondie and the Bumsteads' next-door neighbor, Herb Woodley, were naked and going at it in Blondie's kitchen. A naked Maggie spanked Jiggs's balloon-big buttocks with a spatula. Captain Easy had Mary Worth bent over a car fender. Alley Oop showed Tarzan's Jane what a real ape-man could do. I was amazed and delighted. The entire Sunday comics were roaring with lust, the characters crossing over into one another's lives, breaking every rule of decent comic-strip behavior. I didn't know such books existed. It was like discovering life on Mars, or picking up TV pictures from a UFO.

The best book in this secret library was called *Hormone X,* a short novel that played on the Red Scare the House Un-American Activities Committee had recently whipped up to a fever pitch. In the book, the Commies had dumped a synthetic hormone into the water supplies of all major American cities. The results were spectacular. The hormone caused all women between puberty and menopause to become insatiable sex tyrants. Each chapter was illustrated with yellow-tinted photographs of wild-eyed lunatic housewives, secretaries, cheerleaders—even nuns—hunting down men, taking them captive and making sex slaves out of the happily surprised victims while the national defense went to hell.

The trouble with *Hormone X* was that, while the plot was set up neatly in the first few pages, everything after that was just a series of mechanical repetitions. There was no variation on the theme, no narrative complication. The sex frenzy began to wear thin after Chapter 5. I could sense the boredom of the pornographer, who h ad begun to plagiarize himself. the scene between the First Lady and the secretary of agriculture was exactly the same as the scene between the housewife and the plumber thirty pages earlier. Only the names, locales and furniture were different. Worse, the writer, whoever he was, wrote in a flowery, ornate style that robbed the story of practically all its erotic effects.

After ten readings of *Hormone X,* I put it into its dark place among the shorts and undershirts, heady with the belief that I could have written a better sex novel standing on my head. Being a virgin didn't matter: Sexual knowledge could be borrowed. I had already written a war story, "My Bayonet Sings," based on my reading of *Men at War,* a collection of first-person battlefield tales edited by Ernest Hemingway. My junior English teacher, Mrs. Wise, had called "My Bayonet Sings" "terrifying and convincing," even though she only gave me a C- because of spelling errors and crude figures of speech. I didn't mind. It was the highest grade I'd received in any subject during the school year, a year that would be followed by a summer of boredom so deep and unvaried that uncommon and desperate acts seemed inevitable.

I hung out with Buddy Askew that summer. Buddy was a tall blond boy with the lean, hungry muscles of a sharecropper. His parents had migrated to California from Arkansas during the Dust Bowl era. The memory of those hard days seemed to have imprinted the Askew blood, because Buddy—though born in California—had inherited his father's stark, thin-lipped, hardscrabble face. It was a face that expected the worst, no matter how well things were going. Prosperity, abundance, high wages—these were held suspect in the small, uncompromising eyes of both father and son.

Buddy owned a .22-caliber Remington carbine, and we would walk the dry arroyos in the eastern foothills of the county, shooting randomly at small animals. We'd drive out on Highway 80 to a town at the foot of the Cuyamaca Mountains, fill our canteens with Nesbitt orange soda, then set off into the steep country roads in Buddy's 1936 Ford sedan. Buddy had bought the car the previous summer with two years' of paperboy pay. It was a clean car that had belonged to a grade-school teacher. It had crisp maroon plastic seat covers and a steel sun visor above the windshield. When he bought the car, big freckles of black primer showed through the original gray paint. So buddy and I drove it to

L.A. to take advantage of a $19.95 Earl Scheib paint job. The car came out a dull, light-absorbing seaweed- green. It looked like the staff car for the army of some failing country. We drove back home in tense disappointment. The engine was a small, flathead V-8 that put out a tepid eighty-five horsepower, but Buddy installed headers and twin exhaust pipes along with a pair of twelve-inch glass-packed mufflers called "Smittys" that gave the little engine a darkly sexual throb. The twin-trombone sound of the exhaust somewhat made up for the car's boring appearance.

Sometime after his seventeenth birthday, Buddy adopted worldly airs. I figured it was because of TV. There had been a lot of spy shows that year dealing with foreign intrigue. He became as rigidly sophisticated as an East German saboteur. He had two expressions: Amused Contempt and Cynical Insight, both of which he used with devastating effect.

Most of my enthusiasms made his lips curl with Amused Contempt. Now and then, when I said something I thought was profound, he'd look at me with Cynical Insight, as if to let me know he'd had this same thought years ago but had since discovered its many flaws. Whenever my conversation drifted into the great unknowables—sex, death, life on other planets, atomic weapons, and the future of mankind—he would regard something far away, his eyes narrow with Cynical Insight, and then his lips would curl thinly in Amused Contempt. It was an ego-shattering combination. It was as if he had yet to discover someone capable of discussing with him on an equal footing. His favorite put-down was, "Think again, shit-for-brains."

On one of those cruelly beautiful days in June, we were sitting on a steep hillside looking for targets down in the bottom of an arroyo. We'd already emptied a box of .22 long rifles at bottles and cans, birds and field mice, hitting nothing. The barrel of the carbine was too short for accuracy and the muzzle velocity was so slow you could actually see the curving flight of the bullets if the sun struck them just right.

A light airplane droned in the sky directly above us. Buddy languidly raised the carbine and shot at it. My boredom, which had caught up with me, disappeared in a gut-punching surge of adrenaline. The plane was at least a thousand feet above us, and there was little chance the slow, curving bullet could reach it, but even so, the criminal potential of what Buddy had done woke up every nerve in my body. Then he shot at the airplane again. He amazed me. It was as if shooting at planes was no more interesting or serious than shooting at rusted cans.

He handed me the carbine. "You try," he said. "See if you can put a hole in that rich fucker's aeroplane." I took the gun from him and drew the bolt back as slowly as I could. I was a little nearsighted and saw the plane as a drifting yellow smear. By the time I was ready to fire, the smear was about to vanish over the crest of a hill. I shot at the patch of blue sky the plane had vacated a split second earlier. Buddy looked at me: Amused Contempt.

As we walked back toward the highway, I told Buddy about my discovery of my stepfather's secret collection of dirty books. For once he didn't give me one of his sophisticated expressions. He looked... *blank.* His parents were strict religious people who were always alert for deviant behavior, in Buddy's friends as well as in society at large. Not much in the way of smut got through their front door. I gave him a thumbnail sketch of the plot of *Hormone X.*

"That's a load of bullshit," he said. "There isn't such a thing as a hormone like that." He tried to give me Amused Contempt, but he was too stimulated to make it work. He only looked peevish and alarmed, as if he'd just swallowed a sharp chicken bone.

"I know there isn't," I said. "It's just a story."

Buddy had long legs, and his strides were quick. I had to half-trot to keep up with him. Suddenly he whirled around and fired a shot over my head. I dropped to a crouch as he fired again. "A dove," he said. "I think I winged the little cock-sucker."

I looked around at the empty, birdless sky. Buddy had reclaimed his normal superiority by scaring me and now regarded me with a muted form of Cynical Insight. "You believe everything you read, shit-for-brains?" he said, casually pushing bullets into the carbine's magazine.

"I *said* it was a story," I repeated, but he ignored me, following the line of thought that suited him.

We drove down to Sweetwater Reservoir. Buddy parked on an embankment about twenty feet above the water.

"I guess this is where they'd dump it," he said.

"Dump what?"

The carbine was on the floor, between our feet. He picked it up and aimed it out the window. He sent a visible bullet hooking out across the still waters. "Hormone X," he said.

"There's no such thing," I reminded him.

"Think again," he said, his beady eyes narrowing at invented targets.

"What are you talking about?" I said.

"I'm talking about the Commies. They'd do it if they could, and they proba-bly can. How do you know that book of yours wasn't written by some ex-Commie who had the facts?" Buddy got out of the car and urinated into Sweetwater, which provided half a million people with drinking water. I joined him.

Buddy's father, Terrel Askew, sold electric-eye equipment to large retailers. This was the beginning of the automatic-door era. I had dinner at their house once: macaroni and cheese and yellow Jell-O salad in which fragments of fruits and nuts were suspended. Mrs. Askew put the food on the table and we served our-selves. They weren't a talkative family, but Mr. Askew did ask about my parents.

I didn't tell him that my mother had been married four times, or that my present stepfather and I had different last names. Minutes passed between Mr. Askew's questions. The click and scrape of forks against the Melmac plates filled the intervals. Mrs. Askew cleared her throat several times as if to speak, and her face brightened as if a pleasant thought had occurred to her, but this appeared to be a vestigial mannerism with no present function, a social counterpart of the human appendix. She said nothing during the entire meal.

Buddy and I finished eating first. Buddy asked to be excused. His father scanned our plates, making sure we had scraped them clean, then nodded. We went to Buddy's room. There was a picture frame nailed to his door. There was no picture in it, just a printed sign:

"A BOY IS KNOWN BY WHAT HE DOES WHEN HE HAS NOTHING TO DO"

"You sure pissed off my dad, shit-for-brains," Buddy said.

"What? I didn't do anything!" I was stunned. "What pissed him off?"

"You didn't say what your old man did for a living."

"He didn't ask."

"Don't you know any manners? You don't make someone play twenty questions with you. If they ask you anything at all about your old man, they probably want to know a couple of other things, too."

"Should I go back and tell him?"

Amused Contempt. "Too late now. You blew it."

"Maybe I should tell him my old man collects dirty books."

"Don't be dumb. He'd never let you over here again if you did a dumb thing like that."

I took this as a compliment: Buddy valued our friendship. "Thanks," I said.

"For nothing, shit-for-brains."

He pulled a checkerboard out from under his bed and set it up on the floor. "You're black," he said.

When Buddy and I went out shooting again, I brought *Hormone X* with me. I also brought Ward Moseley's .38. I didn't plan to shoot it; I just wanted Buddy to see it and be impressed. A nickel-plated snub-nosed .38 was far more sinister than a cheap .22 carbine with a short barrel. I wore an old army-surplus fatigue jacket and kept the pistol in one of the big side pockets.

We filled our canteens with orange Nesbitt and headed out into the arroyo. When we sat down in our favorite spot, I took out *Hormone X* and thumbed through it casually.

"What's that?" Buddy said.

I showed him the cover.

"Give it here a sec," he said. He flipped through the pages, looking first at the yellow pictures, then at the text. He frowned hard and his lips began to move. "Crap," he said. "What the hell is 'tume—tume...'"

"Tumescence," I said.

"'Tume—ess—sent member.' What the hell is that supposed to mean?"

"Stiff dick," I said.

He slapped the book against his thigh. "Well, for shit sakes, why don't they just say so?"

I couldn't help him there.

He read on. "'Carlyle gently presented his tumescent member to Vivian's hot...' *What?* Vivian's hot *Volvo?* He's screwing a damn souped-up foreign *car*?"

"Not 'Volvo.' 'Vulva.'"

"'Vulva.'" He shook his head, unwilling to ask me what the word meant. He tossed the book back to me. "This isn't worth the paper it's printed on," he said. "I doubt if it was any ex-Commie that wrote it. Just some dumb fruit who went to college."

He took the book back and opened it to the photographs. "The pictures are pretty good, though," he conceded. "Your old man got any more books?"

"Just cartoons."

He looked at me with Cynical Insight. "Tijuana Bibles," he said. "I've seen them. They're pretty stupid."

He picked up his carbine and stared at it, as if it were a strange device he hadn't seen before. He opened the breech and snapped it shut. Then he fired. I watch the bullet curve across the canyon and chip a large rock about fifty yards away.

I pulled out the .38 and fired three times at the rock. The .38, even with its short barrel, had more muzzle velocity than the carbine, and its report had twice the authority. It bucked in my hand, its power surprising me. Buddy jumped away from me, stunned. Which was the effect I was hoping for. "Damn!" he said. "Where'd you get that thing?"

I started to tell him, but a scream from across the arroyo shattered the air. Two people, a man and a woman, ran in full crouch from behind the rock we had shot at. They were naked. The woman fell and the man stopped to help her up. Then the man looked up and saw us. "You fucking idiots!" he yelled. "I'm going to come over there and shove those guns up your asses!" I squinted hard, to sharpen my vision. He was about thirty years old and big. He ran behind the rock again and came out pulling up his pants. He tossed a blanket to the woman, then sat down to put on his shoes. The woman remained crouched, the blanket pulled tightly around her.

"Let's get out of here!" I said, jumping up.

Buddy didn't move. He reloaded his carbine. Then he fired at the rock again. The man, who had begun to move down his side of the arroyo, stopped dead in his tracks. He looked like he was going to yell at us again, but nothing came out of his mouth. He started backpedaling up the slope, as if he realized he'd misjudged what he was dealing with.

So had I. Buddy had an expression on his face that made my heart skip. A cold hatred mixed with an eerie calm made him look older. He was a stranger to me, someone from another world, a world of piney hills, smoldering resentments, the warring blood of ancient clans. I was suddenly more scared of him that of the man across the arroyo.

"Come on, cocksucker!" Buddy yelled. "Come on over here and shove these guns up our asses!" His whooping voice was high-pitched with a kind of eager delight.

The woman started screaming again. "They're murderers, Philip! Let's get away from this place!"

Philip gathered the woman's clothes and they scrambled up their side of the arroyo. The blanket the woman was wrapped in snagged on some bushes and fell off her shoulders. She left it behind. I looked cautiously at Buddy, who was still sighting down the barrel of his carbine. "Look at that ass wiggle," he said. "I wouldn't mind having me some of that." The dead calm in his voice had nothing to do with me or with anything I knew about. When Philip and the woman were gone, we headed for the car.

"We'd better make tracks," I said. "They're probably going to call the cops."

Buddy nodded but did not hurry. And when we got to the car, he didn't start it right away. He sat behind the wheel with his hands relaxed in his lap, staring thoughtfully out the windshield.

"You know," he said. "I've been thinking. 'Vulva' is maybe the dirtiest word I ever heard of. The way it sounds. I better have me another look at that *Hormone X*.

"Jesus, will you just start the *car*," I said. "We've got to haul ass before cops come."

He looked at me and grinned. Amused Contempt. "You know what?" he said. "I finally got you figured out."

This startled me. But in a way I felt flattered. He'd been thinking about me; I was someone who needed figuring out. I had not been as curious about him. Until now.

"You don't keep your head," he said. "You get all worked up at the drop of a damn hat. That won't do you any good in the long run. You got to remember that you're in the middle of everything around you, kind of like what they call on TV 'the eye of the storm.' If you forget that, then you're just a part of the storm—wind and torn-up trees and scared shitless."

We drove back to town, as if all we'd done was kill another boring summer day. After dropping off the .38 and *Hormone X* at my house, we went to a matinee. A movie theater was as good a place to lie low as any. Then we went to his house. He asked me to stay for supper. His mother had fixed fried chicken and potato salad. The table was already set, but she put down another plate for me.

"Well, son," his father said to me as we took our seats. "How are your parents?"

"Just fine, sir," I said. "They're working tonight, at Convair."

He nodded. "Those B-36's will put the godless Communists back into hellfire where they were spawned."

Buddy glanced at me—a new expression on his face: Provisional Approval. I was learning.

The man from Mankato keeps neurotic dogs—two lank Borzois he calls Trotsky and Nikita—in his six-foot-by-eight-foot patio, right next to my six-foot-by-eight-foot patio. He's friendly enough, successful in his time, but has no common sense when it comes to caring for animals. The big animals need to run, but all they can do is slither from one patio wall to the other like tall and silky iguanas.

He's sixty-six but thinks he looks like Cary Grant at fifty. He works out, swims, tans himself, dyes his hair patent-leather black. His belly is flat but only if he remembers to hold it in. I don't look like anybody. I have thinning gray hair, pot belly, crepey neck, round shoulders, bifocals. We live in side-by-side townhomes in a complex locally known as the Divorce Courts, a stop over for people in transition.

Novias

Like me, he is living with a young woman. He calls his girlfriend his *novia,* which means fiance. His girlfriend and my girlfriend are from Mexico—mine from Juárez, his from Mexico City. His name is Frank ("Francisco," his *novia* sometimes calls him). My name is Aubery. My girlfriend doesn't like the way my name sounds when she pronounces it ("Ow-Berry"), so she calls me "Berry" for short, with r's trilled, the b buzzing like v: Verry. Both Frank and I left angry Anglo wives behind. His, in Minnesota. Mine, in West L.A.

My girlfriend, Ofelia Lozano—I have also begun to call her my *novia*—despises his girlfriend, Maribel Castillo. Maybe because Maribel is white. A sleek, silvery blonde of aristocratic Iberian blood. She is from Mexico City, a chilanga. The big-city chilangos are not revered here on the border. I've seen this bumper sticker: Haz Patria, Mata a Un Chilango—Do Something For Your Country, Kill a Chilango. Border humor. Ofelia, like many mestizos, has a throwback Mayan profile—the beaky nose, the narrow, sloping forehead, the deepset indecipherable eyes.

Maribel won't give the time of day to Ofelia. She has an unrealistic but stubborn sense of her own station in life. She is smart, well educated, and snobbish. She went to school in Switzerland and studied art history in Paris. Her family went broke, or nearly so, in the recent collapse of the peso, and she took a job at Dillard's, the upscale department store, spraying colognes at shoppers trapped in the premeditated bottleneck between the scent islands. That's how she met Frank.

His fibrillations kicked in just as he entered the narrow aisle where smartly dressed young women trigger the seductive aerosols at browsers. The aisle was crowded, the air was dense with musk. Frank leaned on a glass countertop, sucking wind. Maribel sprayed eau de whatever in front of him. He slapped at the sweetened air, opening a passage in it, but then he hunkered protectively over his misfiring heart. Maribel caught his arm and led him to a stool behind the island. She got him a glass of water. He tapped his pacemaker with a mea culpa knuckle, smiled. His heart settled down. "How do," he said, romance fantasies stiffening his neck hair.

Frank Milhollan was a sales exec for a midsize pharmaceutical company and has a million in fixed-rate annuities and another million in municipal bonds, plus a generous "golden parachute" retirement plan. He has two cars, an El Dorado ("My Eldo," he calls it) and a restored 1938 Cord 810 roadster. In his other life he was a Heart Attack Harry, an in-your-face Type-A kind of guy. But he is pacified now in retirement by Prozac, Zantac, and beta-blockers. His dangerous auricular fibrillation is stabilized by a pacemaker. I like him. We're in the same boat. The main difference between us is he still strains at his oar somewhat; I lean on mine.

We had Frank and Maribel over for dinner after Frank and I realized, with what seemed good humor at the time, how similar our late midlife situations were. Ofelia didn't like the idea, but she made red tamales, beef and chicken fajitas, and her specialty, a glow-in-the-dark pico de gallo that would make Satan beg for ice water. I'd driven my Cherokee across the border, all the way to Casas Grandes, to get a couple of liters of Indio Juh Sotol, a mellow but very strong cream-of-tequila-like drink that's cured with rattlesnakes. You can't get it in El Paso, or even in Juárez. They age it in fifteen-gallon jugs. You can see the pickled diamondback coiled on the bottom of each jug. I'm sure the venom leaks into the sotol because you get more than just drunk on it. The FDA, DEA, ATF, or whoever, would make it a Schedule I no-no if they knew about it. I enjoy it, but the day after drinking it I leave blood in the toilet.

The dinner party was a flop. The first thing Maribel said when she looked at Ofelia's colorful buffet was, "This is *Indian* food." She might as well have called it pig slop, judging from her tone. She wouldn't eat it. I quick-broiled a couple of pork chops for her, microwaved some rice, boiled a package of green beans almondine. Ofelia was furious at me for doing this, but didn't let it show. She is a short, compact woman with skin the color of a west Texas sunset after a sand storm, eyes like wet obsidian.

I fell in love with her in a little Greek restaurant on the east side of El Paso. She was there with a man I thought was her husband but who turned out to be her half brother. He left her alone at their table and didn't come back. She started crying, her sobs coming out in desperate gasps. She wiped her tears with heart-breaking little dabs of her napkin. I went over to her.

"*¿Con permiso?*" I said. I made an elegant bow—not a drunk's bow, although I was a little drunk—but an Old-World courtesy bow. "*Puedo ayudarle. Soy un doctor.*"

She shrugged. "I am not sick," she said. "Only sad."

"*Qué lástima,*" I said. "May I sit down?"

I don't really speak Spanish, just a few words and prepackaged phrases, enough to get in and out of trouble. But her English was more than adequate. "Suit yourself," she said. My hands were shaking. They always shake these days. She noticed but didn't dwell on my palsy. It was an inauspicious beginning, but things heated up nicely after that.

Her half brother Lalo, it turned out, had deserted from the Mexican army. They were going to send him to Chiapas to help put down the Indians and he, claiming Zapotec heritage, wanted no part of it. He came across illegally and was heading for Chicago to stay with friends.

After dinner I poured Frank and myself snifters of the Indio Juh. I filled a pair of elegant long-stemmed glasses with membrillo, a candy-sweet liqueur made from quince, for Maribel and Ofelia. Ofelia would rather have had the sotol, but I was eager to find some common ground for the two women.

Frank got drunk quickly and began to hallucinate. Or so it seemed to me. He kept jerking his head to one side, as if reacting to a half-visible threat at the edge of his vision. I get happy and loquacious on any booze, but sotol turns me into a smart-ass visionary. I don't hallucinate, but marginally sensible insights pop into my head, which I feel obliged to voice. I'd come to think of these whipcrack illuminations as my rattlesnake epiphanies. A somewhat loose notion for a defunct neurosurgeon to entertain.

"It occurs to me," I began, "that women are basically greedy, while men are basically selfish. That's why a generous man is a threat to his family, and a woman active in the charities always has a smirking hypocrite or an out-and-out idiot for a husband."

There's a point in your life when you stop worrying about making sense. Relative sobriety has nothing to do with it. You admit to yourself at last that your idea of order, no matter how tidy or self-referentially complete, has always been tied to a runaway horse. I held on too long; I made one mistake over the limit. In neurosurgery the limit is zero.

Frank started to hum to himself and rock back and forth in his chair. "I don't think you should drink any more of that, Frank," Maribel said. She gave me a severe glance, the nostrils of her thin Iberian nose delicately flared. She has the most inexpressive mouth I've ever seen on a woman—a thin red line the corners of which neither lift nor droop.

I poured myself another inch of the snake juice. Frank, who was still relishing his dearly bought freedom, shoved his glass towards me. He'd extracted the fishhooks of propriety and caution from his mid-American soul and wasn't about to get snagged again. I poured him a third sotol.

"I can handle this stuff, Maribel," he said.

To break the tension, I made everybody sit together on the sofa while I got my camera.

I make digital pictures. I use a 24-bit color camera, feed the images into my computer, crop and scale them, then print the results with a tabloid-size printer. It's my hobby. Inspired by the sotol, I took pictures of the group from a dozen angles, then set the camera on a tripod and took a picture of the four of us.

"The dogs are lonely," Maribel said. "Listen, they are crying. We should go home now." The sad warblings of the two Borzois harmonized.

I took the camera into my study and put the disk into the computer. I brought the image up on the screen. Frank looked jowly and tired: Cary Grant bloated and saggy from cortisone and downers. He looked as if he'd just gotten out of a marathon sales conference. Maribel looked bored and impatient, her skin pore-less as wax; Ofelia's expressionless Indian eyes holding back a tide of passionate indifference.

Mine was the only smiling face. The skin around my eyes and mouth is scarred from decades of smiles—reassuring smiles that impart confidence to pre-op patients, congratulatory smiles that reward their post-op stoicism. I made a tabloid-size print and brought it out to the living room.

"There we are, the four *compañeros*," I said. My intentions, I believe, were good. But the pictures were depressing. Old white men—end-of-the-road grin-gos, allied with young Mexican women. A common sight in El Paso. These are usually economic arrangements for the women. The old men are making one last grab at sexual possibility—conquistadors planting their ragged flags on a mortal shore.

Didn't someone once say that the last frontier for colonialism is the flesh? If not, someone should have. I heard a guest lecturer at the local university describe how indigenous populations are dehumanized by the colonialist through the mechanism of "othering." *Othering,* he said, is a subtle process. If they are *other,* then they are not *you,* and therefore they can be *yours.* Like the animals and savannas and rain forests and mineral deposits, all claimed in the name of God and Fatherland, and Manifest Destiny.

Some of this makes sense. But I draw the line at "othering." I have not oth-ered Ofelia. I am not an otherfucker. I am in love with her. I see the smug lec-turer smirking: Your love, doctor, is the love of the Lord Protector. The colo-nized want freedom, but they want security, too. If the Lord Protector can pro-vide security, freedom may be postponed. And freedom postponed is freedom denied.

I plead innocent to his glib cant, but admit Ofelia and I have nothing in com-mon, nothing of consequence to talk about except what is immediate and press-ing—what channel to watch, where to eat, what clothes to wear, who to see and who to avoid. Separated by age and culture, we have no access to a sharable col-lective memory. Forty years ago, when I was a twenty-four-year-old medical stu-dent, I was a Hank Snow fan. She thinks she might have heard of him once. I play my old vinyl disks for her. She listens with respect, but prefers the *norteña* music she finds easily on the radio. It sounds like North Dakota polkas to me, the Welkian accordions wheezing. Yet I love her.

"I used to be quick," Frank said, regarding, sadly, the digital photo. "I was a rather good boxer in my college days. Middleweight. Frank-the-Cat Milhollan. I fought Chuck Davey, back when he fought for Michigan, before he turned pro."

Frank stood up. He took a stance and threw short combinations, his head rocking left and right, his blackened Cary Grant hair shifting stiffly in flat panels. The hallucination in the corner of his vision attracted his attention. He dipped a shoulder and crab-stepped sideways to give it a hard target. "Did all right, too," he said, beginning to suck air. "Davey's problem was his handlers. They brought him along too quickly. The modest White Hope. Kid Gavilan's bolo punches brought the rising star down, pronto."

"We must go home now," Maribel said. "Listen to the dogs. They are grieving."

"About your dogs," Ofelia said.

This was a sore subject. I signaled Ofelia to let it go, but she was still fuming over her unappreciated dinner.

"They bark at night, when we are trying to sleep."

"Dogs bark. They are not cats" Maribel said, coldly, reasonably.

"Davey beat me on points," Frank said, panting dangerously. "He was a classic boxer. Couldn't punch a hole in wet Kleenex, but he could box."

"If they bark again tonight," Ofelia said, "I will call the management tomorrow. Dogs over twenty pounds aren't permitted here."

That night, after Maribel and Frank went back to their apartment, Ofelia and I sat on our patio, drinking coffee under the desert stars. My brain was still toxic with snake-juice insights. For instance: *Romantic love is hormonal and thus fickle, while domestic love is as dependable as the alimentary process.* A colonist would not have such thoughts, would he? A colonist would think in terms of optimal usage and future potential. A colonist would know when to cut his losses. His thoughts would be coolly utilitarian and far grander than mine. The thoughts of an old man in love are humble and ecstatic, predictable and corny. Hopeful, but edged with self-doubt and fear.

Trotsky and Nikita in the adjacent patio began to keen. We went inside. Frank and Maribel were having a major fight. The walls between our apartments are thin. We heard Maribel's rapid-fire Spanish, Frank's feather-smoothing mid-western drawl.

"The Iberian Princess," I said.

Ofelia gave a melancholy shrug.

"It's not a compliment, honey," I said. "I meant it as a joke."

"Es verdad, sin embargo." True, nonetheless.

I reached for her hand. "Let's go to bed, *querida.*"

Querida is our code word for bed festivities. I squeezed her hand, for emphasis.

"Do you think you are ready, Verry?" she said. "It has only been since Sunday. We should wait another two days. You need more time to regain your strength." I am thus reminded that I turn sixty-five next month.

She was only being practical, not standoffish. Geriatric sex needs proper spacing.

"But I feel strong," I said. "I feel colonial. I feel like el fucking Cortés."

She laughed at this. "And you want me to feel like the whore of Mexico, *la malinche?*"

"Sí."

"This is Indio Juh speaking to me, not Cortés or my sensible *chavalo*, the splendid doctor."

Not so splendid, I think.

In the dark my years are gone. She is twenty-seven and I am sixty-four, but in the dark we are equals. I don't care about my wrinkles, or my seborrheic keratoses—the big black molelike growths on my back—or my sprung hemorrhoids, or the gray-haired breasts I seem to be growing. Nor does she. I am proud to have her, and immensely grateful. I will give her all the security she can hold in her brown arms.

I am a thief in this darkened room, and that is half the excitement. A young man should be here with this girl, but he is not. A usurper is in his place, stealing youth. But Ofelia is willing to give her youth to me. To her I am no thief but an old gringo bearing gifts. Does she love me? Does it matter? I have money. The young man, who is only a hypothesis, does not. I have position—at least I had it once and still wear its invisible mantle—and the young man does not. My history is all behind me, and the young man has all his ahead of him, and that would be a gamble for Ofelia, a gamble she is unwilling to take. Yes, she wants security. She has never known it.

Slipping into half dream, I am visited by the woman I maimed. She is young, lovely, plump with recent motherhood, her wonderfully ordinary life ahead of her. She has a chromophobe macro-adenoma, a pituitary tumor big as a damson plum. The op team is going to access it transseptally—through the nose. The ENT surgeon, Dick Freeling, begins our delicate odyssey. He's packed her nose with a four-percent cocaine solution and injected the mucosa of the nasal septum with lidocaine. With his Knight's scissors he makes his incisions in the ethmoid bone, opening the way. He uses his V-chisel to remove a maxillary crest spur. When it's my turn, I insert the bivalve speculum, which provides a stainless steel tunnel to the underside of her brain. I score, then open, the sphenoid floor with my rongeur. "This is where God lives," Freeling, a religious man, says, meaning the region where the optic nerves cross, where the carotid arteries lift columns of blood to the hungry brain. Here, where the master gland, the pituitary, governs the body's capabilities and the heart's desires.

The bed on the other side of the wall began to rock and roll. Frank and Maribel had made up. Trotsky and Nikita continued to rue their exile, their wretched sobs harmonizing. I thought of Frank's weakening heart, his pacemaker, the beta-blocker that will not prevent eventual congestive heart failure. I thought of Maribel, colonized under the heavy collapse of Frank's expended flesh. Colonized now but destined for independence.

But I can't be distracted from the woman whose life I ruined. I see her, supine, her head tilted back, unconscious and unsuspecting. She will never see the faces of her children again because of me. Deep in her skull, I punch through the pituitary floor with the backbiting Kerrison rongeur. The tumor is a big bastard, occupying the sella turcica and crowding the optic chiasma. My hand shakes, my gravel-blind eyes blur. "You okay?" Dick asks.

"Fine and dandy," I say. I'm working in careful concentric circles, from twelve o'clock to twelve o'clock, with ringed curette and blunt dissector, peeling the intruder out, layer by layer.

I've done hundreds of these procedures. I can do them standing on my head. I'm not going to back off now. But I am tied to a runaway horse whose destination is inevitable but not predictable. I stare hard into the operating microscope. My eyes are not what they once were. Floaters, translucent as amoebae, screen my vision. Even so, I proceed. I have to worry my way around the carotids but in doing so I elevate and displace the optic nerves with my unsteady curette, damaging them. I'd done over two hundred transsphenoidal surgeries with decent results. Until now. With luck she might see degrees of gray and approximate shapes. This is the substance of my recurring nightmare: she wakes to a world of laminated shadows. Some move, some don't. None can be recognized.

Trotsky and Nikita wake us at dawn. Ofelia pulls a pillow over her head. The dogs make unearthly sounds. Not quite barking, not quite howls. Something in between, more irritating than either. I get up, get the coffeemaker going. I hear Ofelia in the shower. She doesn't come out until I've finished two cups.

"You okay, darling?" I say. She is wet under her chenille robe. Her long black hair, backlit by the morning sun and coarse as a horse's mane, is beaded with a million sparkling prisms. I feel my heart swell with pride and fear. How long will I be able to keep her? When will she finally wake to her own power and beauty?

"I'm fine," she says. "Now."

"Do you want me to call the manager? He'll make them get rid of the dogs."

"No. I want to leave this place."

I reach for her with my shaking hand. "Oh, baby," I say, thinking the worst.

"I want us to live in Mexico, Verry. You can be a doctor again, in Mexico."

I start to explain how I can't be a doctor anywhere, when someone rings our doorbell, then starts to pound on the front window.

It's Maribel. There's more animation in her face than I thought possible. Her lips are quivering, her cool eyes are wide with panic, red with tears.

I knew—having seen this look before on women of all races, nationalities, and economic strata—that Frank was dead. I told Ofelia to call 911, then went next door in my robe and slippers. I went through the motions, gave the cold body routine CPR, for Maribel's sake, but he was dead, dead for at least an hour.

The man from Mankato died quietly, bravely, not wanting to alarm his *novia*. I see him waking with flash-fire pain racing across his pectorals and down his arm, his breath short, then shorter. I see him reach for Maribel, perhaps touching her one last time, not to wake her but to confirm the reality of this impossible gift he's been allowed these last few months of his life.

When Maribel woke up, she saw that he was dead, and knew he had been dead for some time, but she rushed over to our apartment anyway, hoping that I, a doctor, might alter the fact. I found him pale as the bedsheet, his open eyes fogged by the absence of the animating spirit. His pacemaker was still kicking spikes of electricity into his indifferent auricles, like a mindlessly ticking turn signal on an overturned car.

Of course he had no updated will. His Mankato widow will get everything, including the Cord roadster and his Eldo. Maybe even the dogs. And Maribel will have to go back to the scent islands at Dillard's. Frank had his moment in paradise, but Maribel, who might have had hopes for something more, has nothing but her youth and impeccable pride.

Frank had a few thousand dollars in the apartment. I encouraged Maribel to take it. But she refused. "He made no provision for me. And I did not ask him to." I have a sudden and immense admiration for her, but don't know how to give it words. Her dignity is formidable.

Back in our apartment, the three of us sit in the small kitchen, drinking coffee in silence, waiting for the EMS van to arrive. Maribel is calm now, even relaxed. I give her my best smile, the one that congratulates stoicism and grit.

"That drink," she says abstractly. "That sotol. This is what killed him, I believe."

It isn't an accusation, but even so, I don't want to argue about it. I personally think he died of surfeit: love, freedom, sex, and happiness. It was too much for an old warhorse sales exec to take. His battered old heart could not tolerate the untethering of his soul.

I reach for Ofelia's hand. She grips mine hard, stopping the tremble.

L ittle Biscuit, take a nap now and stop that awful singing," my mother said. She called me Little Biscuit when she was high or in a good mood, otherwise it was Charlie, Chaz, or even Charles. The man she got high with also called me Little Biscuit. We were in his car, a black '37 DeSoto, somewhere in Georgia, heading for Florida and then on to Cuba, where the man would be safe. We were all high, but of course only they were drinking. I got high with them because they got so happy when they were passing the bottle back and forth in the car, or when they stopped to rest in a shady spot along the highway, or later in the day at a motor court. That's why I was singing. I wanted them to be happy and I wanted to be happy too. I was ten years old and thought that people were meant to be happy. Why live otherwise?

On the Lam

We were running from the police and the FBI. The man, who my mother asked me to call Uncle Jack, had done something to someone. Uncle Jack was Jack Bernstein. He was going to work for Mr. Lansky, who owned most of Havana, according to her. She had left my father, Amadeo "Big Biscuit" Biscotti, for Uncle Jack. My father was a gambler who wore tailor-made silk suits and Italian shoes and had his fingernails manicured once a week. She was fed up with gamblers. "They're as boring as accountants," she said.

She was the Maybelline girl in the ladies' magazines. All you saw was her big blue eyes and dark lashes, but you could still tell it was her. Her eyes identified her sure as a fingerprint. There was something in them—a hardened light that could sometimes look cold, sometimes mean, sometimes so lost it made you catch your breath. Even when she was in a good mood, she held something back. It was as if she could not trust the moment, no matter how banked with good luck it was. No amount of surrounding makeup could warm or soften that stony light. Even when she was high and happy you could see that the dark thing that lived behind her eyes could never be really happy or high. It could worry you, if you thought about it too much.

We'd been living on the road for a week and I was tired of it. I wanted to go back to New York, to the Lower East Side, where my friends were. Uncle Jack was nice enough to me. He bought me toys and Big Little books. Once I broke the windwing of an Oldsmobile with a rock. I was throwing it at a bird on a wire, but the rock fell short. The Oldsmobile was parked at the same motor court we were in. Uncle Jack gave the man ten dollars for a new windwing. The man who owned the car was mad and wanted to call the police on me, but Uncle Jack calmed him down fast. "You don't want to do that, sport," he said. Uncle Jack had a big bald head and hairy hands with fingers that looked like they could crush rocks. His black eyes, close-set on either side of his thick nose, looked as if they could burn holes into wood. He carried a gun under his jacket, a .38 revolver with a stubbed barrel. The man who owned the Oldsmobile looked at

Uncle Jack and saw something that made him stop yelling. Then, when Uncle Jack gave him the ten dollars, the man went to his room, apologizing for being such a sorehead.

"I get carried away sometimes," the man said in the doorway of his room where he was safe.

"Relax, sport," Uncle Jack said. "I would've acted the same."

He carried the gun in an inside pocket of his coat. When he hung the coat up, the weight of the gun pulled the coat down to one side and made it look baggy. Once when he left the gun lying on a table, I picked it up and aimed it out the window. It was heavy, and I could barely hold it level with both hands. I aimed it at a man who was crossing the street with long, purposeful strides. He was coming towards our motor court and might have been from the FBI. He was wearing a hat and I aimed the gun at the brim. The man couldn't know a gun was pointed at him, and that I held the power of life and death in my hands. I put my finger on the trigger, and the thought of pulling it made my heart skip beats and my stomach quiver, the way you feel when you step onto the roller coaster at Coney Island.

Uncle Jack took the gun from me and said, "No, Little Biscuit, don't ever touch this gun. It is always loaded, okay? You never want to point a gun at someone unless you are ready to make his wife a widow, you understand what I'm saying? This is not a toy, Little Biscuit." Then he gave me a dime for a Big Little book. I bought a "Tailspin Tommy" at a drugstore, the one where Tommy finds the secret plans of the smugglers and then has to become a smuggler himself for a while to save his life.

When we got to Florida, something happened. Uncle Jack made some phone calls from the Palm Garden Tourist Court in Hialeah while sitting on the bed in his shorts. My mother was taking her bubble bath. Uncle Jack wedged the phone in the thick folds of flesh between his jaw and neck. As he talked, he opened his gun and took the bullets out. He squinted into the cylinder holes, then put the bullets back in. I'd seen him do this before. It was a nervous habit. When he hung up, he went into the bathroom and told her to get dressed. "The deal's off," he said. "I'm suddenly a goddamn leper." He looked sad and worried.

My mother got out of the bathtub and walked naked and dripping bubbles through the room looking for a cigarette and cursing. "Jesus damn it all to hell. This is just what we didn't need," she said, her eyes turning hard. They packed their suitcases while I went out to the parking lot to throw rocks at birds. I hit a car again, this time on purpose. The rock skipped off the hood and made a pit in the windshield, but no one came yelling out of his room. Then we got into the DeSoto and headed back up the highway we came south on.

Uncle Jack drove fast. We had a slow trip coming down to Miami from Manhattan, but everything was different now. We turned west through Georgia, went into Tennessee, and then headed for Illinois. We drove day and night, no stops, except for gas. Uncle Jack kept both hands on the steering wheel and he glanced up at the rearview mirror a lot. He yelled at her and she would yell back. Sometimes she would start crying without anyone having said a word and he would pull the car off the road and put his arms around her. I heard him whisper into her ear, "We'll beat the bastards, Ruta."

We finally stopped near Green Bay. We found a nice motor court called Ole's Sleepytime Lodge. It was next to a small lake and had a bed, a cot, and a kitchenette. My mother went out to buy groceries, and then she fixed a big dinner of rigatoni, sausage, cheese, and bread. The Biscotti women had taught her how to cook Italian. She bought a gallon of red wine and a bottle of Hires root beer for me. She also bought me a toy. Things were suddenly relaxed again and I was glad of that. I waited for them to get high so that I could get high, too, because I needed to feel happy again. They made themselves drinks before dinner, and when we ate, we stuffed ourselves. They drank half the wine and then sat in the small sofa, Uncle Jack's arm around my mother, her hand on his thigh, kneading. They looked happy but half paralyzed with food and drink.

I played with the toy she gave me. It was a bomber, an old Boeing with open-air turrets. It was a windup that fit in your hand. You'd wind it up and it would scream like a siren and sparks would fly out from underneath it. I imagined diving on Germans, the machine guns in the turrets blazing, the bombs falling away. Uncle Jack stood up and belched, then put a nickel in the radio. He found the "Make Believe Ballroom" on an NBC station, and they danced as if they were in New York in some fancy club. My mother was wearing her party dress. Uncle Jack, his big head glowing like a peeled onion, said, "Answer me this. How come an ugly mug like me winds up with the Maybelline girl?"

I was glad to see them so happy, and I sang along with the Make Believe Ballroom orchestra, *Moonlight becomes you.* I sang this slow romantic ballad as I killed Germans, finding them in their pillboxes and blasting them out with firebombs. I swooped down on them, making the *ratatat* sound of the turret guns and the thud and boom of the bombs. I got high on music and the sounds of war.

The radio had a shortwave band, and I got a nickel out of her purse so I could listen to it for another hour after they went to bed. She didn't care, because she wanted me to occupy myself. I listened to foreign-language broadcasts, pretending to understand them. Their bed was by the wall, across the room from me and the radio. My cot was under the window and next to the table that held the radio. They tried to be quiet, but I heard them anyway through the static and voices—the concertina wheezing of the springs and the quick sounds she could not hold in.

I got up early the next morning and went outside. I was surprised to find ankle-deep snow on the ground since it was still summer. The car had a shelf of snow on it, dripping like soft cake frosting off the hood and trunk. The sky was blue, like Florida, but it was also dark. It was as if you could see black streaks of night behind the blue, like this northern blue was thin and couldn't last. Florida blue was thick. You could cut big mile-deep cubes out of it and there would still be blue sky to spare.

"Charlie, come on!" she said. I went back into our room. "We've got to go, but first you get in the shower with Uncle Jack. You stink like a stray dog."

"I don't want to," I said.

"Do what your mommy says!" Uncle Jack yelled, his voice rattling the windows.

I took off my clothes in the bathroom. Uncle Jack was already in the shower, singing, the steam coming out from behind the curtain. I got into the shower at the far end, away from the spray. Uncle Jack was lathering himself with soap, even his bald head. His eyes were shut tight and he was singing, "We did it before and we can do it again," a war song. We weren't in the war yet, but you could see it coming.

The water was hot. I stayed out of its reach. Then Uncle Jack rinsed off and said, "Okay, Little Biscuit, your turn." He saw that I was staring at him, and he laughed. "Don't worry, you'll have a cannon like that someday yourself. Then you'll be a mensch, a real trouble-maker. Remember, the ladies will always go for a real mensch, no matter what." I got under the spray and Uncle Jack gave me the soap. "Get your hair good and clean, Little Biscuit. I think you got lice."

We kept going north, up into Michigan. The farther north we went, the colder it got. It was only September, but the air was crisp and the lakes were clear blue, not tan and weedy like the warm lakes down south.

A police car pulled us over outside of Iron Mountain, and Uncle Jack took his gun out of his coat pocket and put it on the seat next to him, under a newspaper. The policeman looked at Uncle Jack's New York license. "Big city folks, hey?" he said.

Uncle Jack nodded. "We're on our way to my wife's folks, over by Marquette. Ain't we, baby?" He patted her leg.

The policeman, squinting at the license, said, "Bernstein. Jack Bernstein. Not many Jewish boys here in the Upper Peninsula, hey?" He looked into the car, suspicious.

"My wife's a Finlander, officer," Uncle Jack said.

The policeman bent down and took another look at her. *"Hyva aamiia!"* he said.

"Hyva paiva," she said back. "Good to be home," she said in English.

"Küinka se mene?" he said.

"Fine," she said. *"Hyva kütos."*

The policeman smiled and touched the bill of his cap. "Have a good visit, folks," he said. He got back into his car and drove away.

"Shit!" Uncle Jack said. "Jesus!" He took the gun out from under the newspaper and put it back inside his coat.

"Satana!" my mother cursed. *"Perkelle!"*

The trip seemed endless. I got the idea into my head that they would now turn around and head south again, and that's how it would be forever, driving up and down the country, crisscrossing, doubling back, going in circles, coast to coast, border to border, a never-ending run. "Are we really going to Grandma's house?" I said.

"That's right, Little Biscuit," Uncle Jack said. "You are at least." I saw my mother give Uncle Jack a look. I'd seen that look before. It meant *Shut up.* When she wanted to keep something away from me and someone else accidentally blurted out the truth, she'd turn that look on them. She uncapped the bottle of gin and tilted it up to her lips, then she passed it to Uncle Jack. She wanted to get high, and I wanted her to, but I didn't think I'd be able to get high with them. I tried to sing, but my throat was suddenly full of road dust.

I had a sinking sensation, one I'd had before. I felt like I'd stumbled into a hole and was falling straight down into bottomless dark. The hole was always there, somewhere in front of you, like a trap. It made you suspicious of good moods. A good mood set you up for the sudden drop. You'd get high, you'd sing, then the earth opened up, blue sky turned black, and the hole sucked you down.

I was going to get dumped again. This time at Grandma Aiti's house. The first time my mother left my father, I was sent to St. Vincent's, the boarding school in Tarrytown. She said she wanted me out of the Lower East Side. "You talk like a wise guy," she said. "I want you to learn how to be polite and talk proper English. Maybe if you get into the church choir up there in Tarrytown, you'll quit singing like a ruptured mule."

I feared and hated St. Vincent's, and all the other boys there feared and hated it too. We were all rejects, too much trouble for our families. Everyone there feared and hated everyone else. The nuns, who glided through the playgrounds and hallways like huge black and white confections, were nice to us, but nice people can't deal with groundless fear and universal hatred. They can't believe such uncivil energy exists in children. They believe it's a mood or an act, a temporary thing that you can easily drop if you wanted to. The nuns didn't understand that it was the only thing that kept us from disappearing completely.

I had always been afraid of disappearing completely, like someone lost at sea. I already suspected that I was becoming invisible. If I became totally invisible, then I'd be lost forever, *erased.* I remembered being terrified at the movie *The Invisible Man,* starring Claude Raines. He was there, in substance, until he unwound the bandages that covered his face and neck. Then he was *not* there.

His hat floated across a room, his pipe followed the trajectory between what were supposed to be his hand and mouth, but that was never convincing. He was *gone,* a patch of talking air, forgettable as a dream.

Hate was the bandaging that made you visible. I nursed my hatred, I protected it. I used it on the boys who were smaller than me. I made them see me and then I made them fear me. I pretended to be a wise guy. "Beat it, you pissant punk," I'd say, and they'd scamper away. "Gimme a nickel, you little bastard," I'd say, and they'd dig in their pockets.

I couldn't eat nun food. They fed us spinach and boiled eggs, chipped beef and steamed cauliflower, fried liver and pickled beets. I stuffed supper into my pants pockets and flushed it down the toilet when I got the chance. I lived on bread and milk. Once when my mother came to visit me with one of her magazine-model girlfriends, I threw my hamburger on the floor of a Tarrytown restaurant. When they took me to a movie, I unbuttoned my pants and peed in the aisle. These were the most disagreeable things I could think of doing. But they were strong, durable women who had seen the bad behavior of grown-ups. My antics only amused them. They laughed at my pranks. My mother had a powerful laugh. It always brought tears to her eyes. She said, "It's not a life-and-death matter, Charles. Put your wee-wee away, honey. It doesn't frighten us."

She loved my tiny Italian grandmother, Genia Biscotti, who was from Naples, but she'd laugh sometimes at her old-country ways. We'd been living temporarily in a little house on Staten Island with two well-mannered, well-dressed men from Sicily. The men were in New York, for a week, just to rub someone out. They'd been brought over by the mob. They were professionals and were relaxed and businesslike. My grandmother screamed at them in Italian while they were cleaning their guns, a nightly ritual. "Assassins! Murderers!" But the men went about their business calmly, maintaining their dignity and courtly ways. These men did all the cooking, played checkers with me, and read the newspapers out loud to practice their English. But Grandma Biscotti didn't trust Sicilians and looked down on them as social inferiors. My father, who was their host, treated them with respect. My mother told me, years later, "The old lady hated them because they weren't *Napolidan.* If they had been from Naples, it would have been a different story. She would have baked them a cake. Hit men from Naples, as everyone knows, are fine upstanding gentlemen." She laughed her big laugh every time she told this story.

On the playground in Tarrytown I caught butterflies and pulled off their wings, denying them the freedom of flight, turning them back into worms. I bullied the smaller boys and was, in turn, bullied by the bigger boys. The nickels I extorted from the smaller boys were extorted from me by the bigger boys. We lived in a hierarchy of fear. You could smell the anxiety. It was a chemical reek, strong as urine. The nuns had us listen to radio speeches by President Roosevelt.

The nuns, in their innocence, acted as if we were able to care about what the president said, or could be uplifted by his stirring rhetoric. We didn't know what he was talking about and couldn't have cared less. We were castoffs, we were the unwanted, and everyone, including the president, could go to hell.

We routinely fantasized escapes: cutting through the chain-link fence that surrounded the school grounds, or digging a tunnel underneath it, then going on the lam. When we played war, I was a counterspy, blowing up ships, planes, and tanks. When we took prisoners, we tortured them with pinches and Indian burns whether they told us their secrets or not. The object of war was to inflict pain, not establish freedom, democracy, and the American way.

Grandma Aiti's house was on U.S. 41, between Negaunee and Marquette. A forest of maples, oaks, and poplars edged up to the back of the house. My grandpa's 1939 Hudson Terraplane sat out in front of the house like a dream of the future—a future where contoured aerodynamic steel, chrome plating, and brute horsepower would make human flaw irrelevant.

My real uncles, my mother's brothers, worked in the iron-ore mines under Negaunee. They invited Uncle Jack to take a sauna bath with them. The sauna was behind the house and was itself a small house with two rooms and a chimney. One room was where the rock-covered barrel stove was, the other was where you got undressed, and, after your sauna bath, cooled off.

My real uncle, Moose, threw pails of cold water on the rocks, and the steam exploded upward. The steam drove Uncle Jack down to the lowest bench with me. It was kind of a test—to see if we could take it. My real uncles laughed, and Uncle Jack, who was a good sport, laughed too. "You Finlander boys can take the heat!" he said. Then we went into the anteroom and switched ourselves with cedar boughs. Uncle Jack and my real uncles went into the house and drank whiskey and played cribbage. I had cake and milk with my mother and grandma Aiti in the kitchen. Cake and milk and the sober talk between my mother and her mother didn't get me high. I wanted to be with the men, out on the screened porch. I could smell their cigarette smoke and whiskey. My real uncle, Cuss, had taken out his guitar and was singing "Red River Valley." He had a sweet tenor voice, and the other uncles, even Uncle Jack, joined in the singing. Getting high and singing, that seemed like the best way to spend your life.

"Drunk," Grandma Aiti said.

"Drunk," my mother agreed, a statement, not a judgment.

I liked Michigan, but I was afraid of it too. I knew I was going to be left here with my grandma and grandpa. My grandpa, who also worked in the iron- ore mines of Negaunee, showed me how to tap sugar maples for their sweet sap, and how to set snares for rabbits. One day he took me for a walk with Miko, one of his dogs, an ancient milky-eyed spaniel. Grandpa carried a .22 rifle and a shovel.

We walked behind the house and down a path that went through the woods. I asked him where we were going, and he said, "It's time to let Miko go." This gradually sunk in as we walked. He was going to shoot the old dog.

Miko seemed to understand that this was his last walk in the woods. He whined and lagged behind, but followed obediently. When we came to the place where it was to be done, Miko got very agitated. His whines grew higher in pitch. They sounded like human pleas. I wanted to tell him to run, to head into the woods and never come back, but I also knew that Miko, who was half blind and stiff with age, could not survive on his own, a vagabond dog on the run.

Grandpa laid the shovel aside. He pulled a poplar sapling down and pressed it across Miko's back to hold the old dog still. "You stand on one end of it," he told me. Miko started moaning. Grandpa put the muzzle of his small rifle against the back of Miko's head and pulled the trigger. The abrupt thud and Miko's sudden lurch made me slip off the sapling, which sprung back up.

Grandpa dug a hole between two trees and dropped Miko into it. He filled it in and we covered the grave with stones to keep animals from digging Miko up. I cried all the way back to the house, but Grandpa didn't seem to notice. When we got back, Grandpa took a bottle of whiskey out of a kitchen cabinet and poured himself half a glass and drank it down. I watched him closely as he wiped off his mouth. He didn't get high at all.

I met some of the neighbor boys—big Finn boys in bib overalls and bare feet. They laughed at my New York accent. I told them they sounded stupid. I wore my New York clothes to intimidate them—porkpie hat, a pinstripe wise-guy suit Big Biscuit had given me before I left on this trip. I even put on a clip-on tie. The big Finn boys laughed at me. I picked one out I thought I could beat and tried to extort a nickel from him. He couldn't believe his ears. "You go to hell, you damn Dago," he said.

We fought. The buttons came off my coat and my porkpie hat went flying. His name was Aino Keckonen and we rolled around together on the ground, Aino winding up on top. He was too strong for me. I couldn't budge him. "Give?" he said. "Give," I said.

Eventually we all became friends. They got a kick out of my name, Charlie Biscotti. They chanted it, but not to make fun of me. It was as if the syllables of my name were a mysterious incantation. They had names like Kalevi Altonen and Artturi Koskenniemi, which were ordinary everyday names to them.

Indian summer came, and the weather got sultry. One day I was out in my grandma's garden picking corn when I saw a black Ford pull up to the front of the house. Men in coats and hats came to the front door. I heard some yelling, then my mother came out carrying a suitcase. She got into the black car and the men drove her away. I figured they were after Uncle Jack, but he had left for Canada several days before. I ran after the car as it pulled away on U.S. 41, heading toward Marquette. She waved at me through the rear window. Though she was fifty yards away, I saw her eyes, the dark reservoir of sadness in them. I kept running until the car was out of sight. I stood on the empty highway, looking at the dense forest on either side, the dark-blue alien sky, and the white frame house that was going to be my new home.

"*Satana,*" I said. "*Perkelle.*"

I spent another year on the lam. I found the Maybelline girl in magazines my grandma had, and I talked to those untrusting blue eyes. "When are you coming?" I'd say, and the sad beautiful eyes said, "Soon, Little Biscuit, soon."

I learned more Finn words to add to my Italian. My uncle Cuss, who called me *buska hosa*, taught me how to play a few chords on the guitar and sing "Red River Valley." I learned to roll cigarettes with the neighbor boys and how to smoke them. When we couldn't get tobacco, we smoked corn silk. We smoked in the woods where I embroidered stories about New York gangsters, and how my mother was going to prison for being a gun moll, and how when she got out we were going to California where there was a million dollars hidden in a cave. When we got that money, we were going to buy a big house by the ocean and hire servants to take care of us. I showed them pictures of the Maybelline girl, to convince them that my mother could become a movie star if she wanted to.

When the year was over, she came for me. She looked tired, as if she had walked all the way across the country. Her face was drawn and her teeth had gone bad. Her clothes were dirty and didn't fit her. Her eyes weren't Maybelline-girl eyes anymore. She'd been held in the Bronx County jail as a material witness for eleven months. When they finally caught Uncle Jack, they let her go. "I didn't recognize him," she said. "A Canadian plastic surgeon changed his face."

After another month in Michigan, she got restless. She had a need to see new places and do new things. California had been on her mind, too. Bronx County paid her three dollars a day for all the time she was in their jail, and so we had enough money to last a while. I asked her what we'd do when we got to California. "We'll see when we get there, " she said.

We took a bus to Chicago, where we would board a train to Los Angeles. It was an old, noisy bus with bad springs. When it turned corners, it felt as if it would roll over, and when it made stops, its brakes would squeal for a full minute, making you grit your teeth. I remembered Uncle Jack's slick black DeSoto, streaking through Florida. I remembered them getting high, and I remembered getting high with them and singing. In spite of my restlessness and boredom, that had been a real adventure. I wanted this to be one, too.

I asked her what happened to Uncle Jack. "Sing Sing," she said. I didn't understand. "It's a prison, Charlie. "He'll be there for twenty years. I don't think we'll see him again."

She didn't want to talk. She leaned her head against the window and fell asleep. It was dark out, and most of the passengers were slumped down in their seats. A loneliness big as night swept over me. I thought about Uncle Jack, how lonely he must be in Sing Sing. And then I thought of the prison itself—a prison whose name commanded you to sing. I pictured the prisoners, in their cells, singing sad songs while the turnkeys egged them on, their lonely voices rising up out of the cells, over the walls and guard towers, and into the countryside, making people stop in their tracks and think that what they were about to do wasn't so important after all. I started humming, thinking about the singing prisoners.

The man seated directly in front of me had set a shopping bag in the aisle. Every now and then he'd reach into it and lift out a slim dark bottle with a long neck. When he finally fell asleep, and when I was sure everyone else around us was asleep, I reached into his bag and pulled out the bottle. I uncapped it and brought it to my lips. It was sweet wine. It tasted like warm cherry juice. I took a full swallow, then another.

My humming, after a while, got louder. Then I put words to the tune. It was a song about the past and the future. I made it up as I went along. It was a song about staying one step ahead of the thing you needed to get away from, the thing that would always be there.

He woke into light the color of ice. A warm girl was pressed against him. He pushed her away. She groaned and he remembered where he was. He hugged her close. "Did it again," he whispered into her hair. "Late."

He slid out of bed. The cold linoleum shocked his feet. The girl pulled her clock radio close to her face. Gray light came from a small square window in the door of her apartment. "I think it's after eight," she said. He turned on the bathroom bulb, looked at himself. He thought: *Rotten. Very rotten.* Even so, he was happy with this. The girl was a reward he allowed himself. Reward for *what* he could not say. He knew he was not an especially deserving man. His ordeals had been run-of-the-mill by any standard. In any case this affair wasn't going to last much longer.

The girl said, "Does the wife know you're here?" He could barely under-

Seize the Day

stand her. She had buried herself under the quilt, hoarding the diminishing warmth of the bed. He liked the way she always said "The wife." He liked the way she held herself in her own arms when he left the bed. He looked at his several faces in the badly cracked mirror. "Why don't you replace this thing?" he said.

He had a marijuana and Thunderbird hangover. No board in his head, no splinters of glass in his stomach, but he felt assaulted by small waves of giddiness. He needed to think, to organize his thoughts, to put the morning, if not his life, in order. But the thoughts tripped over themselves, digressed, got lost in a traveling pastiche of images and voices.

He looked at his multiple, bloodshot eyes. His many gray tongues. He brushed his teeth with her toothbrush, as she had told him to do. He liked that, too: her domestic commands, her little directives. She did the same when they were having sex, whispered breathy instructions, something his wife could never allow herself to do.

"You better hurry," she called. "I don't want her busting in here with some kind of betrayed-wife act."

He raised his right arm, carefully, because of a new stiffness, then cursed.

"All right, then," the girl said, flapping open the quilt. "Get back in here." He obeyed.

It had snowed. He walked past the feed store which fronted her apartment. His car was hummocked with white. The temperature had dropped to zero. She stood in her doorway, wearing only the quilt. He waved. She took the cigarette from her lips and kissed the crystal air.

She was twenty—fifteen years younger than he. She worked as a waitress in a dim cafe called the Chicken Shack. He'd met her there. She brought him a half-chicken in a basket with slaw and cottage fries. He'd been depressed for weeks, and the accumulation of routine days had made him bold. And he knew this: the weeks would cycle into months, the months into years. The cold certainty that nothing now would ever change for him could not be trivialized by the antidepressants, which, in any case, he had stopped taking.

He'd said the right things to her and she agreed to meet him later on. They smoked some of her reefer, drank the wino wine from Dixie cups in his car. They got wondrously drunk and two-stepped themselves sweaty in every shitkicker bar they could find. Three months ago. It seemed like minutes.

She had a way of looking at things that he could envy if he could believe it. All her obligations, she said, were voluntary. "I stopped living my life for other people when my ma said the only reason she got her breast lump was because I didn't finish nurses' training." People, she had said, hold on for dear life to the thing that enslaves them. "Ma tried to turn that cancer in her tit into an iron ball chained to my leg."

He'd shrugged his shoulders at first, then laughed. She threw a fake karate punch at his chest. "You prick," she said, laughing. "I guess I'm just not a subtle person," he said. She gave him a sidelong pickerel smile, her small teeth needle-sharp, then made a machine gun of her arm and shot him dead. They collapsed into each other, in the direction of the bed.

The storm that had made the city storybook white was receding to the south. The sharp air rattled with the sound of chained tires. He thought of his wife, on the other side of town, making breakfast as usual, in spite of everything, finding comfort in routine, thriving on injustice. He pictured the snappy apartment, neat as a magazine photograph, the Sears furniture, the big Zenith television set heaving early-morning cartoons into the passive eyes of his children, the hanging lamps, the potted plants, everything in its place, accountable. He had no hatred for any of this. This was how it was supposed to be. It made no sense to find fault with it.

He swept snow from the windows of his car with his hands. The girl would be back in bed now, holding herself in her arms under the patchwork quilt, always the satisfied one, each moment adequate, a way he wished he could be. Her radio would be on so that she wouldn't lose track of time. He buried a small urge to go back inside, and started the car. The engine turned over slowly in its thickened oil. It came to life and gave out a ghostly whistle that increased in pitch until it could no longer be heard. The cold plastic of his dashboard hummed.

He turned on the radio and tuned it to the station the girl always listened to. Blues, even in the morning. On Monday morning the striding guitars, the lyrical pain of black and would-be-black voices, seemed exotic in this northern city of Swedes and Indians with French names. He turned the volume up, recalling her warmth. After they had made love in the first light of morning, she was full of advice. She told him he was the whitest man she knew. He wanted to know what she meant by that. "The questions you tend to ask," she'd said. "'Did you get off that time, hon?' 'Do you ever think of me as someone else?'" She laughed at him and said, "It's like you're clueless, you know? Guys like you figure there's always something invisible they got to dig for, like their own eyes were caked over with shit. They only trust a questionnaire. Tell me something, did you have to take Robert Young lessons for this?"

She was always sharp-tongued in the morning. Her cheek was on his arm and her lips touched his chest as she spoke. She was small and dark and not very good- looking. He pulled her tight against his chest, forcing a sigh from her. He resented her needling critiques even though they aroused him. "All right," he said. "Here's another one—do you think I'm a bad man?"

She kissed him and then pushed herself away, her hands careless against his face. "You *wish,*" she said.

Sometimes she seemed depressingly wise to him. Other times he believed her apparent wisdom was an ornament, like the rope and wood wall-hangings in her apartment, but he never challenged her.

He turned the car into the street. The wheels rasped against the new snow, but the car continued to pick up speed. The traffic was not heavy because it was now past the rush hour. He would be late for work this morning, as he had been three mornings out of five for the last several weeks. He had been sent terse memos about this.

He drove through the snowy streets following the already glazed ruts a hundred cars had made before him. The city lurched by him on both sides. Red-faced men shoveled snow away from the doors of shops and offices. The sun was up in the south, a cold white disk stamped against a hard blue sky. There was an honest crispness in the air. The cafes were beginning to fill with early shoppers. The blue guitars and the black voices were another thing. The girl, who claimed to be part Saskatchewan Cree, a native of Moose Jaw, said, "They know where it's at." He doubted it. No one knew where "it" was. The world was made of dazzling, impenetrable surfaces, margined on all sides by oblivion. There was no "it." People wore blinders from birth to death. A condition he could accept. Even so, he liked to humor her.

"Tell me about it," he'd said, lighting a cigarette to cover his grin.

She'd looked at the ceiling, as if remembering something too exquisite to put into words. Then she raised up on her elbows and looked at him. "Yes or no," she said, "does your manhood depend on how I answer?"

He shrugged, suddenly bored with her. "I don't know what my manhood depends on," he'd said.

He was on a bridge that linked the two halves of the city. White mantles of snow-covered ice from each bank did not quite meet in the center of the river. A dark blue snake of unfrozen water serpentined against the encroaching ice and snow.

An old man in a knee-length parka fished with a long cane pole. His face was wrapped in a scarf and his wool cap was pulled down low on his forehead. Only old men fished the river in winter. They fished for whitefish with maggots, standing in a single, bone-stiffening spot for hours. He knew that the old men kept the maggots between their lower lips and gums to keep them alive. He told this to the girl. She had shuddered and refused to believe it. "It's the truth," he'd said. "It's the only way to keep the maggots from freezing."

"You just can't keep this up indefinitely," his wife said calmly, reasonably. He nodded assent. These were easy punishments. She stayed at the sink, her back to him, doing the morning dishes. She worked righteously, her back stiff, her arms busy. She was wearing her red quilted robe, the one with the imitation Chinese ideograms on it.

"Guilty as charged," he said, too softly for her to hear. He wondered what the ideograms might mean, or if there could be such a thing as an accidental language.

Furious images from a cartoon network collided soundlessly on the Zenith. A mechanized triceratops with bloody teeth, a bespectacled alien gutting a sleek blonde, a seductive but sexless dragon wading through gore: corporate child molestation, around-the-clock. The sound was muted now that the children had gone to school. Dishes rapped against each other telegraphically. He read what had come to be a familiar code as he watched the snow slide from his shoes.

"I'm sorry," he said, again too softly to be heard. *I'm rotten,* he thought, wishing it were true. It would make things easier. But he was not rotten. He was a nice guy; he'd been told that often enough by friends and colleagues. His wife was equally well liked. There was nothing wrong with either of them. They had a good life that had been drifting, without hint of self-congratulation, toward a dream of domestic perfection. He oftened imagined himself at sixty—respected, calm, loved, his wife gray but still nimble, sexually responsive, and good-humored. And they would die respected and comfortable after a long, responsibly lived life. *What is wrong with this picture?* he thought. *Nothing. Only a fool would find fault with it.*

She fixed him eggs and a thick slice of ham. She poured coffee, gave him silverware and a fresh napkin that was still warm from the dryer. All these gestures were normal and convincing, but she would not look at him.

"So what is it," she said. "Delayed curiosity? Is there something you need to know? Do you need to fill in some gaps?"

"It isn't that," he said. But it *was* that. It was exactly that.

The places at the table where the children had eaten were messy with crumbs, pieces of toast, flecks of oatmeal. The paper was spread on the floor, open to the comic section. There was a gob of grape jelly on Sally Forth. His wife sponged the mess off the table. Small winds from the sponge's thousand tiny caves sighed as the crumbs went flying.

He poured himself another cup of coffee. He drank half of it in one swallow, scalding his mouth. "I'd better get going," he said.

She went into the bedroom. He expected her to come right out, but she didn't. He finished his coffee, then went into the bedroom to get ready for work.

His wife was on the bed, motionless, face against the pillow, no list of accusations in her eyes. Cold light glowed deceptively warm from the window's yellow curtains. The furnace blower came on with a chuckling gale.

"Is it because she's younger than me?" she continued. "Is it because she's pretty?"

He took a clean shirt from the dresser. He took off his clothes. He put on clean shorts, clean socks. *Yes,* he thought. *No,* he thought. "I don't know," he said.

"Come here," she said, opening her robe. Her whiteness on the dark bed made her seem small and frail, adolescent and vulnerable.

"I have to go to work," he said.

"No. Call in sick. We can have the whole day."

She propped herself up on her elbows, her round breasts and dark nipples were lurid on her child-sized body. Her stomach was still flat and tight. "Make love to me," she said. "The way it was."

"I don't think so," he said.

"Come here, goddamn you. I'm still your wife."

He went to her and she raised her legs. She was thin, and the silky hourglass joining her thighs was darkly obscene against the perilous frailty of her body. He felt suddenly repelled, almost pulled away, but she took him in hand and manipulated him until he was ready, and the possessive vise of her legs hurt his kidneys. As if in a fit of rage, she grabbed him by the hair and pulled his mouth down to hers. He lunged athletically, careless, without finesse, then pinned her arms hard against the mattress in a parody of rape, the only way he could, at this point, stay interested. He nipped blood from her neck, then watched tears slide down her face.

"You bastard," she said as they fell away from each other.

"I'm sorry," he said.

He felt nothing. She heard it in his voice and her face went grim. "You don't care about anything," she said.

"That's a terrible thing to say," he said.

He drove back toward town. Sex fixed nothing, especially when it was frenzied. No help in that for the head or for the progress of the soul. It was a spike on the otherwise unremarkable flatline of life. In marriage it produced the illusion of intimacy, even when it had degenerated into habit and ritual. He knew of people who had tried to breathe new life into their marriages with kinkiness: mate-swapping, picking up third parties in bars, role switching, collars and cuffs, and so on. He had suggested something along these lines to her once, but she had recoiled. And, in truth, he was no sexual adventurer himself. He just wanted...

He didn't know what he wanted. Maybe it was just *Want* itself, a shapeless constant of desire that never attached itself to a specific object. He began to see Want as a demon, a parasite on the heart.

He was driving forty miles an hour and he didn't see the other car. He hit the brakes knowing it was useless. The street was solid glare ice by now, and his car went into a frictionless slide. The other car had been sounding its horn, and after he hit it the horn continued to sound. The wallop of metal on metal punctuated the morning convincingly. His forehead crystallized the windshield, and his car skated a full circle and came to rest against the curb of the opposite lane. The other car slid into a power pole. It was a black Buick, an old Roadmaster, driven by an elderly woman. There were other elderly women in the backseat, and another beside the driver. They were gray and plumpish and wore the same blue corsage, on their way to some gray function. The horn of the Roadmaster continued to alarm.

Other cars stopped. He got out slowly. His knee had rammed the dashboard. "He must've been doing fifty," someone said. He didn't see where the voice came from. Someone else said, "A morning drinker. Couldn't wait for happy hour." The second voice was also nondirectional. Stupidly, he looked up into the sky at the contrails of a jet. Ice crystals winked in the cobalt zenith like tiny weightless diamonds.

The old ladies did not leave their car. He looked into an unshattered window. They were seated as they had been, before the impact. They looked straight ahead as though their drive had not been interrupted. They were very pale. Chalky. They were not speaking. The Buick's engine was racing. The driver seemed unaware of the engine noise or of the blaring horn. She held a painted hanky to her eye and her nose trickled blood. He opened the door and shut off the ignition.

He noticed a spilled purse between the two women in the front seat. Among the compacts, lipsticks, checkbooks, and other odds and ends, there was a roll of currency thick as his forearm. The outer bill was a fifty. He put his hand on it, and an excitement he would not have been able to explain raced through his body. His hair felt like copper wire in a magnetic field. He heard the irregular thudding of his heart. He had to urinate badly.

He backed away from the car and closed the door gently. "You'd better stick around, bud," someone told him.

"I've got to go," he said, and limped away from the accident scene until he found a gas station. He locked himself in the men's room and relieved himself. Then he counted the money. Nine thousand dollars in fifties and hundreds. He counted the money again, then fattened his wallet. He stuffed the remaining bills into several pockets.

He heard the distant wail of sirens. He walked to the rear of the service station, and continued up the street and into a run-down neighborhood of narrow, clapboard homes in need of paint. He ignored the pain in his knee, which was not bad at all. There was a large bump on his forehead and he felt light-headed, but he only had a slight headache. He walked quickly, limping, the accident and the people it attracted falling away behind him.

He walked through this poorest section of town, along the river, past gray warehouses and the small, wretched houses where the unskilled unemployed lived. A slatternly woman with stringy unwashed hair looked at him through her front-room window and, without provocation, sneered. A half-naked child appeared at her side. The child waved at him and the woman slapped the child away from the window. She repeatedly mouthed some words meant for his eyes. He gradually deciphered them: *Move on, trash.* He smiled and returned the insult. *Miss America,* he mouthed.

Then he was on the highway north, heading toward the airport. He was exhausted when he reached the terminal, since the airport was uphill from the town. He went into the restaurant, a franchise called Cody's. The decor of Cody's was Wild West. On the walls, cowboys in silhouette rode ponies or slouched in talky groups against corral posts. A stuffed black bear stood next to the cash register, its glass-eyes fixed in an idiot stare.

He sat at an empty table. When the waitress came, he ordered coffee and a breakfast roll, though he wasn't hungry.

"That's some bump you have there," the waitress said.

He shrugged. "Ran into a cupboard," he said.

The waitress, probably only thirty but her face already creased with fatigue and disappointment, said, "Cupboard my aching rear. You been out doing your reckless buckaroo act, I can tell. My second ex used to come home mornings looking just as worked on as you, if you don't mind my saying it."

He didn't mind. He took it as a compliment. He liked her looks. She reminded him of a song, "Crazy Arms," an oldie. He went to the men's room, where he washed his face and wet his hair down. Stubble darkened his upper lip, and the bump on his forehead was blue. He still felt light-headed, but he also felt self-justified. He was suspicious of this feeling, since there was no way to account for it, but he didn't want to pursue his doubts.

He stared at himself in the mirror and vowed never to pursue his doubts again. Maybe that's what had been wrong with his life up to now. "Relight the wick," he told his reflection. The man in the mirror smiled brilliantly at him, a smile open as a blank check. It took him a second glance to grasp that the uncharacteristic smile was his.

When he returned to his table, his coffee and breakfast roll were waiting for him. "Thought we lost you," the waitress said.

"I was lost but now I'm found," he said, quoting the hymn.

She studied his face for his meaning, then shook her head and smiled. "You're a real card," she said.

"I am that," he said. "The king of trumps."

"Is that supposed to mean something to me?"

He shrugged. "Take it any way you want," he said.

By the time he finished his first cup of coffee, he decided that the waitress was interested in him. She wore a wedding band, but it was on the wrong finger on the wrong hand. That meant something, but he couldn't remember what. It excited his imagination.

She was in need, he knew that. Not just money, but direction. Her life was empty and getting emptier by the year. By the time she was forty, she would have nothing, be nowhere, and the hard good looks would become just hard looks. Bitterness would bleach her blue eyes pale.

"You've got to seize the day," he said to her as she refilled his cup. She looked at him for a long moment, studying him, then went to another table. He hid an urge to smile by raising his cup to his lips. She was obviously ready—as he was—for a major change.

He stood up and limped into the terminal. He found an airline that had a morning flight to San Francisco and he bought two tickets with cash from his wallet. Then he went back to the restaurant.

"Thought you ran out on me," the waitress said.

"Far from it," he said. He put the two ticket envelopes on the table, like a player spreading a royal flush.

He knew she'd come with him. Why wouldn't she? She was fooling only herself now with that prim, all-business act. He could already visualize them seated next to each other as the plane accelerated down the runway. She'd be grateful for her good fortune. He could see the two of them in San Francisco, in a good hotel overlooking the bay. He knew how she'd make love—needfully, edgy with old hurts—and he knew what she'd say afterward, and what they'd do on the second day.

I. RETURN OF THE HERO

My father came home from the Second World War empty. He didn't look empty. He was much larger than when he went away, three years earlier. When he left us for the war, he was a lean twenty-seven-year-old, full of stories and jokes that made me and my little brother, Woodrow, laugh until we hurt. When he came home he was thick with fat and he looked forty. His arms stuck out from his sides, his legs were tight in his wool army pants, and his belly rolled out in front of him like a grievous load someone had forced him to bear. Even so, there was nothing inside him anymore, nothing for us. It was as if an overweight impostor was trying to pass himself off as our happy Dad. We won that war, but he came home glum as the losers.

I didn't understand how war could make someone fat or how victory could make him empty. Woodrow and I thought his antics would be twice as good, now that he'd been to war and had come home safely, but we were wrong. We waited for his long, preposterous stories, his winks and chuckles, but he only sat unmoving in his easy chair, reading or dozing. Or he would go for long walks through town, refusing to let either me or Woodrow tag along. We nagged and pulled at his sleeves. We tried to remind him how generous he had once been with his time, but he acted as if we weren't really there. He didn't know us anymore. He had forgotten us.

The Boys We Were, The Men We Became

It was hard to accept. I reminded him of his story about the airliner that ran out of gas and went down in the Gobi desert and how all the men passengers donated their suspenders so that the pilot could make windup motors out of them that would turn the propellers and allow the plane to fly everyone back to civilization, but he just looked mildly alarmed, as though only some kind of irresponsible idiot would tell such lies to children. We whined to mother, but she hushed us, saying, "Daddy isn't himself yet. He'll be all right, but we need to give him time. He saw terrible things overseas."

I was old enough to imagine sex, and when mother became pregnant with Baby Bart, I was astonished. How could a man as morose and distant as our dad possibly arouse himself enough to have, much less enjoy, sex? But when Bartholomew was born, Dad's spirits sank even lower. And that amazed me, too. He ignored Baby Bart pretty much as he ignored the rest of us. He would sit in his underwear, smoking his cigarettes, staring into the blue nicotine haze. From across a room, I sometimes stared into this haze, too, trying to fathom the vision that had paralyzed his spirit.

We gave him time. But as the years passed, he became more sullen and withdrawn. He acted as if nothing around him had a real existence, including his wife and children. We were just smoky shapes drifting around him and sometimes pestering the quiet, empty spaces that occupied his reverie. The things he had seen in Europe had hollowed out the once-substantial elements of his prewar world. Then one day he packed a single suitcase and left home without a word of explanation, apology, or good-bye.

After a few months, Mother gave up on him. Then she, too, became sullen and indifferent. I didn't know if she was just bitter for being abandoned or if the emptiness of my father had been a contagious thing that had infected her, too. She put on weight, and the heavier she got, the more distracted and heedless of the world around her she became. I looked for signs of it in Woodrow and myself, and even in Baby Bart. Could the same thing infect us? I struck poses in the bathroom mirror that reminded me of my father. I pushed my belly out, wondering if it could bloat. I imagined myself empty, and, imagining it, I *felt* it. Something solid but invisible rose up from my legs, gathered momentum, and assaulted my stomach and chest. It flew into my throat. My mouth fell open and I heard it screech over my tongue and past my teeth. My heart tripped and hammered against its bony confinement. I broke a sweat. I wanted to run, but a cold paralysis held me in its grip.

"What's the matter with you, Bernard?" my mother asked through the bathroom door, tapping it lightly. It was a dutiful question, something a mother would ask. But it was empty of care. "Are you getting sick, Bernard?"

"No, I'm not getting sick," I said. I told her that I was only laughing. "I just remembered a joke," I said, my face in the toilet, the gleaming wet porcelain hollowing out my words until they became brittle shells of sound.

2. INTRUDERS

Time drained some of Mother's bitterness away. She began to have dates now and then. The men she dated seemed generally lifeless to me. I would watch Mother and her dates sitting at the kitchen table over beer and potato chips talking in bored voices about weather or work or relatives. One man named Roger Spydell I remember because of his greenish complexion and his busy, nicotine-stained fingers. He would drum the table impatiently when listening to Mother, and when he talked, his fingers would punch little emphatic holes in the air. Roger drove a long black Packard Eight that drifted down our street like an ebony coffin that had been accidentally launched into a slow river. Mother and Roger would sit in the big car together in the driveway after a date, talking with their mouths almost shut and staring out the windshield as if at the dead immensity of the finite space immediately in front of them. Sometimes they would go into her bedroom, and Woodrow and I would listen at the door, but we heard nothing but the close-mouthed mutter of indifferent conversation, or the slow breathing of sleepers.

Another man she dated was critical of nearly everything. His caustic remarks would descend, in stages, from the loftier subjects of the national government and the state of public morality to the little things he found personally offensive in his everyday life. Criticism was the only form of expression that gave him the appearance of having purpose and energy. When the subject of conversation was not open to criticism, he became inarticulate and confused or openly bored. Words, to him, were cruelly sharp instruments to be used only for cutting away the fat from the lean, and sometimes the lean from the bone. He once actually said that criticism was his gift. He said this with a self-congratulatory smile. He looked as though he was waiting for someone to pin a medal on him.

A man I remember only as "Pincher" seemed, at first, to be full of life and good fun. He was a big pink man with a round hairless head. He was always winking at us and sticking his tongue into his cheek as if everything he observed was a joke. He brought us gifts. He brought Woodrow an imitation samurai sword he'd bought in Tokyo during the Occupation. He gave me a Red Ryder BB rifle, and he gave Baby Bart a Japanese doll-bank with a head that unscrewed. We called him Pincher because he liked to give us pinches. He pinched Woodrow and he pinched me. He pinched Mother until she begged him to stop. He gave Baby Bart little pinches in his crib until he screamed. Pincher pinched expertly and he pinched hard. Once I looked at the back of my arm and saw the blue imprint of his thumb and forefinger. When Woodrow cried after one of his pinches, he said, "Don't be a baby, Woodrow. Maybe you ought to be in the crib with Bartholomew. Or maybe you *don't* want to be a man someday." He laughed when he said this, as if the notion tickled him.

Though I was several years older than Woodrow, Pincher made me cry once, too. I turned away from him so that he wouldn't see the quick well of tears in my eyes, but he forced me to face him. Then he winked, stuck his tongue into his cheek, and tousled my hair. One day I accidentally caught Mother coming out of the bathroom in her underwear and saw that her arms and shoulders, as well as her thighs, were leopard-spotted with blue and yellowing welts.

About this time a shy bully at school named Dolph Hubler singled me out to be his latest victim. At fifteen I wasn't as big or as courageous as I wanted to be. I was a disappointment to myself at five feet seven inches tall and one hundred and thirty pounds. Dolph, who had been set back two grades, was man-sized. He was close to six feet and probably weighed two hundred pounds. He was big and clumsy and forced by his parents to wear faded bib overalls and oversized oxblood wingtip shoes that were obvious hand-me-downs from his father or older brothers. Dolph wasn't a natural bully, but had been forced into the role because of the sly smirks his appearance aroused. To keep these smirks at a respectful distance, Dolph would single someone out now and then in random reprisal.

Dolph would look for me in the crowd of kids loitering in the school yard before the first bell. When he found me, he'd slap the books out of my hands and then show me, and whoever else might be interested, his big raw fist. He made the top middle knuckle protrude as if introducing me to it. Then he would punch my shoulder hard enough to jar my collarbone. The first time he did this I was so stunned and panic-stricken that I couldn't talk or move. Filled with a sick dread I hadn't known before, I smiled at him. My smile was irrational since it had no bearing on my true inner state. Dolph towered over me, annoyed by this inappropriate smile that did not credit his power to instill fear. He had the body of a middle-aged beer drinker. His ears were big and fleshy, and when he walked, he waddled from side to side, the palms of his hands facing backwards, apelike.

Everyone was afraid of him. Each morning when he approached, my friends would drift away as if they had pressing business on the other side of the school yard. None of them wanted to show partisanship for me, knowing that such a foolhardy gesture could only attract attention to themselves as a possible source of future victims.

I ran with a clique of intrinsically cautious boys who liked to pose in rugged approximations of James Dean, Marlon Brando, and Aldo Ray, hoping to distract one another from the discouraging truth about themselves. They would slouch in groups, thumbs hooked insolently into the belt loops of their Levi's, saying, "Well, then, there now," in the breezy, dreamy way James Dean said it in *Rebel Without a Cause*. They would repeat this phrase to each other tirelessly, as if it were real conversation, packs of Chesterfields, Camels, or Lucky Strikes rolled into the sleeves of their T-shirts. Though they moaned at passing girls with the sexual menace of Marlon Brando, they would marry the first or second girl they slept with. They were in love with safety. After high school, they would pursue college deferments from the draft. They would plan sensible careers. And they would do nothing to attract attention to themselves, knowing instinctively that Dolph Hubler existed in the world as a principle, a mindlessly vengeful force, darkly determined to inflict pain and humiliation at random, but always gravitating to the most visible targets.

Dolph Hubler put a serious crimp in the safe allegiances I was in the process of adopting. Dolph was my first crisis in personal relationships. There was no way around him. I couldn't put him out of my mind. I dreamed about him. In one of my dreams we went fishing together. We were wading in a stream. Suddenly I realized the fishing trip had been a ruse. Neither of us had fishing poles. He was going to drown me. I saw it in his face as he waded towards me. I woke up, fighting for high ground.

Dolph homed in on me each morning, knuckle upraised, his small colorless eyes unblinking. My cringe was internal, not visible, but Dolph perceived it anyway and rejoiced in it. Outwardly I pretended that the morning ritual between us was all in good fun and that his shoulder punches were not a great inconvenience. He would hit me and I would say, "Well, then, there now, Dolph," in the casual, unhurried manner of James Dean. It was the way I had chosen to save face. All my friends approved of it. "Attaway, Bernie," said one of them, his voice manfully hoarse in the whispering style of Aldo Ray. "You showed that pissant, Bernie." Such congratulations were offered, of course, only after Dolph had lumbered out of earshot.

The trouble with my strategy, though, was that while it was face-saving to me, it was frustrating to Dolph. He needed to strip me of my James Dean front and expose me to our wide audience as a sissy, even as a crybaby. And so he increased the force of his punches until my lower lip began to tremble under the easy anarchy of my cool smile. He made an ear-piercing falling-bomb whistle to dramatize the ballistic arc of his punch and then the bomb-blast boom when the red knuckle sank into my shoulder deep enough to knock bone. I felt my well-greased hair lifted by impact into comical arrangements. My shoulder became a blue disaster zone of pulverized meat.

Mother's latest boyfriend was a tiny, wiry man named Ducky Tillinghast. Ducky was smaller than me, but he radiated toughness. He'd been in the navy for twenty years and had once been featherweight champ of the Sixth Fleet. Somehow he'd caught wind of my difficulties with Dolph Hubler. One evening, after we'd all had dinner together, he took me aside. "Bullies are almost always yellow, Bernard," he said somberly. "I say almost always because you never know for sure. There's the chance that you have drawn the one in ten who is everything he says he is. But I guarantee you, son, most of them are pushovers when you deal with them properly. Why do you think he picked you, someone half his size?"

Ducky gave me a ten-minute boxing lesson I didn't want. I had no intention of hitting Dolph Hubler back. As I watched Ducky holding up his little fists and shuffling his feet around, I felt a large surge of contempt. Dolph Hubler could pick Ducky up by the nape of his neck and throw him over the school yard fence. It was ludicrous to me, this pint-size man encouraging me to fight a monster the two of us together wouldn't have been able to handle. I guess I was sneering a little at him, but he paid no attention to it.

"You set up the right with the left," he said, pawing at the air. "You stick stick stick with the left, then you come over and stake him with the right." He danced in front of me like a midget Sugar Ray Robinson. He showed me how to make a left jab snap like a flicked whip and how to put body weight into my right. He finally took note of my halfhearted and somewhat disrespectful attitude. It bothered him. We were out in the backyard. He offered me a cigarette. We smoked and talked in the dark among the throbbing crickets. "Look, Bernard," he said after a while. "I can show you a thousand tricks, but if you don't have the belly for a fight, then none of them can help you."

I hated him suddenly. I was glad it was too dark for him to see how red my face had become or how my lip was quivering.

"I'll tell you this, though, Bernard," he said. "If you let it go on, you will eat so much dirt that eventually you will come to think it's the only item on the menu. The world is already full of men like that."

I saw Mother frowning at the cigarette in my hand. She was at the kitchen window, doing the dishes. I took a deep drag, making the burning tip glow brightly so that it would illuminate my face, which was again placid with contempt.

"What do you have to lose, Bernard?" Ducky said.

I pictured the things I had to lose. I saw my teeth sprinkled on the asphalt school yard. I saw my ripped shirt spotted with red. And I saw worse. I saw Dolph dragging me around the school yard by my ankles as girls in their crisp skirts and saddle shoes giggled with forbidden excitement. It was clear to me that I had an awful lot to lose. My friends would understand this. They were going to live by an understanding of it all their lives. They had already become experts in their midteens at cutting their losses. They were learning very quickly how to face the world with a handy smile while the world beat them slowly into pablum.

So, when I actually hit Dolph Hubler, no one was more surprised than me. I'd already decided that endurance was a greater virtue than the will to retaliate. I'd simply outlast Dolph. He'd get bored eventually and find someone more promising. But one morning my fake James Dean indifference suddenly collapsed. Dolph was especially disgruntled with my passive acceptance of his ballistic punches, so he doubled the force and the rate of delivery until he was panting with effort. I felt myself caving in. Something terrible was about to happen—I was going to cry or run away or beg him to stop. To prevent this, I dipped my shoulder away from his falling fist. This small act of resistance alarmed him. He wasn't ready for it. His big, heavily freckled face sagged with surprise. Before I fully understood the movement that dipping my shoulder had started, my left hand was flicking at his nose. It snapped like a whip, just as Ducky said it would. As I jabbed, I rotated my fist so that when it struck, it punished. This was also one of Ducky's many techniques. The feel of soft, yielding flesh under my knuckles was a revelation to me. It was equivalent in magnitude to my discovery two years earlier of masturbation. It was a new, illicit pleasure of the body.

Surprise continued to mount in Dolph's face. Then it began to change into horror. His hands hung helplessly at his sides, paralyzed by this impossible turn of events. I took the opportunity to step towards him. My right foot planted, I was able to put my entire body weight into my right hand. It bounced off his nose with a wet, meaty thump. Dolph sat down slowly, like a man stopping in a wilderness to reconsider the path he'd chosen. A shining rope of blood twisted from his nose. Tears rolled from his eyes.

My friends congratulated me loudly, but their praise was tempered by dismay. An element of disapproval undermined the barking shouts that celebrated my victory. Eventually they drifted away from me. I was no longer one of them. I was untrustworthy, perhaps dangerous. I began to associate with a new, rowdier group. They were grittier than my old friends, but they hadn't been gritty enough to challenge Dolph Hubler.

Exposed now for what he was, Dolph became the school clown. My new friend, Art Bannister, humiliated Dolph on a daily basis. He would punch Dolph on the arms or stomach and make him cry. Art declared one morning to an audience of hooting girls from the seedier section of town that Dolph would be their "Slave For a Day." He would carry their books when asked, he would run petty errands, he would open doors, and he would bow when commanded to do so. Dolph Hubler in his oversized oxblood wingtip hand-me-downs became a living joke. How this flabby, stupidly dressed dork had ever been feared was so great a mystery that we could only deal with it by forgetting it. His past freedom to evoke terror was simply erased from the collective school yard memory.

3. GEMS

Shortly after Mother broke up with Ducky Tillinghast, she took a job as hostess in a restaurant called Chez Frenchy. Her salary wasn't much, but she did very well in tips. Chez Frenchy was owned by Frenchy Bigelow, a tall, hairy, slope-shouldered man who liked to wear jewelry, especially diamonds. He had a diamond stick pin, a wristwatch with diamond hours, a large signet ring with a diamond center, and a pinky ring with a big sapphire in it.

Frenchy liked to talk. He told me all about precious stones. Rare gems, he said, are connected intimately to the history of the world. The ancients believed some rare stones had medical properties. The Arabs and Hebrews, for example, considered the carnelian to be an important prophylactic. The breastplate of the Hebrew highpriests were studded with topaz, beryl, onyx, ruby, emerald, sapphire, agate, amethyst, and jasper. Caesar paid the equivalent of ten million dollars for a single pearl. Caligula adorned his horse with a collar of walnut-size pearls. "But the diamond," Frenchy said, "is the king of rare stones. It has made and broken empires, caused heads to roll, made billionaires of common men. The Koh-I-Noor diamond, for instance, was believed by the Sultan Baber of the Moguls to be equal in worth to the entire world!"

He also said that he'd been in the French resistance during the war. He'd been a right-hand man to Pierre-Michel Rayon, the famous underground leader. He had an autographed picture of Rayon. The picture looked as if it had been torn out of a magazine and the autograph was an unreadable corkscrew of blue ink. Frenchy was a friendly man who liked to recount his wartime experiences, when he was not reciting the histories of rare stones. The war fascinated me and I liked to listen to him tell about it. He said that he'd been responsible for blowing up three German tanks and an entire railroad bridge, complete with supply train. He said he killed an SS colonel with his bare hands. He showed me his large hairy hands and closed them slowly into fists, demonstrating their life-extinguishing power. He regarded these lethal fists with a melancholy that spoke of war's enduring sorrow. He told me how to make a bomb out of a mixture of sugar, acid, and calcium chlorate that could be used to incinerate a German staff car. He explained how to determine the structural weaknesses of railroad trestles. He recalled fondly the selfless courage of the Parisian graffiti artists who covered sidewalks, monuments, and the walls of buildings with brilliantly comic insults to the Third Reich. Frenchy's best friend had been executed in the street after being caught painting a Cross of Lorraine on the door of Gestapo headquarters.

"It's a terrible, terrible thing, this war," Frenchy said as if it were still going on. "But it gives a man his purpose." His eyes would get misty with scenes of heart-wrenching sadness as he spoke. "Your friends die in your arms, and it is very, very sad. But all the time you know in your heart that their purpose still lives and that they *were* their purpose. A man is not a man, Bernard, unless he is also a purpose. Do you comprehend this, my young friend?"

I nodded soberly, but he was over my head.

"Without a purpose, a man can be dismayed by war. War can drown the spirit of a purposeless man."

I was grateful to him for telling me about the war. He had seen things that were just as terrible as the things my father had seen, but they hadn't turned him into a silent brooder. Of course this was ten years after the war had ended and for all I knew my father was able by then to tell stories of the war with equal enthusiasm to some willing listener somewhere in the world.

"Do you understand how important it is to preserve your dignity, Bernard?" Frenchy said to me once. He was visiting Mother and we had just polished off a set of steaks that had cost her a week's worth of tips. He made a church of his hands as he spoke, and the rare stones on his thick fingers flared in the light from the candles Mother had put on the dining room table.

"Sure," I said, but as it always was with Frenchy, this was only his way of opening up a deeper subject.

"It is a ludicrous thing, really. Dignity. why do we insist on it? In the end, none of us have it. In the end, we are a few ounces of humble dust." His rings and diamond cuff links winked richly in the candlelight. "And yet, without dignity, life becomes a monstrous slaughterhouse pageant without meaning."

"Let's change the subject," Mother said.

"No matter what the enemy does to you, Bernard," he said, ignoring her, "you must refuse to submit. His techniques may be subtle, and you may be tempted to bend to his arguments, but you must hold yourself apart from him. Deep within you there is the unviolated place of refusal. You must preserve this, under torture, under bribery, under his vile promises."

"Oh, brother," Mother said, rolling her eyes.

"I tell you, my young friend," Frenchy continued. "Many many went along with the *boche*. Women and men. They licked the boot."

I was very impressed with French Bigelow—from his knowledge of rare stones to his participation in the war. I told Mother this while we were doing the dishes later that evening. We still had on our good clothes and were both wearing aprons.

After listening to me praise Frenchy, Mother said, "Oh, honey, Frenchy's an old liar. He's never been to France, and the jewelry he wears is mostly fake. He's from Detroit. He worked on a GM assembly line during the war."

I found myself rising to his defense. "So *what* if he's lying," I said, "as long as what he's saying is true."

She shut off the water tap and looked at me, drying her hands on her apron. "Listen to yourself, Bernard," she said mournfully, as if I had just proved beyond doubt that my early promise had been the biggest miscalculation of her life. "Just listen to what you're saying, Bernard."

But even though Frenchy was a liar, Mother married him a year later anyway. He was as close to rich as she'd seen, and money had always been a problem for us after my father left home. I don't think she loved Frenchy in any kind of torch-song way, but she got along with him well enough. Frenchy was kind and generous to Woodrow and me and Baby Bart, and in return we were a faithful audience for his fabricated tales of life in the French resistance.

I used some of the knowledge I'd picked up from Frenchy to impress a girl named Sidney Graves. We were both in eleventh-grade chemistry. I'd been watching her from a safe distance since the eighth grade. She was not especially pretty, but she had eyes that stopped my heart. They were amethyst lavender, deep set, and her gaze was steady and serious under her tall, brainy forehead. Her eyes gave you the impression that the mind behind them had never entertained a trivial thought. She had long thin legs and narrow hips, but her breasts were womanly. Her hair was mouse-brown, but closer to gray than to brown. Sometimes, from a distance, she was mistaken for a teacher because of her iron-gray hair, perfect posture, and slow, purposeful stride. And because of this and the slightly English intonation of her speech (an impediment, I found out later, rather than an affectation), she was not a popular girl. Kids called her Lady Graves behind her back. She was the best student in math, chemistry and physics and had already been offered scholarships to Berkeley and Cal Tech.

I was a poor chemistry student, and that was my excuse to talk to her. I asked for help with precipitates and catalysts. We studied together, first at school during lunch hour. I took these opportunities to show off my knowledge of gem, stones.

"Did you know, Sidney," I said, "that the Hindus believed that if you put the powder of ground-up diamonds into your mouth, you wouldn't be struck by lightning? Or that lapis lazuli was prescribed as a laxative by Antonius Musa Brassarobus, the medieval medical scholar?" Her unblinking eyes studied me, assessing my credibility, and I'd feel my confidence start to crumble. "The color of a gem often changes its name," I said quickly. "For example, a red sapphire is a ruby. But a yellow sapphire is called a yellow topaz. You probably didn't know that topaz gets its name from an island in the Red Sea called Topazion." I talked straight into those analytical eyes, hoping for the best. I wanted to bring up my knowledge of the French resistance, too, but couldn't find a way to make the leap from gemstones to underground warfare.

Our study sessions eventually moved to her house. Her house was always empty when we got there every afternoon at three o'clock. Her father was a detail man for a pharmaceutical company and spent most of his time on the road. Her mother worked in a real estate office, sometimes not coming home until after dark.

"You're the only boy who's ever shown any interest in me," she said after our first kiss.

The kiss was an accident hoping to happen. Our heads were close together, bent over the kitchen table as she worked out a reaction formula. I said, "Wait, you're going too fast for me, Sidney." She looked up, we bumped cheeks, our lips brushed together. My heart began to stumble against my ribs and I heard her catch her breath. I said, "I'm sorry." She said, in her unintentional English accent, "It's all right, it's all right," and we kissed again, involving our tongues this time.

These homework sessions gradually degenerated into kissing sessions. Then kissing wasn't enough. We both went exploring. The first time I saw her naked breasts I almost passed out. The only breasts I'd ever seen were the low-slung overworked breasts of native women in *National Geographic*. Sidney's breasts didn't sag like theirs and her nipples hadn't been elongated and chapped from swarms of little mouths. Her nipples were small and pink and alert with virginal anticipation. Staring at them, I started to shake all over. I was having a mild convulsion and knew that I'd stammer if I tried to initiate conversation.

Sidney's explorations were at first limited to her hands slipping under my shirt, but she eventually grew bolder and opened my belt. Her explorations, unlike mine, were conducted coolly, with scientific reserve. She regarded sex as another learning experience, I regarded it as a tightrope walk to joy. When she took my penis in her hand, I came instantly, showering her hand and forearm with hot pearls. She didn't pull away in disgust as I expected but bent closer to see the phenomenon, as a chemist might regard an unexpected catalytic reaction. "Oh, G-Geez—I'm sorry," I stammered. "Don't be," she said. We took a shower together, and under the drumming water, on the slippery tiles, we gave each other our virginities.

These blissful afternoons were the high point of my life, but they didn't last. Her father died suddenly in Cincinnati of a heart attack. Sidney and her mother went back east to live with Sidney's grandparents so that her mother could recuperate and start her life over. I was frantic with grief, but Sidney took the philosophical view. "Our time together was perfect, Bernard. Nothing can change that. We'll think about this years from now and be glad that we didn't let it become a boring thing, ruined by arguments or unfaithfulness. You see?"

I didn't see. "I love you, Sidney," I said.

"I love you, too, dear," she said. "And nothing will change that. I'll change, and you will change too, but these last few months we've had can't be changed by anyone or anything. We'll both keep this time safe in memory, and memory will only make it better."

I didn't understand this or feel consoled by it, but I knew one thing: Sidney Graves was too smart for me and that, had we gone on together, she would have soon left me far behind. I was older than Sidney by three months, but the last time we made love I sensed that something in her was years older than I would ever be. This realization embarrassed me. I felt the displacement of someone who had always been over his head and was just becoming aware of it. I made some choking noises—disguised sobs. Sidney held me in her consoling arms; I buried my face in her iron-gray hair.

We said good bye in a strangely formal way: we shook hands on her front porch while her unsuspecting mother, smiling sadly, looked on from behind the living-room curtains.

4. BABY BART

Mother decided that Baby Bart wasn't normal enough. She took him to the doctor, and the doctor recommended a child psychologist. Baby Bart was nine years old and quirky with goofball behavior. He wouldn't talk for days, and when that passed, you couldn't shut him up for days. He alternated between brooding and babbling from about age six on. And his babbling was weird. He'd want to talk about death and what happens to people after they died or where they were before they were born. Frenchy humored him, but the rest of us ran for cover when he'd start in.

Mother asked Woodrow to show Baby Bart how to do normal things, like building model airplanes or using a compass to find your way out of the woods. Woodrow was an Eagle Scout and knew how to do a lot of practical things with limited resources. But Baby Bart was even too much for an Eagle Scout. Woodrow tried to teach him how to read semaphore flags, but Baby Bart's constant questioning defeated his patience. Woodrow put a paper bag over Baby Bart's head and made him keep it there.

Mother believed Baby Bart's switching back and forth from total silence to annoying babble was a form of epilepsy. All the medical tests, though, turned up nothing. Baby Bart was normal, as far as any of the experts could tell. But he wasn't.

"How can things just *be?*" he said to me once.

I was still grieving over my loss of Sidney Graves, who, I believed, was the only woman I could ever love, and was in no mood to put up with Baby Bart's oddball ramblings. I ignored him.

"Stuff just is everywhere, but I can't figure out how stuff can be stuff, the way it is, like dishes and hair and shoes and light poles and cities," he said. "I mean, there should be no stuff at all, there should be nothing anywhere everywhere. And what is 'where' supposed to mean? Tell me what 'where' is supposed to be, Bernard. Or 'there.' Or even 'here.' What do you think?"

"I think you've been inhaling your own farts under the blankets," I said. "For Christ's sakes, Baby Bart, you should be talking about baseball or playing with your decoder ring. You keep this up, Mom's going to have you committed to a nut house."

The thing about Baby Bart was that he never took insults personally. He was big for his age, tall and wide, but he was also weak and flabby. He had no athletic ability. Not that I had any. I was a lounger, always on the lookout for cookies and other sweets. I'd already had two molars pulled, and fillings in ten other teeth. Woodrow, even though he was an Eagle Scout with merit badges, wouldn't drink milk unless he could spike it with Hershey's chocolate syrup. But Baby Bart was even worse. He sugared everything, even his peanut-butter-and-jelly sandwiches.

I once overheard him talking to Frenchy. They were in the kitchen late one night, having cookies and milk. In his nonstop talking phase, Baby Bart wouldn't go to sleep. He'd roam the house, looking at things, reading a few pages from books randomly selected from the bookcase, or looking out the windows at the nighttime sky. I'd been reading in bed and came down to the kitchen for a glass of water when I heard them. I stopped to listen.

"Do dogs think?" Baby Bart asked Frenchy.

"They certainly do," Frenchy said without hesitation.

"That means they have words in their heads, doesn't it, Frenchy?"

"Well, I don't know about that. Maybe not words..."

"You can't think without words, can you?"

"Hmmm... let's see. No, I guess you can't."

"A dog knows, 'sit,' and 'come,' and 'fetch' and 'roll over,' but that's not enough words to think with, is it?"

"Maybe they can think without words," Frenchy said.

"No, I don't think so. I tried to do, it but it didn't work. You've got to have words to think."

"I guess dogs don't think, then."

"But they look like they are, don't they? When a dog looks at you with his ears up and eyes all shiny, you could swear they are thinking."

"I'm getting sleepy, Baby Bart," Frenchy said. "I think I'll turn in."

Baby Bart banged the kitchen table with his head, startling both Frenchy and me.

"What did you do that for?" Frenchy said.

"Do what?"

"Hit the table with your head!"

"Oh, I was just wondering if I could shake up all the words in my head so that I would think different thoughts."

Frenchy laughed. "Good idea, Baby Bart! You need to think some different thoughts, all right, but you don't have to give yourself a skull fracture to do it."

"I want to try to think like a dog someday," Baby Bart said. "I want to think of something without thinking of it. Wouldn't that be neat? That would be like figuring out a puzzle before you knew it was a puzzle. You'd be ahead of everybody. It'd be like having one of Superman's special powers from the planet Krypton."

"You make me dizzy, Baby Bart," Frenchy said, yawning.

I walked into the kitchen then. "Hey, Bernard," Baby Bart said. "Do you think dogs think?"

"Yeah," I said. "They think about licking their balls, then they think about humping your leg. They're real geniuses."

Frenchy and I made our escape, but from my bedroom, all through the night, I heard Baby Bart roaming the house, rummaging through drawers and cupboards, paging through magazines and books, absorbing the small details of a world that had the inexhaustible power to seduce his sense of wonder.

We never stopped calling Baby Bart "Baby Bart" because he had a baby face that he was never going to lose. When he was stoop-shouldered and gray, that chubby pink face would still be open and naive and stubbornly impressed by the unsolvable puzzle of existence.

5. MARRIAGE AND THE FAMILY

In 1958 the draft caught up with Elvis Presley, but I was safely enrolled in college by then. I got my 2-S deferment by majoring in electrical engineering. In any future war, I would be stationed, on the grounds of my valuable education, well behind the front lines. It was clear, even then, that the gun fodder for future wars would come from the marginally educated legions of aimless young males a society such as ours produces with almost conscious intent.

After I graduated, in 1962, I married the third girl I'd slept with, Beatrice Carns. I got a good job at Lockheed Missiles and Space Corporation in the industrial town of Sunnyvale, just north of San Jose. A year later, Woodrow joined the marines and they sent him to officer candidate school.

Lockheed was the prime contractor for a submarine-launched ballistic missile called the Polaris. I worked in a unit that investigated quality-control problems with parts and equipment that were shipped to us by suppliers around the country. I traveled a lot, sometimes even to Europe. It was an interesting, even exciting job, but Beatrice became unhappy. She didn't like it when I was gone, and she didn't seem all that happy when I was home.

Beatrice was a tall, impatient redhead who had been a star volleyball player at San Jose State. We met in a Sunnyvale bar called the Vertical Takeoff. The bar was named after an experimental interceptor Lockheed was developing. The plane, never put into production, sat on its tail and went straight up a few thousand feet before it leveled off. What it did after that was ineffective.

It was happy hour and Beatrice, along with a few of her friends, was celebrating. She had majored in psychology and had just been hired by Lockheed's personnel department. Mutual friends introduced us. We were both a bit drunk, but we looked good enough to each other to continue what chance had started.

I'd been at Lockheed two years by then, and Beatrice saw me as an insider, someone who knew the ropes. She was ambitious and wanted to become part of Lockheed's management structure. I had no such desires, but I didn't tell her this. In spite of her ambitions, Beatrice quit her job a few months after we were married. She wanted babies and a domestic life. At least that's what she thought she wanted.

We rented a small house next to the railroad tracks on the east side of Palo Alto. The commuter trains roared by every half hour on the dot, shaking the house, making dishes rattle on their shelves. It may have been that simple, conversation-stopping intrusion, rather than any particular fault in either of us, that frayed our marriage bonds.

Baby Bart, who had joined a Christian brotherhood of some kind, came by to visit us once. He called himself a novitiate. He wore a sackcloth cassock, crude sandals, and was tonsured. He was living communally with his fellow brothers up in La Honda, but looked as if he'd stepped out of twelfth-century Europe.

Beatrice made a pot roast, complete with oven-roasted potatoes, carrots, and onions. Baby Bart had grown up to be a very large man. He was well over six feet and probably weighed two hundred fifty pounds, and he had an appetite to match. He put away half the pot roast, six dinner rolls, and most of the potatoes.

He guzzled wine like he did Kool-Aid when he was a kid. There was still plenty of food for Beatrice and me, but Baby Bart's gluttony, along with his ascetic garb, irritated Beatrice.

"God bless this table," Baby Bart said, wiping his gravy-stained mouth on his napkin.

Beatrice put her fork down hard on her plate. "You normally say grace *before* eating," she said.

"The brothers think afterwards makes more sense, don't you agree?" Baby Bart said. "That's when you're truly grateful, when your belly's full and your mind is unwanting and at peace."

Without a shred of self-consciousness, Baby Bart leaned to one side and released a thunderclap of gas. Beatrice threw her napkin down and went into the kitchen. The six P.M. commuter roared by, rattling the windows. It took a while for the train, which was headed north, towards South San Francisco, to pass. When it did, Baby Bart, his voice gravely with mucus generated by the rich food, said, "This table, this excellent fare, God put it here, expressly for us."

From the kitchen, Beatrice said, "Oh, for Christ's sakes."

"You, too, Beatrice," Baby Bart called out. "God put you here. He wanted you to be here, at this very moment. It seems trivial maybe, but it's not. Nothing is trivial. We are all here, together, because God put us here."

Baby Bart annoyed me, too. "So what's your point?" I said, hoping to jettison the subject so that we could enjoy our dessert—cherry pie a la mode.

He turned his huge infantile face towards me, a pink topography of cherubic features. His eyes were large and sad and glazed with Christian love. "No point, Bernard. Just suggesting the obvious. What seems obvious to me, at least."

Beatrice came in carrying a tray loaded with a steaming carafe of coffee, a pint of ice cream, and a deep-dish cherry pie. She was looking forward to ending the evening as soon as possible. "And Hitler?" she said, pouring coffee for Baby Bart. "Is it obvious to you that God wanted Hitler among the Germans? How about Caligula? How about the Boston Strangler?"

Bart sipped his coffee, spooned into his pie. "What is, is," he said, almost too softly to be heard.

"So God has this black sense of humor, is that it?" she said.

"Everything hides God's face. It's all holy, Beatrice."

"Crud," she said. Her skin was very pale, almost transparent. When her temper flared, you could see small veins and capillaries near the surface. The blue pulse in her temple was visible—a danger sign. We fought often and I knew the signals. This evening was going to end badly.

I wanted to lighten things up. "'God is a comedian playing to an audience that is afraid to laugh,'" I said, quoting Voltaire. It made no impression.

"Without horror there can be no bliss," Baby Bart said. He set his coffee cup down and folded his hands in his lap, ready for the siege.

"You don't have to defend the existence of Hitler or anything else, Baby Bart," I said.

"Your religion, whatever the hell it is, is tailor-made for hypocrisy," Beatrice said.

Baby Bart belched lightly. He leaned forward, elbows on the table. "This meal," he said, speaking to Beatrice as if in confidence, "was truly a blessing."

"Bullshit," Beatrice said.

"This house, this furniture, the pictures on the walls, all of it, including you and your husband. Perfectly exquisite. It's what God wanted it to be, and here it is."

Beatrice picked up a dinner plate and Frisbeed it against a wall, shattering it and staining a painting of the Golden Gate Bridge, one that I liked in particular. The sun was under the bridge; the dimpled water dazzled the eye like a chest of gold coins that had been overturned; a three-masted sailing ship plowed west through glittering scallops of gold. "Did God want this, too?" she said, sending another plate flying at the wall.

"Things, not ideas," Baby Bart said. "Things, not events suborned by ideas. You don't know what you want, Beatrice. But no one does, really. It's better not to want at all. Only God rightly wants. God rightly wants these lovely things, but people don't know what they want, even when the object of desire seems so necessary. Thus the general unhappiness."

"You're deeper than whale shit, baby brother," I said, hoping to defuse Beatrice's growing rage. But Beatrice stalked out of the house, got into our car, and drove away into the night.

Beatrice and I began to fight regularly. Our arguments became the chief gossip of the neighborhood. Baby Bart, and perhaps the clockwork commuter trains, only triggered what was bound to happen to us sooner or later. We didn't see eye to eye on most things, and sex became a chore for her, mechanical release for me. Even so, we had a child, a little girl we named Polly Delight. Parenthood did nothing to renew our marriage. In fact, the added pressure of caring for a baby made us fight all the more and with more intensity.

Beatrice had a loud voice that carried well down the pleasant tree-lined street we lived on. I threw a bottle of beer through the front window, and once took a hammer to the plaster walls. She threw dishes at me, screamed until the blue pulse in her temple seemed likely to burst. Once she picked up a bread knife and pointed it at my throat.

Neighbors, alarmed at this chronic racket, called the police more than once, and we had to face that embarrassment, but even the threat of public humiliation was not enough to moderate our behavior. Once I drove out of the garage without opening the door. She ripped the drapes from the windows, burned them in the yard. We found ourselves in an escalating one-up contest of destructive tantrums.

And then, in a moment of drunken candor, I admitted to having an affair with Heide Kreide, the daughter of a German rocket designer in Huntsville, Alabama. Heide hated the way Americans pronounced her name—*Hi*-dee *Cry*-dee, so she changed it to Heather Chalk, a literal translation. For some reason I thought this tidbit of information would somehow lessen the shockwave of my confession. Beatrice was not entertained. "You dirty, heartless son of a bitch," she said, picking up little Polly Delight as if to shield her from the evil emanating from my person.

"No argument," I said, knowing that we were finished at last.

"Things work out for the best," Baby Bart said the next time I saw him.

"Sometimes they do, sometimes they don't," I said, feeling a bit philosophical myself.

Baby Bart had given up his full-time commitment to the brotherhood, got his MBA, and had taken a job at the Bank of America as a loan officer. He still wore his sackcloth cassock on weekend retreats, and saw no conflict of interest between the spiritual and the financial. "It's all of a piece," he said.

6. PRISONERS OF LOVE

A year after Beatrice left me I fell in love with a girl who worked in the Lockheed blueprint library named Inez Pascal. Inez was almost ten years younger than me, but that didn't seem to make much difference to her. We were soul mates. We told each other this often. For the first time in my life I understood what passion was. Inez was small and intense. She did nothing halfway. We would go out for lunch and wind up, hours later, playing the slots in Reno, work be damned. Inez had an apartment overlooking one of Lockheed's parking lots. When I was laid off in 1968 after an argument with my lead engineer over my chronic absenteeism, I moved in with her. The narrow casement windows of her apartment made it seem like a cell. I spent my days there, watching soap operas or gazing out at the mammoth parking lot as it emptied or filled during the shift changes. Then Inez quit her job in protest over the Vietnam War. "*That* is where the war comes from," she said, pointing a righteous finger at the low gray buildings of Lockheed Missiles and Space.

She joined the peace movement and became more intense than ever. She made trips into Berkeley with her new pacifist friends. She asked me to come along, but I refused.

"You're apathetic," she said. In those days the crime of apathy was second only to the napalming of villages.

"No," I said. "I just don't think the nerve center of the military-industrial complex is located in Berkeley." Under my glib words I was mourning her once, pyrotechnic passion, now diverted to the cause of sane international relations.

We argued, and the argument escalated until it included United States foreign policy, the American Medical Association, and Billy Graham's influence (or lack of influence) over Richard Nixon. I finally agreed to go with her to Berkeley, but I didn't join the march on Sproul Hall where the war-mongers were planning the incineration of the world. I was, by this time, thirty pounds overweight, almost thirty years old, and balding. I couldn't see myself tramping along with lean, long-haired kids loaded on pot chanting inflammatory slogans as the lines of bored cops itched in their riot gear. That was no way to end a bad war, or start a good one.

I had a hard time finding another job. Boeing made a tepid offer, but the job was in North Dakota and Inez refused to go there. There was no peace movement of any impact or glamour in North Dakota. I finally took a job in a large department store in a Santa Clara Valley mall as a plainclothes security guard. I had no experience, but I told the interviewer I'd been a brig guard in the marines. He didn't ask to see evidence of my service. I had a boot-camp photo of Woodrow and I was prepared to tell the interviewer it was me, fifty pounds lighter, but he was so happy to have landed someone with real experience in handling security matters that he signed me on without further investigation. It was the Christmas season. If I did well, he said, my job might last until Easter.

It was an easy job. I wore a blue blazer, gray slacks, and carried a can of mace, a walkie-talkie, and a set of handcuffs. I worked in men's clothing and in sporting goods on alternate days. It was a minimum-wage job, but they gave me discount privileges.

Inez spent Christmas Day in the Alameda County jail. I cooked the turkey anyway and ate hot sandwiches out on the steel porch of our apartment. The Lockheed parking lot was full, and the windows of the gray buildings thrived with feverish light. It reminded me of something one of Inez's new friends once said:"The satanic mills will never stop unless we the people stop them, even if we have to use our own bodies to clog the gears and wheels." It was a popular sentiment. I asked the boy who said this if he had ever seen someone who'd had his arm caught in a grain auger. "You fail to grasp the metaphor," he said, dismissing me.

I was becoming, I realized, an object of amused curiosity among Inez's new friends. One of them asked me to give him my draft card. He was going to mail a box of them to the attorney general's office in Washington. I told him no. We were sitting on the floor of a luxury apartment that overlooked the sailboat, speckled bay. The apartment belonged to a professor. Everyone looked at me with expressions ranging from contempt to pity. I said, "I'm Four-A. What's the use? No one's going to draft me anyway. Where's the metaphorical value in that?"

Because I was with Inez, I was treated like a dupe of the warlords rather than one of their toadies. "Poor old Bernie just doesn't get it," said the professor, a Trotskyite with tenure.

I received a phone call at work one afternoon a few days after Christmas. The store was having a sale and every department was mobbed. My supervisor told me to make it quick, two minutes at most. The call was from one of Inez's friends, a boy named Peter Ordway. We had to yell at each other because there was a lot of background noise at both ends of the line—acid rock on his, shopping mobs on mine.

"You're *what?*" I shouted, one hand clamped to my free ear.

"Denver. *In* Denver. Didn't have time to tell you. It all happened so fast. Here, talk to Inez."

"We'll be in D.C. a few weeks, then New York," Inez said, her voice quick with the happy excitement once triggered only by me.

"I thought you were at home, in the apartment. How did you get to Denver?"

"No time to explain. We've got to run to the United terminal."

"*We?* You and Peter?"

"Yes. No. Not just me and Peter. Don't be like that, Bernard. Jealousy's so reactionary. Stay cool, darling. It's not just Peter and me, it's all of us. Everyone. We're going to be doing some serious guerrilla theater. As much as the warlords would like to believe it, the revolution is not over."

"Why did you call?" I said.

"Don't sound so gloomy. The world hasn't ended. I forgot it's winter back east. Send me my wool sweaters, will you, Bernard?"

"Sure," I said. She gave me an address in Georgetown. I didn't write it down.

Just before closing time that day a deranged man entered sporting goods. He was wearing a 49ers jersey and cap. His pants were camouflaged combat fatigues. He didn't have shoes. He was a big man with a dirty white beard. He stood in an aisle, laughing. He had a grand, Mephistophelean laugh that scared most of our customers out of the department.

My mouth went a little dry, but there was enough bitterness in me at that moment to cut fear's paralyzing chemicals. I walked up to him, mace in hand.

"Shut up," I said.

He wagged a negative finger in my face, amused. He was tall enough to look down on me. His sharp blue eyes were dancing with the merriment insanity can sometimes produce. He was benignly attentive to everything before him, like a god well pleased with the material fabrications of his inventive dreams.

I raised the mace so he could see it plainly. But he laughed again—a deep, booming, stagy laugh. He looked like Lee Marvin—rangy, lean, tough with stringy muscle. I sniffed the air between us for alcohol, but I'd been drinking earlier that day myself and couldn't detect anything beyond the fecal stench of the man's ruined liver.

"Come on, sport," I said. "Let's go, okay? It's almost closing time."

"Use it," hissed my supervisor, yards away behind the safety of the canoes. "Use your mace!"

I didn't want to use it. I hated mace, on principle. The madman turned and walked away from me. He overturned a display of golf clubs. Then he sent a rack of executive dumbbells thumping across the tile floor. I tackled him from behind and we went down, hard.

He was as strong as he looked. I tried to stay on top of him, but he lifted me off with a roar and I rolled into a low table stacked with Port-a-Potties. When I got up, I saw him moving with guerrilla stealth, doubled over as if avoiding gunfire.

Then he was coming at me with a duckboat oar. I waved a skateboard at him. It was total war, suddenly. My war. A war I wasn't prepared to wage.

The slow oar stirred the air above my head. I threw the skateboard over his shoulder. He was a graceful, laughing warrior, I was mired in gloom. His war was happy and mine was not.

Then one of his demons nagged at him, complicating his attack. He lowered the oar and scratched his head, bewildered, his laughter slowing to a creaky groan, the residue merriment false. I took the oar out of his hands and laid it down.

His strength, which had been twice mine, was now miraculously atrophied. I handcuffed him easily. His flimsy wrists came together as though they were reeds. The look in his eye was apologetic and puzzled. He was ashamed of himself. The demon that had interrupted his oar-swinging zeal was sanity. It had returned like a dull oceanic depression, bringing with it overcast skies and a mild, enervating drizzle. It made him civil, circumspect, and ineffective. It made room in his heart for fear.

"I'm sorry," he said, his voice surprisingly high-pitched now. "Something must have happened."

I didn't pursue what that might have been. A lot had happened to all of us. I thought of Woodrow, who had been wounded in Vietnam two years earlier and had returned home in love with morphine, then heroin. He lived first in the mountains northeast of Seattle, then in the streets of L.A. where Mexican brown was accessible and relatively cheap. After committing an exotic sexual crime, he spent a year in the hospital for the criminally insane at Atascadero. When he got out, he went to Holland. He figured Amsterdam was a good place to be a junky and whatever else he was in the process of becoming.

I thought of Baby Bart, who had moved into a vice-presidency at his bank. He got married, and his wife, in her first pregnancy, gave him twin boys. In her second pregnancy, she had twin girls. Baby Bart wanted to name the boys Yin and Yang, but his wife, a Mormon farm girl from Logan, Utah, put her foot down. She named the boys Brigham and Joseph. Baby Bart got his way with the girls, though: Blossom and Autumn. They bought a house in Larkspur, a three-story brick with a half-acre yard. "God's half acre," Baby Bart calls it.

I thought of our father, who had gone to the last good war but had returned home from it an empty stranger, having suffered grievous ruptures to the soul's delicate vessel. And I though of our mother, making her bitter way as a sort of home-front camp follower, the question of dignity postponed for the duration, her calculating eyes fixed to a changeless goal—our survival. Frenchy Bigelow, who had built a cloudy fortress of lies against the daily invasions of conscience, never saw her long-range strategies, or the fierce tenacity that made them work. He believed he was simply and happily married to a worthy, hard-headed woman who allowed him, when the profits of Chez Frenchy merited it, small interludes of rest and affection.

And my Inez. She had harnessed her explosive, all-out passion to the ready yoke of righteousness. After her sorties to Washington and New York, and later to Bonn and Brussels, she would have no use at all for doubtful heroes like me who would never fight for the cause of the moment—unless they were caught in its feverish arms and *combat* was the only way out of that terrible embrace.

My prisoner sat on a stool in the supervisor's office, waiting for the police. I sat with him, chain-smoking. He shot shy glances at me now and then. I could tell he had something on his mind.

"What?" I said.

"I used to be married," he said. "She was a good woman. But I—you know..."

"I know," I said.

He smiled, his eyes wise with special knowledge. "I bet you do," he said.

He was quiet for a while, then said, "She called me Doctor Love. I don't mean to brag, but that's the way it was with us."

His grin faded, his eyes fogged over with nostalgia and confusion and regret. "Goddamn bitch," he said.

"I hear you, man," I said.

"You ever notice that time runs backwards in a mirror," he said abstractedly. "You figure that says something?"

"We can only hope," I said.

What grows in your garden of dreams can kill you. Cancer has a thousand different seed beds. The heart will wither and fail in the mildest drought. The brain sits on its slender stem like a delicate white flower. These organs are vulnerable to the soul's harsh seasons. All diagnoses are true. All remedies are quack. The truth is, we were not made for survival. I want to tell Señora Applegate this, but I specialize in lies. I am the one who will save her, but what saves her will be a fiction. Do you think that matters? It doesn't.

Fern Applegate understands this much: Doctors, most of the mainstream AMA types, get impatient with you when you assume knowledge of your own body. They believe they know you better than you know yourself. Your body is the subject of their long, demanding, and costly study. It is a hegemony established over the bloody millennia. It is their turf, and amateur opinions are not welcome. They know that livers, hearts, stomachs,

The Singular We

lungs, bladders, kidneys, and spleens are not open to unlearned public debate but rather are major topological features of a dark interior continent, a continent whose shorelines and inlets and spiny divides have been thoroughly mapped, measured, catalogued, and traveled by the argonauts of medical science since Galen.

Fern ardently believes she is unique: medical science tells her she is not. One femur is virtually indistinguishable from another—once you disregard such local properties as size, shape, density, and relative health. A knuckle is a knuckle, be it Hittite, Hottentot, Mongol, Inuit, or WASP. The history of our tragic descent from the trees is available in any worn-out knee you choose to study. Superficial features aside, we are one body. Individuality, the doctors know, is a romantic myth, a useful energizing principle in politics and the arts. In the operating room, surgeons count on the reliability of sameness. They do not want surprises when they open a chest cavity to replace the wheezing ventricles with sturdy replacements from the anonymous young donor who was good enough to run his two-hundred-seventy-five horsepower Z-300-X into a bridge abutment. Anonymity is a blessing in disguise.

And Fern knew what she was up against: The good doctors see you as a squatter in your own body with limited squatter's rights. You are not simply on their turf, you *are* their turf. Fern may have been a brief candle with a seductive personal luminosity, but her unremarkable wax and wick are theirs alone. And she knew that in doubting her neurologist, Dr. Mike Higgins, she was doubting the compass direction and self-assured thrust of Western Medical Science.

But then every belief system is sooner or later tested. When Fern's MRI showed, indisputably, a "large mass" in the sella turcica, above and behind the sphenoid sinus, camped at the base of her brain and engulfing the pituitary gland, everything she had come to believe about herself threatened to collapse like a house of cards.

At thirty-nine she was a blaze of suntanned health. Blond, firm, tennis-lean, she was chief executive of her own company, The Magic Gourd—A New Age curio emporium—and the wife of a professor of mathematics at the local branch of the state university system. Her symptoms had been almost negligible. A flurry of bright spots, like flashbulbs going off across a stadium, would make a dazzling display now and then in the far left corner of her vision. Her ophthalmologist said there was nothing abnormal about her eye and sent her to Southwest Diagnostic for a brain scan.

Fern didn't smoke or drink, and she ate leafy foods that were organically grown. She read the works of visionary nutritionists who shared the belief that preventive medicine, if not the only medicine, was the best medicine. She also believed that there existed cures for disease that were not recognized by the medical orthodoxy, cures developed over the centuries by the brujos and curanderos of Mexico, the medicine men of Native American culture, as well as the die-hard pagan herbalists of the Old World.

And now, after having endured endocrinological tests and MRIs and CT scans, Fern was told by Dr. Higgins that surgery and only surgery could amend her condition. The tumor had to come out, and soon. "It's in a bad spot, Fern," he said. "It's pushing into the optic chiasm—the place where the optic nerves cross—and its got a grip on your carotid arteries. If there's an infarction..."

Fern never felt better. How could she have a brain tumor big as a golf ball? How could her life be at risk at its peak? She'd never felt sexier or enjoyed sex more. Was it possible that her passion was merely a symptom of a pituitary gland gone wild because of a tumor's influence? Were her enthusiasm, receptivity, and romantic daydreams just chemical accidents? Did her heightened sexiness signify a gloomy pathology?

"...two methods of attack, Fern," Dr. Higgins was saying. "We can do a conventional craniotomy, which might be best, since there's a possibility this tumor might be a menengioma rather than a chromophobe macroadenoma. Or we can do the nondisfiguring transsphenoidal—up the nose. Right now I'd opt for the transsphenoidal. Focused radiation might have been a possibility some months ago, Fern, before the tumor reached its present size. But that would be too dangerous now, since the lesion is elevating the optic nerves."

Fern thought hard. She did not want disfiguring doors sawed into her skull, nor did she want Mike Higgins entering her brain through her nose. She was not ready to surrender her idea of herself, though she liked and respected Dr. Higgins.

"I'm going to try some alternative approaches first, Mike," she said, returning his familiarity.

Mike Higgins had heard such spunky defiance before. He sympathized with these patients, wished to God he didn't have to be the one to give them the bad news. But after years of trying to soften the blow by treating their evasions and fantasies with respect—an indulgence that only made the blow far more devastating when it came—he decided it was best to be up-front and direct. These people were grown-ups after all, and had to be accorded the dignity of having achieved a comprehensive vision of their lives, one that could accommodate the looming presence of mortality. Deeply religious people handled these bombshell announcements best. But self-indulgent dilettantes like Fern Applegate would erect shells of denial to the very end. Oddly, it was all too often the bright and educated who were most likely to challenge diagnosis and treatment.

Dr. Higgins patted Fern's knee. He was a big, fleshy man. His bearlike shoulders sloped with the gravity of his task. "We'll do our very best to make you comfortable," he said. "I guarantee you, your suffering will be minimal, Fernie. I've done hundreds of these."

"I'm not going to suffer at all," Fern said. "I'm going to beat this damn thing, Mike."

Dr. Higgins hated to patronize his patients. But sometimes it was impossible not to. "Yes, we are, Fern," he said. "*We* are going to beat this damn thing." He shook Fern's hand and scheduled another appointment for her.

Fern decided not to tell her husband, Hector. Hector Applegate lived in abstract mathematical space. He paid no attention at all to his body. He ate what he wanted, or whatever junk food was handy, smoked unfiltered Camels, took no exercise, had no interest in himself as a flesh-and-blood entity.

He was something of a child—her illnesses devastated him. He'd lost his preoccupied air when Fern had to spend a week in the hospital after her hysterectomy. A crop of fibroid tumors the size of hazelnuts had been discovered in her uterus. The pain and bleeding from this obtrusive clutter of tissue made surgery a necessity. Fern believed the surgeon's knife had its place. You didn't consult the stars over an ingrown toenail. Fibroids were intruders that required eviction. The surgeon, as the body's landlord, would effect their swift removal. Fern could accept this.

Hector had trembled in the waiting room, going out to the parking lot every ten minutes to light up a Camel. He was a slight man with a large head, not in a freakish way but in a way that made you think of history's great innovators: men who require capacious skulls to accommodate the billowing complexity of their thoughts, men who neglect their bodies because they are hopelessly transfixed by the abstract workings of the cerebral cortex. He smoked and wept, the subtleties of Chaos Theory momentarily overshadowed by the mystifying brutality of ordinary life.

He was a narrow-focus genius. Outside his field of specialization, he was usually at a disadvantage. Just now the macroscopic behavior of phase transitions preoccupied him, but when he set aside his intense involvement with his life's work, he was an ordinary and loving family man.

He rarely got sick. When he did he went straight to his HMO's primary care physician and passively accepted what the doctor prescribed. The doctor appreciated this, understood it as respect. Hector gave the doctor his turf without haggling. Like all good academicians, Hector knew instinctively that one did not question another's area of specialization. His best friend, a historian, was an expert in medieval European kitchen utensils. But when they visited over lunch in the faculty dining room, they talked baseball, the future of American politics, the best way to weatherproof double-hung sash-style windows. At parties, Fern often embarrassed Hector by offering unschooled opinions to colleagues who had spent their entire adult lives achieving what they considered to be small but durable additions to their area of scholarship.

"I think the Africanized bee will wipe out the organic-honey industry of Texas," she once said to a world-renowned entomologist.

Hector winced. The entomologist frowned—the same automatic frown that appeared on Dr. Higgins's forehead when Fern challenged his recommendations. "It's somewhat more complicated than that, Mrs. Applegate," the entomologist said politely.

Hector loved Fern and Fern loved Hector. They had a good marriage. Their children—two teenagers and a ten-year-old—were well-balanced high-achievers. But Fern couldn't tell Hector about her diagnosis because she knew he would side with the experts. Fern had her own experts, but they were not recognized by the sanctioning academies. They were on or beyond the fringe.

To her surprise, Fern was not depressed over her bad luck. She had taken tumor-shrinking herbal teas during the months after her diagnosis, along with a steroid, Decadron, that Dr. Higgins had prescribed. The steroid had side effects, both good and bad. The bad were supposed to be depression, nausea, headache. The good were euphoria and increased appetite. So far she had only experienced the good. She'd gained ten pounds and felt happy about it. She also felt an excitement, like a child waiting for Christmas.

One of Fern's contacts, an herbalist, recommended a curandera near Monterrey, Mexico, on the road to Saltillo. This curandera had a fabulous reputation. Fern packed her Audi and told Hector that she was going to visit her big brother, Louie, who lived in San Antonio. She'd close shop for a few days and bring in Xochi Lucero to run the household. Xochi, their maid and baby-sitter for fifteen years, lived in Ciudad Juárez. She had no green card, but that was a small matter in El Paso, where practically every middle- and upper-middle-class family employed undocumented women to clean, cook, and take care of children. Immigration officials did not pursue this large- scale illegal activity. If they did, half the population of the city would have to be indicted. Most of these Mexican women made fifteen to twenty dollars a day, twice what they could have made in the dozens of foreign-owned factories, the *maquilas*, of Juárez. The national furor over Zoe Baird's use of illegals as baby-sitters and her subsequent humiliation before an inquisitionally minded congressional subcommittee, amused and perplexed most El Pasoans.*¿Qué es el problema?*

Fern's brother, Louis Stanton, lived in the King William district of San Antonio, a neighborhood of extraordinary neneteenth-century mansions. He was a retired air force colonel, having flown sixty missions in Vietnam. Louis, a happy eccentric, was ten years older than Fern. His wife, Kelly, had left him for a hippie minister while Louis was spreading cluster bombs throughout Lu Tan. It tickled him that Kelly's minister had shed the cloth for a three-piece Armani and became an officer of one of the largest S&Ls in Texas to go belly-up. Then Kelly dumped him for another air force guy, this time a brigadier general who was the Pentagon liaison for a company that manufactured the electronics for smart bombs. "Isn't that a kick in the tushy?" Louis said every time he recited this history. "I believe that I was born to implement and then provide an audience for this singular joke. My life's work is done." Louis was a tall, silver-haired, movie-star-handsome drunk who did tai chi to Frank Sinatra records.

"I've got a brain tumor, Louis," Fern told him after their second Beefeater.

"What the hell are you talking about?" Louis said. "We Stantons don't get brain tumors. We get hemorrhoids, ulcers, and heart attacks. In that order."

"They say if I don't have it taken out, it will blind me, or maybe infarct, and kill me. They're trying to worry me, Louis."

Louis took her in his arms. He would have said something consoling had he been able to. But he'd seen too much of hopelessness to indulge in sentimental lying. After a long minute of holding her close he said, "Shit, sis."

The next day, Fern drives south toward Monterrey, Mexico, and then to my little red house halfway to Saltillo. Since we have corresponded, I am expecting her. The cure I will effect will come from her, from the dark cave in her soul where the purifying waters hide.

She is very güera, blond, and guapa, in that gringa way, a way that makes our short dark men stare momentarily, then turn away and smile to themselves. Such self-assurance is always a mask that conceals the face of chaos. The long, confident stride, the frank gaze, the uncompromising cheer and friendliness—all admirable in the geometrically ordered north, but unconvincing, even menacing, here.

I like her, despite this. She is a child of light and has never seen her own shadow—the shadow inside, the second self, the ungeometric one who empowers and disempowers.

"Why have you come to me, señora?" I ask, as I always ask.

"You are a curandera. The best, I've heard. I am here to be cured."

"Wait," I say, and go into another room. She must sit in the hard wooden chair, enduring the heat of my little un-air-conditioned house, while I finish washing my dishes. I expect she will think that the ring and clatter of china is the sound of potion-making. I need no potions, nor does she. We are in the process of inventing a fiction, one that will speak directly to her shadow. Está bien. For this much is true, every human body is unique, despite the convincing similarities. Sameness is the superficial reality that hides the peculiar twists and turns your physiology has been forced to take by a spirit world of good and bad influences. Every diseased organ is diseased because it was the recipient of a dark romance that must be exposed by a darker romance—my fictive art.

Fern sat naked on the short-legged wooden table while Señora Montes held a black chicken over her head. She spoke in a language that was not Spanish, a pre-Columbian tongue that was guttural and lilting at the same time, a language of impossible consonants and hissing, diphthonging vowels. The burning *copal,* the resinous stuff that filled the room with incense, made Fern's eyes weepy. The weepiness of her eyes worked its way down into her chest and she held back a sob as long as she could, then let it out. It was followed by another, and then more tears, a freshet, as if a hidden tap had been twisted open and then beyond open. Through her tears, the room seemed red to her, though there wasn't much red in it, and the *eh, eh, eh,* sounds Señora Montes was making also seemed red.

Señora Montes passed the docile chicken over and around Fern's shaking body, then set it aside and resumed the process with an eagle feather. Fern remembered a scene from her childhood, her father walking down a country path, away from her, she screaming at him to stop. It felt like an abandonment of some kind, an exaggerated mood that could not have meaning, for her childhood had been happy, and her parents loved one another and lived harmoniously, and yet his receding back, how the twilight caught in the folds of his shirt, how he seemed willing to allow himself to be swallowed by the darkness of the trees, moved her to scream at him, as if his peril was obvious only to her. The memory came unbidden, and made her sob again. But how could it have meaning?

Está bien, Señora Montes said, touching Fern's forehead with an egg. The cool egg drew on the skin of her forehead, drew on the bones and the sinus cavities inside the bones, and touched something even deeper. *La limpia,* the cleansing, was now complete. A young girl came in with a basin of water and a coarse cloth. Señora Montes went back into her kitchen and fixed herself a cup of tea while Fern bathed and put her clothes back on. The money was incidental. Fern left it on the table, and later, when the curandera picked it up and put it into her leather wallet, she did not count it.

The operation—an up-the nose transsphenoidal—conducted by Mike Higgins, was a total sucess. The tumor was not a difficult one, not a clinging menengioma, but a fatty macroadenoma he spooned out like a puddle of Jell-O, leaving the neighboring arteries and nerves unmolested. It was more accessible than the radiologist had perdicted, based on his readings of the MRI. "It looks like it de-bulked itself somewhat," Mike Higgins said, attributing the redefined space around the tumor to a steroid he had administered two weeks before the oper-ation. "The magic of modern chemistry," he said.

Fern did not disabuse his of this notion.

She now knows that she is both unique and common. She accepts this para-dox. It is, after all, only one more paradox in life's massive catalogue of para-doxes. In sameness is ordinary imortality. In uniqueness, the singularities of beauty and death.